AN EMPIRE'S SPECTACULAR WEALTH—
DESIRED BY THE WHOLE WORLD!

It begins amid the overwhelming splendor and simmering intrigue of the court of Czar Alexander II a hundred years ago, and explodes into our own day with a climactic battle for one of the world's great wonders. It is the story of a staggering reward as real as rock, yet more elusive than a dream, and the international hunt to capture it.

Martin Toberts wants it, even though the KGB, the French police, and his own CIA want to kill him before he can grab it.

Pell Bruckner wants it, because some things are stronger than honor, stronger than your own skin.

Solange Cordier wants it, because of the whisper of a man long dead—and the embrace of another very much alive.

TAKING LIBERTY

LAWRENCE DUNNING

▲ AVON
PUBLISHERS OF BARD, CAMELOT AND DISCUS BOOKS

TAKING LIBERTY is an original publication of Avon Books.
This work has never before appeared in book form.

AVON BOOKS
A division of
The Hearst Corporation
959 Eighth Avenue
New York, New York 10019

First Avon Printing, March, 1981

AVON TRADEMARK REG. U.S. PAT. OFF. AND IN
OTHER COUNTRIES, MARCA REGISTRADA,
HECHO EN U.S.A.

Printed in the U.S.A.

To Barbara, my wife,
who coped with so many things

Prologue

THE NORTH DELEGATES LOUNGE in the United Nations complex on the east side of Manhattan is a large, high-ceilinged room with wide windows overlooking the East River. There is a liquor bar at one end of the lounge, and behind it is a quiet café-espresso bar where more intimate conversations are possible. The lounge itself, the bar areas, and the corridor leading to the South Lounge are often the locale of serious, high-level discussions between ranking members of various national delegations. Sometimes, of course, the North Lounge is used for more informal conversations—including, not infrequently, the delicate negotiations between lonely male delegates and high-class, expensive female members of an entirely different profession. Accommodations of the latter sort are arrived at much more easily and quickly, as a rule, than those between the representatives of opposing nations in the sessions of the General Assembly.

Anton Kolczak, a youthful member of the Czechoslovak delegation, entered the espresso bar and immediately spotted the man with whom he was to meet—Vladimir Malychev, a high-ranking representative of the Soviet mission. Anton would have preferred a good stiff vodka on the rocks, but because Malychev had suffered from gastric ulcers for years and drank no alcohol, the younger man graciously accepted the sweet, foamy cappuccino from the dour-faced Russian.

They stood together talking quietly about the Ugandan minister's unpopular position publicly taken that morning in the General Assembly, and gradually they began to talk of other things, private things, matters that had little or nothing to do with the General Assembly, the Security

Council, the Secretariat, or indeed any other part of the United Nations organization.

Anton, the student, listened intently as Malychev, who liked to show off, conversationally circled one particular bit of highly classified information with which he had been entrusted by his superiors in Moscow. The information concerned a project known as *Fonarshchik,* which Malychev, again showing off, translated into English as Lamplighter. Malychev, Anton realized, was a basically stupid man who nevertheless served certain purposes of his government well through his seniority with the world body and through his ability, even eagerness, to argue insignificant points interminably.

Anton nodded, smiled, now and then asked a seemingly simple question to lead the gray-haired Russian diplomat down indirect paths toward supplementary information. The Russian was voluble and seemed pleased to be taken seriously. "You will go far, comrade!" Vladimir Malychev exclaimed at one point in an outburst of fatherly goodwill, clapping Anton across the shoulders in a gesture of Communist solidarity between peoples of different countries sharing the same Marxist ideals.

Anton gratefully ordered the second round of cappuccino.

The following afternoon Anton Kolczak took a taxi from the General Assembly Building to Grand Central Station, disappeared into the bustling terminal, and eventually caught the crosstown shuttle to Times Square. Surfacing on Forty-second Street, he walked casually west toward Eighth Avenue, stopping now and then to peer into shop windows and surreptitiously check the reflection of the opposite sidewalk. At the prearranged meeting place, a pornographic movie house devoted primarily to homosexual films, he paid the cashier and walked through a dusty curtain into the stale-smelling theater. After his eyes grew accustomed to the dark, he carefully checked the seats on both sides of the aisle and finally spotted his American friend two-thirds of the way down on the right. There was no one else sitting close to him, which was the way Freddie always arranged it.

Anton slipped into the seat beside him and spoke in low tones directly into Freddie's ear, repeating all that he had learned the preceding day from Vladimir Malychev about the Lamplighter project. Freddie listened intently, his eyes never once leaving the screen. When Anton had finished, Freddie reached over and grasped Anton's hand in a soft embrace, then rose soundlessly and disappeared toward the rear of the theater. Glancing up for the first time at the flickering figures of young boys on the screen, Anton decided to reward himself by staying to watch at least part of the film.

Freddie's apartment on West Eighty-sixth Street was a two-room efficiency—one room of which, furnished and equipped through sterilized CIA funds, served as Freddie's office and photographic darkroom. After converting Anton's information to a typed, coded letter-sized sheet of paper, Freddie photographed the page and, with the aid of a microscope, reduced it onto a piece of film smaller than a postage stamp. He developed the tiny film, wrapped it in plastic, and placed it in a metal Band-Aid box. The sheet of paper he had typed and photographed he burned to ash in a thick metal wastebasket he kept for that purpose.

Later that evening Freddie left the apartment carrying the Band-Aid box in his jacket pocket and walked down West Eighty-sixth Street toward the Hudson River. He crossed Riverside Drive and went into the park, walked north to the first concrete bench past West Ninetieth Street, and sat down. After a while he took the metal box from his pocket and placed it just inside the leg of the bench, where it would not be noticeable. He sat there a while longer, then got up and proceeded north as far as West Ninety-fourth Street. Sometimes there were gangs of boys in the park—toughs, mostly, but some of them not so tough, he had found. Still, he left the park by the most direct route and never once considered looking back.

At precisely eight-fifteen a man wearing a white shirt and a striped tie walked directly to the bench, sat down, felt around the base of the concrete bench leg, and pocketed the tin containing the microfilm. He looked out toward the river as though enjoying the evening air, stood up, stretched, and immediately headed back the way he had come, toward his car parked nearby on Riverside Drive.

The courier raced to La Guardia Airport and just made the last night shuttle to Washington. At National Airport an hour later he was met by a CIA driver and taken directly to the headquarters building in Langley, Virginia, where the night duty officer informed him that Thornton Daniels—in charge of the Paris desk of the NATO section, Clandestine Operations Group (COG)—was waiting for him. The courier was escorted to Daniels's office by an armed guard, and while the guard watched, Daniels accepted the packaged microfilm frame, signed for it in the courier's receipt pad, and thanked the courier. He asked the guard to escort the courier to the floor below, where a Mr. Price at the Tanzania desk had, he believed, a package for delivery to London the following day.

After the guard and courier had left his office, Thornton Daniels took the microfilm frame to an adjoining room. There he mounted the frame, sandwiched between two plastic sheets, in the holder of a microfiche reader-printer; the image was slightly fuzzy and he turned a dial to sharpen it.

The report was brief, as those from his Communist-bloc U.N. source usually were. It concerned a rumored Moscow-inspired clandestine operation of some sort, probably imminent, probably to take place in the eastern United States. Daniels read the report several times. There was no input on the origin of the rumor, or confirmation, but Daniels had a great deal of confidence in Anton Kolczak. He pressed the print button on the machine and instantly produced five copies for internal Langley circulation. On his desk calendar he made a note to call Weston at the National Security Agency at Fort Meade in the morning.

Daniels sat at the counter of the Hot Shoppe in Bailey's Crossroads and stirred the sugar in his coffee, his eye on the front door. When Weston arrived he sat down beside Daniels at the counter and ordered hot chocolate. After the waitress had left he asked Daniels what was shaking.

"I want you to put an outside ear on the Russian U.N. Mission building on East Sixty-seventh Street in New York," Daniels said. "Maybe for a week or so. We're not that curious about what's said—well, we are, of course, but I'm aware that all their transmissions are electronically coded. By the way, your people don't have a handle on it yet, do they, George?"

"We're working on it. Exactly what *do* you want from us?"

"Essentially, we're looking for beam direction of all their short-wave transmissions and a statistical breakdown on the total amount of their communications traffic."

"Who they talk to and how often, in other words."

Daniels nodded.

"We've had a routine ear on them since the mission came to town," Weston said. "Granted, what you want calls for something a little more intense. Besides, I owe you one. How does a twenty-four-hour detail for ten days sound to you?"

Daniels smiled. "I'll let you know when I see the stats."

The battered van had been parked on the south side of East Sixty-seventh Street, in the block between Lexington and Third, for more than a week, but no one had mentioned it to the police. The van was topped by a gaudy wooden sign advertising for Sam's Pizzeria. Hidden inside the boxlike sign were a rotating signal detector and various directional antennas, hooked to several thousand dollars worth of microcomputerized signal-analyzer equipment stored compactly inside the body of the van. Six NSA employees manned the equipment in three eight-hour shifts. They still had two and a half days to go on their assignment, but already the data stats showed a definite pattern of increased directionally beamed communications traffic between the heavily antennaed building diagonally across the street and north-central France, probably Paris, on a frequency easily and clearly received in Western Europe.

Inside the somber stone building housing the Soviet mission to the United Nations several of the sharper-eyed delegates had noticed the van by the second day. First Secretary Vladimir Malychev, in charge of the mission in the absence of the ambassador, ordered an immediate surveillance check run on the van. Technicians photographed it from several windows through telescopic lenses and ran the description and license plate number through the mission's computerized central file of vehicles used at one time or another by various U.S. intelligence agencies. The vehicle file showed that the truck had been used operationally in several eastern U.S. cities by the National Security Agency.

"Undoubtedly they are monitoring our transmissions around the clock," Vladimir Malychev told his subordinates. Still, he did not appear worried; he was used to having their transmissions monitored by various civil, military, and federal organizations. Secure in the knowledge that the NSA had not broken the immensely complex computer code—a fact confirmed as recently as the past week by a KGB agent in place at Fort Meade—he saw no reason to worry about the van, and when it ultimately left the street, not to return, he felt only the slightest relief, as though an annoying mosquito had voluntarily left his arm for juicier flesh.

"No doubt about it," Weston told Thornton Daniels on the secure line between Fort Meade and Langley. "Their communications traffic between New York and Paris has increased tremendously in the past few weeks."

"You're sure?"

"Absolutely. Say, what's all this about? Something going on in gay Paree we ought to be aware of?"

"Thanks for the ears, Weston. I owe *you* one now."

Daniels cradled the phone and was about to ask his secretary to send in Bruckner, when the agent ambled through the door and, uninvited, sat down beside the desk.

"Don't get comfortable," Daniels said testily. "You'll be on the morning flight to Paris. Prepare yourself for an extended stay—a month, several months, it's hard to say. We'll make the arrangements for travel and a contact at the other end. Before you leave I'll brief you on what we have so far—which, I admit, isn't much. We do have the project name . . . Lamplighter."

"Ours or theirs?"

"Theirs. You get to play hotshot journalist again this trip."

"That's what I am—a journalist," Bruckner said, smiling cynically.

"Yeah—so I saw in your resume. We'll fix you up with some accreditation from Sigma Delta Chi, the Overseas Press Club, things like that. You'll be more genuine than Scotty Reston at the *Times*."

"Any, ah, terminations involved in my assignment?"

"We don't anticipate anything violent. Mostly what we need is an unknown face to do a little research, unhampered by undue interest from the other side."

Bruckner snorted. "If there's no more action than I've seen recently, I may be looking for a new job."

Daniels considered his statement. "I know an outfit on the other side that's recruiting," he said finally, "but their pay's lousy. And your prospects for peaceful retirement and a pension are zilch."

"Aren't they anyway?" the agent said, but Daniels did not reply.

ONE

1

THE GIRL WAS YOUNG and rather fragile looking, of that much Toberts was certain. She moved dreamily through the stately, high-ceilinged rooms of the old mansion, her bare feet only sporadically visible beneath the swirling folds of her pale green gossamer dress. Her face was hidden from his view but now and then she laughed, the musical notes rising higher on the scale until they disappeared among the softly drifting motes of dust suspended in the still air.

She seemed to be dancing toward a distant doorway, the movements of her lithe body beckoning Toberts to follow her. He hesitated, some imminent danger pressing palpably upon his chest, warning him, but finally he could not resist the pull of that strange, mystical laughter. The girl passed through the open door and disappeared. Hurrying, afraid he would lose her, Toberts rushed into the adjoining room and, pausing, felt the hot breath of the beast on his neck. Too late, he turned and saw the thing that would devour him, its eyes rolling in a mountainous head. Transfixed by fear, Toberts desperately tried to remember a prayer, any prayer, that might have effect against beasts. But the thing moved toward him, and as it gathered him in to crush his body among its tentacles, Toberts heard once again the girl's tinkling laughter echoing far away in distant chambers of his mind.

The insistent tinkling sound continued, until Toberts raised his head off the pillow and groped blindly for the shut-off switch on the little Bavarian alarm clock. The mansion had disappeared, and the beast, and the girl; and he found himself, as he did every weekday morning, in bed with Jessie in their house in the Rue Bonnet in

3

Montmartre, near the northern boundary of Paris, the City of Light.

He threw off the covers on his side of the bed and padded barefoot to the window. It was raining, for the fourth straight morning, on the celebrated multihued rooftops of Paris, the gentle spring drizzle the French call misting. Toberts rubbed his hand over the heavy bristles on his face, thinking that he would give five hundred francs to see the sun this minute peeking over the spire of Sainte-Hélène. The darkness of the hour and the day depressed him inexplicably.

"Bonjour, le monde," he said to the world outside, but although he had done this every morning of the five years he had lived in Paris, the world had so far not condescended to reply. He padded into the bathroom and scraped away at the bristles with an English Rolls razor until his skin looked pink and felt, even in the deep creases, reasonably smooth to his fingers. Absently touching as he did a hundred times a day the small scar under his left jaw in a place that never grew whiskers, he stared into the mirror above the washbasin. There seemed to be no more gray tinging his short, sandy hair than had been there yesterday. Smiling at his unaccustomed vanity, he brushed his teeth with the new candy-striped American fluoride toothpaste that Jessie insisted on buying at the embassy exchange (although there were French toothpastes available everywhere that were equally as good and cost less; his wife, Toberts often thought, was the most chauvinistic woman he knew) and returned to the bedroom to dress for the day.

Jessie was sitting on the edge of the bed, blinking at the feeble light issuing from the window where Toberts had opened the drapes. "What's it doing outside?" she asked the room.

"Misting," he said, "the everlasting misting." He chose his clothes carefully, as he did every morning, for the kind of day he expected to have at the embassy, taking into consideration such things as visiting dignitaries, whether or not he might be called into the ambassador's office for a conference, the sort of "traveling" he might have to do. Fitzgerald had never been particularly sticky

4

about the way his embassy people dressed—except on the formal occasions, of course—but Toberts simply *felt* better, more prepared, when he knew that none of his colleagues could find fault with his attire.

"Do you want an egg, Martin?" Jessie asked him.

Toberts felt the heat rise in his face. Every morning he had exactly one egg for breakfast, poached, on toast, with either orange juice or grapefruit juice and coffee. Every morning Jessie asked him the same question, as though something might have changed between the time she went to bed the previous night and the time she rose the following morning. He used to think she did it just to annoy him, and possibly she did; but long ago he had decided that, although it may have started that way, it had become an insidious habit—living proof of her insensitivity toward him.

While she was in the bathroom Toberts opened the bottom drawer of the dresser and selected a fresh handkerchief. He pulled away the false back of the drawer and stared at the snub-nosed .357 magnum revolver nestled in the straps and leather pouch of the compact shoulder holster, decided against it, and replaced the wooden panel. Jessie didn't know he had it, he was sure of that, but now and then he felt a need to check on it, as though knowing that it was still safe in its little nest obviated any need he might have had for taking it with him.

In a pink robe and high-heeled backless slippers, her graying hair sleep tossed but somehow appealing, Jessie looked good preparing breakfast, Toberts thought. But then she nearly always looked like a four-color page from *Elle* or *Harper's Bazaar*. He had once, long ago, been genuinely fond of her—loved her, even, he supposed—but in the past few years, since he had been transferred to Paris (though he supposed it had started long before that, having less to do with location than her advancing age) she had become all those things he despised in women—didactic, narrow-minded, bitchy toward the world in general and him in particular, bored and unhappy with her lot in life but too rooted in habit or the deceit of the mythological "good marriage" to do anything constructive about it. And Toberts, admit it or not, had his own hang-ups about what a marriage should be.

"I suppose you don't know when you'll be coming home tonight," she began, sliding a dismal-looking egg toward the no-longer-warm piece of toast on his plate.

"No, I'm sorry," he said. "It's beginning to look like a bloody awful day. Jamison's been on me for a week now about the press kit for the American Filmmakers Documentary Festival."

"I thought you'd already done that."

"You must be thinking of the Hollywood Western Stars Retrospective—we did that last month. This documentary thing is coming up the second week of May, about three weeks from now."

"Does Jamison think all this so-called cultural exchange crap really wins froggy friends for good old Uncle Samuel?"

Toberts winced. "I wish you wouldn't use silly terms like that for our hosts, Jessie. Even around me. One of these days you're going to slip at an embassy reception for the French foreign minister and create an international scandal."

"Oooh, wouldn't that twist your carrot, though!" She laughed hoarsely, two deep barks from a seal. "What do I give a damn for your French officials, anyway? It's a miserable country, Martin, I don't care what you say. Just look at the way we live—the two of us rattle around in this house, but somehow we can never afford servants to take care of it properly. We need it for entertaining, you tell me, but when was the last time we had a really decent party here? Sometimes I wonder what you do with all that money the State Department pays you."

"The ICA pays me, Jessie."

"ICA, yes. International Communication Agency— sounds grand, doesn't it? Used to be USIS, or USIA, I could never remember which. But the point is, you work for the American ambassador in the American Embassy, and that's supposed to *mean* something in the world, isn't it? Even to these frog bastards."

"Jessie, please . . ."

"Please, my ass! I'm sick of it, sick of the way we live

6

—get up in the morning, you go off to work all day, come home or not, dinner generally late or by myself, you go to bed, you get up and start all over again, the same on Saturdays as every other day of the week and like as not Sundays, too. I'm *bored*, Martin. Bored to death with this hideous, monotonous so-called life we're not really living."

"Then why don't you do something about it?" Toberts suggested, in what he thought was a rational tone of voice. "Do charity work, like the rest of the embassy wives. Get a job, even—I'm sure I could get you a work permit through Fitzgerald."

"And exactly what is it that I'm trained to do? I mean, in the way of a paying profession? From what I've seen, the girls walking the Champs-Elysées around midnight don't need any competition from a newcomer."

"You're being ridiculous, Jessie."

This kind of stupid bickering made him feel terribly old, Toberts realized, and when he was *really* tired of it all, like this morning, it seemed to him that it had been going on forever. "Listen, I've got an idea. I know it isn't much fun for you around here— I honestly thought you'd enjoy Paris, though, and the embassy life is what you cut your eye teeth on, as natural to you as your own skin."

"You thought, you thought! This is a filthy city, full of robbers and dirty little men slobbering over every female butt on the street. Why did you think I'd love that? What sort of pervert do you think I am?"

"Well, I just made a mistake, that's all. So what I'm proposing is that we get you and most of our belongings packed up, close the house here, and put you on a plane back to our place in Arlington. I surely won't be kept here longer than another six or eight months, and Brian Jamison can find me a nice little flat somewhere close to the embassy. What do you think? Does that sound reasonable?"

"Reasonable?" she said, staring at him with lifted brows over her coffee cup, her well-pedicured foot nervously dangling one of the mules. "No way, Martin. What makes you think I'd give you an opportunity like that to sniff around every little slut in Paris behind my back? God knows you probably do enough of that already."

"You're not being fair, Jessie—I've never touched another woman since the day we were married."

"Big deal. You want a medal? Get them to strike you off one down at the embassy."

Toberts pushed back his chair hard enough to knock it over and stood up. He was shaking so noticeably that his cup rattled when he set it down. "There's no use talking to you when you're this way," he said, sorry that she could see how upset he was. In his business you weren't supposed to show your emotions—not to friends, certainly not to antagonists. And that's what Jessie seemed to have become, an antagonistic stranger. He walked out into the sitting room to pick up his attaché case.

"Come back here and pick up this chair!" Jessie screamed at him, as though he were a child. "You pigheaded bastard! You know what you are, Martin? You're a stuffy, ultraconservative, poor computerized schmuck of a civil servant who fancies himself a diplomat. With your experience and the years you've put in all over the world, if you had an ounce of push in you you could have been the ambassador here by now, instead of just a press flunky. And we'd have a decent place to live, some decent friends, enough money to take a trip once in a while to some country where they still remember how to speak English—"

"I'll probably be late this evening," Toberts said quietly, not caring very much whether she heard him or not. As he opened the front door, he listened for a moment to the sound of Jessie rattling around in the refrigerator for the sherry bottle. Then he stepped out into the rain and quickly closed the door behind him.

The wiper on the right-hand side of the Peugeot's windshield stuck every second or third arc and made a hideous noise as it dragged its poor broken body across the wet glass. Toberts, knowing that it was technically spring, wondered why he didn't feel more like celebrating the traditional vernal rites, but suspected the damp gray day had a lot to do with it. The winter had seemed interminable; travelers who praised French weather had obviously never spent a winter in Paris, where the cold rain seeps downward from collars and upward from pants cuffs and chills unsuspecting bones from the inside out.

As he guided the six-year-old Peugeot south along the Avenue de Saint-Ouen, which would shortly become the Avenue de Clichy, Toberts considered the state of his life at the middle age of forty-five. A girl was singing a French torch song in a minor key through the tinny speaker of the car radio, and he wondered idly whether he would ever again know the sweet sorrow of a new love affair.

What he had told Jessie was true: No other woman had slept in his bed in the thirteen years of their marriage. That was more unusual than a casual friend might imagine. He had seen classified statistics once, worked up by the agency's personnel staff (motivation and tenure section), purporting to show that the average field officer's marriage lasted something less than 3.5 years. Surprisingly, marriages of convenience or appearance between the agency's large male homosexual coterie and perfectly acceptable women seemed to last, on the average, a great deal longer and to present a more stable base. In other words, Toberts had mused, if you want your marriage to prosper, turn gay.

Slowing for the crush of traffic around the huge Gare Saint-Lazare train station, Toberts turned over and over in his mind the ridiculous argument with Jessie. They *had* been in love with each other at the beginning, hadn't they? Cool, poised, stately Jessie Higham, recently divorced from Sir Graham Higham, a Canadian foreign office official in Ottawa, had been exactly what Toberts had been looking for at that admittedly low point in his life —a woman striking enough in manner and looks to push his career forward a notch or two and, more important, to erase from his mind Laurel's death five years earlier. A permanent cure for the disease of loneliness, he had hoped, if that were possible.

He had met Jessie at an embassy party in Ottawa, which is the way most people in his circle met. He had come by himself, and because of an assignment earlier in the day away from the city he had arrived late for the reception. The usual hands were shaken, words spoken, drinks accepted and sipped at (but never actually and heartily *drunk,* as drinks usually are at real parties; too much was always thought to be at stake to permit the fuzzing of the brain by alcohol when the representatives of real or potential world enemies stood only an arm's length away, munching the same decorative, tasteless canapés). The American ambassador had been away in Washington, but Toberts had spotted the U.S. Information Service chief across the room and had gone over to shake hands in an attempt to feel less conspicuous. There had been a tall, dark woman standing beside the chief; though Toberts remembered the scene as clearly as if it had taken place yesterday, he could no longer remember the chief's name.

"Ah, Martin, here you are—I'd almost given you up," the chief said heartily. "Jessie, this is Martin Toberts. Mrs. Jessie Higham, Martin."

Toberts had taken her coolly offered gloved hand, staring at her a bit, his brain clicking over like the miniature computer that it was. "Higham, Higham . . . not Sir Graham's wife?"

"Former wife," Jessie had said, allowing her hand to be held longer than necessary. "Graham and I were divorced . . . oh, it must be eight or nine weeks ago now." Her eyes, he noticed, sparkled brilliantly under the longest, darkest lashes he had ever seen.

"I didn't know. Forgive me."

"No reason for forgiveness, dear boy. It was common knowledge that Graham and I hadn't been getting along in ever so long a time. It was rumored that he had this showgirl, you see . . ." She glanced at the chief and smiled. "Would you be kind enough to see if someone might fill my glass for me?"

"Of course, dearest Jessie, though I must admit I'm loath to leave you alone with this handsome, unattached lecher."

As the chief went off in search of a fresh martini, Jessie innocently said, "Exactly how unattached would that be?"

The question always made Toberts nervous, no matter who asked it. "My wife died five years ago," he said.

He was never sure whether she had turned slightly into

10

the room then, so that the light was reflected differently from her eyes, or just what; but afterward he was reasonably certain she had suddenly looked at him in an entirely different way. A woman so obviously attractive must have had many admirers; why she should have chosen him he was not sure, but choose him she did.

He remembered that the chief did not return, with or without the promised drink for Jessie; that, too, might have been some kind of plan on the old boy's part to get him interested in the female world again. But when Toberts found her a drink, and then another, and another, so that she was eventually leaning against him intimately, she was so charming and gay that he hadn't the heart to let the suspicious side of his nature wonder whether she might be a borderline alcoholic. And, indeed, he had not been convinced of the fact until they had been married for some years, and he had begun to find the emergency bottles hidden in out-of-the-way places, and word began to spread slowly among whatever present group of embassy wives they were involved with that Toberts's wife never wanted to leave a half-empty sherry bottle at an afternoon card party, and wasn't it sad she was beginning to let her looks go. Things like that never remained hidden for long in the small, insular diplomatic world to which Toberts belonged.

His mind drifted to other things, eventually to Laurel, his first wife. The feeling of despair was still there, after all these years. What marvelously happy times they had planned, for themselves at first, selfishly, and then for the child, who was not to be. Love had had a different meaning when Laurel was alive; it had never been the same with Jessie, even in the beginning. And she was getting more impossible all the time. He wished ferociously that she *would* return to the States—but not so that he could play around, as she had suggested this morning. (With whom? He knew no one he could even begin to be interested in seeing. Oh, now and then a secretary at the embassy might look at him questioningly, but he was never sure if this was because he was a reasonably tall, reasonably attractive man in a milieu of smallish gray men, or simply because he wasn't seen much around the embassy

11

corridors and probably looked as though he didn't belong.) Not that at all, but simply that it would allow him to get out from under this intense feeling of pressure whenever they were together these days, to breathe more freely, to concentrate on doing his job.

Now as he guided the Peugeot into the Place de la Concorde and turned onto Avenue Gabriel, he glanced up automatically at the ramrod-straight Marine guarding the impressively forbidding entrance of the main American Embassy building at number 2. On the high gateposts above the guard were two carved American eagles, and beyond the spacious courtyard an American flag fluttered damply over the doorway of the building. Unimaginatively, in the American way of doing things, it was called A Building.

Toberts turned into a short drive off the street and rolled to a stop beside another Marine guard in a rain poncho standing beside a small gatehouse. Toberts presented his ID card, the guard studied the pleasant, thoughtful face in the photograph and Toberts's own face, inserted the magnetically imprinted card into a slot in a metal box, and handed the card back to Toberts. At the bottom of the incline ahead of the car the reinforced steel doors opened into the embassy's underground garage, reserved for only the highest-ranking employees. Normally the parking perquisite would have stopped at the level of the cultural attaché, but because of Toberts's special job he was also allowed the parking privilege. And there were advantages to the underground garage besides keeping his car out of the weather; the primary one, as far as Toberts was concerned, was that it allowed him to come and go almost unnoticed by the outside world.

He pulled the Peugeot into his numbered slot and walked the hundred or so feet to the elevator, which eventually rose deep inside B Building to a point on the fourth floor only a short walk down the corridor from his office. Toberts's immediate superior in the embassy hierarchy, to whom Toberts was only nominally answerable, was the cultural attaché, Brian Jamison, whose office was on the second floor. Other offices on the second and third

12

floors of B Building had to do with lectures, awards, translations, film, music, and programs such as the Fulbright exchange. The first floor was devoted to the press department, which had writers and editors who occasionally put together a supposedly informative magazine aimed at glorifying the American image for Frenchmen, and who otherwise maintained liaison with the French press.

The entrance foyer of the building, for those who did not ascend in the noisy elevator from the underground garage, was on the next floor down, the ground floor, which also contained the large American restaurant where Army and embassy dependents came by droves to escape the unknown texture of French food and Paris restaurants. Below that was the well-stocked PX, a little bit of San Antonio for homesick Americans. The fourth floor, where Toberts spent his embassy days, contained rows of offices, too, but they were largely unidentifiable by the occasional signs painted on doors or tacked to the walls along the corridor. The fourth floor, Toberts had always felt, had a kind of mystical hum that seemed to emanate from the carpeting in the halls, or perhaps from the region of the ceiling's recessed lighting. It was possible that the sound, if it *was* a real sound, had something to do with the electronic equipment in the communications and cypher room that occupied one large area at the end of the corridor, but he didn't think so; in fact, he had once put his ear against the reinforced steel door of the comm center, to check his theory about the hum, but had heard nothing.

"Good morning, Billy," Toberts said to the uniformed civilian guard sitting at a small desk beside the elevator shaft and the stairwell. As he spoke he automatically pulled out his ID card and handed it to Billy.

The guard looked at the card and at Toberts almost as if he hadn't seen him nearly every weekday morning for the past several years.

"Morning, Mr. Toberts," he said, handing back the card. He stepped out from behind the desk and followed Toberts down the corridor to room B-406. Toberts inserted his key into the top lock and the guard inserted a different key into the bottom lock and returned to his desk.

When Billy wasn't on duty someone else was, twenty-four hours a day, seven days a week. The double-key procedure was a pain in the ass to everyone on the fourth floor, even to Toberts, but he had submitted to the building security chief's recommendation to adopt it because he suspected the idea had originated with Walter Fitzgerald when he had become the new ambassador to France three years ago. There was already enough friction between Toberts's job and the rest of the embassy staff without adding to it unnecessarily.

"Good morning, Mr. Toberts," his secretary, Mme. Joubert, sang out from her little cubicle at one end of the long, narrow room.

"Whatever do you have to be so bloody cheerful about this morning?" Toberts asked her gruffly, but he smiled as he said it. Mme. Joubert was a jewel—fast, efficient, knowledgeable in every area of the embassy, able to deal with a wide range of visitors and callers, from the friendly to the not-so. And her disposition had more than once kept Toberts from the depths of a raging depression, for which he was continually grateful.

"My, but didn't we get up on the wrong side this morning! You remind me more and more of my Henri, getting older and more cantankerous every blessed day. You had coffee yet?"

He shrugged, grimaced.

"Oh, I see," she said, a worried little frown of concern creasing her broad forehead. "Troubles with *la ménagère*. Is she drinking again?"

"More than ever. I'll take a cup of that coffee now while I'm looking over the night's beastly accumulation of Urgents, Top Secrets, Immediate Actions, and Eyes Onlys. Anything hot?"

"The coffee," Mme. Joubert said. "You know I'm not allowed to poke my nose into the crypto cables—Elliott has them all locked up tight in the vault. I glanced at the log, though. There must be a dozen of them."

"Coffee first, remember. And plenty of sugar this morning, to kill the taste."

"I know someone who needs plenty of sugar," she said in reproach.

14

He watched her pour the thin black liquid from a charming hand-painted crockery pot she had brought from her home because, she said, "it'll make the coffee taste ever so much better than that old tin thing you had before I came here, that nobody's washed in a hundred years." The truth was, the old tin thing had been with Toberts in Beirut, Johannesburg, Ottawa, Brussels twice, Lima, and now Paris. He had become very fond of it and, more than that, of the coffee it made, which no one else would ever drink. But Mme. Joubert's brightly glazed pot kept her happy and suitably decorated her space in the office, as it might have decorated the country kitchen of any other pleasantly round-faced, gray-haired, grandmotherly woman of a certain age like Mme. Joubert. And Toberts, in a business where genuinely pleasant words were difficult to come by, needed Mme. Joubert badly.

The telephone rang just as Toberts sat down at his desk. It was fixed to ring at both his desk and Mme. Joubert's, so that either could answer while the other was out; and sometimes both answered at once, which is what happened this time.

"Hello? Who's speaking?"

"Mr. Toberts's office," Mme. Joubert said. "Is that you, Mr. Jamison?"

"Yes, it is. That boss of yours in?"

"I'm here, Brian," Toberts spoke up. "Just trying to get a cup of coffee and a little early-morning love from my secretary. What's up?"

"That Filmmakers Documentary Festival thing. The head man at Cinémathèque Française has been on my back two or three days already this week—'Why hasn't there been any publicity?' he keeps asking me, and I'm a little stuck for an answer. I know you're not much interested, Martin . . ."

Toberts sighed. This dual existence in the embassy—the role he played for Jamison and the staff charts, and that other, shadowy existence that was the only real world he had known for the past twenty-four years—threatened at every turn to draw from him more energy than he had

15

to give. "I thought we agreed I would pretty much stay out of this one, Brian," he said carefully.

"So we did," Jamison said. "It's just that I value your judgment highly on something like this . . . and, frankly, I don't know where else to turn on short notice. Martin, if you've got a minute free this morning, I would really appreciate it if you'd drop down for a little chat."

"What time?"

"Oh, shall we say in fifteen minutes? It won't take long, I promise."

Toberts slowly cradled the receiver and said "Damn!" under his breath, but Mme. Joubert, as usual, heard him anyway.

"Does that Mr. Jamison really think you're the chief of the press section?" she asked him, bringing in his Bavarian mug full of steaming coffee.

"That's what it says on my classification sheet, that's what it say in the official position description, that's what it say on the embassy staff register . . ."

Mme. Joubert shook her head. "Have you talked to the ambassador about it?"

"No. Fitzgerald is not about to take sides against his own cultural attaché. Besides, he doesn't like me very well."

"Oh, nonsense. I think I'll just slip a little word to his executive secretary sometime, you know, find out when his schedule's clear for an hour or so—"

"Please don't do anything foolish. I'll talk to him one of these days . . . he won't listen, but I'll talk to him."

"By the way," he called after Mme. Joubert, who was heading back to her own desk, "this is really quite remarkable coffee."

"I'm so glad you like it," she said, beaming happily, unable to see the wry face Toberts was making over the pallid brew.

The meeting with Jamison was short, not very productive, and about as unpleasant as Toberts had expected it to be. He was caught, literally, between a rock (the ambassador) and a hard place (Jamison); while both of them, and a few other people at the embassy, knew that

16

Toberts was the CIA station chief in Paris, Ambassador Fitzgerald's staff charts showed that Toberts was also head of the press section and, therefore, the ambassador expected Martin Toberts to do a certain amount of press-related work for the embassy. This requirement had been passed along to Jamison, who was delighted to have the Ambassador's backing in order to get Toberts's unwilling cooperation from time to time. Because, as Jamison had carefully refrained from ever admitting to anyone, Toberts was the best writer and best news manager in the place, and both Jamison and the ambassador deeply regretted the extraordinary amount of time Toberts's covert job required of him.

"How was the dragon this morning?" Mme. Joubert asked when Toberts returned to his office.

"Breathing righteous fire, as usual," Toberts said. "They must think my days have more hours than most people's."

"That's just their way of saying how valuable you are to them."

"I'd prefer money," Toberts said, chuckling at his own little joke.

Mme. Joubert handed him a slip of yellow paper with a telephone number written on it. "Mr. Sloan from the Paris *Times-Weekly* called while you were gone—he said to get back to him as soon as possible, that he would be in the office all morning."

"Thanks."

Toberts took the slip of paper to his own desk and dialed the number of the newspaper, which was one of several English-language weeklies published in Paris for the large American community. The editor himself answered.

"Harold Sloan speaking."

"Hello, Sloan. This is Martin Toberts. Did you call?"

"Sure did, Martin. There are some things I've been working on that you might be interested in—might be a good word for the embassy in there somewhere, if you can get Fitzgerald to approve this article series. What do you think?"

"I think Ambassador Fitzgerald would be highly pleased,

Sloan. That is, if the particular *slant* is right; I'd have to see what you've got dummied up, of course."

"Fine, fine. Could you drop by sometime later today?"

Toberts consulted a small desk calendar. "How about lunch? I'll stop by your office and pick you up around noon."

"Fine. You're buying, I assume."

"On my salary? Uncle Sam is not frivolous with the taxpayers' money, Sloan."

"We all know about *that*," Sloan said sarcastically and hung up.

Toberts pushed down the plunger of his telephone, released it, and from memory dialed another number. A man answered in the middle of the third ring, which was one of their signals. "Is Monsieur Duchamp in, please?" Toberts said in his flawless French.

"No, Monsieur Duchamp is out just now, but he will return your call after one o'clock if you will leave your name and number," the man said.

"Merci . . . three-two-six, three-seven, four-six," Toberts replied, inventing a number. When the man did not ask him for his name, which would have indicated some sort of trouble for which caution was necessary, Toberts hung up.

The man who had answered was Georges Maron, one of Toberts's French agents. The code meant that he had news of Cassius and would leave a message for Toberts in the usual place, to be picked up after one o'clock. Toberts glanced at his watch and swore silently, thinking of all the things he still had to do today and wondering where he would find the time.

He went to the massive wall safe across from his desk and worked the combination. There appeared to be a dozen or so new crypto cables which Elliott, the code clerk, had filed through the one-way incoming slot of the security vault, just as Mme. Joubert had said. This arrangement allowed the code clerks on night duty to safely store Toberts's messages in Toberts's own safe, so that he could work them whenever he got to them, night or day, without giving the clerks access to anything else in the safe. Besides the new overnight cables, Toberts also removed a previously decoded cable that had arrived two days ago from Thornton Daniels. The cable had been uncustomarily brief:

FM: CIA LANGLEY (DANIELS)
TO: AMEMBASSY PARIS///FLASH
      PRECEDENCE///TOBERTS EYES ONLY
TOP SECRET (ENCRYPT FOR TRANSMISSION)
PELL BRUCKNER ARRIVES DE GAULLE APRT
FRIDAY, 25 APR, 5:30 PM, TWA FLIGHT 802
FROM DULLES. USUAL RECOGNITION. HAS
BEEN BRIEFED.

That was all. More than a week ago Daniels had discussed sending a new man to work with Toberts on the project Maron was supposed to be checking on, the project code-named Lamplighter by the Russians. Toberts had objected, claiming that he had a man about to make contact with the renowned deep-cover agent known only as Cassius, who could probably tell them exactly what they wanted to know. But Daniels had insisted on flying someone in to help. It was possible, Toberts admitted, that Daniels knew more about the amount of digging that might be involved than he was telling; it wouldn't be the first time Daniels had held back information that Toberts had later found out would have been helpful to him on a particular case. But it had been Toberts's experience that headquarters types always had an exaggerated sense of their own importance, and it didn't much matter what headquarters they operated from. Probably the agents Toberts controlled from his office in the embassy felt the same way about him.

Memorizing the time and flight number and making a mental note of the amount of time required to drive to the Charles de Gaulle Airport northeast of Paris through late-afternoon traffic, Toberts shredded the cablegram into the burn bag for later destruction and settled down to the tedious but, in a way, still exciting task of decoding what might prove to be communications of literally earth-shaking significance. More times in his career than he could remember this had indeed happened—some coded message addressed to him had caused, or ultimately resulted in, the occurrence of some event that later made headlines the world over.

Such a blood-pulsing message was not destined to turn up among the dozen or so received at the embassy during the preceding evening hours, but it took Toberts nearly all morning to discover this fact for himself.

At a little before eleven-thirty Mme. Joubert took a call from the ambassador's secretary, who stated that if it wouldn't be too inconvenient Ambassador Fitzgerald would like for Mr. Toberts to pop over to A Building for a short conference. "That's what she said—'pop over,' " Mme. Joubert reported to Toberts. "That psuedo-British tart!"

Toberts grabbed a pad of notepaper and headed down toward the tunnel connecting B and A buildings. Fitzgerald seldom commanded anyone in the embassy to appear in his office, but it was understood when he summoned you, you were to drop whatever you were doing and report at once. There was a definite military feel about all embassies, including this one, which had bothered Toberts at first but to which he now paid almost no attention.

He surfaced inside the main building and went directly to the ambassador's reception room on the first floor. The room was large and luxurious and, at the moment, empty. Toberts selected a magazine from the round table in the center of the room and sat in one of the comfortably worn brown leather chairs directly beneath an ornate crystal chandelier. On the wall opposite him was a large portrait of a nineteenth-century admiral.

Eventually Fitzgerald's secretary came silently through a door leading to the ambassador's office and whispered to Toberts that Ambassador Fitzgerald would see him now. Toberts held the door for her to pass back through, but after delivering her message, she ignored him entirely.

The room was spacious—perhaps twenty feet by fifty feet—with a fireplace at each end, portraits of American diplomats on the pine-paneled walls, and the same opulent brown leather furniture as in the reception room. The outstanding feature of Fitzgerald's office—the thing that sometimes took away the breath of first-time visitors— was the row of three huge windows facing onto the broad Place de la Concorde, with its flags fluttering in the breeze, its swirling traffic, its fountains and statues, and its almost palpable sense of the past five hundred years of French history. Toberts liked the room and had learned to feel comfortable, as many others of the embassy staff had not, with its occupant.

"Come in, come in, Martin!" Fitzgerald said heartily, pushing aside a pile of mostly unopened correspondence on his huge desk. "Just catching up a bit from being up north last week. How are things in the press section?"

"Just fine, Ambassador," Toberts said. Fitzgerald had asked Toberts to call him Walter shortly after the ambassador had taken over the post, but Toberts felt more comfortable with "Ambassador" and steadfastly stuck to it. "A little busier than we'd perhaps like to be—"

"Fine, fine—Jamison tells me what a splendid job you've been doing for him."

Toberts was sorry to hear the ambassador say that. He had wanted to bring up his concern about the impossibility of doing two jobs well and how Jamison had been imposing on him, but now it would have to wait.

"Martin, there are a couple of things, one in particular I wanted to get your reaction to—although the way the problem has been presented to me I don't think we have much choice. First, though, I get the distinct but highly subjective impression that some project or other is on the immediate horizon with possible wide-scale ramifications for the U.S., but I also get the feeling that no one wants to talk about it yet. What, if I may be so bold, is the CIA saying of interest these days?"

Toberts smiled disarmingly. "Haven't I always told you everything of importance that I know?"

"No, you have not," Fitzgerald said, "and most of the time that is precisely the way I prefer it. But, Martin, once in a while you could volunteer an insignificant bit of yesterday's news to pacify the old ambassador's vainglorious ego, couldn't you? So that I don't end up looking the fool at some diplomatic bash next week or next month."

Fitzgerald stared at him with a serious face, and finally Toberts said, "I thought we'd agreed that I would tell you in general terms, through progress reports and so forth, what we were up to and would show you all of the outgoing cables that I thought you'd be interested in, but that that would be pretty much it. Are you saying you want to change the ground rules?"

"No, no. Not at all. I've been told you're extremely good at your job and, frankly, I would just as soon *not* know how you plan to carry out Langley's diabolical assignments, or who your sources of information are. I mean, bribery, blackmail, listening to other people's private conversations, photographing them through keyholes, for God's sake—it all sounds a bit infra dig to suit my image of what the gracious American visitor to these foreign shores should be. And France is an *ally*, don't you know!"

"The cold war has never officially ended, Ambassador. Someone has to listen, someone has to look, someone has to write the reports. I truly think the side with a monopoly on intelligence-gathering will eventually have a monopoly on everything else as well."

Toberts chuckled, as if to disparage his own seriousness. "I don't mean to plead that if I didn't do this despicable job someone else would. It's no doubt true, but I happen to like my job and I'm better at it than almost anyone I know. That doesn't mean there aren't parts of it that infuriate or disgust me at times, but then I don't believe I know anyone who isn't discouraged by his job once in a while. Even you, I imagine, have your off days."

The ambassador exhaled toward the ceiling. "All the time, Martin, all the time." He dug among the piles of envelopes on his desk and came up with one that he waved at Toberts. "Here, for instance. A woman from Indianapolis wrote to me personally about her son who was recently traveling alone through France and who has, according to the woman, been treated abominably by the Paris police simply because he happens to wear his hair long and an earring in one ear. I did a little investigating and found that this lout of a son of hers stole a taxi near the Tuileries and almost beat the driver to death in the process. What does she want me to *do?*"

"Send him on his way with a warning, probably."

"Yes. What was it we were discussing before? Oh, yes, keeping me on top of things locally. After all, Martin, I *am* the ambassador; it doesn't look well for me to be the most ignorant member of the staff."

"Ambassador, I promise to keep you informed of anything big I come across if the State Department is involved," Toberts said, though he knew he probably would not. "What was the other thing you wanted my reaction on?"

"Oh, that. I think I indicated it's pretty much a closed loop now, out of my hands. Building security briefed me on a potential security problem the other day and I've already informally agreed to Coleman's proposed solution."

"Knowing Coleman, I'm sure it's a beauty," Toberts said.

"He's a good man, Martin, knows his job inside and out. Anyway, as soon as you okay it I'll sign the official memorandum of agreement with our French nationals liaison officer in the Foreign Office. What Coleman recommends is that we immediately post the entire fourth floor of B Building as off limits to all French nationals employed by the embassy."

Toberts frowned. "You're talking about almost half of the embassy staff. What's the latest personnel figure—two thousand?"

"About that."

"I hope that liaison officer is a genius," Toberts said, "because we're going to have nearly a thousand angry women on our backs."

"They aren't all women, Martin."

"Ninety percent of them are. And most of those are typists used to transcribe, research, and file unclassified messages. They all have the usual State Department security clearance, too. Don't get me wrong, Ambassador, I'm not disagreeing. For once I think Coleman had a good idea—actually, I've thought we ought to do something

23

like this for a long time. Forgive me for saying so, but Langley does not accept State's routine background investigations as anything like secure enough for their purposes."

"I'm quite aware of the uneasy truce between our two agencies, Martin. The fact is, perhaps we're finally recognizing that CIA has a valid point in this area. Or perhaps State is merely attempting to protect its financial investment in the fourth floor—the coding and communications equipment, et cetera. Whatever the reason, may I assume we have your support then?"

Toberts sensed a trap, something slightly out of order in their very ordinary conversation. It had to do with the fact that the ambassador was not usually so solicitous of Toberts's opinion on a matter that, like this one, lay entirely within the ambassador's prerogatives to order into effect by his signature without anyone else's concurrence. A single buried fact began to worm its way forward through the accumulated debris of factual material stored in Toberts's retentive mind: Coleman, the building security chief, had once made noises about his lack of trust in Toberts's secretary, Mme. Joubert.

That had to be it, Toberts thought.

"I assume Coleman will keep in mind that my secretary, Madame Joubert, will be exempt from any such order," Toberts said evenly. "After all, she's an American. From Sandusky, Ohio, I believe."

The ambassador shook his head. "Her place of birth doesn't matter in this case, I'm afraid. Were you aware that her husband is a French citizen?"

"Of course. That's never been any secret."

"And were you also aware that Madame Joubert gave up her United States passport several years ago and is now legally a citizen of France? *Only* France?"

"I know that, too, Ambassador. Madame Joubert has had more security checks run on her—by State, CIA, FBI, even the State of Ohio—than anyone else in the embassy, including you and me. I can absolutely vouch for the fact that she's as clean as anyone human can be."

"Martin, I'm sure what you say is true," Fitzgerald said. He rose from his handsome desk and stood facing

24

the magnificent view of the Place de la Concorde through one of the huge windows, his hands clasped behind his back. "But the fact of the matter is, we simply cannot make an exception, in the case of Madame Joubert or anyone else. I think you can understand why. If we did, tomorrow we would have twenty requests of the same nature from others on the fourth floor. No, Martin," he said, turning to face Toberts, "it's simply out of the question."

Realizing the tactical advantage the ambassador held simply by standing while his adversary was seated, Toberts himself stood and faced the ambassador squarely. "If Madame Joubert is forced to leave, or to work somewhere else in the embassy, it would take me six months to find a suitable replacement and have her checked out thoroughly, and another six months before she would know enough about our operation to be of any use to me. Ambassador, I cannot afford the luxury of postponing my assignments for a year. The intelligence capabilities of the U.S. would suffer immeasurably, I guarantee that. Madame Joubert, in my opinion, is necessary to our mission in France, and I cannot believe that you would jeopardize that because of some blanket order by a little dictator like Coleman."

"Coleman's competence is not the issue here. We're discussing the basic fairness of a ruling that you would like to apply to some people but not to others in the same category."

"There is no one in the embassy in Madame Joubert's category," Toberts said angrily. "There is only one Central Intelligence station chief in Paris—me. And I have only one administrative assistant—Madame Joubert. Notice that I didn't say secretary. Madame Joubert is much more than that. Ambassador, I want you to know that I officially withdraw my support of Coleman's plan. And I also want you to know that if you go ahead without my concurrence, I will be forced to cable Langley with the particulars so that they may lodge a formal complaint with State."

"Do you realize how foolish that would make us look? *All* of us, Martin—you included."

"I'm willing to take that chance, Ambassador—it's that

important to me. The question is, are *you* willing to risk it?"

Looking somewhat puzzled, the ambassador sat down behind his desk again. "I didn't realize this was such a touchy matter with you, Martin. I can see I'll have to get back to Coleman before we reach any final decision. I want your word on something, though. I want you to promise me that, whatever I decide, you'll agree to live with the decision and not fight me, or Coleman, any further."

"That's a promise I can't make, Ambassador. I think you know why."

"Then you leave me no choice but to mention this discussion in my next cable back home."

"I'm sorry you feel that way, Ambassador. Was there anything else?"

The ambassador stared blankly at Toberts for a moment, then smiled broadly, as though their entire argument had been erased from his mind. "Yes, Martin. I wanted to remind you about the press reception for the new Ghanaian chargé d'affaires at their embassy tomorrow night. Jamison will be there, as will I, and I'm sure the press contingent will be expecting you. It should be fun—they're one of our few friends left on the Dark Continent."

"Full dress, wasn't it?" Toberts asked, knowing that it was—Jessie had had her dress for the occasion selected and bought more than two weeks ago.

"Of course. These Africans are absolutely *delighted* with the formal trappings of diplomacy."

"And we're part of the floor show," Toberts said.

The ambassador smiled cordially—already practicing, Toberts thought, for tomorrow night. "Sometimes that's the way it seems, Martin. But as you so aptly stated before, if we weren't doing it, someone else would have to."

Toberts shook hands with the ambassador and walked back through the tunnel to his own building. With Mme. Joubert's help he quickly cleaned up most of the work left over from the previous evening and prepared to go to lunch. During a lull Mme. Joubert asked him what the ambassador had wanted, what they had talked about for such a long time, and Toberts replied, "I was mostly trying to save someone's job."

"Here at the embassy, you mean?"

Toberts smiled at her. "Don't be a snoop, Madame Joubert, or you'll be joining those other girls in the bull pen."

On the way out of the building Toberts passed by one of the large secretarial pools of young, cute French typists, and when one of them complimented him on his suit and tie he beamed happily, as though suddenly remembering that this was the way Paris in the springtime was supposed to be. He consciously pulled in his stomach, because although he still had a solid, muscular frame, he knew he was getting flabby around the middle from too many desk jobs. He was still smiling when he entered the *Times-Weekly* office and collected Harold Sloan for lunch.

2

THE SMALL PARK WHERE Georges Maron and his wife frequently took their five young children was less than two blocks from their apartment on the Rue des Poitevins, between the massive gray academic structures of the Sorbonne and the colorful Quai Saint-Michel. The park was large enough for playground equipment, which the children enjoyed, and there were benches, trees, and a few walkways for adults to use as they desired. Although one saw an occasional student sprawled on the grass, asleep with his head resting on a pile of books, the park was usually populated only by boisterous children and their harried mothers.

Such was the case this Friday morning, a day and an hour when most men were hard at work behind a desk in some musty office across the river. It amused Maron to be able, because of the nature of both his official and his unofficial jobs, to do things differently from other people, other families, although sometimes he wondered whether his children considered him quite normal. So far, their questions had caused him only a minimum of anxiety.

"Watch me, Papa, watch me!" his youngest son Jean-Paul squealed happily, turning a scary, inelegant somersault over a low metal bar.

Maron smiled. "Bravo, Jean-Paul. You will be able to join the circus next week." Still smiling, he turned to his tiny, dark wife who sat happily beside him on the bench, watching their two daughters on the swings. "He's going to be the biggest one of them all, Marie, and the strongest. You'll see. Didn't I tell you that on the day he was born?"

Marie smiled and clasped Maron's veined, wiry hand.

28

"You said he was the ugliest piglet you had ever had the misfortune to set eyes on. The sisters were shocked at your language and thought you must be drunk. Don't you remember?"

"I remember," Maron said. As he spoke he turned his head toward the shrubbery at the northeast corner of the park, from behind which a young man wearing a blue beret appeared and stood for a moment. Maron watched him inspect the park and then walk slowly toward a nearby bench. The young man sat down and took a rolled-up picture magazine from his jacket pocket. Slowly he began to turn the pages.

Maron stood. "I shall return shortly," he told Marie, who held onto his hand perhaps a moment longer than she should have. She, too, had seen the young man in the beret and had not been fooled at all by his studied casualness. "Be careful," she whispered. She was, thought Maron, becoming almost a professional, if only she wouldn't *worry* so about him.

Maron strolled through the park and eventually sat beside the young man on the bench. "You have news for me, René?" he asked conversationally.

The young man looked up from his magazine without smiling. "We have located the agent Cassius; he is in Paris—now, today. The Hotel De Luxe, 26 Rue Chevert, near the Invalides. Room 342. The register shows he arrived Wednesday evening, after six P.M., and is using the name Jean Petit."

"Is one of the others there now?"

"Yes. We are sticking like a second skin—I told them how important it is."

"And he has no knowledge he is being watched?"

"So far, we do not believe so."

"Hmm." Maron nodded. "I would not be complacent, René. Cassius has been at this business longer than all of us put together; the fact that he has survived is testimony enough to his skills. Perhaps he wants us to *believe* he has not been spotted, for purposes of his own. We shall see."

"There was one visit, other than short, routine walks for food, newspapers, and the like. Late yesterday afternoon he left the hotel and walked to Avenue Duquesne, and from there toward the Place de Fontenoy—"

"He was heading toward the UNESCO complex?" Maron broke in.

"We . . . are not certain, Georges. As he turned south a second time he simply disappeared."

"You lost him," Maron said, nodding his head as though he could have expected it. "Probably our friend Cassius paid a visit to one of the UNESCO offices, which would be of extreme importance to our uncle—particularly if he does not already know of this connection, or if Cassius does not himself inform Uncle of the connection—and you let him get away from you. From *us,* in fact, since I will ultimately be held to blame."

René blanched at Maron's words; he did not like to be caught in an unprofessional moment, though as only a runner for Maron his responsibilities were somewhat less than Maron had implied. Spot, report, run periodic incidental surveillance on a subject—that was all he and the others were being paid to do. René and one or two others were the only ones who even knew who was paying them, and none of them cared about the source of the funds.

"Perhaps," he told Maron, "Cassius merely wished to view the buildings—"

"As though he were a tourist, you mean? Don't be an ass, René. Cassius had business there, with someone, of some unknown nationality, to discuss some particular thing of greater or lesser importance, probably greater. Cassius does not deal in minor matters."

Maron shook his head and glanced over toward another part of the park where his children played happily on the equipment and where Marie waited anxiously for his return. "Tell me this, René—do you know where he is at this minute?"

"I was about to tell you. He took an early morning walk and returned to his hotel not more than half an hour ago, having stopped at the delicatessen on the corner for a bag of croissants and eel pâté. He is still inside the hotel."

"Marvelous," Maron said. "Eel pâté. You never let an unimportant detail slip by you. Isn't that so, René?"

Without another glance at the young man beside him on the bench Maron rose and walked directly back to his family. Marie stood to meet him, the look in her eyes an uneasy combination of love and fear.

"Get the children," he said to her, "we must return to the flat immediately. I'm expecting a telephone call." He turned toward the swings and shouted, *"Allons, enfants!"* There was more command in his voice than a stranger would have thought likely to come from such a small, fragile-looking man.

As soon as they reached the apartment Maron checked his watch again and saw that it was still early for the call he expected. He thought about what René had told him, and how one of the runners—perhaps René himself, although he hadn't admitted it—had bungled what ought to have been a simple shadow job on the familiar sidewalks of Paris. Cassius was good, there was no doubt of that. Now somewhere between fifty-five and sixty years old, the short, bearded agent of undetermined nationality had operated at one time or another in most of the major cities of Europe and the British Isles. Martin Toberts had mentioned him to Maron once, telling him only that Cassius was of immense service to the West from time to time and that he was to be given whatever professional assistance he required, whenever he required it, from Maron and his men.

There were only three children at home now, the two oldest having gone off to school from the park. Maron asked his wife to send them outside to play while he used the telephone, and she did as she was told, just as she always did. It was hard on all of them, he knew that, but it was especially hard on Marie. The children, even the oldest ones, probably thought he was engaged in some kind of elaborate game of hide and seek, but Marie knew nearly everything that Maron knew about his secondary business. She was miserable knowing, but she would have been even more miserable if he had kept his secrets to himself.

He looked up the Hotel De Luxe in the directory and dialed the number. When a clerk answered he asked for

31

room 342; he could hear the tone buzzing and counted nine of them before a hoarse voice said, *"Qu'est-que c'est?"*

Maron waited until he heard the click indicating the clerk had left the line, then said slowly, "I have news from our uncle."

There was a pause. "I dislike the way you have stirred up these little ants around me—if they are not very careful they will be stepped upon."

"We had to find you quickly," Maron said by way of apology.

"That is too bad. I would have found you soon enough. What news?"

"Uncle wishes urgently to speak with you about an extremely important matter. It seems there is the smell of smoke between New York City and Paris, along the bear route. The smoke means fire, ultimately, Uncle is certain of that. The question is, what is the nature of the fire that the smoke portends? Uncle thought perhaps you had heard something useful in your travels."

Cassius uttered a sound of disgust over the line. "You are a fool to call me here, at my hotel—there are many who would give a great deal to know my location at any given moment. And do you really believe your juvenile attempts to disguise your conversation would mislead even the rankest newcomer to the profession? You are as naive as these ants you have sent to watch me."

"Yes, that may be. One of the ants, as you call them, saw you yesterday afternoon walking toward the buildings of UNESCO on the Place de Fontenoy. He would have approached you with a message, perhaps, but you disappeared."

"That is almost certainly because I was not heading toward UNESCO but was merely stretching these old leg muscles, as I do every day in decent weather, walking as far as the Avenue Garibaldi before returning to my hotel. The ant was mistaken."

"That is possible," Maron agreed.

"Have you told our uncle about any of this yet?" Cassius asked.

"No. Why?"

"I implore you not to do so until we can meet and

discuss a matter of utmost delicacy. Do you know a safe place?"

"Of course—the Maron Travel Agency, on Rue Washington just off the Champs-Elysées."

"Very well. Shall we say in half an hour?"

"No, I cannot possibly be there before two this afternoon."

"At two, then."

"Oui. Merci," Maron said, but Cassius had already hung up and the line was dead.

Maron was debating how much to tell Marie about the meeting when the telephone rang beneath his hand. He let it ring a second time and snatched up the receiver in the middle of the third, which was a signal.

A man's voice said, "Is Monsieur Duchamp in, please?"

"No, Monsieur Duchamp is out just now," Maron said, recognizing Toberts's voice, "but he will return your call after one o'clock if you will leave your name and number."

"Merci," Toberts said, and hung up after giving Maron a fictitious number. It meant that Maron would leave a message at the drop in the Bois de Boulogne before one.

As he sat beside the telephone Maron's wife looked at him and frowned. "What is it, Georges? Is something the matter?"

"I don't know," Maron answered. "I was just talking to a man called Cassius who is working for our side. He knows Toberts—the CIA seems to have given him implicit clearance throughout this entire part of the world but . . . I don't know. He wants to meet me later this afternoon at the shop—he says he has some urgent news to pass along to me. He seemed to be annoyed that René and the others spotted him."

"Perhaps that is simply professional pride," Marie said. "I know how you are—like little boys playing your games of war and bandit, memorizing secret codes, secret hiding places . . . Admit it, Georges, you enjoy the secret part of your life much more than you enjoy your travel agency work, or your family . . ."

"That's not true!" Maron said, going to his wife to hold her small body in his arms. But even as they held on to each other and rocked back and forth in the hall outside their bedroom he knew that perhaps it was true—else, why did he do it? Certainly not for the money, though the CIA's small subsidy of his travel agency did put roast veal on the table occasionally instead of sausage. But there were other reasons, going back to the friendship of the Allies during World War II.

"Is this man Cassius dangerous?" Marie asked him.

"Yes, I believe he might be if he were not on our side," Maron answered honestly.

Marie looked into his eyes for a moment. "Please be careful, Georges. I don't know what we would do without you."

"Nothing will happen, little dove. I am very careful in my secret games, I promise you."

But it was not true. Toberts had warned him several times, and Maron himself knew that by nature he was not a suspicious man. For instance, the call to the hotel where Cassius was staying—any good agent would always assume that his home telephone was tapped by the opposition, yet Maron repeatedly used it for just such secret business calls. Someday, he thought, holding Marie closer to him, someday something bad would happen to him because of a momentary lapse of carefulness. His only hope was to somehow put aside enough real money soon enough that his dear Marie and their five beautiful children would be taken care of when that time came.

3

As he had promised, shortly after noon Toberts picked up Harold Sloan at the *Times-Weekly* offices on Rue Réaumur, which happened to be near both the Bourse stock exchange and *France-Soir,* one of Paris's leading daily newspapers.

They walked to a small restaurant nearby that Toberts had visited once or twice before, where they asked to be seated at a corner table with a view of the street. They ordered the daily special, a lamb casserole, and a bottle of light rosé, which they sipped slowly as they talked.

"Tell me about this Pell Bruckner you're handing me," Sloan said. "When's he due in?"

"Soon," Toberts said. "I can't say exactly when I'll be able to bring him by your office—it depends on a number of things. But soon."

"Can he write?"

"Sure. You think we'd throw in a ringer just because we need him?"

Sloan smiled. "Hell yes."

"The man is a veritable Horace Greeley. Thirty-five years old, from a tough neighborhood in East Los Angeles—the fact that he grew up at all tells you something about him. His mother raised him after his father took a powder when the kid was six or seven. Somehow, with the help of a partial Air Force ROTC scholarship and a job in a sorority-house kitchen, he managed to snag a journalism degree from UCLA—that was in 1967. He saw service in Vietnam for a couple of years in Air Force Intelligence—that, as you may have guessed, was where we recruited him. He took to the secret life like a spaniel to water, apparently."

"I take it you didn't personally recruit him?"

35

LAWRENCE DUNNING

"I've never met the man, Sloan. You know how that goes—they sent me a cable with his dossier all neatly summarized. Somehow our paths have never crossed. He's ten years younger, of course. I gather he's spent time in London, Belfast, Geneva—lots of civilized places."

"What's he like in his spare time?" Sloan asked. "Or is that something they don't put in dossiers?"

Toberts smiled, remembering the details from Thornton Daniels's cablegram from Langley perfectly, as though they had been burned into his cerebral cortex: "Bruckner was with AF Intelligence 1968–69, where he repeatedly volunteered for search and destroy sorties with Montagnard hill troops. Was known as something of a killer, i.e., when the option existed for routine capture and transport of prisoners, passive interrogation in place, or termination, he usually went for the jugular. Recruited by one of our own in Saigon; after brief training on the Farm we sent him straight back to Vietnam for two more years. Not married, no permanent female attachments that we know of. One or two notations in the file of occasional violent outbreaks of temper, but these are class three unsubstantiated comments. Another class three mentions possibility of homosexual predisposition but we doubt it. Drinks too much but can hold it better than most. The occasional woman he has is apparently for sexual relief only. None of these things has ever, to our knowledge, affected his performance on the job, which is considerable. Has a deserved reputation for being ruthless but effective—we've used him on three Terminations With Extreme Prejudice and there was never a hint of moral ambivalence. Also, he was never in any way later connected with the bodies. He has deep personal drives that we've never been able to dredge up in the flutter-box sessions. As far as we know, he's a clean, cool, logical machine—just don't expect him to love you."

Toberts smiled again at Sloan, who was apparently waiting for an answer to his question. "Well, all I know is that he drinks, has an occasional woman, skis and climbs well, likes fast cars, flies anything he can get off the ground. And, of course, he eats babies for breakfast, like all of us do."

36

Sloan laughed. "He sounds like he'll fit in just fine."

"As I told you, though, he won't be around much, so don't fire any of your regular reporters. Too bad, in a way. The irony of it is that, given a different set of circumstances, Bruckner might have made a first-class investigative reporter in the bare-knuckles atmosphere of a city like Chicago or Saint Louis."

"Or Paris," Sloan said. He eyed a fresh-looking young girl and her boyfriend who sat down at a table not far away, and Toberts, when it was convenient, glanced back over his shoulder at the same table. There seemed to be nothing disturbing about them; noting things that occurred around him was simply habit for Toberts, a habit that Sloan had imitatively picked up over the months and years of their association.

"Any special instructions for the paper, Boss?"

"I told you not to call me that, even joking," Toberts said grimly. "No, nothing special. We may have something in a couple of weeks—the State Department's going on another tour of Third World countries and I have a feeling we'll need a boost from the press. Play it neutral for a while—we don't want to turn off any unsuspecting readers."

"That's something else," Sloan said. "Circulation's dropped two percent since I talked to you last. If something doesn't pick us up we'll be eating into capital before you know it."

"Don't sweat it, Sloan," Toberts said. He reached into the inside breast pocket of his suit jacket and withdrew a fat envelope, which he laid casually on the table, not looking at it. They continued to talk about various social and political events of the day in Paris and throughout France—events of the kind that would make the news columns of all thirteen Paris dailies as well as Sloan's *Times-Weekly*. "I assume you'll be covering the press reception for the new chargé d'affaires from Ghana tomorrow night?" Toberts asked him.

Sloan shook his head. "I've got a date with a little beauty I met last week at the theater opening. I think she goes for sexy bald-headed men."

"Forget the French floozie," Toberts said, in a tone of

voice that let Sloan know he wasn't kidding. "I want you to be there, where a conscientious newspaperman ought to be on a fine April Saturday night in Paris. Your *country* wants you to be there, Sloan, and without the floozie. Otherwise, I'm afraid your country will cut off your business."

"In the financial or metaphorical sense?"

Toberts smiled. "Probably one after the other. I don't make the rules, Sloan, I just see that they're followed. The embassy needs your support, and we can't very well get it if you aren't there. Just keep thinking 'African sphere of influence,' over and over. I guarantee it'll make you forget all about women."

Sloan nodded. "Okay, Martin. We'll do a good story for you."

"You'd damn well better," Toberts said. "I'll bring Bruckner around when I get the chance. I doubt if you'll have any worries there—he's got the technical know-how and we've fixed him up with every journalism card there is. Just remember to check with me before you try to send him out on a story."

"Sure, Martin. You know me."

"Fine, Sloan. I'm going to leave now—you stay put for a little while, okay? No use taking chances."

As Toberts got up and walked quickly to the exit, Sloan stared at the money Toberts had left on the table to pay for their lunch. Casually he put down his wineglass, signaled for the waiter, and pocketed the plain white envelope that, as usual, Toberts had filled with crisp new hundred-franc bills for another two weeks' operating expenses.

Toberts walked slowly along the street the restaurant was on, in the opposite direction from where his car was parked. He stared into shop windows, bought a newspaper at a corner kiosk, then crossed the street and slowly walked back up the other side, looking all the while for anyone who seemed to stop when he stopped, or an occupied car that hugged the curb, waiting. When he was satisfied that he wasn't being followed, he strolled briskly to the Peugeot and drove off in the direction of the Bois de Boulogne, the huge park at the western edge of the city that Parisians used in much the same way New Yorkers used Central Park.

The misting rain had stopped earlier and the sun was trying to force its way through the clouds. He felt good, as though extraordinary events were about to occur over which he would have a more than customary measure of control. Being in control was important to him; it had been his experience that he rarely got hurt when he was able to directly control an operation or at least that phase of an operation in which he was involved. The bad times he remembered had invariably been caused by the interference of people or events of which he had had no prior knowledge, and therefore no way to control.

He drove into the Bois and headed for the large centrally located meadow called the Pré Catelan, near the buildings housing the Racing Club of France. He found a parking place, left the car, and began walking along one of the numerous footpaths in the area. On the way he stopped to watch a lovely young horsewoman posting her fine roan mare down a nearby bridle path. The girl's long chestnut hair blew freely about her face, and as she lifted her hand to brush a wisp from her eyes, she turned in his direction and Toberts thought she smiled at him. In any case, she had smiled at *something,* and it made him feel younger, happier, more alive to think that the smile had been intended for him. When she was gone he resumed his walk at a faster pace.

At the southwest edge of the Pré Catelan stood an imposing chateau with gateposts the height of a man. Toberts stood beside the left gatepost for a moment, surveying the meadow and the few people along the walkways. When he was sure no one was watching, he reached up to a ledge just beneath the concrete ball atop the post and felt blindly for the small metal cylinder that he knew would be there. Maron had had plenty of time to leave a message for him inside the cylinder, as he had promised, but sometimes things happened that made a change of plans unavoidable. He unscrewed the cap of the cylinder and pulled out a folded sheet of thin paper covered with Maron's familiar scratchy handwriting. Toberts had discovered once that the scratchiness was caused by the fact that Maron, whenever possible and despite the ubiquity of ballpoint pens, still insisted on using an old-fashioned steel-nib pen and bottled ink, usually brown.

The message was short. Maron's runner had located Cassius in Paris at the Hotel De Luxe, 26 Rue Chevert, room 342. He had arrived sometime Wednesday evening; there were people watching the hotel. Maron had contacted Cassius directly, and they were to meet later in the day to discuss the matter at hand. Maron would return to the same drop point in the Bois after the meeting; Toberts could leave instructions for him, or Maron would request a meeting with Toberts to relay whatever information he had learned from Cassius.

Toberts put the message in his pocket and on a page torn from a small spiral notebook he always carried with him he wrote his own message to Maron: "You should not have made direct contact without my prior knowledge, but what's done is done. Meet me tomorrow morning (Saturday) at 9 o'clock in front of the giraffe run at the zoo in the Jardin des Plantes, *without fail.*"

He folded the page and placed it in the cylinder, replaced the cap, and returned the cylinder to its former hiding place atop the gatepost. He left the chateau and wandered for a while through the park. At a secluded spot behind a clump of bushes near the Shakespeare Garden he took Maron's message from his pocket, lit a match, and touched the flame to the corner of the thin paper. The paper curled and turned brown in his hand from the nearly invisible flame, and in a few moments the ashes blew from his fingers and dispersed in the breeze. He retraced his steps along the bridle path, hoping to see the young girl again, but when she didn't appear he reluctantly returned to his car and left the Bois.

He drove to a public telephone and called Mme. Joubert at the embassy. "Anything hot?" he asked her.

"Oh, the usual," she said cheerfully. "Where are you calling from?"

"A pay phone, but don't let that lull you into a false sense of security. As I've told you before, we've long suspected the Quai d'Orsay agents, the Sûreté, and God knows who else have tapped the city lines out of the embassy. What's up?"

"Well, Stanley dropped by—about the visitor from the south. He wanted to know if you wanted him to handle it."

Stanley was another agent who worked out of the embassy's fourth floor under Toberts, and the "visitor from the south" was an African agent the CIA, mostly Toberts, had been running for several years. A meeting had been planned two weeks ago, to take place in Paris during this weekend, but Toberts was certain he would not be able to make it. In fact, he was reasonably certain he was going to have to transfer a good number of more or less routine assignments to Stanley over the next several weeks —however long it took to come up with some answers on Project Lamplighter.

"Madame Joubert, tell Stanley he's to take over all my routine stuff for a while, until I inform his otherwise. That includes briefing the visitor from the south—the papers and notes are in the file safe. Anything else?"

"I don't believe so. Oh, that Mr. Coleman from building security dropped up for a minute, but he didn't seem to want anything special, just looked around and then left. I asked if I could help him, but he didn't even say scat to me. I think he's a rude man."

"Bastard!" Toberts muttered.

"What did you say? I didn't quite catch that."

"Never mind, Madame Joubert," Toberts said. "I'll be out of touch the rest of the afternoon, but I plan to drop by the office sometime this evening before I go home. Leave me a note about anything that comes up, will you?"

"I will. But can't you just go home when you've finished what you're doing? Your wife doesn't see that much of you, I know, and if I were in her place, I'd worry myself sick about you."

"You're sweet, Madame Joubert," Toberts said, "but Jessie doesn't worry about me. She has her . . . compensations. Tell Stanley to carry on like a good boy."

"I certainly will *not!*" she said, but she was laughing anyway.

"*Au revoir,*" Toberts said, and hung up the receiver.

It was three-thirty when Toberts got back into the Peugeot and headed as rapidly as the heavy traffic would allow straight across Paris to the northern edge of the city.

At the sign for the little airport town of Roissy-en-France he turned off the highway and pulled into a parking place at exactly five-fifteen. It would take him at least ten minutes to reach the terminal building and find the right gate, and then of course there was the problem of picking out of the crowd of deplaning passengers a person he had never met. The signal was to be a copy of *The Washington Post* folded diagonally under Bruckner's arm, but since the TWA flight originated in Washington, a good many of the passengers could be expected to have a *Post* in their hands as they went through customs.

He found a chair near the international flight customs inspection area and sat down to smoke and wait. Since a large majority of the flights in and out of the airport either originated in or were destined for some country other than France, the customs area was always busy, and this afternoon was no exception. Toberts watched the entrances and he watched the exits; he stared unobtrusively but thoroughly at each person in the room and at each new arrival, and though several were carrying newspapers, there were no diagonal folds and none of the men looked right anyway. The hope of the intelligence agents of every country in the world was to look like anything but agents, but somehow those who had been in the business a long time were usually able to recognize their counterparts at a glance.

Toberts waited until six o'clock but no one matching Bruckner's description appeared. Thinking that Daniels or someone in his office had screwed up again—that, or else that someone had recognized the infamous Mr. Pell Bruckner and had taken him out of circulation while the plane crossed the Atlantic—Toberts smoked a final cigarette, then walked out to the TWA flight information counter and checked the closed-circuit television listing for arrivals. Beside flight 802 from Dulles was the single word *dévié*.

"Diverted where?" he asked the pert young attendant behind the counter.

"Pardon? Oh, flight 802—*oui,* it has landed at Orly Airport about one-half hour ago. One of our radars is not working and we have sent several flights to Orly this afternoon. No one has told you before?"

Toberts, sighing, shook his head. "Unfortunately, no."

The girl looked genuinely sorry. "Is there anything I can do to assist you, monsieur?"

Toberts stared at the long lashes drifting periodically down over her lovely brown eyes and felt a momentary pang of desire. Twenty-two or twenty-three, he judged—certainly young enough to be his daughter. Why had he had the thought at all?

"No . . . no thank you, there's nothing to be done about it now," he told her, realizing that now he'd have to wait for Bruckner to contact him. He started to ask the girl if there was news of any *incidents* aboard the flight, incidents perhaps involving a slumping corpse? A door blown out with a man lashed to the handle? But of course he couldn't really ask those things, much as he wondered about the possibilities. He thanked her again and left the terminal building.

It was on the way back to Paris, where he planned to stop by the embassy, that some fool of a produce truck driver cut in front of him so sharply that he had to slam on his brakes and swerve off the highway onto the shoulder. As he sat gripping the wheel with the engine idling before starting out again, an almost mystical feeling of dread came over him that frightened him by its intensity and uncommonness. If his relationship with Bruckner had started this badly, he thought, there were surely much worse things to come. But because he was not a man for whom mysticism held any fascination, he shook off the foreboding and pressed his foot sharply against the accelerator, sending a spray of loose gravel onto the roadway behind him.

4

THE PILOT OF TWA international flight 802 from Washington, D.C., received word over the radio shortly after crossing the English Channel that number one and two approach radars at Charles de Gaulle Airport were malfunctioning and that his aircraft was being diverted to Orly. The old airport was actually closer to Paris than the new one by about five miles, but the two, being in opposite directions from the heart of the city, were more than eighteen miles apart. The passengers would not be pleased, particularly the ones expecting someone to meet them at de Gaulle, and they would probably irrationally blame the pilot; but that, he supposed, was why they paid him $84,000 a year.

Under the CIA's new travel rules Pell Bruckner was seated in about the middle of the 747's coach section (instead of in first class as was the former custom) and he was not enjoying it in the least. Toward the end of the boring flight he heard the click of the plane's intercom speaker system followed by the sound of someone blowing twice into the microphone, and even before he heard the stewardess's pleasant, unemotional voice he braced himself for trouble.

"Good afternoon, ladies and gentlemen," the stewardess cooed. "We have an important announcement for all passengers of flight 802 scheduled to deplane in Paris. The pilot has just received word from flight control operations at Charles de Gaulle Airport that, due to problems with their radar, for your safety we will be landing at Orly Airport instead. TWA regrets any inconvenience this unavoidable change in plans may cause you. If you would like assistance in making arrangements for ground transportation from Orly, please check with one of the three

44

stewards wearing red tags who are stationed throughout the aircraft. The pilot advises that landing time at Orly will be approximately the same as originally scheduled—that is, seventeen-thirty, or five-thirty P.M., Paris time. Thank you."

Damned radars, Bruckner thought, always fouling things up. He had a basic distrust of machines or anything else that he could not directly control. When he had only himself to depend upon he always knew he would be all right, because he took great pains to see that his physical and mental responses would be as perfect as it was humanly possible to make them. Emotions he discounted entirely as being nothing more than excess baggage a person in his profession could not afford. Working on the emotions of *other* people, manipulating them through their uncontrolled emotional responses, was, of course, something all good intelligence agents were trained to do, and Bruckner had learned his lessons well. The sight of a man or woman dying, horribly, right in front of him at this moment would have caused him no more consternation than the sight of a fly being swatted by a stranger. But the unexpected shift in arrangements concerning this flight, about which he had certain misgivings in any case, upset him more than he would have cared to admit.

His contact, who was to have been at de Gaulle, was only a name to him—not the kind of situation he would have preferred. And now this mix-up about airports. He wondered whether the contact would have checked on the flight early enough to have done something about meeting him at Orly instead of de Gaulle. He hoped so, because he had not been to Paris in several years and he was always slightly uncomfortable operating in an unfamiliar locale. But he supposed, with characteristic cynicism, that no one would have checked, and that he would therefore be left stranded at a dimly remembered airport outside a strange city.

As the plane deviated imperceptibly from its scheduled flight path, Bruckner went over again in his mind the instructions and information passed along to him by Thornton Daniels at Langley. Another job of pretending to be a working newsman. Bruckner sometimes wished he had

45

a more interesting or exciting cover. Once he had even suggested to Langley that they let him cover as a racing-car driver, actually entering races in various parts of the world as the need arose. But someone had quickly vetoed the idea as being impractical because, for one thing, the sport was too dangerous to risk the health and life of one of their top covert agents in a non-mission-oriented way, and second, the logistical difficulties of fitting CIA missions around the availability of a scheduled race in the right place at the right time would have been so enormous that Bruckner was told to forget the idea and concentrate on keeping his journalistic skills current.

After all, there was hardly a place on the globe without a newspaper or two, and nearly all of them eventually saw, or could be convinced by CIA funds to see, the wisdom of an English-language edition. More newspapers had been started or kept going this way than anyone outside the agency even began to suspect. Bruckner had smiled at the possibility that someday, following the meddling of some congressional committee or another, all CIA support might be summarily withdrawn from the world's newspapers and newspapermen. Overnight the total news outlets internationally might, he suspected, drop by half, and almost no one would be able to figure out why. Fortunately, the agency had been able to soft-pedal the recent public outcry about clandestine operations of the American intelligence establishment, so that while a few sops were thrown to the protesters in the way of public censure and scattered firings of officers who had lost their usefulness long ago anyway, in truth the agency continued to operate just about as it pleased. There were simply going to be a great many things no one would talk about in the future to anyone, particularly congressional oversight committees. The gullibility of the American public to believe what they saw printed in their daily newspapers was legendary and, in Bruckner's opinion, grossly underestimated.

He lit a cigarette and stared out the window, remembering the time years ago, as a student at UCLA during the mid-sixties, when he had actually wanted to become an investigative journalist. He had seen it as a way to collect and wield a vast amount of power over other people's lives, and with that kind of power you would have to be a fool not to be able to convert it into money, large sums of money. Who was to say whether the money so obtained would have been any more dishonest or illegal than the under-the-table funds with which most political parties and corporate businesses seemed to operate these days?

He had had to live, during those college days, with a vast feeling of inferiority that it had taken him most of the rest of his life to overcome. He would not have been able to attend college at all without the partial ROTC scholarship, and even then he was perpetually ashamed of his poor educational and cultural background, his lack of the right clothes, his lack of the large amounts of spending money that all his classmates seemed not only to have, but to take for granted. Even now he sometimes wondered whether any of his acquaintances during those years noticed that he wore his ROTC uniform much more often than was required by the rules. It was only after graduation that he found his proper niche in life when he was assigned to Air Force Intelligence under Vietnam combat conditions. There, he had felt almost immediately, was the life he had been born to lead, and nothing so far had caused him to change his mind. He still wondered when his chance at working his way into a really lucrative deal would surface, but he knew that the secret life offered many such opportunities for undisclosed personal gain, and that he would immediately recognize such an opportunity when it came his way.

As the 747 began to dip slightly above the cloudy skies of France, stewardesses came bustling down the aisles, making sure that all their passengers had their seat belts fastened and cigarettes extinguished for the impending descent. Adjusting his already fastened belt a fraction tighter, Bruckner ground out the glowing ash of his own cigarette, and out of years of habit split the paper with his thumbnail, shredded the unburned tobacco into the ashtray on the arm of the seat, and rolled the paper into a ball that also went into the tray. Maybe, he thought, something about the project he was being sent halfway around the earth to work on—the KGB's Project Lamplighter—would result in a door being opened, a contact made, a secret discovered that would ensure his financial independence for the rest of his life. Just maybe. And if it did, he would damned sure be ready for it.

The customs check at Orly was the usual miserable mess. Bruckner could hardly believe that anyone would be so stupid as to put a false bottom in a suitcase as a nesting place for smuggled gems or drugs, yet the papers were always full of juicy little items about how some local customs inspector, on nothing more than a hunch, had turned up a quarter of a million dollars' worth of very good cocaine hidden in a secret compartment of some second-rate actress's overnight bag.

Bruckner himself knew at least a half dozen ways to smuggle things across international borders that would seldom if ever alert the usual customs agent. As he stood waiting in line for his baggage to be checked, he thought of some of his favorite ruses. One was to secrete small objects beneath a full wig. Women's wigs were always suspect, men's almost never were. It was for this specific reason that Bruckner wore his own hair cut almost unfashionably short.

Another hiding place he had used on a number of occasions was inside the body of a pet to be shipped on the same plane he was riding. He had heard that customs people had sometimes found contraband jewels by digging through the feces of some poor German shepherd fed the bright stones in a handful of raw hamburger. But hardly anyone would think of, or have the stomach for, removing stained bandages from the haunch of a bedraggled-looking cocker spaniel and probing the fresh wound with medical instruments to remove the foreign matter carefully buried in the dog's flesh. The dogs always died when Bruckner recovered his property; perhaps he was not as gentle as he might have been, but that was just as well, since he would have been obliged to kill them in any case.

Having been passed cursorily through the inspection, Bruckner wandered to the main part of the terminal building, his copy of *The Washington Post* folded diagonally under his arm as he had been instructed. He checked his quartz digital watch against the wall clock; both agreed it was two minutes before six P.M. since, as he customarily did, he had set his watch for his destination time zone almost the minute he had stepped on the plane at Dulles. He continued to circle the waiting area for another thirty minutes, stopping now and then at a kiosk to flip through an English-language publication or to stare at the pictures in a French one. He had learned French years ago, of course, but it was not one of his usual working languages, and since there hadn't been time to take a refresher at the CIA language school, he would have to brush up on it here in Paris. *Damn Thornton Daniels!* he thought, remembering that Daniels had promised to cable Toberts at the Paris Embassy immediately after they had talked. Well, Daniels couldn't have known about the faulty radar at de Gaulle, he supposed, but *someone* should have checked it out.

He made one more slow circuit of the terminal building and then collected his baggage and thrust it into the back seat of a taxi waiting outside in the queue. "Hotel Crillon," he said to the driver, giving the name of a famous old Paris landmark on the Place de la Concorde. Daniels had mentioned it to him as a possibility, though carefully pointing out to Bruckner that it was quite expensive; that, as much as anything, had made up Bruckner's mind for him that he would have to stay there. And should anyone at Langley question his expense vouchers, there was also the fact that the Crillon was only a stone's throw from the American Embassy on Avenue Gabriel.

The taxi driver was voluble in both French and a kind of gutter English, and when his passenger did not respond with more than an occasional grunt, he even tried what was probably the one phrase of Yiddish that he knew, to no effect. The remainder of the ten-mile ride was made in a kind of grudging silence on the driver's part, while Bruckner carefully kept an eye on the cars behind them, and even those waiting for traffic lights at intersections through which they passed.

They crossed the Seine on the magnificently broad Pont de la Concorde and made the traffic loop around the statues and fountains toward the hotel. The doormen and porters treated Bruckner as though he were royalty, which pleased him immensely. It seemed that their greatest desire was only to serve him in such a way that, during his stay with them, no matter how brief, he would want for nothing. The atmosphere of the richly decorated lobby was so compellingly tasteful that he marveled at how easily a former East Los Angeles resident could adapt to it, as though he had been accustomed to rooms like this all his life.

He was lucky, the reservation clerk told him, there had been a cancellation within the hour. Bruckner was escorted to his room on the fourth floor west by an immaculately uniformed porter. Though plainer than the lobby downstairs, the room was decorated in what appeared to be blue velvet and antique oak, with paintings on the walls that, for all Bruckner knew, might have been original old masters.

When the porter was gone, after having been tipped the exactly correct amount, Bruckner went to the window and stared down at the street below. In his hand was a map of the city that he had purchased while waiting for his contact at Orly. The street had to be Rue Boissy-d'Anglas; directly across the street was the imposing structure housing the American Embassy.

He studied the building a moment or two, then went to the telephone and asked the hotel operator to get him a certain extension at the embassy. While it rang he glanced at his watch and saw that it was seven o'clock; he had eaten a light mid-afternoon snack on the plane, but he would need something more substantial than that shortly, and he most certainly could use another drink or two. A light misting kind of rain speckled the window and the patterns of light reflected by it. He felt the salutary effects of the hotel already beginning to wear off.

"Two-six-five, seven-four, nine-one," a young man's voice answered after the connection was made.

Bruckner waited for the operator to click off, then said, "Is Mr. Toberts in? This is Pell Bruckner, with the Paris *Times-Weekly*."

"Oh, Mr. Bruckner, I'm sorry," the young man said.

"Mr. Toberts isn't in just now—in fact, I believe he said something about meeting you at de Gaulle Airport this afternoon."

"That's dandy," Bruckner said. "Except that I wasn't *at* de Gaulle—my plane landed at Orly. Does this kind of screw-up happen often here?"

There was a momentary pause at the other end. "About as often as anywhere else, I presume."

"What's your name?" Bruckner said abruptly. "Or aren't you allowed to use it?"

"I'm Stanley, sir. Would you, ah, care to come over to the embassy and wait for Mr. Toberts? I'm sure he'll return shortly."

"I'm tired, Stanley. I've had a long trip."

"It's just across the street, sir. You *are* calling from the Crillon, aren't you?"

Bruckner frowned. He had told no one he was staying here, in fact had not even definitely made up his mind about it until he was in the airport. "Yes," he said, "I am. How did you know?"

"I believe Mr. Daniels told us you would be staying there."

"Well, I'm still tired. You tell your Mr. Toberts that I'll be in the Crillon bar indefinitely—anytime he decides to come back on the job he can call me there."

"Yes, sir, Mr. Bruckner. I'll tell him when he comes in."

Bruckner held onto the phone for a moment, listening to the various clicks and buzzes that were sometimes an important part of his life. He wondered where they found the terribly green adolescent agents they were hiring these days, nice young men like Stanley who didn't have the foggiest notion what it was all about and never would know. Probably out of some Ivy League fraternity house, he thought with a touch of the old bitterness.

He hung up the receiver, unpacked the small bag that held most of his essential travel gear, and went downstairs in the elevator to find a drink.

The bar at the Crillon exuded an atmosphere of wealth, position, and immense satisfaction with itself, from the opulent burnished woodwork to the perfectly correct, professionally detached bartender. There were three older couples and one table of noisy men in the room when Bruckner entered and took a seat at the bar off by himself. The men he assumed were newspaper reporters—Thornton Daniels had mentioned that the place was frequented at five in the afternoon by English-speaking journalists. Bruckner glanced at his watch, confirming that it was nearly eight. "They're mostly a harmless bunch of drunks," Daniels had said, "but I'd avoid them if I were you. No sense raising unnecessary questions, and some of them are still sharp enough to smell a phony from a mile off. Your credentials are good, but not *that* good."

Bruckner ignored the loud group and began to drink steadily, relieved to see that Chivas Regal was available here, as it was nearly everywhere else in the world, if you were willing to pay the price. He drank it on the rocks, undiluted, believing that the addition of anything, even water, to the pure essence of Scotch whisky would have been to desecrate what he considered the nearly perfect drug.

The loud group left after a while and the room became considerably quieter. Somewhere in the middle of his third Scotch Bruckner noticed that a girl with red hair had taken a stool at the same end of the bar, and that when the drink she ordered was set before her, it was bright blue and frothy. The bartender spoke briefly to the girl, then came over behind the bar to where Bruckner sat. "*Pardon, monsieur,*" he said. "The young lady wishes to know if she may buy the handsome American gentleman a drink."

Bruckner looked at the girl, who was dressed in the sort of flashy, expensive clothes that were the almost universal badge of the higher-class prostitute. "Only if I may buy her a drink in return," Bruckner said.

The bartender passed along his message to the girl, who smiled broadly at him across the empty stools. In a moment she picked up her blue drink and moved to the stool beside him.

"I'm afraid I don't speak much French," Bruckner told her, knowing it was better to get the language thing out of the way early.

"Neither do I," the girl said. "I'm German, actually. Sometimes I claim to be Swiss, but only because the French are such poor sports. Are you from Detroit?"

"Detroit? No—why did you ask that?"

"No reason. I met a very nice young man from Detroit once—he was a student at the Sorbonne. He had red hair, and a funny red beard that tickled."

The girl laughed, remembering, and showed her incredibly bad teeth. She should have kept her mouth closed, Bruckner thought, aware that the price she would settle for had just dropped fifty percent from what she would ask. With her lips together she could have been an angel—long auburn red hair, cut in bangs, green eye shadow, a lustrous, healthy look on her cheeks, and lips that could, he imagined, perform small miracles on a man's body. Her body was the kind that would always attract attention, at least for a few more years, her breasts still young enough to be high and well-spaced without the hindrance of a bra, her buttocks large and rounded with deep visible cleavage, the latter immensely erotic to Bruckner.

He stirred on the seat. "What's that terrible thing you're drinking? That blue thing."

"*Noyaux* egg fizz. It's delicious, if you like the taste of almonds. You wish to try it?"

"No," Bruckner said sharply, disliking her playful attitude. "Drink the damned thing in a hurry and let's go."

The girl's eyes opened wide. "Go where?"

"Upstairs, of course. You didn't think we were going to sit here and discuss French politics or the weather, did you?"

The girl tossed her head and gave him a weary smile. She took from her purse a small card printed with her name—Ilsa—and a telephone number and handed the card to Bruckner. "In case you like me and wish to see me again," she explained needlessly.

Disregarding the girl's previous offer, Bruckner paid for both drinks and led her by the arm toward the elevator. He had the feeling she knew her way around the Crillon a great deal better than he did. On the elevator she asked his room number, and when they reached the fourth floor she automatically turned in the right direction.

Once inside the room the girl quickly surveyed the bed and the suitcases and began to undress. Bruckner disliked the inevitable discussion of money, but it was always better for such a discussion to take place before the ceremonies, not after. "What is your usual charge?" he asked her matter-of-factly.

She looked at him with slightly raised eyebrows. "That depends."

"On what?"

"Several things. The gentleman in question, for instance —whether he appears to be clean, free from disease—"

"Never mind about that," Bruckner interrupted her. "I assume I take more of a risk there than you do."

"Then there are the different preferences of the gentleman in question." She was naked now, and he could see that she did indeed have a magnificent body. She ran her hands lightly over her breasts and down her flanks, smoothing the skin in order to show herself off to best advantage.

Bruckner became impatient. "I would like for our lovemaking to be something of a surprise for you. How much for whatever pleasures we shall decide upon as we go along?"

The girl looked at him again, and this time there was nothing of the flirtatious coquette in her eyes; her manner had turned hard and businesslike. "Three hundred francs," she said without hesitation.

Bruckner translated that into dollars in his head: between sixty-five and seventy. She was obviously worth at least that much, and probably could have gotten more from almost any man she approached. She was either new to the business or, for some reason, had taken an interest in him, Bruckner, personally. The latter possibility bothered him slightly but for only a moment; dismissing it as the effect of too many hours in the air and too much alcohol, he quickly stripped off his clothes, pulled the quilt, blanket, and top sheet to the floor and more or less pushed the girl onto the bed.

She lay on her back, staring up at Bruckner above her, then slowly began to caress his body with her hands, doing what she was paid to do. She drew up her knees and parted her legs, displaying for him with painted fingers her inner beauty. But Bruckner was not interested. Roughly he turned her over face down on the bed and elevated her buttocks by shoving her knees up beneath her freely hanging breasts. Excited now, he entered her anally with one short jab, causing her to scream in pain.

"*Graisse!*" she yelled. "*Graisse, bâtard!*"—begging Bruckner to use some sort of lubricant to keep from hurting her. But he continued to hold her upper thighs in his powerful hands and with each short, forceful stroke entered her body more deeply. Helpless, the girl tried to muffle her screams with the knuckles of one hand stuffed against her mouth, but with each new assault against the dry internal membranes her breath was expelled in sharp gasps as audible pleas for mercy.

It continued for a while, until Bruckner, with a deep groan, completed the act and withdrew. The girl sobbed quietly on the bed. Disgusted, Bruckner left the bed and took three hundred francs from his wallet. "Here," he said, holding out the bills, "take this and get the hell out of here."

The girl looked at him from teary eyes, but when she did not immediately move from the bed, Bruckner leaned over her curled-up body and shouted, "Now! Unless you want me to begin again."

Undeniably frightened this time, the girl darted from the bed and threw her clothes on hastily. She no longer looked, Bruckner thought, as though she would be worth three hundred francs to anyone. He suddenly felt foolish, as though he had been grossly overcharged for an inferior product, and took a step toward the girl with the idea of taking some of the money back. But she had already stuffed it into her huge purse, and with a departing look of fear and deep hatred for Bruckner she burst through the door into the hallway and disappeared.

Sorry that he had gotten involved with her, Bruckner went into the bathroom and cleaned himself. What did prostitutes expect? he wondered. You paid them to let you do things to them, and then when you did those things they acted as though you were some kind of monster without feelings. He couldn't imagine anyone being stupid enough to become emotionally involved with a whore.

What he had done was simply the only way he could have sex with a woman, and over the years he had come to realize that the violence involved, and the fact that the women usually were screaming with pain, contributed powerfully to his enjoyment of the act. It hadn't been like that with the young Montagnard hill boy Giap in Vietnam; though brief, their relationship had been more like a love affair than anything Bruckner had experienced since, and each time he thought of Giap being blown apart by the freak artillery round in the middle of a hot, bright afternoon, he felt more pain and sorrow than anything else in his life ever caused him. What he needed now, he decided, was another drink, and he dressed quickly and returned to the bar off the lobby of the hotel.

But as he sat drinking the straight Scotches, one after the other, more painful images flooded his mind and he didn't seem able to control them. The most disturbing was his memory of a time years before when he had been on assignment in Belfast. After several months in the wet, cold climate he had taken a week's leave and gone to lie in the sun on the Algarve coast of southern Portugal, and while there had drunk enormous quantities of the local brandy. One morning, drunk on the brandy and sun and the sea air, he had somehow met and then had sex—the same kind of sex as with the prostitute—with a dark-haired, huge-eyed girl who could not have been more than eleven years old. There was no question he had been drunk out of his mind, but sometimes, as now, he remembered the little girl so clearly he felt that he could almost reach out and touch her smooth dark skin. What had happened after the incident was lost in waves of alcohol and years of purposeful forgetting; and except for times like this, sitting in some bar waiting for a contact, he actually did manage to forget a good many details of the incident that some overzealous security man from Langley would have given a week's pay to get his hands on. But that would never happen.

Sighing heavily, Bruckner ordered another Scotch on the rocks and waited for the man named Martin Toberts to join him.

5

TOBERTS STOOD QUIETLY AT the entrance of the Crillon
bar and took in everything of interest, all the little details
that most people who were not trained observers would
never notice. He saw a table of older tourists, two women
and a bald man wearing thick corrective lenses, Belgian,
speaking Flemish; one of the women was the man's wife
and one was his sister, though since he treated both with
equal dislike it was impossible to tell which was which.
There were three reporters huddled together in a corner
whom Toberts instantly recognized—two from *The Washington Post* and one from *Newsweek*—who shared Paris
offices on the Rue de Berri in the eighth arrondissement.
They had obviously been in the bar a good while and were
now quite drunk—whether drunk enough not to recognize him, Toberts could not tell.

There were a few other people spotted around the room,
but none looked interesting to Toberts. Pell Bruckner was
not here; he knew that instantly. Toberts imagined he
could pick out another agent from a group just by viewing
any ten men standing perfectly erect and motionless in a
straight line. Something about the quickness of the eyes,
the set line of the jaws and lips . . .

When he had returned to the embassy after the abortive
attempt to meet Bruckner at de Gaulle Airport, Stanley
had told him about Bruckner's somewhat testy call from
the Crillon, and Toberts had decided simply to walk over
to the hotel rather than have Bruckner paged in the bar.
Paging always called attention to people; Bruckner should
have known that. As Toberts was deciding whether to ask
the bartender about a person who might have been at the
bar earlier, a man wearing an expensive-looking cashmere

jacket came from the direction of the restrooms and re-
claimed his seat at the bar. He was slightly taller than
Toberts—about six feet two inches, he judged—thinner,
and a good ten years younger, probably around thirty-five.
He had dark hair and bright electric-blue eyes, and from
what Toberts could see in his movements it appeared that
every inch of his trim body was muscle. Daniels had indicated that Bruckner was a health nut, constantly keeping
in shape by running, lifting weights, using portable tension
bars in his hotel rooms, exercising his hand and wrist
muscles by squeezing a firm rubber ball at odd inactive
moments. There was no question that the man was Pell
Bruckner. Walking directly toward the bar, Toberts wondered whether, should the occasion ever arise, he would
be able to take Bruckner in *mano a mano* competition.

"I believe you were expecting me," Toberts said, standing
beside Bruckner's stool. "Martin Toberts. Sorry about the
mix-up at the airport."

He extended his hand and Bruckner, unhurried, glanced
at him and finally shook the hand. "Pell Bruckner. Actually, I had nothing better to do than hang around the corridors at Orly for an hour."

He was smiling, as if to let Toberts know that he was
joking, but Toberts wondered.

"Let's go over to a booth—it's a little quieter, I think,
and we can talk better there."

"Yeah, I saw them, too," Bruckner said, motioning
toward the table of reporters.

As Bruckner slid into the booth, the drink he was carrying spilled on the table and he cursed in English. He
glanced up quickly at Toberts and smiled in the same
boyish way again. "Hate to waste this stuff," he said. "Do
you have any idea what they get for a small glass of
Scotch here?"

"Yes, I do," Toberts said. He had ordered a whisky-
Perrier at the bar, which the bartender now brought over
to him. "I hope you ordered whisky instead of Scotch—
you get the same thing, but usually a lot cheaper."

Bruckner nodded. "You mean that generic bullshit. No,
thanks. I like to know what I'm getting. Or getting into."

"That I can understand," Toberts said. He offered

Bruckner one of his cigarettes, which Bruckner accepted. "What's the news from the States?"

Bruckner leaned closer across the table. "Funny stuff. Weird stuff. I don't know how much Daniels told you in the cables."

"Bare outlines, mostly. Why don't you give me what you've got?"

"What would you do with a dose of syphilis?" Bruckner asked him, laughing with adolescent good humor at his own joke.

Toberts stared at him, wondering whether he was drunk and to what extent he could trust this unknown quantity thrust on him by Langley, in their infinite wisdom.

"No, I'm not *borracho, amigo,*" Bruckner said, seeing Toberts's expression. "Just a little jet lag, nothing more serious than that. I have something of a reputation for being a drinker—I suppose that was in the dossier Daniels forwarded to you—but, believe me, I never let it get in the way. *Never.* Understood?"

"Duly noted, as we say in the Foreign Service."

"I thought your cover was the Communication Agency."

"Same thing, almost. You were about to tell me . . . ?"

"Yeah—the poop from Group. Okay, Langley's been talking to the comm spooks at Fort Meade, and I guess between them they know several things. There's been unusually heavy message traffic between New York City and Paris, originating at the Russian U.N. Mission building, on KGB channels. Nothing unusual about the KGB tie-in, as I suppose you know. Half the Russian U.N. delegation have been positively identified as KGB plants. The odd thing is there's also word through direct CIA channels that something big is being planned by the Russians to take place before long in the eastern U.S., incredible as that sounds. Langley understands the KGB has given it top priority, and they've even got an operational code name—Lamplighter."

"Yes. *Fonarshchik,*" Toberts said. "I'm sure Langley has run it through their language permutations computer for significance, although the KGB doesn't often give hints to the opposition that way."

"Maybe they feel secure," Bruckner offered, and

Toberts had to agree that was possible, in light of the small amount of information available up to this point.

"Anyway, Daniels thought I might be able to help you dig up something here to tie in with the Paris traffic. It could be no more than a relay point, of course; Paris itself may not be an objective at all."

"Naturally. We've thought of that, too. But there isn't anything else to go on. Did Daniels say exactly what he expected you to help me *do?*"

"Oh, research, interrogation, the usual analytical stuff. I don't know whether you're aware of this, Toberts, but analysis is not my usual bag."

Toberts gazed intently into Bruckner's amazing blue eyes. "I understand that several CIA connections, both sides, have died of the measles immediately after they were seen talking to you. Let's see—there was that car accident north of London a couple of years back, a fatal case of brucellosis in a previously healthy Swiss athlete in Geneva, somebody fell off a five-story ruin in Athens ... You really get around, don't you, Bruckner?"

"I happen to be between assignments—Daniels said I was to tell you that."

"So I wouldn't worry," Toberts said gravely. "Okay. Now about your cover while you're here—"

"Daniels fixed me up with a walletful," Bruckner said.

He started to pull them out but Toberts stopped him. "Press cards and passes are great for window dressing, but there's no way you're going to fool some of the old-timers here. And what one foreign press journalist knows, they all know, sooner or later—it's a tight little world here."

"So I'll keep my mouth shut."

"You'll have to do better than that. Here's the dope: The Paris *Times-Weekly* has been around long enough to be accepted as an established English-language paper with a middle-of-the-road editorial policy, though normally pro-U.S. They—meaning Harold Sloan, the editor—have been on our payroll for several years and they know which side their bread is buttered on."

"Is there any possibility they're also on the take from the other side?"

"We don't think so. Sloan's no fool, he knows we're watching him and the paper—every word of every issue —as closely as we watch anything in Paris. The man is a pragmatist. I don't think he'd want to blow a good thing by doing anything to cast suspicion on his operation."

Bruckner laughed sourly. "I wish I had a dollar for every 'pragmatist' I've known who's been caught working both sides of the street."

"Nevertheless," Toberts said, "trust Sloan. He's your link with the real world, and sometimes with me. Because of my press connections there's nothing wrong with my being seen with you from time to time, but it can't be a continual thing. We suspect that our phone line into the embassy is being tapped, certainly by the French Foreign Office and possibly by the KGB as well. In other words, treat it like you would any other open line."

"What kind of working hours am I supposed to keep with Sloan?"

"Why? You got a hot date in Paris you didn't tell us about?"

"You know what I mean, Toberts. Although no one said I had to spend twenty-four hours a day on this project."

"If that's what it takes, that's what we'll spend," Toberts said, in a tone of voice he hoped would give Bruckner the message. He watched with interest as Bruckner wet his fingers and pinched out the ash of his cigarette, then split open the paper of the butt lengthwise, shredded the tobacco into the ashtray, and rolled the paper into a tiny ball which he flicked away from the booth. It was called "field stripping" by military people; Toberts hadn't seen anyone do that to a cigarette in years.

"You won't be in the *Times-Weekly* offices much," Toberts continued. "I've cleared that with Sloan. And you shouldn't have any more than necessary to do with the other reporters and assistant editors. It's a small operation, not more than a dozen staff members total. Just keep out of their way; Sloan will pass the word to the others that you're an expert on long-term digging, the really deep investigative stuff. Who knows, we might even give you some bits and pieces from time to time that Sloan can dummy up as though you'd turned the stuff in yourself. You won't have time to do any actual writing for them."

"Does Sloan know what I'm really here for?"

"No. Neither do I, but that's beside the point."

Bruckner smiled, and the blue almost disappeared from his narrowed eyes. "Langley has its little ways, Marty."

Toberts winced at Bruckner's use of the nickname he hated. "Martin will do fine, Pell. Or Toberts, either one."

"Yes, sir, Mr. Martin Toberts," Bruckner said with mock humility. "Is that 'Junior' or 'Senior'?"

Toberts was considering whether and to what extent he should assert his authority over Bruckner now, and perhaps forestall later angry repercussions, when he noticed a pretty young girl with long red hair cut in bangs and two large, rough-looking men with decidedly unfriendly faces approaching their booth rapidly from the doorway. Bruckner, too, had noticed them; a frown crossed his face and he glanced at Toberts.

"This is trouble," he mouthed almost silently.

The girl approached the table first and seemed to be addressing herself only to Bruckner, as though she knew him; but since she spoke in rapid German, which was not one of Toberts's major languages, he could only catch every third or fourth word. It seemed to have something to do with the fact that Bruckner had treated her badly, and now she had brought friends along to teach him a lesson in manners.

"Does she speak English?" Toberts asked Bruckner.

"Yeah, sort of. Listen, Toberts, she's a whore. She works the hotel here. We had a little . . . misunderstanding a while ago. But she got her money, every cent she asked for. I don't know what her beef is."

"Whore?" the girl shouted, showing a mouthful of bad teeth. "You call me a whore, you goddamn pervert? My friends here will teach you a little respect for a decent woman." And as she spoke she stepped back and the two ugly men moved in close to the edge of the booth on Bruckner's side, effectively trapping him.

"Now, just a moment, please," Toberts said in his most unctuously diplomatic manner. "I'm sure this unfortunate matter can be cleared up without any unpleasantness.

However, I suggest we continue our little talk outside, as I believe the bartender is about to call *les flics*."

It wasn't true— in fact, the bartender was watching them with something like amusement on his placid face —but Toberts was afraid the table of drunken reporters in the corner might at any moment wake up enough to take an interest in the argument, which he wanted to avoid at all costs. He scooted out from his side of the booth and, smiling, motioned to the two men and the girl to follow him. For a moment he wasn't sure they were going to, but then Bruckner shrugged and smiled at the nearest man, the burlier of the two, and apparently convinced them that he was not going to be a problem for them.

As the group moved warily toward the exit, each eyeing the others suspiciously, Toberts began to doubt that Bruckner, in his present condition, would be much help with the two toughs despite his earlier assurances. But as soon as they were through the lobby and out on the dark street several things happened simultaneously. The girl rushed at Bruckner with a flash of metal in her hand which, though it turned out to be only a nail file, Bruckner quickly dislodged with a short downward chop to her wrist; the girl screamed in pain, and the largest of her friends, moving remarkably rapidly for his bulk, sent an open meaty hand crashing toward Bruckner's throat. Bruckner grunted, catching only the edge of one finger as he neatly backstepped the blow, and suddenly his right leg was in the air, rigid as steel, describing an arc that ended, at the outside edge of his shoe, buried deep in the huge man's genitals. The other man advanced toward Toberts with something like murder in his tiny piglike eyes.

Although he knew he was in excellent shape for his age, Toberts was not and never had been a street brawler, preferring to settle difficult matters with his brain instead of his fists whenever possible. But there were times when no amount of talk could take care of a problem, and this seemed to be one of those times. Intensely conscious of the other man's reach and manner of movement, Toberts let him get almost within striking distance before changing

63

his own position from one of passivity to one of total muscular concentration.

Remembering the startling technique of his karate instructor, Mr. Takichi, at the CIA training farm, instead of screaming the usual *haieee!* or some variation thereof, Toberts, mentally screaming, quietly spoke the single Japanese word *dozo,* which meant "please." And it had the proper effect. For that one vastly important fraction of a second in a physical contest of this kind his opponent almost stopped his forward motion to puzzle out Toberts's purpose in speaking the foreign word, and while the man's balance was less than perfect, Toberts smashed his rigid hand flat against his opponent's carotid artery, nearly splitting the man's neck in two.

Bruckner and Toberts looked at each other and Bruckner smiled. "I didn't know an old man like you had it in you."

"I wasn't too sure about you, either," Toberts said. The girl, holding her damaged wrist, stood against the wall staring down at her two companions, who were definitely not going to be of any further help to her for some time. She looked up at Bruckner, the cause of all her problems, cursed at him in German and English, spat at him but missed, and went off down the street still cursing loudly.

"You must have done something to make her that angry," Toberts said to Bruckner. "You sure you paid her enough?"

"I'm sure," Bruckner said coldly. "What do we do with these two?"

"Leave them. My car's parked over at the embassy— I'll call the French cops anonymously and have them picked up and taken to a hospital. First, though, I'm just curious about something . . ."

He bent over first one, then the other of the two men, removed their billfolds, and flipped rapidly through their identification papers. "French, apparently. Nothing unusual looking. I thought maybe, you know—"

"Yeah, I thought about that, too," Bruckner said. "I think the lady was just mad at me for some reason; maybe she had a tough night." He laughed. "Lady, hell."

"Okay, let's accept it at face value," Toberts said,

replacing the billfolds exactly as they had been after carefully wiping off his prints. "Get a good night's sleep, Bruckner—we've got a year or two of digging ahead of us, starting tomorrow."

"Maybe yes, maybe no," Bruckner said. "We'll see."

As Bruckner disappeared into the hotel entrance, Toberts began walking back toward the embassy. At the corner of the Rue Boissy-d'Anglas he turned and stared back at the Crillon's impressive south face. As he did so, he caught sight of a lighted outdoor telephone booth in the middle of the block. Inside it was the girl, Bruckner's whore, who with some difficulty because of the wounded hand was attempting to make a hurried and apparently secretive call. She was crouched low in the booth as though attempting to stay out of sight and, as she clumsily dialed the numbers with her left hand, repeatedly turned her head to stare out through the glass at the street behind her. She spoke only a few minutes, then hung up and walked up the street, away from Toberts, who was standing in the deep shadow of a fountain.

A cold knot began to form in his stomach as he watched her walk away. She might or might not be a coincidence, he thought, but in almost twenty-five years in this business, if it could be called a business, he had never run across an occurrence of any importance that he would have called a genuine coincidence.

6

"MONSIEUR JEAN PETIT TO see you, sir," the secretary said, standing in the open doorway to Colonel Alexis Balachov's inner office within the complex of UNESCO buildings on the Place de Fontenoy. Because of Colonel Balachov's high rank as the chief Soviet delegate to the U.N. organization, the office had one of the better locations in the complex and was beautifully appointed. And because of Colonel Balachov's other high-ranking position—that of the KGB *rezident* or chief of station for the Paris area —his secretary, who was rather short and broad with curly graying hair, was, in her own right, a major in the KGB.

"Ah, yes, show Monsieur Petit in," the colonel said graciously.

The agent Cassius walked through the door without waiting for the secretary to show him in; he understood Russian perfectly and had very little time to waste on formalities. "Colonel Balachov," he said, extending his hand in greeting. They had seen each other only the day before so there was little need for extended greetings.

"What is it you have for me today, comrade Cassius?" the colonel asked him, after the secretary had closed the door. "I assume it is of some importance, to risk a return to this office so soon."

"I believe it is, yes," Cassius said. He had never felt altogether comfortable in Colonel Balachov's presence. Even seated it was obvious the colonel was a big man who, when standing, was a good eight inches taller than Cassius's five feet six inches. The material of the colonel's business suit, Cassius noted, in the meticulous way he noted everything about everyone he came in contact with, was far inferior to his own, though perhaps almost as expensive. KGB colonels had never been noted for their sartorial splendor, and most wore ready-made, even ill-fitting clothing.

"I've been contacted by a CIA agent named Maron—I believe you know of him?"

"Yes. Georges Maron. He's one of Tobert's subagents."

"In any case, he called me at the hotel where I'm staying —a second-class firetrap over by the Invalides—to tell me that one of his runners had found me there, and that 'Uncle,' as he put it, wished to speak with me about an urgent matter."

"*Fonarshchik*," Colonel Balachov said. "Or, as our Mr. Toberts refers to it, 'Lamplighter.' There seems to have been a leak somewhere in our own channels—I suspect we shall eventually trace it to the Soviet U.N. mission in New York City."

"Quite so. Maron also indicated that another of his runners followed me part of the way here yesterday afternoon before I lost him. It is also possible, though highly doubtful, that one of Maron's people might have seen me visit the Sorbonne before I registered at the hotel."

"Tell me again what progress you made there, comrade."

"Very little, I am afraid. Strangers are not really welcome at the university, particularly strangers without credentials and without academic sponsorship who wish to poke about in official papers of any kind. If I were a professor it might be a different matter."

"Then perhaps," the colonel said, looking over the tops of his reading half-glasses, "we shall have to recruit a professor. Eh, Cassius?"

"As you determine, Colonel." Cassius felt that he was being made the butt of some joke he did not quite understand. "In any case, I do not believe the CIA is yet suspicious of me or my actions. Maron indicated that he had not contacted Toberts about the runners' reports on me. I told Maron that I had important news for him before he spoke to anyone else. We are to meet at his travel agency shop on the Rue Washington at two o'clock."

The colonel nodded. "So, Cassius, what is it you wish of me? Surely you did not come here merely to tell me of this scheduled meeting with a minor subagent of the

CIA who, by your own admission, knows nothing except that you possibly visited UNESCO yesterday afternoon."

"Certainly not, Colonel. I would not waste your extremely valuable time with so minor a matter. But, in fact, Maron and his runners are a problem to us—and in any case if Maron makes his report, Toberts or some other member of the CIA Paris apparatus will put two and two together, and will probably come close to a class A unsubstantiated supposition that I am doubling for you. If Toberts ever believes that, my useful life as an agent, and probably my physical life as well, would, I suspect, end rather abruptly."

The colonel chuckled. "Oh, the Americans are not above using many of the 'despicable' tactics they so publicly deplore. But I sometimes wonder, Cassius—I wonder whether they might not already know of your dual status and are simply playing you back to us. With or without your cooperation."

Cassius scowled. "That remark was unworthy of the trust and confidence built up between us, Colonel. I put it out of my mind, as the result of pressures you undoubtedly face in your two important posts."

"Yes, perhaps," Colonel Balachov said. "Were you in fact asking my opinion earlier on what to do about Maron?"

"Essentially, yes."

"My suggesion, Cassius, is to do whatever you think you must. Maron is of no importance to us, but your double role—and particularly your current involvement in *Fonarshchik*—must be preserved at all costs. Meet with him as planned, see what he wants, and use your good judgment as to how best to dispose of the matter. You have been resourceful in the past; I assume you will continue to be so."

"Thank you, Colonel," Cassius said as he stood to go. "I shall keep you informed of my actions."

"I expect no less," the colonel said, without smiling or extending his hand to the world-famous agent.

The Rue Washington, off the Champs-Elysées, was an excellent location for a Paris travel agency, and Maron's shop, though small, had the same intriguing airline posters in the window as its more opulent neighbors. Cassius found a parking place close by for the small gray Simca he had rented earlier and sat motionless behind the wheel, watching passing pedestrians as he waited for thirteen minutes to elapse. At precisely two o'clock he left the car and entered the Maron Travel Agency, smiling inwardly at the thimble-sized bell that tinkled as the door closed behind him. How typical of the small businessman's mentality, he thought. A frail-looking Frenchman who was obviously the proprietor came to the front of the shop to greet him.

"Monsieur Maron?" Cassius said.

"Oui?"

"I believe you are expecing me."

"You would be Monsieur . . . ?"

"Cassius—not Monsieur, not Mister, not Señor. Cassius alone."

Maron stared at the man in awe, shifting his gaze from the steely gray eyes to the full beard. "I have heard much about you . . . Cassius. I am honored to meet you at last."

"Thank you. Now, could we please get to the business at hand? I am afraid I have many pressing matters to attend to during my stay in Paris."

"Of course—this way, please." He led Cassius to the rear of the shop and pushed open a heavy door leading into a small back room. It was furnished simply with a desk piled high with ledgers, a bubbling coffee pot beside a small refrigerator, and a bare cot. "How long *do* you plan to be in our city, monsieur?"

"Shall we close the door?" Cassius said, ignoring Maron's question.

Maron offered Cassius the one chair, then closed the door and seated himself on the cot. "What was the important news you had for me?" he asked Cassius.

Cassius looked at him. "You said you had not passed on the information your runners obtained about my being in the vicinity of UNESCO. Is this still true?"

"Yes, certainly. I am a man of my word, monsieur."

"I was sure you were." Cassius glanced around the tiny

room. "Is this conversation being taped or otherwise recorded, may I ask?"

"No, it is not."

"Good. Then what I have to say will go no further than the two of us. There are things about your contact, Martin Toberts, that are not as they seem. For instance, I have recently come into possession of certain correspondence that—"

He stopped abruptly when the telephone on the desk beside him rang loudly. As it continued ringing he lifted his eyes toward Maron, who seemed to be weighing the wisdom of answering in a stranger's presence. Finally he crossed over from the cot and picked up the receiver. *"Oui,"* he said quickly.

It was one of the runners, Emil, with recent news of Cassius. "He was definitely spotted entering UNESCO this morning, about ten-thirty," Emil said. "Not only that, but he was followed inside to a point suspiciously close to the office of Colonel Alexis Balachov, who is known to be the KGB *rezident*. Actual entry cannot be confirmed because our man somehow raised the suspicions of a building guard and had to retreat out of sight."

"Merde!" Maron whispered into the phone. "Tell me, where is he now, this minute?"

"I do not know—I thought you would need to know what we have found out, so I left my post in front of his hotel to find a telephone to call you. You were not at home and your wife would not say where you were. I finally thought to call you here. I assume Cassius is still in his room at the hotel."

Maron nodded grimly. "Thank you, Emil. I suggest you return as soon as possible."

With a quick glance at Cassius, Maron hung up the phone and stood abstractedly beside the desk. Finally he said, "Excuse me, please, Monsieur . . . ah, Cassius. I apologize that I must interrupt our conversation for a moment to check the front of the shop for customers."

He closed the door of the back room behind him and went directly to the second telephone on the front desk, where he quickly dialed a number from memory. When a man answered with nothing more than the number repeated, Maron whispered as loud as he dared, "Martin Toberts, please. It's urgent."

"I'm sorry, Mr. Toberts is not in at the present time," the voice said. "Would you care to leave a message?"

"No, thank you," Maron said. He hung up and turned back toward the small room. Cassius stood in front of the open door, watching him.

"That was very careless of you, Maron," Cassius said. "Calling your control on an open line from your place of business—even rank amateurs are trained better than that. I detest amateurs, Maron."

"I was only . . ." Maron faltered, then suddenly snatched at the handle of the middle desk drawer and frantically pawed inside.

Anticipating the move, Cassius covered the distance between them in a fraction of a second and, leaping in the air, kicked the drawer shut on Maron's hand. He hurled the shouting Frenchman away from the desk and pulled from the drawer the heavy U.S.-issue Colt .45 automatic that Maron had been trying for.

"Into the back room, Maron, and stop the yelling," Cassius ordered.

With no other options open to him now, Maron complied. When Cassius had closed the door behind them, he removed the full clip from the handle of the automatic and ejected the shell from the chamber, letting the bullets fall to the floor harmlessly. Grasping the automatic by the barrel, he forced Maron's injured hand down flat on the desk and calmly smashed it with the steel handle.

Maron's face turned white from the pain but he did not cry out as Cassius expected he would. "I want to know everything that the CIA—and especially your Mr. Toberts —knows about me. I want to know if they suspect me of being a double agent. You will answer me fully, now, or I will kill you by degrees. The pain, I might add, will be quite unbearable."

When Maron trusted himself to speak through clenched teeth, he told Cassius, "I've seen worse than your kind during the Occupation. Fascists or Communists, you're all the same filthy pigs!"

Cassius brought the heavy automatic down sharply

71

again, this time catching Maron's hand behind the wrist, breaking the large bone. Maron screamed and he would have fainted if Cassius had not held him upright, slapping him hard across the face several times. "Now you will begin to tell me what I want to know, or the pain will go on and on. You really have no choice, Maron."

And since what Cassius said was obviously true, that all choices for Maron had been eliminated, the little Frenchman finally whispered brokenly, "Yes, I will tell you . . . anything you want."

"Who called you a few moments ago?"

"Emil—a runner."

"And what news did he have for you?"

"He said ... . that you had been followed to the office of Colonel Alexis Balachov."

"And you, being a bright intelligence agent, decided that that means I am a double agent for the Soviets."

"Yes."

"And does Toberts know of this?"

"No—I do not think so."

"Will the runner inform anyone other than you about his observation?"

"No. They work only for me . . . answer only to me. They know no one else in the employ of the CIA."

"Have you made notes of your discovery, or recorded what you consider to be facts in any way?"

"No."

Cassius stared hard at Maron, trying to determine whether the little man was capable of lying to him under the presence and threat of so much physical pain, and decided finally that although Maron's ideals were undoubtedly strong, his frail body was much too weak to stand extended physical torture.

"I believe you," Cassius said, laying the empty automatic down on the desk. "If I later find that you have lied to me, I will do even worse things to your wife and children than I have done to you. Knowing that, is there anything you wish to add?"

"Nothing," Maron said with all the dignity he could muster. "Except that I trust your punishment will be in hell. May I call my wife now?"

72

"Not just yet," Cassius said. "First I want you to call your runners and tell them to stop all surveillance on me and my hotel, that you have no further instructions for them at present."

Maron hesitated only briefly before dialing a number and relaying to René essentially what Cassius had told him to say. When Maron hung up, Cassius said with exaggerated politeness, "Thank you." He picked up the automatic again, but instead of striking Maron, he turned to a glass-front bookcase beside the desk and tapped the glass with the gun just hard enough to shatter it in several large jagged pieces. He plucked one of the triangular-shaped pieces from the molding around the case and held it in his hand, running his thumb carefully along one splintered edge to test its sharpness. Then, before Maron could move or even protest, Cassius forced the little Frenchman's chin up with his left hand and drew the razorlike edge of glass slowly across his throat, severing the jugular as easily as he might have carved a tender roast of veal. Mouth open, his stricken eyes bulging, Maron clutched at his throat helplessly with both hands.

"You may call your wife now," Cassius said, watching the blood spurt through Maron's clawlike fingers. Maron made one final, bubbling sound and collapsed at Cassius' feet.

Carefully, Cassius wiped the automatic with his handkerchief, broke the triangle of glass under his heel to destroy his prints, and tossed the gun contemptuously toward Maron's body. He closed the door of the back room behind him, wiped the handle clean, and before leaving the shop flipped over the sign hanging in the front door so that it read CLOSED. Maron, he reflected on his way to the rented car, was now one less problem for him to worry about.

7

SATURDAY, UNLIKE THE PREVIOUS morning, dawned gloriously across the multihued slate rooftops of Paris. Toberts was up early, dressed, and had finished his breakfast before Jessie had awakened. He left her a note, saying that he would be working on a special project most of the day but would return in plenty of time to change clothes before the press reception that evening at the Ghanaian Embassy. He clipped the note to the refrigerator door with a small pineapple-shaped magnet, thinking as he did so how much he disliked embassy food, no matter whose embassy, and the customary hassle—attempting to eat while standing up in a room full of people, your left hand holding a drink and your right hand balancing a plate heaped with things that invariably looked either brown and squishy, or bright blue from someone's imaginative use of food coloring.

He left the house and drove directly to the Hotel Crillon. Bruckner was waiting on the sidewalk for him on the Place de la Concorde side. He was wearing a black turtleneck sweater under a light tan chamois suede jacket that must have cost three hundred dollars. The black turtleneck seemed a little too much like dressing the part of Superspy to suit Toberts.

"What's on the schedule?" Bruckner asked, swinging easily into the right seat of the creaking Peugeot.

"Good morning," Toberts said. "First, the giraffe enclosure at the Jardin des Plantes—we have to meet one of my agents there at nine o'clock sharp, and we may just be able to make it."

"What's his name?" Bruckner asked.

Toberts looked over at Bruckner. "He's a little Frenchman named Maron, Georges Maron. He's done some good things for us in the past. You may as well meet him since you're going to be around for a while—he has friends, he might come in handy if you get hung up sometime."

Bruckner almost smiled. "I don't plan to get hung up, old sport. Here in Paris or anywhere else. But thanks for the tip."

"You're welcome," Toberts said. He turned the conversation to a sight-seeing guide's description of the things they passed as they drove through the crowded streets. Every few seconds he checked the rearview mirrors, but if anyone was following them he was damned good at it, too good for Toberts to spot. They drove along the quays past the Louvre to the broad boulevard that crossed over the Ile de la Cité to the Left Bank. The boulevard continued through the cluster of University of Paris buildings known as the Sorbonne. "Next Thursday this area will be pretty exciting to be in," Toberts said. "If you like excitement."

"Why next Thursday?"

"It's the first of May—May Day. I suppose you're aware that it's celebrated all over Europe as a kind of Labor Day, but in Paris it has special connotations for the leftist students. Some years they've nearly torn up the city."

"So I've heard," Bruckner said. "The cops here must be getting as soft as they are everywhere else in the world. If they'd just kill about five hundred of them a couple of years running, I doubt the problem would continue."

Toberts glanced across at Bruckner to see what sort of expression was on his face. "You're some kind of humanitarian, aren't you, Bruckner?" he said stiffly.

"No, just a realist," Bruckner said. "Animals understand force better than they understand long-winded arguments."

"And humans are the most stubborn of animals. Is that about right?"

"In my experience, the *most* stubborn," Bruckner said.

Having had his mood spoiled, and therefore the day, Toberts drove the remainder of the way in silence. He found a place to park the Peugeot near the entrance of

75

the Jardin des Plantes across from the Gare d'Austerlitz, and from there they walked slowly along the lovely formal paths through the flowerbeds of the botanical gardens, attempting to look like horticultural experts or, failing that, like tourists. "Somewhere around here is the oldest living tree in Paris," Toberts said, continuing his tour-guide role. "I've forgotten what species it is, but I remember someone telling me it was planted before 1650."

"Fascinating," Bruckner said. He was staring around them unobtrusively, his eyes flicking up and down the walkways constantly, never attentive for long, never still.

Toberts glanced at his watch; it was ten minutes after nine. They hurried past the alpine garden and into the zoo area, past the elephant house and the aviary toward the vivarium. "The giraffes are over that way," Toberts said, nodding to Bruckner.

They found the enclosure and Toberts was relieved to see that the giraffes were outside; the one hazard of a zoo as a meeting place was the possibility that the appointed meeting time might be the animals' feeding hour, or resting hour, or for some other reason they simply might not be where they were supposed to be. And nothing could be more conspicuous than a grown man staring into an empty cage, anxious to leave but afraid to miss an appointment.

They stood watching a group of three giraffes—a mother and her baby, and probably the father. The baby seemed to want to play, but the parents had other things on their minds, primarily the rack of hay stuffed into a high rock crevice that they could reach easily without bending their long necks. Bruckner consulted his own watch, a Rolex Oyster that Toberts had admired the first time they met. "Is this guy of yours usually prompt?" Bruckner asked.

Toberts nodded. "Always. Never misses."

"It looks like he missed this time." He stared off to the right, where a sign lettered SINGERIE with an arrow underneath pointed the way to the monkey house. "Do you suppose you ought to check around the area? Maybe he thought you said lions."

"I was thinking about doing that," Toberts said. He strolled slowly down the path to the right and in the space of about fifteen minutes made a complete circle of the animal enclosures. Bruckner was standing alone when he again reached the giraffes. Toberts shook his head, and Bruckner shook his in turn. Somehow, Maron had failed to make the contact, and because it was the first time since the beginning of their relationship Toberts was uneasy.

"Let's go," he told Bruckner, and quickly led the way to the entrance of the gardens, back the way they had come.

On the way to the Bois de Boulogne Toberts shook off Bruckner's questions about Maron and tried to keep the conversation simple and, if possible, entertaining. "Did you like the giraffes?"

Bruckner laughed. "You've seen one giraffe, you've seen them all."

"I'm sorry we missed the bears," Toberts said. "After the Revolution the people brought all the animals here from the royal palace at Versailles—it was the first time Parisians had ever seen lions and tigers. But then during the siege of the city in 1870 the starving Communards slaughtered most of them for food. Imagine eating a tiger steak!"

"I've had steaks I thought came from an elephant, or worse," Bruckner said. "Not, fortunately, on this trip."

"How are the accommodations at the Crillon, by the way? I've been meaning to ask you."

"Excellent. First rate. But for what they charge they ought to be."

"How do you afford it, Bruckner? Uncle doesn't pay that well, last time I checked."

Bruckner looked across the front seat at Toberts, one eyebrow cocked. "Are you implying anything that I ought to know about?"

"No, not really. It's just that you're not here on vacation, there are lots of cheaper hotels in the vicinity, and nobody knows how long this could take. Your financial arrangements are your own affair, of course."

"Yes, they are. But my reasons are simple enough—we only tour this planet once, I'm told, and I plan to make the most of it. I have no family, no heirs—what would *you* do in my situation, Toberts?"

Toberts grinned at the thought. "Sleep at the Crillon, I guess. I understand they have a marvelous champagne brunch on Sundays—perhaps you can make it tomorrow, if you're not tied up with anything urgent."

"Thanks for the tip," Bruckner said, sounding entirely serious.

Having avoided most of the city traffic by taking the southern portion of the Paris ring road, Toberts shortly drove his car into the park and stopped beside a small pond. "Be back in a minute," he said, leaving Bruckner so abruptly that there was no time for questions. He was sure Bruckner understood, though; even though they worked for the same agency and used, from time to time, virtually the same methods, Toberts had no desire to show Bruckner exactly where one of his active dead drops was located. It was simply part of their tradecraft, this business of keeping secret as much as possible of their secret world. Bruckner, he knew, would have done the same.

But when he reached the drop and retrieved the metal capsule from atop the stone gatepost and opened it, he saw that the note he had left for Maron the previous afternoon was still there, folded exactly as he had folded it and, so far as he could tell, untouched. Maron would not have read the note and left it there—that was never done. No wonder he hadn't showed at the Jardin des Plantes, Toberts thought. He debated a moment about leaving the note there, in case Maron checked the drop later, but decided against it. For some reason he did not believe that Maron would be coming back anytime soon.

He replaced the empty capsule and walked quickly back to the parked car, frowning because of a pain that clutched at his intestines like an icy hand.

"Something's wrong," he told Bruckner, climbing behind the wheel.

"Oh? Since when is a missed drop a national tragedy?"

"Since this time. Give me credit for a little intuitive feeling about a man I know as well as I know Maron. He doesn't miss scheduled drops."

"Maybe he was held up in traffic or something."

78

"It's been nineteen hours—even Paris traffic isn't *that* bad."

But as Toberts left the Bois on Avenue Victor Hugo and drove straight for the Arc de Triomphe, it gradually became obvious that Paris traffic might actually be that bad. The little Peugeot joined the mad scramble of automobiles circling the arch in the Place Charles de Gaulle, and Bruckner, for whom this was a new experience, whistled appreciatively. "The news reports about it are true, aren't they?" he said.

"Yes," Toberts agreed. "It's a little like a mechanized rodeo—every man out for himself and eager to dump the competition. The main thing you learn is to stay well away from cars with four crumpled fenders –their drivers just don't *care*."

They made it safely around the arch and out onto the broad, beautiful Champs-Elysées. A few blocks farther on Toberts turned into Rue Washington and drove slowly down the street past the Maron Travel Agency, staring hard at the sign hanging from the door that said CLOSED.

"Where are we?" Bruckner asked.

"Maron's shop," Toberts said, nodding. "Sometimes he insists on using it as a safe house. I've told him repeatedly not to do it, not to assume that it isn't bugged and isn't being watched, but he has a peculiar blind spot about it —probably because it's his own shop."

"The tradesman mentality," Bruckner said. "I've never trusted people like that."

"He was a good man," Toberts said, then quickly caught himself. "*Is* a good man. We bring in people to do an electronic sweep of the shop every so often. Of course that only picks up bugs that happen to be transmitting at the time. The KGB's gotten smart and uses intermittent transmitters almost exclusively these days— damned near impossible to sweep them out. I told Maron it was too dangerous, but he just wouldn't listen."

Having driven around the block, Toberts came back along the front of the shop and found a parking space. "That's his car over there," he told Bruckner, pointing across the street to a tiny Renault. "He must be here."

The door was unlocked and they entered the shop

cautiously, Toberts leading the way. Venetian blinds had been pulled down across the front windows and the shop interior was dark and shadowy after the bright sunlight outside. Toberts and Bruckner made their way through the empty room toward a door at the rear of the shop. Toberts listened at the door a moment, then pushed against it; it seemed to resist his touch. He pushed harder against whatever was holding it and slipped past the edge, closely followed by Bruckner.

"My God!" Toberts breathed when he saw the little Frenchman's blood-soaked body propped partly against the door. There was congealed blood spattered on the door, across a small desk in the room, and on the nearest wall, as well as a sizable pool of it beneath the body. "That's more blood than I've ever seen before in one place," Toberts said, unconsciously whispering. "Poor little guy."

Bruckner bent low over the body and put two fingers through the congealed red mass around Maron's throat. "Absolutely dead," he announced, as though there could have been any doubt about that. "Throat's cut—whoever did it got the jugular the first try. Very neat, very professional." He looked up at Toberts. "Is this Cassius's work?"

Toberts shook his head. "Maybe. Or the Russians. Or some half-crazy Algerian who wanted to go into business for himself."

He, too, stooped over the body, and almost immediately noticed that Maron's right hand was bent at a highly unnatural angle. He reached out and gently felt the bloody wrist. "Whoever it was, they worked him over first," Toberts said. "I hope he didn't try being a hero."

"If he didn't," Bruckner said, a tinge of disgust in his voice, "they now know everything he knew. Which I assume was considerable."

Toberts stood and wiped his hand with his handkerchief, which he then passed to Bruckner. "Didn't anyone ever tell you there might be human considerations more important than following some agency code of behavior, Bruckner?"

"No, no one ever did," Bruckner said. "And I doubt if

the folks at Langley would be pleased to hear you saying a thing like that."

Toberts studied the younger man's face a moment. "I'm sure you're right," he said finally. He glanced at Maron's body once again and then, using the handkerchief, dialed a number from memory on Maron's desk telephone. When a man answered he said into the receiver, "Martin Toberts, Doctor. We have an emergency. A Monsieur Georges Maron, proprietor of the Maron Travel Agency on Rue Washington, eighth arrondissement, died sometime yesterday afternoon of natural causes. Maillot will handle burial preparations, as usual. He will need the death certificate this afternoon, if possible."

After a moment more Toberts nodded and said, "Thank you, Doctor." He pushed the plunger to free the line and dialed another number from memory. "Yes, Maillot, it's me, Martin Toberts. We have a little business for you at Maron's Travel Agency, Rue Washington off the Champs. Quickly, if you please. An unmarked van will do nicely . . . What? Yes, all right, the laundry truck, then. But hurry. And Maillot? Be discreet, will you? The deceased's wife will present rather a problem, I'm afraid . . . Yes, you'll have the certificate by five, I promise. Thank you."

Toberts pushed the plunger yet again and began dialing, but then frowned and hung up before he had completed the connection. "I was going to call Madame Maron," he told Bruckner, "but I think we should go to the house instead. For some things a telephone seems slightly inhumane."

"How will she take it?" Bruckner asked him.

"Badly. We'll try to be as gentle as possible, of course."

"I despise scenes of maudlin sentimentality."

"Yes, I'm sure you do."

Bruckner poked around the shop as though idly curious about the travel business. He unfolded a huge four-color map of Spain and Portugal and squinted at it in the dim light, trying to see where the Algarve was. A quick, almost subliminal image of the eleven-year-old girl, her dark eyes huge with fright, flashed through his mind; he willed it to disappear. "What was Maron's relationship

81

with Cassius?" he asked Toberts, carefully refolding the map.

"There was very little relationship. I never saw the need to inform Maron that Cassius was a double—the more people who know something like that, the more chance there is of the principal discovering your knowledge. I fed Maron only things that we felt sure Cassius either knew or wouldn't care about."

"And you play the humanitarian role," Bruckner said caustically.

"What do you mean?" Toberts asked him, but of course he knew what Bruckner meant—having a social conscience only when it was expedient to have one was almost worse than never having developed one at all. But he wouldn't give Bruckner the satisfaction of hearing him admit publicly what had often worried Toberts in private about the duplicity inherent in his agency job. "It was better, strategically," he said aloud, "for Maron not to know more than he absolutely had to—it made his reactions to unexpected situations more natural if he didn't have to pretend so much ignorance."

"Bravo, Toberts. Right out of the old manual—*What Every Good Case Officer Should Know about Handling the Agents He Runs.* Unfortunately for Maron, you got his little French ass killed."

"That's a lie!" Toberts shouted, smashing his fist into his palm. "Nobody could have foreseen *this* . . . this *horror.* It was simply a routine operation that went wrong —even you've had your foul-ups from time to time, I imagine."

Bruckner raised his eyebrows but said nothing.

"I don't know what happened," Toberts continued, "but I may be able to dig something out tonight at the reception. Cassius's KGB contact will be there—he must have approved or even ordered the snuff job."

"Goddamned little frog bastard!" Bruckner shouted, and suddenly he began to rip posters off the walls, scatter papers from the desk, overturn chairs and wastepaper baskets as though possessed by a demon. Toberts lunged for him and grabbed his right arm. "What the hell are you doing?"

"Maron must have known something hot to warrant this," Bruckner said, allowing Toberts to think he had calmed him. "Maybe something even you weren't aware of. Maybe he hid some papers or notes in the shop here somewhere."

"I doubt it," Toberts said. "You know yourself, sometimes we just get fed up with an unfriendly agent always being in our hair. And then, sometimes, we have to do something drastic about it."

"Just the same—"

"Come on," Toberts said, "I don't want to be here when the clean-up crew arrives. Besides, we owe Madame Maron a visit."

Slightly more than an hour later the two of them were again in Toberts's Peugeot after having visited Maron's wife. Though Toberts had assured her that everything would be taken care of by the U.S. government, including burial with full French military honors, if that was what she wanted, in almost any cemetery in France, Mme. Maron's tearful anger was not appeased.

"Murderers!" she had shouted at them. "Filthy secretmongers! You have killed my beloved Georges, our children's father, with your lies and deceitfulness and treachery. I curse your bastard government, I curse *you!*"

And Toberts, mouthing the smooth, unfeeling words required of him by his government in situations of this kind, experienced through the hysterical outpouring of suffering by this small, plain French woman, the wife for seventeen years of unlucky Georges Maron, a keen sense of irrevocable loss for his former agent. But there was nothing, now, that he could do about it; and so, businesslike, he had pressed her for any information she might have that would shed light on Maron's murder, but she was too distraught to answer such harsh, logical questions. They had departed soon after, leaving Mme. Maron alone wih her sorrow.

But still, Toberts brooded about the degree to which he might have been responsible for Maron's grisly death. Bruckner, however, was as cool as ice.

"I think, old sport, that we will have to deal with this

Cassius very soon. We owe the KGB a little something for Maron."

"A quid pro quo, you mean," Toberts said.

"What?"

"An eye for an eye."

"Yeah. Damned right."

"No. Not until we have no further use for him, and maybe not even then," Toberts said. "You are to make no move, do nothing along these lines unless I specifically tell you to. Is that clear?"

Bruckner's thin lips curled in a lopsided smile. "Regardless of what you've heard or may think, I'm not a homicidal maniac."

"Perhaps not. I think you might enjoy killing, though —the true blood sport."

"Sometimes," Bruckner said. "Still, it's all part of the job, isn't it? If I didn't do it, someone else would, and that someone else would also be pocketing the very nice money Uncle pays his helpers."

"Except as a tactical necessity to save your own life, killing as an operational end is never justified, no matter whose intelligence service we're talking about." Toberts shook his head sadly. "I'm aware that now and then people are killed because of things I've done—other agents, political figures, sometimes even innocent bystanders. I've never killed anyone myself, did you know that, Bruckner? But occasionally I've given orders to others that I knew beforehand would result directly in a killing. And while there are all sorts of ways I justify such things to myself, the truth is, I've never felt good about it. I've never felt that I was doing a noble and righteous thing, for God and country, all that bullshit."

"The agency doesn't require that you always agree with them," Bruckner said flatly. "They only require results."

"Sure," Toberts continued. "I've had to make decisions, sometimes damned tough ones, mostly on my own; and I usually found that I simply did what was expected of me in order to achieve broad policy objectives laid down for the agency at levels much higher than my own. When you're dealing on a daily basis with steps toward a goal with which you basically agree, it's easy to lose sight of the fact that you're also dealing, in a God-like way, with human lives. Sometimes, a day or a week later, I've thought seriously about quitting the agency for just such reasons."

Bruckner lit a cigarette. "Why didn't you, then?"

"I'm not sure," Toberts said. "Because this is what I do, I guess. This is the only thing I'm any good at—it's the same for all of us, I think. It's simply what we *are*."

"You mean," Bruckner smiled, "professional spies, killers, secret-mongers, dealers in high-level filth?"

Toberts smiled too. "Something like that. Let's go see where Cassius lives."

Toberts stopped beside a public telephone on Rue Chevert, a half block away from the seedy-looking Hotel De Luxe. Bruckner stepped out of the Peugeot, looked up a number in the book, dialed, and in a moment was back in the car. "No one answers in room 342. I let it ring a dozen times or so. Either he's in the shower or he's out."

"In a joint like this the shower, if there is one, is undoubtedly down the hall," Toberts said. "Well, let's take a look."

Walking rapidly down the sidewalk, they entered the hotel's front door and continued their pace down the hallway toward the stairs. An elderly concierge stuck his bald head out a hastily opened side door and asked what they wanted. *"Plus de problème, merci,"* Toberts said over his shoulder without slowing down. If he acted as though there were no problem, perhaps the concierge would also believe it.

They took the stairs two at a time, both having experienced often in the past a similar situation when their quarry disappeared out the back door of some establishment while they were entering the front. Of course, this was different; Cassius had no reason to suspect Toberts of anything but friendly intentions. Still, in this business one prepared for what one did not expect.

Toberts placed his ear against the thin wood of the door to room 342, then shook his head at Bruckner. They used a standard pick on the flimsy lock and were inside with

85

the door shut behind them in less than fifteen seconds. A quick inspection showed that Cassius still occupied the room but was not presently at home. Carefully they searched through the clothes hanging in the closet, the personal items, the few books and papers in the room. Cassius appeared to be an extremely neat and fastidious individual.

"Here's something," Bruckner said, bringing over a travel booklet on Paris for Toberts to see.

"Anything underlined?"

"Nothing."

"I wouldn't think so—he's too good an agent for that," Toberts said. He took the booklet and held it loosely between thumb and forefinger at the spine, waving it back and forth in the air to separate the pages. The booklet spread open at a section describing the Sorbonne.

"Nice trick," Bruckner said. "Does that mean anything special as far as you know?"

"Nothing at all. You'd better put it back where you got it. Do you remember exactly how it was facing and where it was located?"

"I think so."

"You'd better," Toberts said. "Cassius is the kind of agent who would deliberately position something innocuous in a room a certain way and then check later. If it's been moved by so much as a millimeter, he'd know his ground had been penetrated and he'd be doubly careful from then on. We don't need to alert him if we can help it."

Bruckner smiled. "You mean you don't want to have to match tradecraft with him on an even basis?"

"Not particularly."

"You make him sound like John Superspy. What's his motivation?"

"No one knows for sure. My guess would be money, pure and simple."

"Simple, maybe. The pure part I doubt."

Toberts looked at Bruckner. "Speaking from experience, Bruckner?"

"Observation," Bruckner said.

"Come on," Toberts said, surveying the room once

again before he quietly closed the door behind them. "I've got to drop you off at the Crillon and get myself home. Do you think you can find the Ghanaian Embassy tonight for the reception?"

"If the taxi driver knows where it is."

"It's at Eight Villa Said, a few doors off the Avenue Foch in the sixteenth arrondissement. Nine P.M. sharp —don't be late. We'll get together sooner or later, as we logically would, but don't make it too obvious. The place'll be full of spooks, friendly and otherwise, and not all of them are entirely stupid."

"Anybody special I should hook onto?"

"Try Colonel Balachov, the chief Russian delegate to UNESCO, or anyone standing close to him."

"Why? Does he know where everyone's skeletons are buried?"

"He should," Toberts said, nodding to the concierge as they passed by on their way out of the hotel. "He's buried quite a few of them himself. You see, he's the KGB *rezident* in Paris. The American tourists are the only people in town who don't know about it."

"Doesn't sound as though there's much point in his even trying to keep it a secret, then."

"No real point, of course," Toberts said. "Except politically. The world press would crucify him if he ever admitted it."

"And what is it *you* do for a living, Mr. Toberts, sir?" Toberts smiled. "I work for the telephone company."

8

PARKING, AS TOBERTS HAD suspected it would be, was a problem around the Ghanaian Embassy that evening. A long line of chauffeur-driven limousines deposited their illustrious occupants at the doorway, where they were given into the care of an official greeter; the emptied vehicles then moved slowly away toward the Square de l'Avenue Foch. Toberts guided the Peugeot past the curbside madness and continued down the Villa Said, looking in vain for a place to leave the car.

As usual, Jessie complained bitterly about the unfairness of it all. "I can't imagine why that ass Brian Jamison should rate a limousine when you don't—are you sure you couldn't persuade Fitzgerald your image is as important as the cultural attaché's?"

"Yes, Jessie, I'm sure," Toberts said, wondering why it was she could never learn to accept the fact that his job demanded a very low profile. "We'll find a place in a minute or two—it's early yet." He looked across at her in the front seat, the light from the street lamps reflected dazzlingly from the rhinestone prisms of her pendant earrings. She had bought a new and very expensive emerald-green dress for the occasion and, he had to admit, she looked as lovely as he'd seen her in years. "Don't worry, you'll still get to make your grand entrance—every male in the place will envy me."

"Yes, I'll bet," Jessie said. "Especially those ridiculously self-important darkies."

"Goddamn it, Jessie, if you make some asinine comment like that when we're inside, I promise I'll embarrass us both. I won't stand for it!"

"You won't do a thing, Martin, dear, and we both know

88

it. You're much too proper for your own good—or have I told you that before?"

"About twenty times a day, on the average. At least I don't wander around in a drunken stupor most of the time, saying insulting things to friends and strangers alike."

"You don't know what you're missing—it's really a marvelous experience to call an asshole an asshole. Besides, when you're drunk people forgive you almost anything."

"Unfortunately, that's true," Toberts said. "How many drinks did you have before we left the house tonight?"

She looked at him across the dark seat. "Not quite enough, obviously. I can still hear you."

Eventually they found a place to park, and although it was a clear, beautiful night and only a three-block walk back to the embassy, Jessie whined continually about her mistreatment. They were shown inside the building where a second functionary checked their names off a huge master list of those invited, then were led to the end of a slowly moving receiving line. "It looks as though just about everyone who doesn't count for anything is here," Jessie said in a mock whisper that Toberts was afraid would carry across the room. He looked around at the faces, nodded to a couple of people he knew, and tried not to think about the possibility that any minute now one of the embassy guards, splendidly uniformed in white with gold braid, might firmly grasp his and Jessie's arms and ask them, politely, to leave.

Gradually the line moved toward the honorees. The new Ghanaian chargé d'affaires, for whom the reception was being held, was a tall, serious-looking black man in evening dress whose name was Akwasi Quahdo. The Tobertses were introduced to Quahdo, and he to them, by a short, lively young man named Charles Mbuma, the Ghanaian Embassy's press secretary and, for the past two years, a good friend of Martin Toberts's. Although Toberts had never attempted to recruit Charlie Mbuma to U.S. intelligence work, he felt that the possibility existed should the need arise. It would probably mean, as it usually did, the loss of a friend, but sometimes that couldn't be helped.

Still, Toberts wanted to delay the change in their relationship from social to professional as long as possible.

"Mr. Toberts and I are old friends in the press-relations business," Charlie told Quahdo. "I consider Martin Toberts one of the finest representatives of the American diplomatic staff in Paris, of absolutely unimpeachable integrity. He also plays tennis better than I do."

Quahdo smiled at Toberts. "We shall have to talk further, Mr. Toberts," he said in perfect British English. "About integrity . . . and tennis." He smiled again, this time at Jessie, and held her hand perhaps a fraction of a minute longer than was required, while his gaze, Toberts noticed, wandered interestedly in the vicinity of Jessie's partly exposed breasts.

"Filthy old coot!" she whispered to Toberts when they had left the line and were heading toward the refreshment table. "I thought he was going to reach in and grab one."

"It was probably the green dress," Toberts said, amused by Jessie's discomfort. If Quahdo hadn't been black he could imagine Jessie leering back at him, perhaps making clandestine arrangements for a later private meeting. Although he was not aware of any such affairs on her part, he would no longer, he thought, be very surprised to learn of their existence.

He tried without success to persuade Jessie to eat something from the sumptuously laden tables. The Ghanaians had provided a feast, a banquet for the eyes as well as the palate, just as Toberts had known they would; but as fast as Jessie could empty one cocktail glass (Manhattans, usually, though she wasn't really all that particular), she had Toberts get her another, or simply lifted one from the endlessly circulating silver drink trays carried about the room by Moroccan boys dressed in white tunics. Toberts, as had become his custom at these affairs, took one colorless vodka and tonic at the beginning of the evening and, with periodic judicious replacement of the ice, made it last a very long time. Evenings such as this were, for him as well as certain of the diplomats present, more in the nature of work than pleasure.

Jessie spotted someone she knew and drifted away from Toberts. He glanced professionally around the room, noticing who was speaking with whom, who was *not* speaking to whom, who was being ignored. A few moments earlier he had seen Bruckner being guided through the reception line by Harold Sloan; it was nice to know that Bruckner had made it. Indirectly, Toberts had seen to it that Bruckner was included on the Ghanaian Embassy's list of acceptables—this was done surreptitiously through Brian Jamison, the U.S. cultural attaché, as though the request had come from Sloan to break in his newly accredited reporter right away. As press chief, Toberts himself would ordinarily have handled these arrangements, but Jamison knew someone who owed him a favor and, besides, Toberts did not want it to appear that he was pushing for special consideration or support for the agent.

He made it seem accidental that as he wandered idly across the room, he just happened to be passing the refreshment tables where Sloan and Bruckner were helping themselves. He caught Sloan's eye, then stopped as though searching for someone across the room; Sloan dutifully appeared at his elbow with Bruckner in tow.

"Martin, good to see you!" Sloan boomed, shaking hands. He was a large man with thin hair and a ruddy complexion. "Martin, I want you to meet my new man, a hotshot reporter from the States—Pell Bruckner. Pell, this is Martin Toberts, chief of the press section of the International Communication Agency. ICA's offices are in the U.S. Embassy by the Place de la Concorde—we'll have to get you over there one of these days for an orientation tour."

Toberts shook Bruckner's hand. "By all means—we'd love to show you around," Toberts said loudly, and to Sloan, almost in a whisper, he said, "I think you're overdoing it a bit, Harold."

They chatted awhile about topics a newspaper reporter would be interested in—inane newsfeature subjects, mostly, that the Paris dailies, and Sloan's weekly, had covered during the past week. Aware that he was expected to know nearly everything about nearly everything, for both his cover and his actual job, Toberts had long made a practice of reading all of the papers every day, clipping items of special interest for later rereading and study.

Having trained his memory by the special techniques taught by the agency, he was, in fact, able to converse intelligently on virtually any subject that had recently received journalistic attention.

As they continued to talk a little longer than Toberts thought necessary, he caught a flash of iridescent green from the corner of his eye and turned in time to see Jessie approaching them with a sexy walk that seemed half knowingly flirtatious, half boozily don't-give-a-damn. He was surprised to see that she apparently had her eye on Bruckner.

"Introduce me, darling," she said, not once looking at Toberts.

He made the introduction to Bruckner and pointed out that she had met Sloan at previous receptions. "Oh, have I really?" she said, allowing Sloan to kiss her hand. "You must be very careful of this man, Mr. Bruckner—he prints awful things about people and no one seems to know how he gets away with it."

"He gets away with it because he happens to be a damned fine newspaperman," Toberts said quickly. "Harold it one of the best editors in the business, Mr. Bruckner— here or anywhere else. I'm sure you'll find working with him a genuine pleasure, as well as a short course in journalistic imperatives."

"I'm sure I will, Mr. Toberts," Bruckner said.

"And if that doesn't work out," Jessie said, smiling brilliantly and just slightly off-center at Bruckner, "then perhaps Martin could find something for you to do at the embassy." She glanced sweetly at her husband. "Licking boots, or whatever it is they do over there all day."

Toberts excused himself from the group and went to join Walter Fitzgerald, who had corralled the new Ghanaian diplomat for himself. During the ensuing long and somewhat dull conversation with them, Toberts noticed that Jessie, far from tiring of Bruckner's lack of charm, was now holding his arm tightly and leaning against him, while still managing to hold on to her drink. Toberts was sure it was not the same drink she had had when he left her.

Edging away from the two career diplomats, Toberts

knew it was time to stalk his real quarry for the evening, whom he had seen engaging in serious discussion with several different groups of foreign officers and press representatives. Their eyes had met once across the room, as though the other man had similarly been searching for Toberts, if only to keep track of his movements. Colonel Alexis Balachov and Toberts were two of a kind—two of exactly the same kind, in fact. Both had cover positions with their governments that gave them access to all sorts of important functions, such as this one tonight, though usually the functions themselves were far less important than the opportunities for contacts that they provided. Both men, no longer young, had worked in their respective intelligence services for many years, and each respected the other for his professionalism and dedication, while distrusting the other implicitly for his devious methods. Yes, indeed, thought Toberts, walking toward the colonel, we are much more alike than anyone at Langley would be comfortable knowing.

"Good evening, Alexis," Toberts said, extending his hand and smiling broadly as though they were old friends, which in a way they were.

"Martin, my dear fellow," the colonel exclaimed, beaming over their good fortune in running into each other like this. By mutual agreement they spoke English to each other; Toberts's Russian was shaky at best, while Colonel Balachov's English was unimpeachable.

The man Colonel Balachov had been talking with was a second secretary at the Norwegian Embassy. Toberts knew him slightly and had no respect whatsoever for his intellectual capacities—if Balachov was attempting to recruit him to their side, he would be getting a bad bargain. Toberts was pleased to see the Norwegian nod politely and wander off to join another group nearby.

"I believe we have a little matter to discuss, Alexis," Toberts said. "At your convenience, of course. I understand a mutual friend, Jean Petit, is in town."

The colonel stared noncommittally at Toberts. "Who?"

"Petit."

"A Frenchman, I presume."

"Possible, but not likely."

"In any case, Martin, I have not had the pleasure of the gentleman's acquaintance."

"Oh, I think you have. Perhaps you know him by another name . . . one of ancient Caesar's assassins?"

"Ah," Colonel Balachov said, "I seem to remember a fellow by the name of Cassius, a legendary spy . . . operated out of the Middle East during World War II, I believe. Of course, I never met the man personally, but I did hear stories. He must have been an interesting fellow."

"Brutal, crude, totally lacking in any ordinary human emotions. That's the way I heard it, Alexis. Hardly the stuff of legends."

"Legends die hard, Martin. People are so willing to believe—I've often thought what an easy time novelists must have, since it is no trick at all to convince a gullible public of the most outrageous lies."

Toberts was not smiling. "That may be true, but once the gullible find they have been deceived, they frequently turn vicious, exacting terrible retribution against the liar. Haven't you found this to be true?"

"I don't believe I understand exactly what you are saying, Martin."

"How about this: 'Beware of false friends.' "

"Certainly wise advice," the colonel said. "And speaking of false friends, I've been noticing that your wife, the lovely Mrs. Toberts, seems to find that new reporter for the *Times-Weekly* fascinating, and he her. I wonder what she sees in him? American reporters are dreadfully dull people, don't you think? He *is* American, isn't he?"

"That's what he said," Toberts said. "It may sound strange to you, Alexis, but I try to believe what people tell me whenever possible."

"Speculation about truth is always interesting," the colonel said.

A thin-lipped, dark-haired man appeared from somewhere behind Toberts and handed Colonel Balachov a folded piece of paper. "Thank you, Boris," the colonel said to the unsmiling aide, who disappeared as quickly as he had come.

The colonel unfolded the paper and read what was

94

written on it, then slipped the note into his pocket. "I *am* sorry, Martin, but an emergency in one of the UNESCO directorates apparently requires my presence. We shall have to continue this fascinating discussion at another time."

He shook Toberts's hand and went directly across the room to make his apologies to the Ghanaian chargé; then with several other people, including his wife and the thin-lipped man, he hurriedly left the embassy. Toberts watched them go, certain in his own mind that the note had had nothing to do with UNESCO. But it had to have been damned important.

The room was crowded enough that he had to push his way through to where Bruckner stood with his back against a wall. Jessie was nowhere in sight. "I have a little job to do with our friend the Russian colonel," Toberts whispered through a phony smile. "Please take Jessie home when it's time to go, and make any apologies necessary for me, though I doubt that anyone will notice. Say I got a sudden chill from a flu virus I've been fighting all week."

"In other words, lie for you," Bruckner said, his smile seeming more of a smirk. "I assume the lady does know where she lives?"

"You may assume so," Toberts said. "And if not, who knows? She'll probably think of something."

"Resourceful lady," Bruckner said.

Outside the embassy Toberts saw the colonel and his group standing well up the street at the head of a long dark line of limousines. He supposed they were waiting for their own car to be brought around; in any case, they hadn't yet seen him. He tucked his head down and walked rapidly in the opposite direction, and upon reaching the intersection, he darted around the corner and broke into a dead run for his car.

He was panting heavily by the time he found the Peugeot and dropped into the driver's seat. As soon as the engine caught he roared out into the street and began to retrace his steps in the car, pulling into the intersection where he had begun his run just in time to see Colonel Balachov disappear inside a huge black limousine. He waited until the driver had closed all the doors and the limousine was pulling away from the embassy before he cautiously turned the corner and began to follow them.

Unlike most of the smaller cars on Paris streets, the limousine was not difficult to follow. The driver was obviously in a hurry, sometimes not even bothering to slow down for red traffic lights when the intersection appeared to be clear. South of the Avenue Foch they headed toward the Seine, passing through the Place Victor Hugo and the Place du Trocadero and eventually crossing the river at the Bir-Hakeim Bridge. Immediately after reaching the left bank, they turned onto the Quai de Grenelle and, because traffic seemed much lighter here, Toberts slowed down and let more distance accumulate between them.

Eventually the limousine also slowed, as though the driver were looking for an address or a particular building among the warehouses of the area. When they turned in toward an open space leading toward the docks and a small unlighted warehouse, Toberts drove on past and then pulled into the first parking place he saw a block farther on. He walked back quickly to the spot where he had seen them turn, and although the limousine was not in sight, he assumed that its driver had pulled around behind the small building. There was a door at the side with a tiny overhead light, and now he could see what he had not been able to see from the street—a dull glow of yellow light coming from a single window frosted by years of grime and neglect. He crept closer to the window and searched for a crack that would allow him to see inside. For the first time in a long time he regretted not having brought a gun. Without knowing how many people were inside, whom the colonel was meeting, and who might be wandering around outside the building, Toberts felt entirely vulnerable.

He found a large crack at one edge of the glass where a piece of the pane had fallen out. By placing his right eye almost into the hole, he could see that the window gave onto a small bare room that contained only an empty packing crate and an unshaded light bulb clamped to a pipe against the wall. On the packing crate sat Colonel Balachov, looking terribly incongruous in this setting because of his immaculate evening clothes, and standing next to the colonel was the agent Cassius, talking animatedly in French. As nearly as Toberts could make out, he was telling the colonel about his recent encounter with little Georges Maron, the travel agent.

"The body is gone," Cassius was saying. "I suspect Toberts must have arranged it."

"No doubt," the colonel said. "We lost the tap on Maron's office telephone a week ago and it has not yet been replaced. Now I suppose there is no reason to do so. Did you have anything else to tell me?"

"No, for the moment that is all."

"Then listen carefully, Cassius. I've just been speaking with our Mr. Toberts this evening at an embassy affair, and I'm very much afraid he suspects your involvement in Maron's death. That, for the moment, cannot be helped. However, I would like you to call Toberts and set up a meeting with him—tell him it concerns information you have about who killed Maron. *That* should whet his appetite. Implicate some neutralist national, if possible. The real reason for the contact, of course, will be to find out exactly how much the CIA knows about *Fonarshchik*— Project Lamplighter. Also, determine if possible what resources they plan to devote to unraveling the mystery, and whether they are working against any sort of deadline of which we are unaware. It would also be very helpful if you could manage to misdirect their efforts. Do you think you can accomplish this, Cassius?"

"Of course," Cassius said testily. "I will contact Toberts tomorrow through the U.S. Embassy."

"Discreetly, I trust," Colonel Balachov said, rising from the packing crate.

"Naturally, Colonel. I am as anxious to bring this project to a successful conclusion as you are."

"Metaphorically, perhaps," the colonel said, "but in fact your interests are quite secondary to ours. Monetary payment alone is never the most compelling incentive."

Cassius smiled. "It will do until something better shows itself."

In order to hear the last words of their conversation Toberts had stayed at the window longer than he should have, and when the colonel opened the door beside the window, Toberts barely had time to slip around the front corner of the warehouse out of sight. He watched the colonel walk toward the limousine parked in back; a moment later the engine started and the limousine swept past him and out onto the street.

Still Toberts waited, knowing that Cassius was somewhere inside the building. Finally, fifteen minutes later, the agent came through the same door Colonel Balachov had left by. He seemed intense, alert, wary—almost as though he expected someone or something might have been left behind to do him harm. When he at last appeared satisfied, he pulled the door closed behind him and walked out toward the lighted street where, Toberts assumed, he had parked his car. When Cassius passed unsuspectingly within a couple of feet of where he stood in the shadows, he was tempted, momentarily, to become quite unprofessional—to leap out upon the small bearded man and perhaps deftly break his spine in retaliation for Maron. But other things were more important than revenge; they always were, Toberts thought. He let Cassius go by untouched, and waited until he heard the distant sound of a car being driven away before he left the comparative safety of the darkness surrounding the building.

He drove to the first public telephone he saw and dialed his own number at the embassy. Stanley, his too-efficient assistant, answered with the dialed number, and for one brief, uneasy moment Toberts wondered whether Stanley did, in fact, ever eat or sleep or do any of the normal human activities. He would not have taken such a bet just now.

"Hello, Stanley," Toberts said. "Glad to see you're on the job."

"Yes, sir?"

"Stanley, I want you to be sure and relay any messages you receive for me from a 'Jean Petit' or 'Cassius'—or anyone unidentifiable—to my home number immediately. I'm going home to bed now, and I intend to relax a bit tomorrow if possible."

"Don't worry about anything, sir—I assure you things will be tightly under control here."

"Yes, Stanley. Control is a great asset in our business. Good night."

He hung up the phone and returned to his car. As he drove through the silent Paris streets, he thought about the events of the last two days and how, recorded on paper as they ultimately would be in some highly classified report, they would be accepted and digested in the bowels of the headquarters building at Langley. Losing Maron was a liability, they would say, but a small one; he was replaceable. As for the rest, Bruckner and he seemed to be heading in the proper direction at a decent pace, and with any luck at all when they met with Cassius, they might be able to file an elaborate report on Project Lamplighter within the next few days.

But there was still something terribly unsatisfying to Toberts about dismissing Maron's death as an accidental hitch in an otherwise workable plan. Maron had been a good man, and now he was no longer any kind of man; he was dead, simply a pile of meat waiting for the worms. And Langley didn't care, and Stanley certainly didn't care, maybe no one cared except the poor wife and children, a few friends, and Toberts, the man next in line to answer for his death.

Suddenly overwhelmed by thoughts of unnecessary death, Toberts sped home. He found Jessie in bed asleep, or more likely passed out, and was glad, though slightly surprised, that Bruckner had at least been a gentleman about that.

9

HAVING SLEPT FITFULLY, AMORPHOUS dreams tumbling in and out of his consciousness all night to bedevil his rest, Toberts was finally awakened for good Sunday morning by the church bells of Sainte-Hélène and Notre-Dame-de-Clignancourt to the east and, farther south, the basilica of Sacré-Coeur. All of Montmartre seemed to be ringing in his bedroom. He rolled over in bed and touched Jessie's shoulder gently.

"Jessie, wake up. It's Sunday morning."

She stirred, raised her head slightly and opened one eye partway. "Are you crazy? What time is it?"

"Nine o'clock. Look, the sun's even shining. It's a beautiful morning, Jessie. We ought to take a walk somewhere."

"What I need," she said, flopping back heavily against the pillow, "is about eight hours more sleep. Close the curtains, Martin."

He got out of bed, pulled the dark curtains together to block out the streams of sunlight pouring into the room, and slipped back beneath the covers. But he knew there was no chance, now, that he would be able to return to sleep.

A quarter of an hour later the telephone rang, and he hurried to answer it before it disturbed Jessie. It was Stanley at the embassy, calling to tell him that a Monsieur Petit had just called to inform Monsieur Toberts of a proposed press junket to Dresden next month, sponsored by the European Newspaper Alliance. "He said you were to contact him at your convenience," Stanley told Toberts. "He also indicated you knew where and how to reach him, and he wouldn't leave a number. I asked."

"Yes, thank you, Stanley," Toberts said. "I know the number."

In fact, there was no number; the entire conversation of "Monsieur Petit" was simply a signal from Cassius to Toberts to use the Paris blind drop they had set up years ago for just such purposes.

Making as little noise as possible for Jessie's sake, he dressed in comfortable old clothes, fixed a hurried breakfast, and left in the Peugeot.

Eventually he reached his destination on the far side of the historic Père-Lachaise cemetery and stopped the car. He walked to the place to which he had come so often in the past and wondered, as he always did, whether anything had changed, whether someone might have discovered the drop, discovered Cassius's message, even, and what he or the unknown person would then do about it. By the side of the impressive marble tomb he stood for a moment and looked around, then stooped and retrieved from a low protruding ledge an ordinary carbonated drink can with one end nearly cut away. He lifted the jagged metal disc and removed a folded piece of paper, which he unfolded and then stood up to read.

Maron's death has reached my ears, Cassius had written. *I know you were his control and must want his killers badly. I have information that leads me to believe I know who is responsible, including written proof. Shall we meet at the entrance to the columbarium later today? If not, I will expect you to leave other instructions. Will recheck drop at noon.*

Toberts crumpled the note in his pocket and withdrew the spiral notebook, from which he tore a page and wrote with his ballpoint pen: *Columbarium no good—too public without capability of excluding the public. Try Opéra metro station, left concourse, maintenance room just past the passenger platform. Noise a security factor. At 8 this evening (Sunday)—should be few people at that hour.*

Toberts put his note into the can and replaced it on the ledge. He had just straightened up when he saw a man and a woman—obviously American tourists by their dress and manner—approaching along the path he had used earlier. He folded his hands reverently in front of him and stared up at the marble monument. More than 130 years ago some master stonemason had carved on its gleaming face the name of the tomb's occupant: Frédéric François Chopin, 1810–1849. Toberts, a lover of classical piano, had chosen this location because of his affinity for the life and music of the Polish national who had chosen to work and die in Paris. "If God has given me tuberculosis," the composer was reputed to have said to his mistress, the novelist George Sand, shortly before his death, "then I consider it a fair bargain that He also gave me you."

Shaking his head, Toberts walked back to his car, suddenly and irrationally jealous of Chopin's stormy love affair with one of the most brilliant women of his time. Where, he wondered, was his own George Sand?

He stopped at a public telephone and called Bruckner at the Crillon, but though he allowed the room phone to ring more than a dozen times, no one answered. There was no place he could think of that Bruckner would be, but of course he hadn't told him to stay inside, either. Deciding to chance a trip across town for nothing, Toberts headed west on the avenues toward the Place de la Concorde. In the lobby of the hotel he used the house phone to call Bruckner's room again and found him in. "Where were you?" he asked him. "I tried to call earlier."

"Having breakfast, down the avenue," Bruckner said. "Even with my unlimited wealth I find eating every meal in the hotel dining room an expensive bore."

"Well, I hope you're dressed because we have a little scouting to do. Shall I come up and get you? I'm just downstairs."

"No, no," Bruckner said quickly. "I'll be down in five minutes. Nothing formal, I assume?"

"We'll be visiting the subway, if that gives you a clue."

Toberts wondered about Bruckner's reluctance to have him come up to the room, but wondered about it only briefly, since almost every agent he had ever known had been odd in some way. The personal quirks of others bothered him very little so long as they did not get in the way of the job to be done.

When Bruckner finally joined him, they walked to

Toberts's car and drove to one of the Americanized shopping centers Toberts knew of that was open on Sundays. There he purchased several hardware items, about which Bruckner asked nothing. They then drove to the Opéra area, parked, and walked through the standard lacy entrance to the metro.

Toberts pointed out to Bruckner the colored glass mosaic decorations and the window displays that were part of the general plan to upgrade all Paris subway stations. "They're even installing rubber tires on the trains to try to keep the noise down," he said, but their conversation was interrupted by the arrival at the station of a train from the Palais-Royal.

When the train had departed, Bruckner said, "It doesn't seem to have helped much."

"Not much," Toberts agreed.

He led Bruckner down the platform almost to the end of the concrete walkway, past the end of the platform onto a narrower catwalk that disappeared into the black hole of the train tunnel. A door in the side wall led to an equipment-maintenance room: Toberts tried the handle and found that it was locked, as he had thought it would be. "I've used this before," he told Bruckner. "Once. The lock isn't the best quality."

He took a small hammer and a cold chisel from his pocket. Inserting the chisel between the door frame and the bolt, he tapped it hard with the hammer and the door sprung open, the frame no more than dented.

"You do much of this breaking and entering?" Bruckner asked him with a smile.

"Not unless I have to," Toberts said. "I mostly leave that kind of thing to people who enjoy it more than I do."

He led Bruckner into the dimly lighted room and closed the door behind them so that they would be out of sight of anyone on the platform or on a passing train. Taking a roll of electrician's tape from his pocket, he cut off a short piece with his pocket knife and pressed it against the edge of the door to hold the bolt out of the way.

"They won't get around to repairing this door, or even noticing that it's broken, for several days," Toberts said, "but we'll be using it tonight and we don't need any impediments."

He examined a heavy metal slide-bolt lock screwed securely to the inside of the door. "I installed this last time I was here, and I guess they left it," he told Bruckner. "It was insurance against unwanted attention from some maintenance engineer while we were conducting our business." He threw the bolt, grasped the inside handle, and pulled hard several times. The lock held.

Bruckner glanced from Toberts to the rest of the small room and the things in it. Overhead pipes of different sizes paralleled the ceiling. There were two generators in one corner that probably operated an emergency pump, as well as filthy canvas cloths and buckets of paint, tools of all kinds, cans and bottles of grease and solutions, and rusted pieces of metal that might once have been parts of trains. "Who are we entertaining?" he asked Toberts.

"My friend Cassius. I intend to have a very serious discussion with the gentleman, about my friend Maron as well as certain other matters in which we have a mutual interest."

"Lamplighter?"

"Precisely. And this should be an excellent place for our conversation—with those trains roaring past just outside the door no one could possibly listen in, no matter what kind of electronic ears they're using."

Bruckner nodded. "You realize, don't you, that if you press him on these sensitive areas in a way that shows your distrust, his usefulness as a presumed double for our side will come to a screeching halt?"

"Of course," Toberts said. "I suspect his usefulness has been over for a long time, whether we knew it or not."

Bruckner nodded. "I'll bring a gag and some rope to the party tonight, and maybe some party favors."

"Rope to tie him with? Adhesive tape's much more secure."

"I'll bring that, too."

"Anyway, I don't plan any rough stuff. I expect our friend will fold readily enough when we confront him with what we know."

"Just the same," Bruckner said, "you never know when a length of rope will come in handy, eh, old sport?"

"As you say," Toberts agreed, not sure what Bruckner meant.

They closed the door behind them and left the metro station.

There were only two people on the passenger platform at eight o'clock that evening besides Toberts—an older woman carrying a cloth bag and a young girl, probably the woman's granddaughter. The girl was very bright and active and had inquisitive blue eyes; Toberts, wary of bright children, kept his back to them and hoped a train would come soon to take them away.

Hearing the sound of footsteps on the stairs, he turned slowly and saw Cassius coming toward him. Simultaneously a train whooshed into the station, grabbed up the woman and girl, and sped noisily away again. Without speaking, Toberts made sure Cassius recognized him and then walked down the empty platform toward the maintenance room. For a moment he heard only his own footsteps and was afraid Cassius was not following him, but then the other, hesitant sound began again, and he slowed to let the agent catch up with him. He pushed open the door into the dim little room and walked inside. Cassius halted momentarily, glanced behind him down the platform, and continued to stand at the edge of the door.

"Hurry!" Toberts said quietly from inside the room. "There'll be other passengers here in a minute. The trains furnish the best security there is."

As if on cue, another train roared into the station out of the dark tunnel ahead.

Apparently convinced, Cassius walked into the room. The door slammed behind him, and Bruckner sprung from his hiding place to pin Cassius's arms while Toberts pinched the little agent's cheeks with powerful fingers, forcing him to open his mouth so that a rag could be pushed between his teeth. Quickly they removed his jacket and taped his arms behind him, then taped his feet together. Securely trussed, he could stand but could neither move from that spot nor speak.

"Welcome, Jean Petit," Toberts said. "Or Cassius . . . whichever. I'm sorry to say I was not able to be quite honest with you. We've brought you here because we need information from you, and you must tell us what we need to know."

Cassius raised his thick gray eyebrows questioningly.

"No, I'm afraid there are no alternatives this time," Toberts continued. "The trains arrive every eighty seconds—we've timed them. For a period of some twenty-five seconds, until the train leaves the station, this room is quite soundproof. If you shout you will not be heard. That is why I am going to remove the gag from your mouth and hold a quiet but serious discussion with you about certain matters, and you must give us your full cooperation."

Cassius shrugged his shoulders as if to say, But I always *do.*

Toberts ignored him. "We know your contacts with the KGB are for their good, not ours; we know that you receive a great deal of information from them, but that you pass on to us only a part of that information, and sometimes even that has been carefully fabricated by Colonel Balachov and his people. We've known for some time what you are, Cassius, *mon petit,* so you have nothing to conceal from us any longer. It will be a relief to you, I assure you, to give us what we ask, without pretense, without attempting to calculate the consequences. We are all civilized people in this room, after all—quite unlike your KGB butchers."

Toberts took a small, battery-operated tape recorder from the pocket of his raincoat and switched it to record. "What we must know, Cassius, are all the details of Project Lamplighter—the Russian word for it is, I believe, *Fonarshchik.* Shall we begin?"

He glanced at the second hand on his watch and looked at Bruckner, who also checked his watch and nodded. Toberts gripped the rag in Cassius's mouth and pulled it free just as the sound of another train coming into the station rattled the maintenance-room door. The noise was nearly deafening.

Cassius shook his head, ran his tongue around his

106

mouth and lips to moisten them. He shook his head again, side to side. "I know nothing about any *Lamplighters*," he shouted over the noise. "The Russians do not trust me with information of the level in which you are interested. I am sorry, I would be happy to tell you whatever I know about it—but unfortunately I have never heard the term used before, by anyone. I am as ignorant of this matter as you are."

He looked appealingly from Toberts to Bruckner and back to Toberts, as if to say, We are all good fellows here, in the same business and everything, and ought to be helping each other instead of hurting, trusting instead of questioning.

As the train outside pulled away from the station Toberts rammed the gag back into Cassius's protesting mouth. Toberts shook his head wearily. "He's going to be difficult," he said to Bruckner. "I had hoped he'd co-operate."

"Probably prides himself on his ability not to crack under pressure," Bruckner snorted. "Little turncoat piss-ant."

Bruckner opened his sport jacket and revealed a twenty-five-foot length of rope coiled tightly about his waist. He loosened one end and pulled the rope free, then tossed one end up over the sturdiest looking heating pipe near the ceiling. He pulled on the free end until both lengths hung about evenly over the pipe, then fashioned a work-able slipknot in one of the rope ends lying loosely on the floor.

"What, exactly, do you have in mind?" Toberts asked him.

"I think we'll do a 'body lift' on Mr. Cassius there—it should make him extremely talkative."

"I'm not familiar with the term."

"You desk types really ought to get out in the field more often," Bruckner scoffed. "Help you keep up with the latest techniques. All you need is a rope and a place to hang it. Of course, there are refinements—have you ever seen a man hoisted by his genitals?"

"Listen—" Toberts began, then broke off whatever he was going to say to watch with a kind of horrified fascination as Bruckner lifted the immobile Cassius as if he were a board and laid his body flat on the floor, stomach up. He then pulled Cassius's pants down to knee level and tightened the rope slipknot snugly around the little man's surprisingly large penis and scrotum. Bruckner then stood and tested his system by pulling on the free end of the rope, noticing with apparent satisfaction how the genitals responded by stretching upward as though they would like to climb the rope toward the ceiling pipe. Cassius's head jerked back involuntarily as he comprehended exactly what was about to happen to him.

"I don't know that this is necessary," Toberts said. "It seems so barbaric—"

"And you honestly think you can talk it out of him?" Bruckner asked. "Don't be a fool, Toberts, we have no choice."

"I suppose. But does this make us any different from them?"

"Not at all. We're exactly the same—us and them—in almost any way you can name. Technology, methods, dedication, ruthlessness when it comes to that—did you really think we were somehow different? A better class of torturers? What?"

Toberts stared at Bruckner and shook his head. "No, I don't think we're different, at least not in any important ways. You're right, Bruckner, we do our jobs—horrible jobs, sometimes, but for good ends, we like to tell ourselves. And then we go home to the wife and kiddies and pretend we're just ordinary family men."

"Some of you do," Bruckner corrected him. "I've never found a need for that kind of self-delusion."

He took a stethoscope and a blood pressure cuff from his pocket, stuck the earpieces of the stethoscope in his ears, and listened to Cassius's heartbeat. "One hundred and four," he announced to Toberts. "Not bad for an old man under as much strain as he's in right now. Let's see about the blood pressure." He tightened the fabric cuff around Cassius's upper arm, inflated the cuff with the bulb while he watched the needle on the pressure gauge climb, then placed the diaphragm of the stethoscope against the inside of the elbow just below the cuff and released the pressure. The needle dropped slowly, kicking periodically as the blood began to flow again.

"One-ninety over one-twenty," Bruckner said aloud. "Say, Mr. Cassius, did you know you have a serious medical problem? I'll bet you haven't been taking your hypertension medicine, have you? That's unfortunate, in view of what's about to happen here. Most unfortunate. Your best bet, old man, is to hope for a massive coronary before the pain makes you spill your guts to us. But, of course, that's why I'll be checking you continuously . . . we wouldn't want you croaking off too soon, now would we?"

"Cut the cute talk, Bruckner, and get on with it," Toberts said angrily.

Bruckner smiled. "You haven't been reading your interrogation manual, have you? I'll bet old Cassius here knows what I mean—the more you talk about the terrible things that are going to happen, the more unstrung your subject gets and the more likely he is to make the procedures unnecessary. In effect, you make him do your job for you. Isn't that right, old sport?"

Bruckner suddenly seized the free end of the rope and gave it a back-straining jerk, lifting Cassius clear of the floor by the noose around his genitals. With the gag in his mouth making him unable to scream, his head simply jerked furiously side to side, his eyes nearly popping from his skull.

Bruckner tied the end of the rope he was holding to a bolt protruding from the wall to maintain the tension, and again checked Cassius's heartbeat and blood pressure. "I think he'll last a few minutes—not much more than that," he informed Toberts. "He's settling down a bit—the human body can get used to almost anything after a while—but all you have to do is give the rope a little jerk now and then, and I guarantee he'll babble for all he's worth on any subject you choose."

"Nice," Toberts said, unable to conceal the disgust that he felt. He checked his watch, saw that it was time for the next train, and said to the pitiful Cassius dangling halfway to the ceiling, "When I remove the gag you start

109

telling me about Lamplighter, as quickly and accurately as you can."

When the approaching train began to rattle the door, Toberts pulled the rag from Cassius's mouth and pushed the tape recorder closer to him. Incredibly, Cassius uttered a single obscenity in Turkish and spit at Toberts's face.

"You stupid little prick!" Bruckner yelled, jerking the rope up and down while Cassius screamed in pain.

"Stop it!" Toberts yelled at Bruckner. "He can't take any more of that."

When Bruckner hesitated, Toberts shouted, "Now!" Reluctantly obeying the obvious command, Bruckner took his hands off the rope. Toberts heard the train pulling out of the station and replaced the rag in Cassius's twisted mouth, then checked the heartbeat and blood pressure himself. "I think we ought to let him down all the way," Toberts said. "If it gets any higher he'll blow up."

"Not until he talks," Bruckner said. "You saw how he was—we just have to keep the pressure on him."

Remaining silent with his dark thoughts, Toberts checked his watch and waited for the next train.

After two other episodes of Cassius refusing to talk and Bruckner hurting him badly, it was obvious to Toberts that Cassius, perspiring heavily now as his entire body twisted and jerked convulsively at the end of the rope, was about to go mad. "Tell us, Cassius," Toberts said again, removing the gag, and the tough little agent, thoroughly broken, began to babble almost incoherently about Lamplighter.

"Old archives in the Kremlin . . . Russians found recently . . . indicate that some of the Romanov crown jewels were stolen one hundred years ago . . . taken out of Russia by Princess Yurievskaya, after death of Alexander the Second . . . stolen in Paris . . . transported to United States and hidden . . . never left there."

"You mean," Toberts said, "these jewels are supposed to still be hidden somewhere in the United States?"

"Yes," Cassius mumbled.

"Who stole the jewels, Cassius?"

"Don't . . . know. Rumor a history professor at Sorbonne involved . . . 1881."

"What was his name?"

"Maurice . . . Cordier."

"Is that C-O-R-D-I-E-R?" Toberts asked him, spelling it out. Cassius twitched, indicating he neither knew nor cared. "He . . . may have left . . . coded papers."

"How much are the jewels worth?" Bruckner asked.

Again Cassius did not answer. Infuriated at the man's stubbornness, Bruckner started for the rope, but Toberts shouted "No!" at him and knelt to read the heart rate again. "He's just barely alive, Bruckner—I don't think anything else you do to him will make any difference now. Cassius, why the name 'Lamplighter'?"

"Not . . . sure, but may be your Statue of . . . Liberty somehow involved."

"My God!" Bruckner said. "You suppose any of this is true?"

"Anything else?" Toberts asked.

"No."

"One more question, Cassius," Toberts said then. "Did you do the job on my little friend Georges Maron?"

Cassius's eyes narrowed but he would not speak. "Answer me!" Toberts shouted with rage, but still Cassius was silent. Toberts nodded at Bruckner, who jerked the rope hard. Seeing Bruckner going for the rope, Cassius had started to answer when a scream came up from his throat, drawing the single syllable *Yes!* from his stretched lips like a protracted nightmare.

Toberts pushed the rag into his open mouth, no longer caring what happened to him, what Bruckner or anyone else did to him. Ultimately, he supposed, it all came down to the ancient law of an eye for an eye, a tooth for a tooth—to which every intelligence agency he had ever heard of subscribed implicitly. You hurt one of ours, we hurt one of yours, the custom proclaimed, and no one ever thought to criticize or question it.

Eyes still open wide, Cassius's head and neck muscles suddenly went slack. Toberts bent over to check blood pressure again, but the needle on the pressure gauge refused to kick. Hurriedly Toberts checked the heart and pulse,

111

but there was not even a whisper of life in the old agent. "I think he's dead," he told Bruckner, who came over to check Cassius himself.

"Heart attack or stroke," Bruckner said. "It happens. At least you got the information you were after."

"I didn't plan to kill him."

"He planned to kill your friend Maron. Just keep thinking about that."

"Yeah," Toberts said. "I'm trying to."

Without discussing it with each other they both knew what they had to do now. Bruckner loosened and removed the slipknot from Cassius's body, replaced his pants, and dragged him toward the door. Toberts turned off the tape recorder and put it back in his pocket. He opened the door wide, simultaneously flipping off the dim light so that the room would be dark behind them. Patiently they waited in the open doorway, each of them holding one of the dead agent's arms.

Finally they heard the train coming toward them from the pitch-black tunnel. As it roared up almost abreast of them, its single bright eye swaying crazily, they tossed the body onto the tracks in front of the hard-rubber wheels the French ministry of transportation was so proud of. Then they closed the door behind them and walked up the long platform to mingle with the few people either getting on or getting off the train.

As they hurried up the stairs toward the street, they heard the train move out of the station and they looked at each other, knowing that it would be a while before anyone discovered the body.

10

The following morning Toberts arrived early at the embassy and began plowing through the cable traffic that had accumulated over the weekend. Mme. Joubert made fresh coffee in the flowered pot and clucked appreciatively as Toberts drank down the first cupful in one long gulp, not realizing that this was a method he had devised for getting the caffeine into his system without having to taste her coffee.

A little after nine o'clock Mme. Joubert took a phone call from the secretary of the embassy's building security chief. She put the woman on hold and whispered across to Toberts, "It's that snoopy Mrs. Weems—she says Mr. Coleman would like for you to come down to his office when you have a minute."

Toberts disengaged his mind from the cable in his hand and tried to focus on the argument he had had last Friday with the ambassador concerning Coleman. It seemed like a long time ago.

"Tell him I'll be down in a half hour," he told Mme. Joubert.

Still holding the receiver against her bosom, Mme. Joubert frowned. "It's not proper, Mr. Toberts. You outrank Mr. Coleman and you both know it—he's supposed to come up here if he wants to see you."

"It's all right, Madame Joubert, this is a special occasion. Tell him I'll be there, please, like a good girl."

He worked another ten or fifteen minutes and then decided his mind wasn't on the cables because of this thing with Coleman that would affect his secretary. Better to get it out in the open than let it drag on any longer, he thought, and grabbed his coat off the rack. "I'm off

113

to see the wizard," he told Mme. Joubert. "Please have Elliott round up all the morning Paris newspapers he can find—the later the edition the better. I *shall* return, bloody but unbowed."

"I'd like to bloody *him*," Mme. Joubert said. "Give him a good sock in the jelly beans for me, will you?"

"I promise," Toberts said, feeling like a traitor for not telling her that the conversation with Coleman was going to be about her.

Coleman's office was on the ground floor of A Building, straight down the narrow hallway and not very far from the ambassador's suite. Location like that meant something, Toberts knew, in embassies the world over, and could count for a good deal more in the politics of internal embassy bickering than anyone would guess from reading the foreign service manual. Besides, Coleman was a rigid regulation follower, one of the army of small-minded clerks whose devotion to established rules was awesome, whether the rules made any sense or not.

Coleman's secretary kept Toberts waiting just that extra minute that destroyed any possibility of an amicable discussion of the problem between them. When Toberts was finally admitted to the small office of the security chief, Coleman was on the telephone, his heavy brows knitted as if over a delicate, extremely high-level decision that only he could make. Toberts wondered whether there was anyone on the other end of the line.

"Hello, Toberts," Coleman said finally after hanging up. "What can I do for you?"

Toberts's teeth grated. "You called me, remember? About Madame Joubert, I imagine—that silly business about not letting her remain on the fourth floor."

"Yes," Coleman said, his downcast eyes searching for something in the papers he shuffled from hand to hand. "Well, the ambassador doesn't think it's silly, Toberts. In fact, he asked me to have this talk with you to see that you understand why he cannot allow Madame Joubert, a French citizen—"

"An American from Sandusky, Ohio," Toberts added hastily.

"—a French citizen, married to a French national

114

of undetermined loyalties, to remain in her present position where, as you surely know, she has access to all the top secret traffic off the transatlantic telex, in addition to hundreds of coded and decoded memos. The woman could steal everything from the latest NATO assessments to the CIA's prognosis for an extraordinary vintage crop in Bordeaux, without even leaving her immediate area."

"But of course she doesn't have *access*, as you claim; she sees the logs and that's about it. Anyway, Coleman, Madame Joubert has worked for me almost five years now—I would honestly trust her with my life."

"We're discussing U.S. state secrets now," Coleman said stonily. "I believe you have signed an oath which states in no uncertain terms that such secrets are much more valuable than an individual life and are to be guarded accordingly. No, Toberts, we cannot allow Madame Joubert to remain. I'm afraid I must ask you to have her signed resignation or transfer documents on my desk no later than COB tomorrow. Otherwise, the ambassador will have to be informed of your refusal."

Toberts nodded. "You're a sweet guy, Coleman, you know that?"

"I do my job."

"Yes, indeed. You do a job on just about everybody," Toberts said bitterly, and left Coleman's office before his anger overcame his reason.

When he returned to his own office, he noticed Mme. Joubert staring at him and wondered if she had heard something—it wouldn't be unlikely, given the ease and speed with which office gossip invariably got back to the affected party. He saw that Elliott had collected the morning papers—*L'Aurore, Le Figaro, L'Humanité,* the *Herald Trib, Le Parisien Libéré, Le Matin de Paris*—and that Cassius's death had made all of them, though his badly mangled body had apparently still not been identified. The police were working on the theory that it was a suicide.

Toberts got the tape of their session with Cassius from his office safe and inserted it into the small player on his desk. Using earphones, he monitored the entire tape, making notes to himself on a piece of paper. When he came to the protracted scream of the agent he punched the fast-forward button on the player to skip ahead, his stomach churning with the knowledge that he had been responsible for the man's unbearable pain and, ultimately, his death. When the tape was over he replaced it in the safe and studied his notes, attempting to assign different weight to various factors: the imperial Russian court, the jewels themselves, Professor Cordier, the Sorbonne, the Statue of Liberty. There were few obvious connections; much more information was missing than was present. The next step was to figure out where to start looking for the larger missing pieces.

As prearranged the previous evening, Toberts took a walk from the embassy to the Place du Marché where he met Bruckner at a restaurant near the covered market. Over lunch they discussed the newspaper accounts of Cassius's death, and how they were to proceed with attempting to verify the agent's story—which had perhaps been manufactured by the KGB specifically for the purpose of confusion, with just enough factual embellishment to lend a certain credence to it. Or perhaps, as Toberts believed, the Russians were just as ignorant of the details as they were, and would gladly allow the CIA to uncover whatever facts they could through original research and then steal those facts at the first opportunity.

"I don't get the Statue of Liberty connection at all," Bruckner said.

"That part could be wrong, or twisted around somehow," Toberts said, admitting he also had a hard time making sense of Cassius's reference to the statue. "Maybe they were using it in a metaphorical sense, to mean the United States, or some part of the United States."

"In any case, we've first got to substantiate one or several of the factual leads by any means we can—otherwise we've got either a hoax or a fairy tale on our hands."

Toberts nodded agreement. "If there were records kept by this Professor Cordier a hundred years ago, they might still be stored at the Sorbonne. I'll try to check out that aspect. I think you ought to get with your boss Sloan and kick around the theory that Cordier, if he existed at all, must have lived in a house somewhere in Paris during the eighteen-seventies. Maybe the house is still there—it might even be owned by present-day relatives of the professor. And maybe this would give us a lead to his personal papers. In any case, Sloan will know how to go about checking Paris city records from the year one. We'll meet tomorrow noon at the spot I showed you in the Luxembourg Gardens, by the Medici Fountain. Can you find it again?"

"Of course," Bruckner said. "I'm not in the habit of forgetting rendezvous points."

"Neither am I," Toberts said, and paid the check.

11

THE OFFICES OF THE Paris *Times-Weekly* on the Rue Réaumur were as cluttered as most other newspaper offices the world over. There were always people coming and going who looked like reporters, copy editors, rewrite men, layout artists, and makeup editors, but somehow, even the first time he had seen the place, Bruckner had instinctively known that there was something different here, something that was not quite right. What was lacking, he finally decided, was a certain sense of urgency about the employees' activities, that communal spirit of involvement in large affairs.

Harold Sloan didn't seem to notice the lack of vitality shown by his staff. As often as not he would spend the better part of a working day locked in his tiny private office with only a faulty venetian blind over a glass window separating him from his employees. Bruckner had stood close enough to the glass several times to see clearly that what Sloan mostly did inside his office was drink whiskey from a bottle he kept in his desk drawer, and sleep with his head tilted back and his feet propped up on the desk. And yet Bruckner also sensed that Sloan was not a stupid or lazy man; his actions would have puzzled Bruckner if he had ever allowed himself to speculate on the motives or personalities of individuals who were not targets in his job.

"I know just the place to start the search, Pell, m'boy," Sloan said when Bruckner approached him with Toberts's idea about the professor's house. "We'll taxi over to the Archives de la Ville de Paris, on Quai Henri IV."

"What is it?" Bruckner asked him.

118

"City records. They keep stuff going way back before Napoleon's time—it's just a question of digging it out."

"And they let just anyone in to paw through all that material?"

"They let *me* in, and that's what's important. It's down by the Ile Saint-Louis—that's an island in the middle of the Seine. Come to think of it, there are a couple of pretty lively cafés nearby."

"This is work, Sloan. Does Toberts know how much of the time you spend drinking and goofing off?"

"Oh-ho!" Sloan said, eyebrows raised. "You wouldn't be thinking of putting in a bad word for old Harold, would you? That is a decidedly unfriendly attitude."

"Friends, Sloan, are a luxury I can't afford. Business associates are another matter entirely."

Sloan glanced sharply at Bruckner and nodded. "All right, *Mister* Bruckner, let's get down to business."

The taxi ride wasn't far from the *Times-Weekly* offices but was still, Bruckner thought, quite expensive; obviously Sloan charged it off to the U.S. government, as he undoubtedly did many other unwarranted expenses. Bruckner made a mental note to speak to Toberts about it.

Though housed in a classically designed building, the Archives were still a governmental function, and the office of the director into which Sloan guided him was very much a civil servant's domain. Although Bruckner missed whole sentences of the director's rapid official French, his manner would have given him away anywhere in the world; he seemed to be telling Sloan, whom he obviously knew quite well, that his request was all highly irregular and was really quite out of the question. Then it was Sloan's turn; he was apparently offering the traditional gift, or bribe—in this case it appeared to be tickets to some new musical the newspaper had received free—and the director's manner suddenly and magically changed to one of gracious cooperation.

Sloan and Bruckner were led to one of several identical research rooms and were introduced to a woman who served as custodian of all the records in her part of the building. She wore a long black dress and black low-heeled shoes. Her eyeglasses were attached to her black

119

and white blouse by a silver chain, and there was a long silver knitting needle pushed through the thickest part of her gray hair, which she wore in a tight bun.

"What can I do for you gentlemen?" she asked them.

Sloan told her, in French, that they were looking for records of housing that might have been occupied by a Professor Maurice Cordier. "He taught at the Sorbonne, around 1881," Sloan said. "As important and respected as university professors have always been in France, we feel sure there will be records of where he lived."

"Perhaps," the custodian said. "First we must determine the existence of this Professor . . . Cordier?"

"I'm sure he exists," Sloan said. "Could we just get on with the—"

"I shall check the university's records first," the woman said. "It is standard procedure, monsieur."

She allowed them to follow her to a section of old ledger books that turned out to be the individual tax assessments of Paris residents for the decade between 1880 and 1890. Eventually, with Sloan and Bruckner looking over her shoulder, she ran a bony finger across a fading hand-written sheet to the entry *Cordier, Maurice L., Professeur de l'Histoire, Université de Paris (Sorbonne)*. Following this information were figures that might have represented the professor's income and tax liabilities for various years, but there was no information about his family or where he lived.

"It appears your Professor Cordier did exist," the custodian said grumpily, as though angry because this would add to her workload. She went to a different part of the huge room. Pushing aside a pile of musty loose records bound together with wire, she began picking through a row of leather-bound volumes of the history, teaching staff, and graduates of the Sorbonne. The volume she finally unearthed contained records for the years 1850 through 1895. Once again Sloan and Bruckner hovered over the woman's shoulder as she turned pages of the great record book, causing her to look up and scowl at them every few pages. Though they found numerous references to Maurice Cordier, the illustrious

professor of history, once again there was no indication
that he had any existence outside the university.

The custodian closed the book, a puzzled look on her
face. "It becomes more and more a mystery," she said
to herself. "Perhaps the Sûreté would have records, but
I doubt if they go back that far, and in any case they
would not allow you into their files. No, I think we have
reached an impasse, gentlemen. Sorry."

Bruckner looked at Sloan. "What about military service? Wouldn't they have had to know the address of his
relatives, in case of death?"

Sloan nodded. "Brilliant!" He proceeded to ask the
custodian about possible military service records, and
suddenly she, too, looked as though a light had been
turned on somewhere behind her metal-rimmed glasses.

She led them to yet another obscure alcove of the
room, and there, finally, in a thick book of original documents signed at the time of conscription into the French
Army, they found what they had been searching for.
Cordier had been drafted in 1854, at the age of twenty,
to fight against the Russians in the Crimean War. Though
his military service had been undistinguished, the records
did show the address of his family home in Paris—49
Rue Veilleuse, in Montparnasse.

Bruckner scribbled the number in a notebook, and he
and Sloan thanked the custodian. They were about to
leave when, holding the military record book braced across
her chest, the custodian raised her eyebrows and said
directly to Sloan, "It is customary, monsieur, to show
your gratitude for the labor involved in these detailed
searches by a small payment to the custodian of records."

Sloan pulled some francs from his pocket and handed
them to her without counting them, and Bruckner made
a mental note that that, too, should perhaps be discussed
with Toberts at some future date.

They took a second taxi to the address Bruckner had
written down, and as soon as Sloan saw where they were,
he shook his head. "Something wrong here, Bruckner,"
he said. "The numbers don't seem to run right—there's
no number forty-nine at all."

The block where the house should have stood was the

center of a modern commercial area of shops and cafés. Sloan asked the driver to turn around and cruise back slowly the way they had come. But it did them no good —the missing house number was still missing.

"How long have these shops been here?" Sloan asked the driver, who was old enough to perhaps remember something useful.

The driver shrugged. "Who knows? Ten, maybe fifteen years. Before that it used to be houses, very old houses, some of them. One day the machines came in and tore everything down—imagine, one entire block destroyed in the space of an afternoon! *Merde!* Notre-Dame may be next."

Sloan nodded in sympathy with the driver's feelings about urban progress. Bruckner, to whom nothing older than last week had ever been sacred or even worth worrying about, remained silent. He hoped that Toberts would have better news.

At the next corner Bruckner left the taxi and found a pay telephone. He dialed Toberts's home number and when a woman answered asked for him although he knew Toberts was not there. For a while, because he had nothing better to do, he talked to Toberts's wife, and when he left the telephone booth, he was nearly smiling.

Colonel Alexis Balachov sat tilted slightly backward in his executive swivel chair and stared at the woman facing him from a high-backed leather chair in front of the desk. A huge, rough-looking man wearing a totally inappropriate suit jacket with mismatched slacks stood beside the chair; one side of his beefy face was bruised and swollen.

"Good of you to come," Balachov said, lighting one of the Russian cigarettes he brought into the country duty-free by the case. "The police are now admitting that our friend Cassius suffered an apparent stroke or coronary attack before being run over by the metro train. An accomplished observer in my employ was permitted to view the body closely in the police morgue, and his report indicates that poor Cassius's scrotum was nearly pulled from his torso. I think we must conclude that, in all likelihood, the CIA were attempting to wring whatever

122

information they could from him by torture, and that ultimately they killed him."

"And are you certain that your 'accomplished observer' correctly interpreted the marks on Cassius's body?" the woman in the leather chair asked. Leaning forward in her intensity, she brushed the long red bangs impatiently from her eyes.

"Yes, Ilsa, quite certain. Boris knows what he is doing —I don't doubt that he himself has used the same methods in the past. But, in fact, even if Boris were wrong in his diagnosis, it would not alter the situation. We need to know about the progress Mr. Toberts and his friends are making on *Fonarshchik.* We need to know where they are looking for information and what their plans are." The colonel looked at the standing man. "It is unfortunate that Relka suffered a ruptured artery at the hands of Toberts and the new reporter—what was his name?"

"Bruckner," Ilsa replied.

"Yes—Bruckner. His arrival in Paris at this time is rather a coincidence, don't you think? In any case, Fon, I trust you will not let happen again what happened to you and Relka at the Crillon. These are not amateur street fighters we are dealing with; they are trained killers. I hope you appreciate the fact that you are lucky to be alive at this moment."

The huge man named Fon clenched a hamlike fist and nearly growled when he spoke: "If I ever meet this Toberts again he will suffer greatly before I allow him to die."

"No, Fon," the colonel said patiently, as though to a child. "We do not wish to kill Mr. Toberts, at least not yet. The CIA would, I fear, take such an action personally and could do great damage to our operation here in retaliation for his death. Ilsa, do you have someone in mind at the American Embassy who might help us out, with or without being blackmailed?"

"I have a contact, yes."

"Is this 'contact' by any chance on the fourth floor of B Building? I understand the most interesting things regularly occur in that location."

"No, Colonel. But my contact is reliable and has, by the nature of his duties, multiple access throughout the embassy. He should be able to find us a candidate for *sanctification.*"

"I trust that is true, Ilsa. After bungling your last assignment you need to restore my confidence in you. Yes, and it must be done without physical harm to Mr. Martin Toberts. In addition to my fear of massive retaliation, I have no desire to see him replaced just now. We know and understand each other well, Toberts and I—it would be such a time-consuming bore to have to tame a new chief of station from the sewers of Langley."

"He deserves to die!" Fon said, grimacing.

"And so he shall, in due time," the colonel said. "And so shall we all."

Having returned to the embassy to pick up his car after the lunch with Bruckner, Toberts drove across the river to Boulevard Saint-Germain on the Left Bank and followed it past Boulevard Saint-Michel to the Rue des Ecoles along the north side of the University of Paris buildings known, since the year 1253, as the Sorbonne. After some difficulty he found a parking place a few blocks away and shortly entered the building, where he was immediately stopped by a caretaker who demanded to know where he was heading and what he wanted there.

"I suppose I don't look much like either a student or a professor," Toberts told the old man. "In any case, I do have an appointment with the library director. Here's my card."

He produced his embassy identification card, which was impressive enough that it got him into all sorts of places where he technically had no business being. The caretaker nodded, said, *"Oui,* monsieur," and with a little bow allowed Toberts to go on his way.

This was not the first time Toberts had been in the Sorbonne, which was fortunate since he would have felt more than a little foolish now asking the caretaker where the library was.

He soon found himself inside the huge Sorbonne collection of books new and rare, documents, periodicals dating

124

from the fifteenth century, unbound dissertations, and stack after stack of papers, loose and seemingly disorganized in folders. The library itself was a room of interesting proportions and more little alcoves and side areas than were visible from any one location. Except for its size, it reminded Toberts of the dark, musty old city library in Albuquerque, New Mexico, when he was growing up.

He approached a young man with rimless glasses who was sitting on a high stool behind a desk faced with card catalog drawers. "Pardon me," Toberts said, "do you mind if I look through the catalog cards?"

"Of course not," the young man said. "Is there something I could help you with?"

"Actually, there may be. I'm looking for anything written by a Professor Maurice Cordier, who I understand was associated with the Sorbonne about a hundred years ago—particularly around the early eighteen-eighties."

"If we have the book we have a card on it," the librarian said. He hopped down off his stool and walked around the desk beside Toberts. "Of course, you understand everything in our collection is not on display here in the main room. We have two or three annexes as well, and a basement room nearly twice this size filled with older, less-used materials."

"Would those also be cataloged?"

"That's hard to say. If they are books, then probably so, but many of the papers and loose documents are simply stored in boxes and there's probably no card on them."

"Then how does anyone ever find what they're looking for in those boxes?"

The young man smiled and shrugged. "Perseverance," he said. "Some of the boxes are labeled or marked with crayon, some aren't. Occasionally the labels are either misleading or, for whatever reason, entirely erroneous."

"Sounds like a wonderful system," Toberts said.

"It isn't as bad as it sounds. When funds are available we hire extra catalogers and classifiers to sift through the older, disorganized parts of the collection. We've made great headway over the past twenty or thirty years."

"I suppose," Toberts said, "when you've been in the same business and the same location for the past seven hundred years, an extra twenty-five or thirty really doesn't make all that much difference. Can we look up Professor Cordier now?"

"Of course."

The librarian went to a bank of file drawers and began riffling rapidly through the cards. "Ah, here we are," he said at last, adjusting the glasses on his thin nose. "Cordier, Maurice L. It seems he was a professor here from 1865 to 1907. We have . . . four books written by him in our collection, all in the field of comparative history. Since he was employed here at the Sorbonne, I assume we would have everything he published."

"Then that's it?" Toberts asked.

"That seems to be all," the librarian said.

"What about the uncataloged documents in the basement?"

"Well, as I told you, there could be almost anything down there. You would have to research the boxes yourself."

"I would be happy to do that. May I go down and take a look now?"

"I suppose so," the librarian said. "I'll need your faculty card number."

When Toberts frowned, the young man in turn frowned and said, "You mean you're not connected with the Sorbonne? You simply wandered in here off the street? I should call the guards, I really should . . . the very idea!"

"No, no, you don't understand," Toberts said. "I'm with the American Embassy—here's my identification card."

The librarian glanced perfunctorily at the card. "You are still unauthorized to use the library except under the supervision of a resident librarian."

"But *you're* a resident librarian, aren't you?"

"Certainly. However, that rule applies only to the main collection. It is impossible for anyone not a staff member of the university to use the protected collection. I'm sorry, monsieur."

"So am I," Toberts said dejectedly. "I guess I'll have

to cultivate someone on the staff. Do you have any suggestions?"

"No, I know of no one who might be interested in your Professor Cordier, an obscure history instructor a century ago. His published works are not exactly household items."

"So it would seem." Smiling ruefully, Toberts turned to leave, when the young man, saying the name Cordier under his breath several times, called out to Toberts. "I knew the name sounded familiar for some reason. There's probably no connection, but I remember now that there's a woman here who teaches in the Romance languages department who might be willing to talk with you."

"And why is that?"

"Her name is also Cordier . . . Solange Cordier. Here, you can reach her at this extension in her staff room when she's not busy with a class. Don't ask me when that would be."

"Thanks," Toberts said, taking the slip of paper on which the librarian had written the number. "Thank you very much. You've been a great deal of help."

"I don't see how," the librarian said as Toberts hurried out of the room.

The cafeteria was nearly empty as Toberts went through the line and picked up a paper cup of black coffee. He had purposely come early so that he could look for her, instead of the other way around; that, too, was part of the tradecraft, being the first to arrive at a rendezvous and thereby gaining a certain slight advantage, sometimes real and sometimes only psychological, but in any case useful.

On the telephone Mlle. Cordier had sounded pleasant but somewhat hesitant when Toberts introduced himself as the International Communication Agency press chief from the American Embassy. She wanted to know why he was calling her, and he was afraid to tell her immediately. He was afraid she would cut him off peremptorily, the way anyone whose privacy is suddenly and inexplicably invaded might, and he felt that he would have a much better chance with her if he could speak with her face to face. And so he had simply said that it was a matter of some importance, implying that the embassy, and perhaps even French-American relations, might suffer if she refused to speak with him. She had agreed to meet him here, after her final class of the day and for a few minutes only, as she was expected elsewhere in a short while.

The coffee was bitter and flavorless. Toberts added both milk and sugar, which he avoided normally because of his recent tendency to put on a few pounds around his waist, hoping this would improve the coffee to the point where it would be drinkable. He sipped it slowly, thankful that at least it was hot, as he carefully watched the two entrances.

When he saw her come in he had no doubt that it was she, though exactly why he could not have said. Her voice on the phone had sounded quite young, perhaps early twenties, but the woman who, having spotted his upraised hand, was now walking toward him was certainly in her mid-thirties, and could have been even older. She wore a cloth coat, as though she had either just been outside or was preparing to leave the building, and from what he could see she had a becoming figure and very pretty legs—which would have been even prettier, he thought, if she had worn somewhat higher heels. Her hair was short and dark and bounced with a life of its own when she walked.

He stood up, smiled, and offered her a chair. "Mademoiselle Cordier?"

"Yes," she said. "You must be Monsieur Toberts." Her voice was low and quite pleasant, though Toberts suspected she was even more reserved than he had thought on the phone.

"May I get you a cup of this terrible coffee?" he offered, and when he saw that she was smiling back at him he knew it was going to be all right.

He brought the coffee and she thanked him and pushed the money for it across the table toward him. He started to protest that it was his pleasure, but something about her manner stopped him, so that he merely shrugged, smiled, and pocketed the coins.

"The coffee served here is a kind of medieval test of courage," she said to him. "If you survive more than one cup, the common wisdom is that you are well on your way to conquering the world."

He found himself smiling broadly into her intelligent gray eyes. "This is my second cup," he said.

"Congratulations. Just what is it that you wish me to do for you, Monsieur Toberts?"

"I'm sorry I didn't explain more about it on the phone. My job at the embassy involves a great deal of sometimes tedious research into French cultural activities, from which I prepare various articles for the French press as well as English-language Parisian periodicals and newspapers."

"Oh, then you are a writer as well?"

"Yes, among other things. Sometimes I'm directed by others to do things that make little or no sense to me personally, but I'm supposed to believe that they all fit into some grand and complex scheme of greater cooperation between our two countries. In this case now we have a Fulbright exchange scholar in history coming over shortly, and one of the things he specifically wished to know was whether there might be in existence any remaining personal papers of a former professor here at the Sorbonne, about a hundred years ago, named Maurice Cordier. The librarian suggested I contact you, the obvious reason being the surname you have in common."

The story sounded entirely phony to his own ears; he half expected her to laugh at him because it was so preposterous. But instead she cocked her head at him and said, "He was my great-grandfather. Maurice Cordier was an interesting old man in many ways. Did you know he published four rather huge works of comparative history during his tenure here?"

"Yes, I saw them listed in the card catalog," Toberts said. "I must confess I haven't read any of them."

She managed to smile and pout in the same enchanting expression. "No one has read them for about seventy-five years now, I'm afraid."

He nodded. "When, exactly, was Professor Cordier here at the university?"

"Let's see . . . from about 1876 until sometime after the turn of the century. As I remember it was slightly more than forty years."

"And do you plan to emulate him?"

"In scholarship, perhaps. Certainly not in length of tenure . . . although there are less pleasant ways to spend one's declining years."

"In any case that's something you won't be concerned with for a long, long time," Toberts gallantly offered.

"Thank you, monsieur," she said, her gaze direct and honest instead of coyly shy as it might have been in so many other women. Unprofessional as it was of him, Toberts found himself being drawn to this woman more and more as they talked. He had almost forgotten the reason they were seated here in the nearly deserted cafeteria, chatting amiably like two old friends.

"Tell me, Mademoiselle Cordier, is it possible that Professor Cordier might have left some personal papers —notes for additional books, perhaps, observations on the times, even material in the form of diaries—stored here at the Sorbonne or somewhere else?"

"Yes, that is possible," she said. "Monsieur Toberts, I know you have told me you represent the American Embassy, but—"

"Oh, forgive me, of course you would want some sort of verification." He took his ID card from his wallet and held it out to her so that she could see that he did, indeed, work for the U.S. government's International Communication Agency.

"The photograph is a good likeness," she said, glancing from the card to his face and back again. "Unusually so, for an official identification. The photo on my driver's license would frighten small children."

"I doubt that," he said, once again being gallant in the offhand way American women seemed to expect.

"Oh, no, it's true!" she said. "Here, I'll show you." And she reached into her purse and extracted a small blue billfold from which she took the offending license with photograph.

He smiled at the picture, which really wasn't very

flattering. "It's awful," he agreed. "The police photographer should be shot."

"Well, whipped unmercifully, anyway," she said, laughing.

"Now," he persisted, "about the papers . . ."

"Yes. *Arrière-grand-père* Cordier was a prolific writer and documenter. At least two or three boxes of his papers have been preserved, uncataloged and unresearched, in the basement of this very building for all these years. I personally have only been told that the boxes exist; I know nothing of their contents. I keep meaning to take a half year off someday and go through the boxes thoroughly, but there just never seems to be an opportunity."

"And other things seem more interesting to do with your time," Toberts said, looking at her.

"You have touched my guilt, Monsieur Toberts. You are most perceptive."

"Then perhaps we could go downstairs together and search through the old materials of your great-grandfather—now, if you want."

"No, that is not possible." She looked down at her cup of no longer warm coffee. "I live with my widowed mother, monsieur. She is somewhat infirm and demanding —she worries when I am late from my classes by even a few minutes. I must go now."

"Then what about tomorrow?" Toberts persisted. "Or the next day?"

"Impossible," she replied. "But wait—today is the twenty-eighth? Then Thursday is a holiday, May Day. Is it for you, too?"

"Not exactly—the ambassador never knows what to expect on May Day, particularly from the students, and I think he feels more comfortable with lots of us around in the building. But I can certainly get back here, if you'd be available."

"Then let's say Thursday morning, about ten—since it's a holiday I plan to sleep at least two hours later than usual."

"But won't the building be closed up?"

"Probably, but no matter—I have an access key."

"Wonderful!" Toberts said, not trying to conceal how

131

pleased he was. "You're sure you don't mind spending a busman's holiday here?"

"I'm not familiar with the expression, Monsieur Toberts, but if you mean do I mind coming back to the Sorbonne when I am not required to by my teaching schedule, the answer is no. I often spend my free time here, doing research in the library, grading papers . . ."

"Sort of a second home, you mean."

She smiled at him and stood to go, wrapping her coat around her. "More of a first home, really," she said, her voice sounding wistful.

Toberts also stood. "May I offer you a ride home?"

"No, thank you, I have my little car outside. Until Thursday, then."

She turned and walked back through the entrance by which she had arrived, and Toberts stood looking after her, a vague uneasiness deepening the lines in his face.

12

AFTER CONSULTING HIS COPY of the Michelin red guide
for starred restaurants in the area, Bruckner walked from
the hotel on the Place de la Concorde north for three
blocks along the Rue Boissy-d'Anglas to the Chez Tante
Louise, where he dined well on *confit de canard*—preserved duck cooked in its own fat—along with a casserole
dish made of white beans and condiments.

It was almost ten o'clock and had been dark for some
time when he walked back to the Hotel Crillon bar and
settled in for an hour or two of serious drinking. For
whatever reason he was beginning not to like Paris very
much, but as long as their supply of Scotch held out he
assumed he would survive. He was barely into his second
Scotch-rocks when he glanced into the mirror behind the
bar and saw, approaching him, the girl Ilsa, the prostitute
with red bangs, with whom he had had sex the first night
in the hotel. He thought perhaps she was merely working
the bar again on some kind of regular schedule, and
maybe she was, but there was no mistaking the fact that
she had already singled him out. There was an empty
seat beside him, and he knew before she did it that she
was going to sit down.

"Hello, baby," she said to him, brushing his elbow with
one large sweater-covered breast as she settled in beside
him. "Want to buy a thirsty girl a drink?"

"Not particularly," Bruckner said, but the waiter was
already hovering and took her order for a champagne
cocktail—just like the B-girls back home in L.A., he
thought.

"Baby, I'm sorry about the other night," she said in
a kind of cooing, singsong voice. "Those two goons were
my brother and his friend—they made me come back be-

cause I was feeling bitchy. I complained about you having hurt me with the sex, and they wanted to teach you a lesson."

Bruckner glanced up into the mirror. "I hope they're not planning to come back tonight to finish the job."

"Oh *no*, baby," she said, running her long red nails up and down his arm. "I just came back to tell you that if you want Ilsa in your bed tonight, you may have her— the same way as last time, if you wish, because I have even prepared my body with grease. You see, I found that I did not mind the strangeness of it so much as I had thought at first."

Bruckner sneered at her. "Business must be terrible— what's the matter, you been giving out free doses of the clap?"

"Clap? Ah, the VD. No, chéri, I have myself examined regularly by the clinic. Ilsa is very clean for you."

"How did you know I'd be here tonight?"

"Oh, well . . ." She seemed to be thinking about that. "As you say, business has not been too good lately. I refuse to lower my prices, and these pigs refuse to pay. How about it, honey? Shall we go to your room?"

"I'll bet you remember just where it is, too, don't you?" Bruckner said. "No, thanks, not tonight." He smiled at her, thought of something else, and added, "I have a splitting headache."

"Ilsa knows how to fix that in a hurry," she said, but when she saw that he was not really interested she began a long rambling conversation that Bruckner couldn't always follow, but that seemed to have something to do with her family, who still lived on a farm outside Hamburg.

A well-dressed man with gray hair sat down at the bar several seats away and almost immediately began giving Ilsa the eye, smiling and finally beckoning to her. She haughtily turned in her seat so that her back was almost toward the man and continued making small talk with Bruckner, only now there seemed to be a kind of direction to her conversation. "I hope," she said, "that you were not hurt the other night by my brother and his friend."

"No, not at all. But I suspect they were slightly unwell for a while."

"That doesn't matter, chéri. And what about your friend—what was his name?"

"Martin."

"Oh—Mr. Martin?"

"Just Martin—I never did know his last name," Bruckner said. "He wasn't hurt either, if that's what you're asking."

"I'm so glad. What does your friend Martin do?"

"He drinks, but not well. And he has a wife, which is probably why he doesn't like women."

"Do you mean," Ilsa persisted, "that he perhaps likes young boys?"

"I doubt if he really likes anything," Bruckner said, and then, because he didn't wish to say more about Toberts, some of which might end up being true, he told Ilsa, "And that's all I know about him, okay? End of conversation. Why don't you get lost, lady—I have some serious drinking to do."

Ilsa lifted her enormous fake eyelashes and said, condescendingly, "Then perhaps some other time, baby," and slipping gracefully off the seat she went to sit beside the middle-aged lecher down the bar, which seemed to make them both happy.

After a while Bruckner noticed Ilsa and the man get up and leave the bar together. He quickly paid his tab and followed them outside. At first he thought he had lost them, but then he saw the headlights of a car that was just pulling away from the curb, and it was definitely being driven by the middle-aged man from the hotel bar. Ilsa, Bruckner saw, was sitting beside him in the front seat. Suddenly a large black car pulled up alongside them, blocking the man's way, and Ilsa, shouting something at the man, leaped from his car and into the larger car, which, Bruckner now saw, was being driven by a burly man who looked familiar.

Sinking back into the shadows of the sidewalk, Bruckner scrawled the license plate number of the large black car in his pocket notebook, and suddenly remembered why the driver looked familiar—he was one of the two muscle men who had tried, at Ilsa's insistence, to beat up Toberts and him in this very spot outside the hotel the other night. "Fucking bitch!" Bruckner said to himself, knowing that he had been set up and hating himself for having let it happen.

He watched for a long time as the well-dressed man in the little car sat very still until long after the other car had roared off, wiping his perspiring face with a white handkerchief that showed up quite clearly from Bruckner's vantage point. The engine died and still the man sat there with the headlights burning, until Bruckner, sure that the man had been nothing more than a spur-of-the-moment mark for Ilsa, returned to the Crillon bar and several more glasses of Chivas Regal.

13

In a way Toberts was glad for the two-day hiatus in his pursuit of Lamplighter. Since Mlle. Cordier had said she couldn't possibly help him search through her great-grandfather's papers at the Sorbonne until Thursday at the earliest, and since the trail that Bruckner and Sloan had been following apparently led nowhere, Toberts was glad to get back to his office at the embassy and catch up on some of the paperwork he felt he had been neglecting. Although Lamplighter was undoubtedly important, perhaps vastly so, he did have other work to do and no one else to do it. There was Stanley, of course, but Toberts never felt quite comfortable leaving top secret assignments or assessments in the hands of his second in command.

One of the first things Toberts did the Tuesday after his afternoon at the Sorbonne library was to check out the license plate number Bruckner had handed him when they met, as prearranged, by the Medici Fountain in the Luxembourg Gardens. For something international Toberts would have cabled the number and description of the car back to Langley for a run through their mammoth ID computer bank. But since he had a feeling it was local, he used their own CIA resources at the embassy—a small central computer for which he had a secure on-line inquiry terminal at his desk. As he had suspected, the automobile, a Citroen, proved to be one known to be used periodically by the KGB apparatus in Paris. The fact that the girl, Ilsa, was working for Colonel Balachov did not surprise Toberts at all. They would simply have to be more careful of her in the future.

On Thursday Toberts left the embassy and drove to the Sorbonne for his appointment with Mlle. Cordier, glad to get away because of all the elaborate preparations being made by the embassy security staff to counter the expected May Day riots by leftist students and their backers.

Surprisingly, the main door of the Sorbonne was open. Toberts approached a doorkeeper inside and asked for Professor Cordier; the guard dialed a number on an intercom set and spoke a moment, then hung up and told Toberts to wait there in the foyer.

Presently he heard the unmistakable tapping of high heels on the steps of the wide main staircase behind him, and he knew without seeing her that Mlle. Cordier had come down to vouch for him.

"Good morning, Monsieur Toberts," she said with a smile. Her voice was every bit as pleasant as he had remembered it was.

"Good morning . . . Professor?"

"The title is correct but much too formal. Mademoiselle is perfectly acceptable."

"And you may call me Martin," he said, pleased at his progress—it should make the search project much easier.

"I believe Monsieur Toberts will do nicely for the time being," she replied, and though her tone was anything but coy, he could not help smiling at her seriousness.

"Well," she said, "shall we go downstairs and see what we can find of my great-grandfather's papers?"

"Yes, right," he said. "There wouldn't happen to be a cup of coffee somewhere handy, would there?"

"I'm sorry, the cafeteria is closed today, as well as everything else, actually. I saw a fellow instructor upstairs earlier, but besides the guard I believe you and I are the only ones here now."

"It doesn't matter. My secretary at the embassy forgot to buy the coffee this week, and I missed having my usual four cups this morning."

She laughed. "Four cups! Then you must be suffering. I know—there's coffee up in my little office and I just now unplugged the pot. It should still be warm, if you don't mind that it is reheated."

"Wonderful." Toberts smiled. "Unless it's been reheated three or four times I don't even notice."

Following her up the stairs, he had an opportunity to confirm his initial impression that her legs were really quite lovely. Even if he had not needed her for access to important material in the Lamplighter project he would have found it no imposition at all to flatter this young woman, to resurrect the dimly remembered techniques for igniting the spark of some kind of romance. He wondered whether she would act as dry kindling to such a spark—in which case he doubted that *he* would know how to encourage yet control the resulting fire— or whether, as he suspected, she had no use for men to clutter her life and might even resent his trying to flirt with her. She wore no wedding band—he had noticed that immediately. Perhaps she was even a lesbian, he conceded, and it surprised him that the thought should disturb him as much as it did.

They left the staircase at the third level and she led him into a neat but still academically cluttered little office that, except for the soft flowered print of the curtains at the one window, showed no sign that it was occupied by a female rather than a male professor. Rather pointedly leaving the door propped open, she plugged in the green metal pot and sat in the wooden swivel chair at her desk, offering him the straight wooden chair beside it.

"Is this where your students come to beg for mercy?" he asked her, trying to get them off what he considered a far too formal basis.

She smiled at him rather condescendingly, he thought.

"Most of my students take my language classes because they want to," she said. "They are good students, they work hard, and they have no need to 'beg for mercy,' as you implied."

"Sorry, I was trying to be funny. Do you enjoy teaching?"

"Yes. Immensely."

"Have you been at it a long time?"

She smiled that distracting smile of hers again. "If you're attempting by this line of questioning to discover my age, you are going about it rather clumsily. You might try the direct approach."

He cleared his throat. "Mademoiselle Cordier, how old are you?"

"That's not any of your business, Monsieur Toberts,"

she said matter-of-factly. Then, perhaps noticing something in his face, she added, "Thirty-four, if it will do you any good."

"You were right, it wasn't any of my business," he said. Unable for the moment to look directly at her, he studied the bookshelves lining the walls of the room. "You must read a great deal."

"Yes, I do," she said. "Not in my field, particularly—I mean, not linguistics or semantics—but I do read in the languages themselves. Novels and biographies, mostly."

"No history, like your illustrious great-grandfather?"

"History I find interesting only to a point—I suspect we keep resurrecting the past primarily because we are dissatisfied with the present, and frankly I am much more interested in the present, and of course the future, than I am in what happened five hundred years ago in some obscure Abyssinian village. *Personal* history is another matter—although as I told you I haven't pursued great-grandfather Cordier's private file of papers in the basement library, I am actually quite glad you happened along to ask about them. Now perhaps I'll find out something about my namesake predecessor here—I'm sure it would make my mother happy, if nothing else."

"What about your father?"

"He's been dead for many years. My mother lives with me, or I live with her. I'm not sure which is correct. In any case, we live together."

She swiveled in her chair toward the coffee pot, set a clean cup in front of Toberts on the edge of the desk, reached for her own stained cup, and poured jet-black coffee into both. From a lower desk drawer she produced packets of sugar and powdered imitation milk, which Toberts refused. The coffee was only lukewarm and looked remarkably like the awful stuff Mme. Joubert made in her little flowered office pot, but the flavor of this coffee was so rich and good that Toberts, amazed, shook his head and smiled. "It's delicious," he said. "Simply the best coffee I've tasted in a long time."

"Yes, I know, everyone says so. But thank you for the compliment."

"Do you use a special ingredient of some kind?" he

asked her. "Come on, Mademoiselle Cordier, what's your secret?"

She smiled at him then, not the condescending smile of before, but the much more genuine and satisfying smile of a person being complimented on something they do really well and enjoying the attention. "I do nothing special to the coffee, Monsieur Toberts. It must be simply the way of the pot. I know the coffee's not hot enough, but that's the best this little pot will do. I've thought of taking it somewhere to have a repairman tinker with it, but I'm afraid that when I got it back, it would make very hot, very bad coffee. I prefer it this way."

"So do I," Toberts told her, meaning it. He noticed for the first time that the color of her eyes was very odd —soft gray, tinged with flecks of orange. "I suppose that the same people who rave about your coffee are always telling you this, too, but are you aware that you have the most remarkable eyes?"

The color rose instantly in Mlle. Cordier's face and she turned away, toward the open door of the office. "I expect that if you've finished your coffee we should go see what *arrière-grand-père* has left for us to discover," she said. "My time is not entirely unlimited."

"Of course," Toberts agreed. As they left the little office she locked the door behind her.

The basement archives were more disorganized, at least in appearance, than Toberts had been led to believe by the librarian. Mlle. Cordier unlocked the door with her own key and after switching on the overhead lights allowed him to enter first. There was one large main room, off which several other smaller rooms opened, all of them as cluttered-looking as a storage warehouse that had not been used for years. Everywhere there were cardboard boxes stacked three and four deep with a series of numbers written on the side of each in black crayon. Sometimes there were other things written on the boxes in an attempt to identify what might be found inside, but mostly there were just the numbers.

One section of the room had floor-to-ceiling metal shelving into which had been crammed thousands upon thousands of file folders filled with papers. There were labels on the end shelves indicating that the folders were arranged alphabetically by author; it appeared to Toberts that once, perhaps a long time ago, someone had started an ambitious project to arrange everything in the room neatly according to a system that a librarian could understand, but for some reason had given up before the project was a third of the way through. Some of the shelving was only half filled, and several racks were completely empty.

Mlle. Cordier stood in the center of the room with her hands in the pockets of her jacket, smiling at Toberts's perplexed expression. "Can you see why I've never had the courage to begin searching for my ancestor's papers down here?" she said. "Particularly when I didn't expect to find them of much personal interest to me?"

"Yes, I certainly do," Toberts said. "My God, how could any self-respecting library let things pile up like this?"

"Lack of money, and lack of time. I suppose the first implies the second."

Toberts pushed a few of the boxes aside to make a kind of path into the center of the cardboard jungle. "So how do we go about finding what we're looking for? Do you have any idea what these code numbers on the boxes mean?"

"Yes, fortunately I checked with the main librarian upstairs," Mlle. Cordier said. She pulled a slip of paper from her pocket. "She told me to look for these numbers —now all we have to do is find the proper boxes."

"No problem at all," Toberts said, laughing as he extended his hand toward the hundreds of identical cardboard containers. He took off his suit jacket and folded it across the back of a chair at one of the three or four tables scattered around the room. "Why don't you sit here and tell me what we're looking for."

She cocked her head at him. "Whose great-grandfather is this? I certainly can't let you do all the work." And she removed her own jacket and placed it beside his on the back of another chair. "You realize, I assume, that we will both need baths when this is over, Monsieur Toberts."

He smiled broadly, the thought of taking a bath with her circulating pleasurably in his mind. Together they began checking the boxes.

It was about an hour before Toberts's analytic mind grasped the fact that there was a semblance of order in the way the boxes were arranged, based on the alphabetic and numeric values of the codes printed on each. Once he had determined that the old professor's papers should be stored somewhere in the northwest corner of the room, it was another half hour until they located three boxes inscribed with the number the librarian had given Mlle. Cordier. Toberts lifted the three boxes out to the table, they then settled down to see what was hidden inside the dusty cartons. After a few moments of randomly pulling out a paper here, a folder there, they established that these were, indeed, the private papers of Professor Maurice L. Cordier, who had held the comparative history chair at the Sorbonne from 1865 until June of 1907.

The professor's great-granddaughter sat across the table from Toberts, beaming. "Suddenly I'm terribly excited about this!" she cried. "Just think what marvelous things might be hidden inside these boxes—it's like opening Christmas presents."

"I doubt if we'll find anything very spectacular," Toberts said.

She frowned at him. "Exactly what is it that you're looking for, Monsieur Toberts? You never told me, you know."

"That's right, I guess I didn't," Toberts said, trying to remember what cock-and-bull story he had invented the other day for her benefit. "The Fulbright scholar—remember?"

"Yes?"

"Well, he wants to research a particular aspect of your great-grandfather's work as it applies to the historical bases for the current East-West détente situation. The Embassy considers it rather high level and somewhat secretive work, I'm afraid, which is why I'm being so evasive. In fact, though, I won't be sure myself what I'm looking for until I find it—if I do. Does that answer your question?"

"Poorly," she said. "But I suppose that's the way diplomats are trained to conduct their business, by befuddling the public."

"Thank you," he said. "I suppose I deserved that."

"Yes, you did." She stared into his eyes intently for a moment, then grabbed a handful of papers from one of the boxes and flipped through them with her thumb. "So, what is our plan of action, *monsieur le général?*"

"I think," Toberts said, "in order to keep from mixing things up we'd better read through the papers in sequence, not simultaneously. What I mean by that is—"

"That one of us reads a page, then passes it to the other—yes, I am neither a child nor a simpleton, Monsieur Toberts. The question is, which one of us reads first?"

Toberts nodded. "Since I know what I'm looking for and you, by your own admission, are merely *perusing* out of curiosity, if you trust me I would say it makes more sense for me to read first. Is that agreeable?"

"Not particularly, but your diplomatic twaddle *is* convincing. I still think you're hiding something. But do go ahead."

And before she could change her mind, Toberts picked a handful of papers out of the first box and began poring over the outdated and academically formal French words written by Professor Cordier a century before.

At the end of three grueling hours they had worked their way through only a little less than half of the first box of papers. Toberts's eyes were swimming; he had seen nothing of any interest to him, and was beginning to think this whole brilliant idea was a waste of time. The professor's opinions, when he expressed them, seemed about right for his period and station, Toberts thought. Perhaps a bit more leftist than he would have imagined, but these were mostly papers from the earlier academic period around 1869, when the professor would still have been a relatively young man. There was a curious gap in the papers from mid-1870 until the end of 1871, about which Toberts questioned Mlle. Cordier.

"Oui, that was during the bad time," she told him.

144

When she saw Toberts didn't understand she explained. "The Paris Commune. After the Prussians defeated Napoleon, a provisional government was established here, in Paris, at the City Hall. Thousands of Communards were subsequently murdered—it was one of our bloodiest periods in history. My great-grandfather may or may not have been a Communard himself, but from what I've read here today I suspect he was an ardent sympathizer. During that awful year and a half or so of siege Parisians were too busy trying to find something to eat for them to worry about keeping up with their diaries."

"Then that probably explains it," Toberts said. "I'm beginning to think your ancestor may have been an unusually interesting figure of his day."

"A very private figure, I would judge. His feelings probably went mainly into these papers and a few personal letters. I doubt if he had much public life—or private life, either, for that matter."

"Speaking of which," Toberts said, glancing at his watch, "my stomach tells me it's time for lunch. Will you join me?"

She, too, checked her watch. "It is closer to suppertime, I believe. Thank you, Monsieur Toberts, but I must be getting home—which means, I'm afraid, that you must also stop for the day."

"No chance that I could stay here alone and work?" he asked, smiling at her in what he hoped was an ingratiating manner.

"None whatsoever," she said. "My, but that was a dazzling smile—I assume it works marvelously well for you when you are chasing young girls."

Toberts started to protest but Mlle. Cordier was already carrying one of the boxes back to the shelf where they had found it. He marked his place, carried the remaining two boxes, and left the archives room with Mlle. Cordier, who locked up behind them.

"At least let me walk you to your car," he said as they passed the door guard on the main floor on their way outside.

She smiled at Toberts and nodded.

They had walked no more than half a block from the

145

front door when an empty bottle suddenly crashed against a stone wall behind them, showering them both with shards of glass. A mob of student-aged young people singing the Communist *Internationale* loudly and badly charged raggedly down the center of the street, blocking what little traffic there was and verbally harassing the drivers and pedestrians foolish enough to find themselves out in the street with the students. Toberts watched one driver apparently decide to take matters into his own hands. A short, beefy man, he hopped from his tiny automobile ready to do battle with the entire student population of Paris, only to be hit suddenly and violently on the head with the staff of a red flag carried jointly by two students.

Almost simultaneously an official blue cruiser with flashing lights rounded the corner and jerked to a stop, disgorging several blue-helmeted riot police waving long, thick sticks and carbines loaded with hard rubber bullets. The students, perhaps from overexposure to television coverage of previous years' riots, knew that in any such encounter with the elite squad of the Paris mayor's forces they would surely lose and lose badly; their already disorganized ranks broke apart into individuals running in the opposite direction from the police cruiser.

Even in his haste one bulky young man speeding past Mlle. Cordier took the opportunity to swing out at her with a heavy hand-painted sign. Toberts deftly stepped in close to the young man and managed to clip him neatly in the forehead with his own sign. The student went down heavily, a huge blue knot already swelling above his right eye. Toberts grabbed Mlle. Cordier's hand and pulled her along the sidewalk away from the retreating mob. They turned the corner at the next intersection and were suddenly in another world—a quiet, sunny May day on a tree-lined street of ancient buildings, a man and a woman holding hands, walking beneath the flowering buds of huge old chestnut trees.

Self-consciously, Mlle. Cordier withdrew her hand from Toberts's hand. "Thank you, monsieur," she said, referring to his having dispatched the angry student.

"I will accept your thanks only if you start calling me

146

Martin," Toberts said. "After all we've been through together . . ."

She smiled, nodded. "You did that rather well, as though you've had experience of that kind before—as though perhaps you have rather a lot of occasion to defend yourself with your hands. Do you, Martin?"

"Oh, you know," Toberts said, brushing it off. "The State Department offers all its embassy people a course in self-defense."

"Of course," she said skeptically. "By the way, since you saved my life, or at least some of my skin, I suppose you may call me Solange."

"Solange," he repeated. "It's a very pretty name. I thought you'd never ask."

"I wondered whether I ever would."

She led him to her car, a tiny old Renault of the type the automobile company had never been able to sell in the States. After agreeing to meet again the following Saturday morning at the Sorbonne, Toberts left her and returned to his own car.

It took him more than an hour and a half to drive through the parade- and crowd-clogged streets from the Left Bank north across the river to his house at the northern edge of Montmartre. Jessie was home, alone with a bottle, as she was more and more often these days. She tried to hide the drinking, even from him—*did* hide the bottle, usually, when she heard him drive up to the house—never apparently realizing that when her breath stank of alcohol, when her sentences were slurred and her bodily actions misdirected and awkward, there was no need for anyone to see the bottle tilted against her lips to know that she had been hitting it again.

"Well, well—nice of you to stop by," she greeted him, sweeping an unsteady arm low to the floor as though curtsying before royalty. "Been to any good parties lately where you don't want to be seen with your wife?"

Toberts exhaled slowly. "How much have you had, Jessie?"

She made a short, chopping motion toward her throat. "Up to here is where I've had it with you, Mister High-and-Mighty. What the hell do you mean, not leaving a number at the embassy where I can reach you! What if there'd been a bloody emergency? Fat lot of good it'd do me to call that trained seal you call a secretary." In a falsetto voice she mimicked Mme. Joubert: " 'I'm *sorry*, Mr. Toberts is out of the office just now. If you'd like to leave your number, I'll give him the message when he calls in.' That harpy! Doesn't she know where you are, either, or does she just cover up for you?"

"Jessie, you know my job takes me all over Paris. I'm in and out of half a dozen offices every day, sometimes more. There just isn't any way to leave a trail of numbers where I can be reached. And I *do* call in and get my messages, as often as I can."

"And what about all the nights you claim to be working? What am I supposed to believe, that you *don't* have some little French floozy out on the town? Who are you trying to kid, Martin!"

"Certainly not you, Jessie. You're way too sharp for that." Glancing at her to see whether she could even begin to guess at the depth of his sarcasm, he went to the kitchen, hoping that she might have begun to think about preparing some kind of dinner for them. But there was nothing out except the breakfast and lunch dishes. "Were you planning to eat tonight?" he asked her, knowing what her answer would be.

"I thought we'd eat out tonight—it's too much bother to prepare the kind of gourmet meals you seem to require, without having a full-time cook."

"You know that isn't true, Jessie. I don't require anything much in the way of food, except that it not be either raw or burned to cinders. Lately those have been the choices—when you weren't too drunk to even remember about dinner. You've got to straighten yourself out, Jess— I can't do it for you. I still think you ought to sign on for the detoxification program at American Hospital."

"And have you spreading awful stories at the embassy about your drunken wife that they had to carry off to the padded ward? Not on your life, sweetie."

"It hardly makes any difference—you've been spreading the same kind of stories about yourself for some time now. I'm sure you know that."

148

On the way out of the kitchen he glanced at the notepad beside the telephone. "Mr. Bruckner called me here?"

"Yes. Why shouldn't he?"

"No reason, I suppose. Did he say what he wanted?"

"Just for you to call—he said you'd know where." She brushed past him, retrieved her bottle from the cabinet under the sink, and poured herself half a tumblerful, into which she splashed a few drops of mineral water from the large green Perrier bottle in the refrigerator. "What's he like, Martin?"

"Who, Bruckner? He's just a reporter on the Paris *Times-Weekly*—one of the people I have to deal with in my job."

"He's a gentleman," Jessie said over the rim of her glass, which she held onto with both hands. A coy little smile played across her lips. "It might surprise you to know that he thinks I'm a lady, too."

"That would surprise me," Toberts said, wondering what sort of daydreams she might have been having. "I would be very surprised if Mr. Bruckner had any conception of what constitutes a lady."

"I think you're horribly jealous! Horrible *and* jealous. He makes most of those stuffed-shirt friends of yours look sick by comparison."

"Well, that wouldn't be too difficult. He has led a rather interesting life."

"And he isn't married, is he?"

Toberts looked at his wife coolly. "Not that I know of, Jessie, but if you'd like I'll ask him."

Jessie took a large swallow of bourbon. "I just thought we should try to introduce him to some nice girl," she said too quickly.

"I'll ask Madame Joubert to recommend someone," Toberts said, opening the evening edition of *Le Monde*. While he read the statements about the day's events in Paris, in France, and in the world beyond, a mental image of Solange Cordier floated before the words printed on the newspaper, and he smiled to himself until, realizing what he was doing, he turned the page and assumed a studious frown.

*   *   *

At the Sorbonne on Saturday Toberts noted with pleasure that Solange Cordier seemed almost as happy to see him again as he was to see her. At her insistence they repeated their routine of the previous Thursday by first going upstairs to her little office for a cup of the marvelous lukewarm coffee. She talked at some length about her work and, with unobtrusive encouragement from Toberts, seemed to relax noticeably from the tension of the first two times they had been together. He genuinely enjoyed listening to her talk—about anything she pleased, he thought later, surprised at his own uncharacteristic patience when the work wasn't exactly progressing. But of course the work *was* progressing, in a way, because Solange was coming to trust him more and more, he could sense that. And, in ways that he couldn't even imagine yet, he was certain that she could be of enormous help to him in ferreting out the secrets surrounding the Lamplighter project.

Later, almost reluctantly, he picked up the notebook he had brought along and reminded her of the boxes of her great-grandfather's papers waiting for them in the basement archives.

They worked for several hours in near silence; the only sounds were the shuffling of brittle, century-old papers between them and an occasional remark by one or the other concerning something in the old professor's work that they found unusually interesting. Strangely, Toberts found himself wanting to explain to Solange what he was looking for and why, to destroy this deception that stood between them like an iron door. Now and then she would pass something back to him that he had already seen, asking if he had noticed a particular line or section that, from what little he had told her, she thought might be applicable to the "Fulbright scholar's project." And he longed to take her cool, efficient-looking fingers with their blunt clear-polished nails in his own large hands, and look deep into her astonishing eyes and tell her everything he knew about Lamplighter. It was the first time in his twenty-four-year professional life that he had ever wanted completely and absolutely to blow his cover; yet here he was, for reasons he understood only vaguely, having to

150

forcibly hold himself in check and apart from someone he had known only four days. The well-guarded secret of his life—and, in fact, that life itself—seemed to be slipping away from his formerly impregnable system of controls.

Eventually they found themselves talking to each other again, as they had in her office, and not completing the review of very many papers. They both realized at almost the same instant what they were doing, and both laughed simultaneously, at themselves and at their good fortune. "I think we've done all the work we're going to do today, don't you?" Toberts asked her, closing the notebook in which he had taken very few notes.

She nodded. "I'm sure of it. There will be other days."

Toberts looked at her, trying to decipher some possible hidden meaning in her words. "I hope so," he said. He returned the checked papers to the proper boxes and returned the boxes to their nook in the dark corner. "You're sure I can't just take these boxes out overnight, photocopy the papers I need, and return the whole mess to you the next day—tomorrow?" he asked her, trying to make it sound like an offhand request.

But Solange was not fooled, as he had known she wouldn't be. "I told you, Monsieur Toberts, that you may take as many notes as you like, but no actual papers must leave the building and no photographs of the pages. In the academic world we call all this"—she extended her hand toward the boxes stacked on the floor—"basic research materials. They are *never* allowed outside the archives, for obvious reasons, since most of them are irreplaceable. *Comprendez-vous?*"

"Oui," he said. "I promise not to bring it up again if you promise never to call me Monsieur Toberts again."

"Fair enough," she said, smiling as she clicked off the overhead light and closed the door behind them.

The guard at the front door of the Sorbonne smiled at Solange and even nodded to Toberts, who considered the gesture real progress in his bid to become an accepted and familiar face at the university. As they walked side by side in the fading afternoon coolness, Toberts knew he did not want to leave Solange just yet, and did not want her to disappear into that shadowy life away from the Sorbonne into which she had given him only small disconnected glimpses from time to time. He decided to risk another escalation in their relationship.

"Solange?"

"Yes?"

"I would consider it a great honor if you would have an aperitif and supper with me—anywhere you choose."

He could see the phrase *"Non, merci"* forming on her lips as she turned to look at him. But something in his face must have changed her mind, because suddenly she smiled broadly and put her hand lightly on his sleeve. "Thank you, Martin, that would be very nice. But you are the man—you choose the restaurant. I promise not to eat too much."

"If you don't I'll be very disappointed," Toberts said, placing his own hand on hers and experiencing once again a kind of cool electricity flowing between them that he found both pleasant and disturbing.

They walked to a place called Le Chat—"the cat"— that Toberts had noticed driving through the Montparnasse area near the Sorbonne. The bar was quiet, as was the dining room later. Solange ordered something she called a kir, which turned out to be white Burgundy wine with a dash of black currant syrup. The dim lights shining through the small glass of kir were beautiful; he held his up before Solange's face and moved it slowly from side to side, watching her features slide refractively through the velvety deep-red liquid.

She inclined her head to one side, a slight frown forming creases between her luminous eyes. "I know almost nothing about you, Martin," she said very seriously. "You wear a gold band so I assume you are married, but that is not much information."

"Enough, probably." He toyed with the corner of the tiny paper napkin on the table. "I met Jessie, my wife, a long time ago at an embassy reception in Ottawa. She . . . fits in very well with the diplomatic crowd."

"And you do not?"

"Oh, I probably do. Sometimes I just get tired of everyone I meet, everyone I talk with, being so everlastingly

152

on their guard with every syllable they utter. It becomes a kind of game, after a while, to try to deduce who's telling the truth and who isn't. You have to make a game of it to keep from going a little crazy."

Solange shook her head. "I wouldn't like that."

"Jessie was married to a diplomat previously—a real one—so she knows the drill. In the thirteen years of our marriage she has never tired of attending the obligatory parties. I sometimes wonder why she stays with a stodgy career civil servant like me."

"That's very refreshing."

"What?"

"To be spending the evening with a man, a married man, who doesn't say or at least imply terrible things about his wife."

"Do you spend many evenings with married men who run down their wives?"

"I used to—far too many. And then I decided that male companionship over drinks or dinner wasn't worth what I had to go through."

"Tell me about yourself, Solange," Toberts said, an urgency in his voice that sounded strange even to him.

"Later, perhaps. We were speaking of *your* life. Somehow, I have the feeling that Jessie was not your first love. Am I correct?"

Toberts drained the small glass of kir and ordered two more, giving himself time to decide whether he could trust this woman—about whom he knew so little, really —with any of the details of his life, past or present. He was so used to lies, covers, false explanations for every facet of his existence that exploring the truth with another human being—even if he was certain it would be harmless —came very painfully to him. He smiled tentatively at Solange, unable to visualize her in a compromising liaison with Colonel Balachov's organization. Of course, *swallows* —as the KGB called their stable of female agents used for sexual entrapment—were all very desirable, intelligent women; their profession demanded no less.

"I grew up in a town in the state of New Mexico called Albuquerque," he began, stopping himself to assess how it felt to be telling someone an innocuous truth that he had not told anyone in nearly twenty-five years. It feels okay, he told himself, but his stomach muscles tightened nevertheless.

"I have heard of Albuquerque," Solange said. "We Parisians are not so provincial as you seem to think."

"All right. My father was a foreman at a large electronic component assembly plant. When I graduated from high school in Albuquerque I managed to get an academic scholarship to the University of California at Berkeley. My father was so proud of me he used to bring his co-workers from the plant home just to meet me. I knew if I didn't make my grades at Berkeley it would kill him. I worked harder that first year than I've ever worked at anything since."

"And what were you specializing in?"

"My major, you mean? Economic and political science. I had some idea that I wanted to save America first, and then give the rest of the world the benefit of my wisdom."

"And have you accomplished what you thought you would have by this stage in your life?"

"No—no one ever does, I guess. Oh, once in a while I pull off something I'm a little bit proud of, but I don't kid myself that most of it will ever make any real difference."

"And what about your mother? You didn't mention her."

"She died when I was twelve years old. I was an only child."

"Tell me about your girls, Martin. Were you always the handsome heartbreaker, with more women around than you could possibly want or need?"

"Never more than I wanted," Toberts laughed, "but often more than I needed. Thank you for the compliment, incidentally."

"I was simply stating a fact—you are a handsome man and I suspect you know that. Who was your first real love?"

"Her name was Laurel," Toberts said quietly, "my first wife."

It was strange how speaking her name aloud for the first time in so many years brought back to him a sudden rush of emotions so intense and powerful that he became momentarily disoriented. Eighteen years without her, eighteen years of seeing girls who reminded him of Laurel in some particular way in the streets and parks and hotels and shops of cities all over the world. And always the keen disappointment when the half-glimpsed young women became, upon closer examination, not his Laurel at all, of course, but imposters with presumed lives of their own —husbands, children, lovers. Why did he go on looking for her? he wondered sometimes. But in the depest part of his being he knew why; it was simply that he had never loved anyone, nor did he expect to, the way he had loved Laurel.

"I met her in my sophomore year at university, and from then on we were inseparable. She was a year behind me, and she stayed on an extra year doing graduate work in art history. We were married in Santa Barbara, her home, the day after she graduated, and two days later we were settling into our first apartment, in Washington, D.C."

"Where you were learning to be a career diplomat," Solange said.

Toberts smiled but didn't answer. "We traveled a great deal, shopped for things for the dream house we expected to have someday, planned for our family, planned to stay in love for at least a hundred years . . ."

Frowning, Solange shook her head. "I think I am not going to want to hear further about this love of yours. The tone of your voice makes me terribly sad, and I don't even know the ending."

"We were doing so well," Toberts continued. "Four glorious years together, then Laurel discovered she was pregnant with what would have been our first child. We wanted that baby so much . . . we had such love to give it, and we knew that, far from coming between us, it would only serve to deepen our love for each other. Six and a half months into the pregnancy Laurel began to have pains that we ignored too long, in our ignorance; one early morning her appendix ruptured, and she was dying long before she reached the hospital. The fetus survived a few hours, less than a day. It was a little girl, they told me later . . ."

Solange, her eyes moist, reached across the table and

laid her hand gently on Toberts's hand. "I knew it would be an awful story. I'm so sorry for you."

He shook his head. "You needn't be—it was a long time ago, as I said. It's simply a part of my life that I don't think about much anymore."

Solange, nodding, withdrew her hand as the waiter approached. "Old wounds can remain painful for a very long time," she said.

Their table in the dining room was ready now, the waiter told them, and they moved into an adjoining high-ceilinged room with the look of a country château, perhaps in Normandy. The difference between this light and airy place and the dark, cramped bar was so immediately striking that they both burst into wide smiles. "Oh, Martin, it's lovely!" Solange said, taking his arm.

They ordered, at Toberts's insistence, the best of the offerings on the small but interesting menu. The sommelier suggested a Fleurie wine, which turned out to be delicate and fragrant.

"I'm enjoying myself more than I have in a very long time, Martin," Solange said, her eyes bright above the sparkling stemware.

"I'm so glad. Tell me, what did you mean about old wounds remaining painful?"

"Oh, *that* . . . nothing, really." She stared down at the table and played with a heavy silver spoon. "No, that isn't true—why is it, do you suppose, that I have no secrets from you?"

Guiltily, because of his own complex secrets, Toberts shrugged and smiled. "I don't know, but it makes me feel . . . special."

"Yes. I think perhaps you are special, Martin. About the other—I was simply referring to a time in my life, years ago, that I consciously avoid thinking about, even after all this time, because I am afraid it will hurt too much."

"Tell me . . . please. If you want to."

"It's odd, but I *do* want to," Solange said. She sipped at her wine for a moment. "A long time ago, when I had been out of the university only a short time. I met a young instructor of biology by the name of Jean. We became friends, and then lovers. Our lives, we thought, were the most beautiful works in the universe; we lived only for each other and could not bear to be separated for even short periods of time. One summer the department persuaded him to go with a field tour to the Italian Alps. He was to stay with the group four weeks, doing in situ research, and then I was to join him by train and we would go off on holiday together. Everything was arranged —even my mother had agreed, because, I think, she believed we would be married by autumn.

"The week before I was to leave for Italy, the head of Jean's department stopped me in the hall one day and took me to his office, where he showed me an official-looking letter he had just received from the Italian foreign ministry. I read it three or four times before I realized what it had to do with me. At an elevation of 3,650 meters—less than one hundred and fifty meters from the top of the Piz Bernina—Jean had crawled out onto an overhanging ledge to take casts of several small animal tracks. The ledge crumbled and Jean fell nearly a hundred meters onto the rocks below. His companions said he had refused the rope in his haste to complete the research—they said he had vowed to finish his segment by the end of the week because . . . because his intended was to visit him.

"I took the news very badly, refusing to believe it, sending telegraph messages to the Rome officials asking for confirmation . . . I even tried to fly there, until others talked me out of doing so. They sent his body back to Paris on the same train I was to have taken to meet him, except that it was traveling in the opposite direction, of course. I wore black for a year, did not smile for two, and became, I am afraid, a mean-spirited recluse in my mother's house. It has only been in the last few years that I have returned to something of a normal life. I had lost a great deal of my will to live, you see; what I eventually gained was a personal independence that I have learned to protect with all the ferocity of a mother lion protecting her cubs. I do not wish to be hurt in that way ever again, Martin. Can you understand what I am saying?"

Toberts nodded. "Quite well, Solange. I feel . . . I don't know, as though there were a powerful bond of shared sadness between us. Do you feel it, too?"

She reached across the table and took his hand in hers. "I've never told anyone else what I've just told you—not in that detail. Somehow it seemed right that I tell you. Does that answer your question?"

He covered her hand, pressing it between his. All of his senses told him that Solange Cordier was an extraordinary woman, a person he could trust implicitly, talk with endlessly and without hesitation, and perhaps fall insanely, gloriously in love with. But the old pressures of secrecy bore in upon him, automatically, involuntarily, so that he removed his hands from around hers and lifted his wineglass quickly to his lips.

"This looks delicious," he said, scooping up one of the asparagus spears on the end of his fork. "I'm glad we came here."

Frowning slightly, Solange lifted a bit of steamed truffle to her mouth and declared that it, too, was delicious. The mood of closeness between them having been broken, they finished the beautiful meal in comparative silence. Afterward when Solange suggested that it was getting late and her mother would worry, Toberts decided not to prolong the evening by offering her a dessert or a liqueur.

L'addition—the bill—including a fifteen percent service charge, came to two hundred and forty francs, or about fifty-three dollars. It was a lot, but not unreasonable in view of the quality of the meal. Toberts paid with his American Express card and they left the little restaurant. On the street, walking back toward where their cars were parked, Toberts again took her hand in his. At first she seemed not to mind, but then she freed herself to search through her purse for something—what, if anything, Toberts never knew—and after that she kept her hands to herself, out of his reach.

The night was almost balmy, with only a slight breeze rustling the new growth on the rows of chestnut trees along the curb. A number of people were enjoying the air of this May evening by strolling slowly up and down the pleasant streets of the Latin Quarter section of Montparnasse, which were lined with bistros, restaurants, and cabarets. Many of the people on the streets were quite young, young enough to be students, which was perhaps why Toberts began to pay attention to a heavyset middle-aged man walking the same direction they were on the opposite side of the street. His pace seemed to slow when theirs slowed and quicken when theirs quickened. As nearly as Toberts could tell, the man had not looked their way even once.

The lighted windows of a jewelry shop gleamed and twinkled beside them and Toberts, on impulse, pulled Solange inside the shop to browse among rows of diamond earrings and pearl necklaces and fantastic, jewel-encrusted bracelets like something Cleopatra might have worn. After a short time Solange protested and Toberts took her back outside on the street. The heavyset man was nowhere in sight; sighing with relief, Toberts smiled apologetically at Solange.

A few minutes later, stopping to look in at the hanging pork sausages in a *charcuterie*, Toberts glanced back down the sidewalk behind them and saw another man, thin and wearing a hat, who had also stopped to peer into a shop window. He looked nothing like the heavyset man, yet Toberts would have bet heavily that they were working together as a team, or part of a larger team, and that their objective was himself.

Instinctively ducking his head slightly, he took Solange's arm and hurried her along toward the parking lot. She glanced at him once, frowned, and asked him what was wrong, but he shook off her question. When he had an opportunity to look behind them again, the thin man was still there, maintaining a uniform distance between them.

At the parking lot Toberts nearly pushed Solange into her car and, promising to call her office at the Sorbonne, watched her drive off down the street until the taillights of her car disappeared in traffic. He stood beside his own car and slowly lighted a cigarette, giving himself ample time to survey the immediate area. It did not really surprise him to see, standing against the corner of a building out of the streetlight's glare, the heavyset man whispering to still a third man and jerking his head toward the lot.

Suddenly Toberts flipped his cigarette to the ground and hopped into the Peugeot. For once the engine cranked over almost before he had inserted the key into the ignition. There was no one parked in front of him and he drove straight ahead, through the parking lot, and out the other side into a busy stream of traffic. Slowly he maneuvered his way across to the opposite side of the street and drove carefully around several blocks, coming out sometimes ahead of where he had started and sometimes behind, until he was reasonably sure he had lost whoever it was—assuming they had actually followed him in a car of their own.

But he knew that it depended entirely on what sort of people they were. If they belonged to the KGB, as he suspected, then maybe they were still with him, somewhere back there among the headlights, because Balachov had been known to put as many as six pavement artists on one target if the target was considered important enough—the first dropping off, to be replaced by a second, and he by a third, until the target supposedly grew tired of searching so many different faces or began to think himself paranoid. God knows it was a technique that frequently worked; Toberts himself had sometimes had occasion to put a large team of agents on a single suspect, though for around-the-clock surveillance the cost in street manpower alone was nearly prohibitive and had to be justified very carefully to Langley.

In a way, he thought, turning at last toward his house in Montmartre, it was flattering to think that someone like Colonel Balachov thought him important enough to use up agents this way. They were obviously waiting for him to discover something important about Lamplighter that they were not yet aware of. A thought flashed through his mind and lingered a moment before he brushed it away and concentrated his attention on the traffic. But it returned to burrow deeper into his mind's speculative hiding places: Was it possible that Solange was somehow feeding them information about his progress, that she was, in fact, leading him exactly where her KGB bosses wanted him to go?

The subtleties of treachery that would have to be involved in such a scheme reminded him acutely of his feelings for Solange and, uncharacteristically, depressed him nearly to the point of tears.

14 _____

ALTHOUGH HE FELT GUILTY about doing it, the following Monday morning Toberts sent a coded cable from the embassy asking Langley's central files section for a complete scan of anything they had on Mlle. Solange Cordier of Paris, France. It was the way he had been trained to operate, and not to have done so would have disturbed him even more than his feeling about Solange. He couldn't help hoping the files would turn up empty.

He had had to make the coffee himself this morning because Mme. Joubert had not yet arrived, which wasn't like her. In all the years she had been his secretary and office manager, she had never once, that he could remember, come to work late, and always when she was too sick to come in at all, she telephoned Toberts directly as soon as she thought he would be in the office.

He gave her another half hour and then he called her home number. Her husband answered, sounding even more frail and ill than Mme. Joubert had led him to believe. "She works in the American Embassy," the old man managed to tell Toberts. "You can call her there."

"I'm *calling* from the embassy," Toberts said. "This is her supervisor—did she leave for work at the regular time this morning?"

"She always goes to work at the embassy," the old man continued, as though Toberts had not spoken. "She likes it there."

"Thank you." Toberts hung up, genuinely puzzled now. There could have been an accident, he supposed, although since Mme. Joubert didn't drive she usually took the metro or bus; only rarely did she feel she could afford a

161

taxi. He checked outside in the hallway and walked down to the guard's station.

"Morning, Billy. You haven't seen or heard anything of Madame Joubert this morning, have you?"

"Morning, Mr. Toberts. Say, didn't they tell you? Mr. Coleman said I wasn't to allow Madame Joubert on the fourth floor for any reason, today or any other day. He said you knew all about it."

"I certainly did *not* know all about it!" Toberts shouted. "Who the hell does Coleman think he is? Where did Madame Joubert go, Billy?"

"I told her to go on down and see Mr. Coleman in his office, just like Mr. Coleman said I should. Boy, she was mad! Fit to be tied—I've never heard so much bad-sounding French in my whole life!"

"That's nothing compared to the English you're going to hear shortly. Coleman's office, you said? Thanks, Billy."

Toberts hurried down the stairs to the basement level and used the tunnel to cross over to A Building, where Coleman maintained his empire. He spotted Mme. Joubert as soon as he opened the door, sitting dejectedly in a small anteroom by herself. She looked up, saw who it was, and almost leaped to greet him.

"What is going on around here?" she wanted to know. "Is everyone crazy? They wouldn't let me on the fourth floor—that guard Billy practically threw me back down in the elevator, said it was Mr. *Coleman's* orders. Do you know anything about this?"

"Not a thing, but I'm sure as hell going to find out," Toberts said. He ignored Coleman's secretary, who was busily buffing her nails at a desk larger than his own, and burst into the inner office. Coleman was leaning back in his desk chair going over a thick report marked SECRET at the top and bottom of the cover page. When he saw Toberts, he slowly allowed the chair's mechanism to return him to an upright position, stuffed the report into his middle desk drawer, locked the drawer with a key from his pocket, and only then acknowledged Toberts's presence by nodding brusquely.

"What can I do for you, Toberts?"

"You can stop jacking my employees around, for one

thing. Who the hell gave you permission to bar Madame Joubert from the fourth floor?"

Coleman dipped his head slightly to stare more comfortably at Toberts over the top edge of his half-glasses. "Ambassador Fitzgerald, of course. Walter and I were in complete agreement about the deplorable state of building security vis-à-vis our foreign national population."

"Damn it, Coleman, don't you understand yet that we're the foreigners here?"

"Not in this building, we're not." Coleman's smile was slightly off-center. "You should read the foreign service officer's manual sometime, Toberts—the embassy is considered to be the territory of its sponsor. You, believe it or not, are standing right this minute on American soil. Why else do you think they let us have our own flag here?"

Toberts shook his head. "You're crazy, Coleman, you know that? Certifiable, as far as I'm concerned. I think I'll speak to your friend Walter about having you committed to a home for the criminally stupid. Don't you think you owed us both—me and Madame Joubert—some kind of explanation of what you intended to do before you did it? Haven't you ever heard of fair play?"

"This isn't a schoolboy's game of some kind, Toberts, like they probably played at your Ivy League prep school . . ."

"Albuquerque Senior High, if you're interested."

"In any case, you were supposed to have been notified yesterday afternoon. There must have been a screw-up in my orders somewhere along the line."

"I doubt it, Coleman. And I am going to speak with the ambassador about this."

Coleman nodded and, unlocking the desk drawer, took the secret report out again. "I don't think he'll be too happy to see you, Toberts, but you do whatever you want. And I wouldn't advise you to try getting even with me over this matter."

"Not everyone is as petty as you are, thank God," Toberts said. He left Coleman's office and, after collecting Mme. Joubert, walked quickly down the hall the short distance to the ambassador's office before his better judgment could stop him.

"I think you'd better wait here," he told Mme. Joubert. Leaving her in the waiting area, he asked the ambassador's secretary to announce him.

"He's very busy this morning," she said with her customary professional cool.

"Just tell him I need to talk with him—two minutes ought to do it," Toberts said. He would have liked to tell her to cut the crap, but there were certain conventions that almost literally had to be observed in an embassy setting.

After speaking into her desk phone, she nodded to him and he entered the magnificent working place that Walter Fitzgerald called his second home.

"Good morning, Martin," Fitzgerald said. "What's on your mind?"

"Good morning, Ambassador," Toberts said, and somewhat too abruptly launched into his subject. "Did you give Coleman permission to throw my assistant Madame Joubert bodily off the fourth floor?"

"Bodily? Oh, come now, Martin, I'm sure Mr. Coleman would never do such a thing."

"No, you're right—he had Billy the guard do it. Madame Joubert is very upset, naturally. *I'm* very upset—no one told either of us about this."

"Well, now, Martin, that isn't quite true, is it?" the ambassador said reasonably. "I mean, you do remember being here in my office discussing this very question about a week ago?"

"Yes, sir. I was under the impression you would reconsider in light of my arguments against such a decision."

"Yes . . . unfortunately, my decision was to stand with the, ah, previous decision. I believe Mr. Coleman is correct in assuming that when we have foreigners running around our top security areas unchecked, we have a potentially dangerous and largely uncontrollable problem. Mr. Coleman simply thought of a way to control the problem. I believe his solution is a good one, a relatively painless one."

"From whose standpoint?"

"Mine, Martin. The United States government pays me this rather handsome salary at least partly on the basis of my being able to make just such decisions as this and to exert the necessary force to back them up. It may seem somewhat tyrannical but, I suspect, only to those whose immediate ox is being gored."

"Madame Joubert is not an ox, Ambassador."

"Quite right, Martin. Merely a figure of speech, as I'm sure you know."

Toberts sighed with the knowledge that he was definitely beaten. "May she be allowed at least to go up today and clean the personal things out of her desk? I guarantee to protect the sanctity of the fourth floor against this vicious little woman civil servant."

"That kind of sarcasm doesn't become you, Martin. I assume it's because you've been working too hard again. Yes, take Madame Joubert up with you, by all means, but stop by Mr. Coleman's office first and pick him up, will you? We've already discussed this, and he wants to be there with her while she disposes of what must be a fairly volatile collection of sensitive government papers. Langley, I assume, would wish no less."

"Thank you, Ambassador, you've been most kind and understanding," Toberts said, unable to keep the vitriol from showing in the tone of his voice and not really caring. In fact, as he knew, it was probably true that Langley, given a choice, would have preferred Coleman's alternative.

The three of them returned to the fourth floor of B Building, where Toberts watched Coleman watching an angry, frustrated Mme. Joubert tearfully going through her desk. Unable to stand it any longer, he went back over to the A Building lower level and bought a bottle of good perfume in the PX, which he had them gift wrap and which he took back up to her.

If he had known how it would affect her, he wouldn't have bought it. She cried for ten minutes straight, pouring out between sobs her feelings of loyalty and dedication and near-slavish love for Toberts as the best and kindest employer she had ever had, one she would never forget as long as she lived, and how she hoped that if he ever needed anything, anything at all, he would simply contact her wherever she might have found a nook for herself, whether in the embassy or elsewhere, and she would do everything in her power to satisfy his needs. If she had been a younger woman, Toberts thought, her impassioned speech—which seemed to make Coleman ill—would have had definite sexual overtones. As it was, Toberts felt terribly sorry for her and wondered whether, as Coleman had indicated, they really would try to find her another job in the embassy. If not, she and her invalid husband would very likely be in a bad way.

Eventually everything was sorted into piles, which Coleman started to paw through until Toberts stopped him with a large, firm hand on the shoulder. Coleman then listened to Mme. Joubert explain what everything was and what should be done about it—this for Toberts's files, that for the burn bag, quite a lot simply for throwing away, and a small pile of things she intended to take with her. After Coleman carefully examined each item in the latter group, the two of them left Toberts's office and disappeared down the hall.

Shaking off a nagging feeling that he should have done more for Mme. Joubert, protected her somehow, Toberts checked the top secret safe and saw that Elliott, the code clerk, had left him a reply to his Langley cable about Solange Cordier. The unscrambled message was about as brief and to the point as a complete file search printout from the huge IBM 370/609 computer at Langley ever got:

FM: CIA LANGLEY
TO: AMEMBASSY PARIS///FLASH
    PRECEDENCE///TOBERTS EYES ONLY
TOP SECRET (ENCRYPT FOR TRANSMISSION)
OPERATION: COMPLETE FILE DUMP.
NAME: MARIE SOLANGE CORDIER.
PRESENT ADDRESS: UNKNOWN, ASSUMED
    PARIS, FRANCE.
OCCUPATION: PROFESSOR OF ROMANCE
    LANGUAGES, SORBONNE, PARIS.

FAMILY STATUS: UNMARRIED; HAS
DEPENDENT MOTHER.
OVERT POLITICAL ACTIVITY: NO RECORD.
COVERT ACTIVITY: NO RECORD.
RECENT CONTACT WITH U.S. CITIZENS: NO
RECORD.
PASSPORTS VALIDATED FOR U.S. TRAVEL:
NONE.
END OF RECORD

Other than telling Toberts that Solange's first given name was actually Marie, the message was uninformative but clear: Solange had never, for anything she had done or anyone she had known, come to the attention of a vast network of U.S. agencies, each with its own computer files and to each of which the Langley computer terminals had direct and immediate access. Toberts was more relieved to learn that than he would have thought.

He picked up the telephone and called Harold Sloan at the *Times-Weekly,* asking him to find Bruckner, wherever he was, and meet him for lunch at the restaurant in Au Printemps department store on the Boulevard Haussmann. They agreed to meet in one hour. As Toberts was about to hang up, he heard the disconnection of Sloan's line and then something else, a double-toned *click* that meant either Sloan's telephone line, or Toberts's own line from the embassy, was being intercepted and monitored mechanically. Such a possibility was not as unthinkable to Toberts as it would have been to Walter Fitzgerald, for instance, since over the last quarter century Toberts had lived with the probability that at any given time his private words to someone were being recorded to be played back to someone else. But still, the thought of a new threat just now did not please him, and during the next hour or so while he cleaned up some of the work piled on his desk, he brooded off and on about the identity and motivation of the listener.

The Square du Printemps, on the top floor of the department store off the busy boulevard, was a charming and inexpensive restaurant basking in the filtered light from an enormous stained-glass dome. Around the central seating area were a number of individual self-service stalls dispensing a large variety of different food specialties, from American-style hot dogs to full-course meals. Toberts found Sloan and Bruckner waiting for him near the perimeter of the luncheon tables, and when they had each decided on a meal and paid for the items selected they carried their food back to the center of the restaurant under the dome.

"I'm sorry the thing about old Professor Cordier's house didn't pan out," Toberts told Sloan. "It was a good idea, though. Keep cranking up that brain of yours for another angle, will you, Harold?"

"Sure," Sloan said. "I've been wondering about that Russian princess you mentioned hearing about—what was her name?"

"Yurievskaya," Toberts said.

"Yeah," Bruckner added. "I looked her up in an encyclopedia—her real name was Catherine Dolgoruka. She seems to have been the czar's little bimbo."

"Anyway, you said she was supposed to have come to Paris back when," Sloan said. "Maybe there's something there."

"Good. Check it out, even if it seems crazy," Toberts told him.

Bruckner looked at Toberts. "How are things at the Sorbonne? You romancing the lady prof, or what?"

"She's been very cooperative. She trusts me," Toberts said, realizing how much he objected to Bruckner's insinuating tone. "If there's anything there, I should be on to it in a couple more sessions."

"On to it?" Bruckner repeated, laughing. "I like your choice of words, old sport."

Tempted as he was to grab a handful of Bruckner's shirtfront and impress upon him that he was nobody's "old sport," Toberts forced himself to remain outwardly calm. "There's some chatter on the line— yours or mine, I don't know which," he told Sloan. "I heard it this morning, just after you hung up. I've been trying to think who uses mechanical intercepts these days, the science of electronics being what it is. There's the KGB, of course, but I doubt it—too obvious anyway. Maybe that little group in the French foreign ministry we learned about last year —but there again, those people are too good at what they do to be that obvious. It's possible some lower-echelon French office might be doing a solo on us for their own purposes."

"Why French?" Bruckner asked. "Aren't they supposed to be our allies or something? Don't they trust us?"

"Of course not," Toberts said. "Anyway, it's just another quid pro quo—we intercept and monitor all their communications, inbound and outbound, from their Washington embassy. Why shouldn't they do the same to us?"

They discussed other possibilities in the Lamplighter project until they noticed that, lunchtime being over, the crowd had pretty well cleared out of the restaurant and left the three of them, huddled together at a center table, feeling uncomfortably exposed. As they started to leave, Sloan motioned to Toberts with his eyes toward the corner of the restaurant where, Toberts knew, the *pissoir* was located. Toberts excused himself and said he would be right back. After he was gone, Sloan too excused himself, saying he might as well join Toberts, and left Bruckner at the table with money to pay the bill.

In the restroom Toberts and Sloan made sure they were alone. "I don't trust that Bruckner of yours, I can't exactly say why," Sloan said quietly. "He's a strange bird—I don't believe I'd want him angry at me."

"Don't worry," Toberts said, "he comes highly recommended. Just let him do his job and help him when you can. And, since I agree with you, try not to do anything to make him angry. Okay?"

"Okay, I guess," Sloan said. He used the urinal and flushed it, and when he came back to wash his hands he saw that Toberts had left him another long, white full envelope beside the soap on the basin.

The page finally found Mme. Joubert sitting forlornly in one corner of the embassy personnel office, where she had been waiting over an hour for one of the clerks to review her personnel file and discuss another job in the embassy with her. "We'll find you something, dear, don't worry," the clerk had told her, but Mme. Joubert knew enough about the way things worked in government offices to worry a lot about her future.

"There's a call for you on Mr. Toberts's line," the page told her. "Nobody seemed to know where you were."

"I'm not surprised," Mme. Joubert said. "Can you ask them to transfer the call here?"

"Sure, no problem," the page said. He picked up the nearest phone and gave the operator the instruction. After he hung up, the phone rang back and he picked it up again to listen, then held the instrument out for Mme. Joubert and left the room.

"This is Madame Joubert," she said into the phone.

"Good," a woman's voice said. "This is a friend, Madame Joubert. It is urgent that you meet me beside the front entrance of the Jeu de Paume Museum at the northwest corner of the Tuileries Gardens in half an hour. Do you know the museum?"

"Yes," Mme. Joubert said, not at all sure what this was about.

"It is only a short, pleasant walk from the embassy across the Place de la Concorde. You should have no trouble."

"Yes, but who are you? And why should I meet you, at the Jeu de Paume or anywhere else?"

"Why, to discuss your husband's future, Madame Joubert. Believe me, your husband wishes you to do exactly as I say, immediately and without telling anyone. This is extremely important to both of you. I will be expecting you shortly."

"But—" Mme. Joubert started, then realized that the line was dead. Puzzled, she punched an outside line and called her house, but although the telephone rang many times, there was no answer. That frightened her badly; Henri, her husband, who had been frail and infirm for many years, never left the house without her.

Quickly Mme. Joubert wrote out a message for the personnel clerk that she would return shortly and left the embassy. She crossed the broad Place de la Concorde and entered the Tuileries close to the museum grounds, suddenly realizing that she had no way of recognizing the caller, whoever she had been. Walking slowly in front of the imposing building, she stared carefully into the faces of the people walking up the steps to view the national collection of impressionist paintings. On her second traversing of the front walkway a heavily made-up woman with long, dark red bangs rapidly approached her and took her arm in a firm grip. "I'm the one who called you, Madame Joubert," the woman said, her voice as inflexible as her grip. "Come with me, please, we must make a telephone call."

The woman led her to a public telephone booth around the corner from the museum. After inserting coins, the woman shielded the dial from Mme. Joubert's sight and dialed a number. "Fon?" she said. "Put him on."

She handed the receiver to Mme. Joubert, who put the instrument to her ear. There was a whispering sound at the other end, but at first no words. Then she heard the unmistakable but very weak and sick-sounding voice of Henri, calling out over and over again his pet name for her: "Jou-Jou? Jou-Jou?"

"Yes, Henri, it's me."

"Jou-Jou, please . . . do whatever they want. They will kill me . . . Jou-Jou, I do not want to die . . . please, save me, save me from these madmen . . ."

"Yes, Henri, I will. Henri, do you know where you are?"

The woman snatched the receiver from Mme. Joubert's hands and hung it up. "You see, we have your husband in a safe place," she said. "Safe for the moment, but only if you cooperate. I want you to return to the embassy and gather up all the papers, notes, whatever your superior Monsieur Toberts has concerning the Lamplighter project. Secretly make a copy of each page and bring the copies to me—I shall designate a place when I telephone you tomorrow."

"But that isn't possible!" Mme. Joubert said. "You do not understand—I no longer work for Monsieur Toberts. They have transferred me out of his office. It would be quite impossible for me to—"

Without warning the woman slapped Mme. Joubert hard across the face. "Enough of your lies! We know that

171

you are Monsieur Toberts's secretary—you have access to the office, his desk, everything. Do not try our patience, Madame Joubert, or you will never see your husband again—at least, not in a condition you would recognize him. Is that clear?"

Sobbing, Mme. Joubert nodded, knowing that anything else she said to this monstrous woman would only be a waste of her breath. Later she would try to figure out a solution.

The woman also nodded. "Until tomorrow, then," she said, and gave Mme. Joubert a shove in the direction of the American Embassy.

15 _____

EARLY THE FOLLOWING MORNING Toberts received a call from Mme. Joubert from somewhere inside the embassy. "Did they find you a new office yet?" he asked her.

"No . . . well, a temporary one," she said, "but I don't want to talk about that." Her voice sounded extremely agitated.

"I'm sorry, Madame Joubert," he said, misunderstanding the reason for her anxiety. "There was simply nothing more I could do. Coleman had the ambassador's ear the entire time, I'm afraid."

"No, no . . . Mr. Toberts, could you meet me for lunch in the cafeteria? About eleven-thirty? There's something I have to talk to you about. Privately."

"You mean here, in the embassy? All right, Madame Joubert. Eleven-thirty." He hung up, wondering what more she thought he could do for her since Coleman had banned her from the fourth floor.

At eleven-thirty he put aside the papers he had been working with and went across to the other building. The cafeteria on the ground floor was routinely used by a majority of embassy personnel and their dependents. He battled his way through the line without paying much attention to what he put on his tray and finally found Mme. Joubert seated along a wall. "Sorry I'm a little late," he apologized, though in fact he was early.

"No, Mr. Toberts, I was early," she said. "I can't eat or sleep or even think about anything else. They've got my husband, you see, my Henri." And she proceeded to tell him about the phone call from the red-haired woman, the meeting in the Tuileries, the other call to her poor husband, and then the threat. "I don't even know what

173

this *Lamplighter* thing is all about," she said to Toberts. "I told the woman I didn't work for you any longer and had no way to get back into your office, but she simply wouldn't listen. I believe she is a most evil woman, who would certainly hurt my Henri badly if I failed to bring her what she wants. What am I to do, Mr. Toberts? You've got to help me."

She was sobbing openly now, and as she searched through her handbag for a tissue Toberts lent her his handkerchief. "It's going to be all right," he said, reaching across the table to hold her plump, damp hand in his. "The first thing is for you to get control of yourself, Madame Joubert. I know it's difficult, but I promise you I know what I'm talking about—you absolutely must be in control of your own emotions. I've been involved in a good many ransoms and exchanges of people and objects—I know the psychology involved, I know why kidnappings work or don't work. This woman said she'd be in touch with you again?"

"Yes . . . today sometime."

"Very well—here's what we'll do. I can't tell you much about my work on Lamplighter, except to say that calling in the police is definitely out. We'll have to handle it ourselves. I'll make up some phony notes that ought to look real enough to fool them, at least long enough to get Henri back. We'll copy the notes on my office copier, as you were supposed to do, and when they arrange for a transfer, I'll be there with you."

"Just the two of us?" Mme. Joubert asked, looking frightened. "I don't believe they were lying to me about hurting Henri—not that I don't trust you, Mr. Toberts—"

"But you'd like a little extra protection," Toberts finished the thought for her. "All right—I think that can be arranged. When the call comes through for you in my office, we'll switch it to you directly. I hope you understand that it will all have to be tape recorded."

"Yes, that's all right." She looked across the table at him, a frown drawing her brows together. "I'm sorry to be involving you in this, Mr. Toberts—I know you have better things to do. I don't even know how they got my name . . ."

174

"We probably never will know that," Toberts said. "People in this business always know people . . . it's their stock in trade, what they have to sell."

He patted her hand to reassure her. "I'm sorry this had to happen to you because of me and my work. You know I would have helped you in any case."

"*Merci*," she said, her voice only a whisper of fear and sorrow.

When the call came through shortly after two o'clock, Toberts had one of the "unpurged" secretaries answer it, switch on the induction recorder, ask the calling party to wait a moment, and motion to Toberts that everything was set. He, in turn, contacted the switchboard on a separate phone and had them patch in the previously arranged conference-call phone so that both his office line and Mme. Joubert's, four floors below in the other building, would remain open. It had taken the ambassador's direct order to accomplish this, but for some reason besides the usual professional ones of carefulness and secrecy, Toberts had not wanted the ambassador or anyone else in the building to know what was going on or why. And so he had invented some ridiculous story about having to record a long and detailed listing of statistics concerning the French printing industry, with open phones to two offices, because, as he had told the ambassador, "You took my secretary away and left me no one to do routine dictation and transcription." The ambassador must have known this was stretching the truth at best, but possibly because he felt guilty about his earlier treatment of Toberts he approved the plan without questioning it.

Through earphones plugged into the monitoring jack on the recorder, Toberts heard the click of Mme. Joubert's receiver being lifted and then her voice saying, "This is Madame Joubert."

"This is your friend from yesterday afternoon," a woman's voice said. Toberts recognized the slight accent as German, but beyond that there was a familiarity to the voice that puzzled him.

"Listen carefully," the woman continued. "Do you have the material I asked you to get?"

"Yes, I have the copies."

"Good. Bring them to us this afternoon after work—you must not arouse suspicion. Your quitting time is five o'clock, I believe. You will meet us in the Jardin d'Acclimatation in the Bois de Boulogne. Go to the terminal for the miniature railway and at exactly five-forty-five buy a ticket. Get on the next train—sit in one of the first three rows of the second car. You will be contacted before you reach the terminal at Porte Maillot; hand over the material to the person who says to you, 'Does this train stop at Neuilly?' Your husband will be waiting for you when the little train stops. You will then both be free to go. Are the instructions clear?"

"Yes," Mme. Joubert said. "But how do I know that I can believe what you say about returning my Henri to me, safe and unharmed?"

"We have no wish to harm either of you," the woman on the phone said. "Just do as you are told—you have no choice in any case."

Toberts, listening on the earphones, wondered whether Mme. Joubert would remember what he had asked her to do, but at that moment she answered his question for him.

"You said *us* a moment ago—are there more than one of you who will be meeting me?"

"That is no concern of yours," the woman said abruptly. "Remember—five-forty-five, if you wish to see Henri again!" The line clicked dead.

Toberts listened until Mme. Joubert had also hung up her receiver, then took the earphones from his ears and shut off the recorder. They were playing it very close to the vest, he thought with grudging admiration for the tradecraft involved. The train, being open, made it virtually impossible to conceal anything that happened aboard it, which in this case would work in their favor. He would certainly have to be on the same train. Yet there was no way either he or Mme. Joubert could know whether Henri was in fact waiting at the Maillot Gate terminal until they arrived, and that would probably be too late, because if he *wasn't* there, Toberts would have to retrieve the phony papers before their validity could be checked or good-bye Henri. And retrieving the papers might not be possible in any case, since Toberts knew that if he were conducting the operation, he would have at least two agents on the train—one to get the papers from Mme. Joubert and one to have them handed off to surreptitiously. The possibilities were infinite.

Toberts glanced at his watch. He had about three hours to come up with some kind of plan. Certain that he could use all the help he could get, he informed Stanley that he would be out of the office the rest of the day and left the embassy for Harold Sloan's newspaper office, where he intended to spend some time talking with Pell Bruckner. On the way out of the building he stopped off in the supply room and filled out a requisition for two portable transceiver walkie-talkies that he thought might come in handy.

At five-thirty Toberts and Mme. Joubert entered the Bois in Toberts's car. He parked as close as he dared, for Mme. Joubert's sake, to the main entrance of the Jardin d'Acclimatation, which was a children's amusement park. As she had been instructed by both Toberts and the woman caller, Mme. Joubert, carrying a brown folder full of papers prepared by Toberts, walked alone to the terminal ticket office of the miniature railway and bought a train ticket at almost exactly five-forty five. Toberts, of course, was somewhat behind her; the little train pulled into the terminal while he was still in line and he watched Mme. Joubert get on the first seat in the second car. By the time he got to the train the two seats behind her were filled and he took a seat in the fourth row. Several children with balloons on sticks were sitting in the row ahead of him, obscuring his view of Mme. Joubert more than he would have liked.

There was a certain amount of switching of seats before the train moved off. Several children left the train, only to run back and leap into their previous seats as a kind of daring game. A burly man asked the person on the end of Toberts's row if they could make room for him and everyone, including Toberts, slid over so the man could sit down. Another man leading a small boy by the hand approached the rapidly filling train and looked from one end to the other for space. Finally he leaned in and asked someone in the row behind Mme. Joubert if there was room for his son; the good-natured people sitting in that row moved over enough for both son and father. A woman with reddish hair stopped beside their car and seemed to search for someone, then moved to the car ahead and found an empty seat.

Toberts studied each of the people he saw around him, trying to put himself in the place of a KGB agent with a specific job to do in the next fifteen minutes. At least one of the very ordinary people on what was essentially a child's play train was undoubtedly such an agent, undoubtedly dangerously intelligent, undoubtedly a killer.

The little train blew its whistle four times and started with a lurch, heading out along the green garden paths of the amusement park and then out into the Bois itself. From time to time Toberts leaned out far enough to see Mme. Joubert through the forest of balloons in front of him, and each time she was twisting nervously in her seat as though she would have given almost anything to turn around for one quick glance behind her, but dared not do so. No one within his view had made any kind of move that he considered dangerous or threatening.

It was tempting simply to relax and enjoy the ride through the park. It was one of the things Toberts had missed by never having had children of his own—the opportunity to return briefly to childhood pastimes without having to feel guilty or foolish about it. Not many adults without children in tow rode this little train, or visited the children's park for any reason. If he, as an agent, were planning an operation on such a train, he mused, he would certainly try to bring along or borrow a child for cover. Like, for instance, the man who had gotten on the train late with a small boy and had sat almost directly behind Mme. Joubert. Remembering this, he felt the hairs on the back of his neck rise.

The man, seemingly pleasant enough, was leaning forward and talking with the boy beside him. Suddenly he reached out his hand and tapped Mme. Joubert on the shoulder, causing her to jump. The man said something to the side of her face; she nodded once, picked up the folder of papers from her lap, and handed it to the man over her shoulder. It seemed to Toberts that she must have glanced at the man and immediately looked away.

Toberts slipped the small CB unit from his breast pocket and flipped the transmit switch. "Three-forty-two," he said into the microphone, and in a moment Bruckner's voice answered with the return code: "Three-forty-four." A little girl sitting beside Toberts heard the voice from the box and stared at it seriously for a moment, then stared up at Toberts. He turned slightly away from her and spoke to the box again. "The transfer has just been made, midway as planned. No other apparent action imminent." The box crackled and answered with the code number, and Toberts slipped the unit back into his pocket. There was nothing to do now but wait.

The little train's whistle blew several times. Suddenly the man behind Mme. Joubert leaped off the side of the train and began sprinting across an open meadow. Stumbling across several pairs of feet, Toberts finally reached the same side and he, too, made the same running leap as the man had. This was not part of any plan, and that was what made it so dangerous.

Toberts pounded to a halt. Of *course!* he thought, and began racing back toward the train. The man he had been pursuing had not been carrying the folder, which was large and should have been plainly visible. There must have been a second agent on the train after all, someone sitting close to whom the man had handed off the folder and who was undoubtedly still on the train, within easy reach of Mme. Joubert.

The train had gained a little speed after rounding the curve, but Toberts, panting heavily, managed to jump up on the flat board railing that ran beside the seats the length of the train. He was standing on the last car, with two cars between him and Mme. Joubert. There was no way of telling who had seen him leave or return to the train, but he had to assume that the second agent was now aware of who he was and where he was, which gave the unknown agent a distinct advantage over Toberts.

Grudgingly, as the train came in sight of the Maillot Gate, Toberts admitted to himself that their little diversionary action had been tactically brilliant; if he had continued to follow the decoy he would have been effectively neutralized, but in any case he was now known to the enemy. He hung onto an upright post with one hand and wrestled the CB unit from his pocket with the other. With no time for the code routine he simply said into the microphone, "Tricky people—they've spotted me but as yet I cannot identify. Will be at Maillot within one minute."

Toberts felt the train beginning to slow down for the terminal ahead. Since there was no way to beat the train to its destination he remained where he was, his muscles and nerves becoming taut once again for the action he knew was coming. The thought crossed his mind that he was demanding, all of a sudden, a great deal from a forty-five-year-old body that in recent years had accommodated itself to desk work rather than the rigors of the field. Besides, he might be competing physically with men almost half his age, although KGB field men tended to be older, by and large, than the average CIA covert agent, who in some cases was no more than a year or so out of college. He would, in any case, have to use his brains better than they used theirs.

As the train's brakes began to squeal and the cars slid to a stop beside the platform at the terminal, passengers, particularly the children, were already jumping off both sides of the train with such commotion that it was difficult to tell what was happening. Toberts swung down quickly and ran up toward the second car, where he spotted Mme. Joubert just stepping down to the platform. A young man was helping her down; she turned to smile at him, but then her smile faded. The young man did not release her arm, but instead seemed to be propelling her in a direction that he wished her to go. The thing Toberts noticed, and suddenly remembered from the train, was the hat the young man was wearing—a green felt Tyrolean model with a yellow feather stuck into its band. He had been sitting in the middle of the row behind Mme. Joubert, adequately close to both her and the other agent who had left the train.

From the corner of his eye Toberts spotted Bruckner sitting behind the wheel of Sloan's borrowed tan English

Ford. He could tell that Bruckner had seen him, and had also seen Mme. Joubert being guided toward another car parked casually in a no-parking area across the wide crowded roadway. The second car was a large black Citroen with a license number that was instantly familiar to Toberts—he remembered running it through the CIA computer file, coming up with a positive KGB identification. Inside the Citroen was a large man behind the wheel and a woman with red bangs sitting in the back seat, both of whom he recognized from the scuffle at the Hotel Crillon. Beside the woman, and seemingly being propped up at the near window by her, was a very old man with thin gray hair who had to be Mme. Joubert's husband Henri.

Mme. Joubert must have spotted him at about the same instant. She screamed, broke away from the young man in the Tyrolean hat, and dashed to the car window through which Henri peered unsteadily, shouting, "Chéri! Chéri!" though he showed no sign that he heard or even saw his wife. The young man, shouting something toward the car, came up behind Mme. Joubert and knocked her away from the window, then made a dive for the front seat. Dazed, Mme. Joubert lay on the ground beside the car, still shouting plaintively at her husband.

Toberts motioned to Bruckner in the other car and went to see how badly Mme. Joubert had been hurt. As he helped her to her feet, the black Citroen leaped to life, roaring past Toberts so close it nearly bowled him over. In the English Ford Bruckner cut through the crowd of gaping parents and children and braked expertly beside Toberts, who, after helping Mme. Joubert into the car, jumped in himself. The car was moving off in the direction the Citroen had taken even before Toberts's door was closed.

"I don't know what spooked them," Toberts said. "Maybe they saw you sitting there watching us, or maybe it was just the fact that I was there so close behind her."

"Or maybe," Bruckner said, "they never intended to hand him over. Maybe they have other uses for the old gentleman."

"Ohhh!" Mme. Joubert groaned in anguish. "Why

would they keep my Henri? They said they'd return him—
I gave them the papers as they asked. Did you see me, Mr.
Toberts? On the train, handing the folder over to that
man behind me? And then he jumped off and I didn't know
what to think, but at the terminal all of a sudden there
was that awful man in the hat."

"It's going to be all right," Toberts said, turning around
from the front seat to comfort her. Bruckner looked
across at him as if to say, What a rotten liar you are, and
Toberts himself did not believe that there was much chance
of everything being all right.

They chased the Citroen through the crowded evening
streets of Paris, down the broad Avenue de la Grande
Armée toward the Arc de Triomphe, around the circle at
Place Charles de Gaulle, dodging in and out of the other
traffic. Bruckner kept a reasonable but constant distance
behind them even though the Citroen could have outrun
the little Ford easily on a straightaway. Obviously Bruckner was used to this sort of thing, and once again Toberts
had to accord him a certain amount of grudging admiration for his technical skills.

They continued on the Champs-Elysées, at times hitting
one hundred and ten kilometers per hour through traffic,
and Bruckner never once lost them by slowing for a
traffic light or dodging automobiles and pedestrians. The
Citroen eventually cut to the right on a side street, roared
across a bridge over the Seine, and continued to speed
down the increasingly narrow streets. Toberts oriented
himself by the lighted grillwork of the Eiffel Tower off to
the right. "They're heading for Montparnasse," he said. "If
they have some safe place in mind they could lose us
pretty easily around the Latin Quarter—some corners are
so sharp you have to turn back on your own rear wheels."

"That's their problem," Bruckner said through clenched
teeth. "If they want to lose me they'll have to kill me!"

As if someone in the car ahead had heard Bruckner's
words, there were two quick, bright flashes from the right
front window of the Citroen, and a bullet crashed through
the upper part of the windshield over Toberts's head.
"And me with no gun," he said, ducking.

Bruckner took one hand off the wheel long enough to

reach inside his jacket and hand Toberts a .38 Special
with silencer attached. "Present from Sloan," he said, by
way of explaining his having a weapon that Toberts had
neither approved nor known about. Making a mental note
to speak to Sloan about it, Toberts took the gun in his
right hand, cocked it, rolled down his window, leaned out
to brace his hand along the chrome window molding, and
squeezed off three nearly noiseless shots. Two of them
went through the Citroen's rear window and the third
lodged in the trunk.

Mme. Joubert grabbed Toberts's shoulder from the back
seat and screamed. "Please, Mr. Toberts, don't shoot! You
might hit Henri!"

"Look, lady, we're doing you a favor," Bruckner said.

As the Citroen careened through the narrow streets and
around impossible curves, Bruckner only car lengths behind them, Toberts imagined that his answering shots
through the window had caused a hurried conference
among the KGB agents. He had no idea what they might
do next, but felt that from their point of view, it would
have to be something spectacular. He also felt strongly that
they were now interested almost entirely in getting away
with their skins—plus the phony papers on Lamplighter, of
course. The pains they were taking to get their hands on
Toberts's notes had to mean that they were groping for
information which they themselves did not have and
could not, apparently, get. They would want to protect
the supposedly valuable notes at all costs.

What they eventually did was both simple and effective.
As the Citroen roared through an open square the back
door flew open and M. Joubert rolled—or more likely was
pushed—out onto the glistening cobblestones. Toberts
yelled at Bruckner to stop; without removing his foot from
the accelerator Bruckner shouted something about Toberts
being crazy, they had no need for the old guy.

"I said stop!" Toberts yelled in Bruckner's ear, the .38
by now pointing noticeably in Bruckner's direction, and
the Ford slithered and skidded toward Henri Joubert's
unmoving form, stopping only a scant few inches from his
body as Bruckner's right foot pressed the brake pedal
into the floor.

When they were stopped Bruckner took his right hand off the wheel and pushed the barrel of the pistol away toward a neutral corner. "Don't ever do that to me again unless you plan to kill me," he said, looking murderously at Toberts.

"Don't ever make me do it again," Toberts said. He hopped from the car and bent over Henri's inert form, feeling for a pulse. Mme. Joubert was beside him, and then Bruckner, who was staring not at Henri, but at the receding taillights of the escaping Citroen. "He's still alive," Toberts said, lifting Henri's head to the Ford's headlights and peeling back the old man's eyelids with his thumb. "I think he's been drugged. We've got to get medical help."

While Mme. Joubert, sobbing, rubbed the old man's unresponsive skin with her hands, Toberts and Bruckner lifted him into the back seat, where Mme. Joubert cradled his head in her lap. Bruckner drove where Toberts directed, back into the center of Paris to the combined home and office of the doctor the CIA customarily used. Fortunately, the doctor was home. He told them to bring Henri into what looked like a fairly complete examination and operating room behind the reception parlor, and asked them to wait outside while he and his wife, who was also his nurse, examined the patient.

In the next room Toberts and Bruckner discussed the possible ramifications of this operation as far as the KGB was concerned, while Mme. Joubert wept quietly into her handkerchief. "They must certainly think the notes are genuine, since we went to so much trouble to prevent their taking them," Bruckner said.

"Not necessarily," Toberts said. "They know we were after Monsieur Joubert, too. Not returning him as promised was a big mistake on their part, and they must realize it by now. In any case, I have no illusions that my bogus notes will keep them off our backs for very long. They want what we know—which so far isn't much of anything."

"It's got to be damned important to them—this proves it."

Toberts nodded. "We've known that all along, I believe."

The doctor opened the door from his examining room and closed it behind him. "I, ah, am very much afraid that the gentleman has not survived," he said. "He was old and tired, the drug was powerful and perhaps carelessly administered, and his heart simply could not stand whatever stresses have recently been required of it. He died without uttering a word."

Mme. Joubert looked at the doctor, uttered a soft moan, and collapsed, suddenly and completely. Toberts, supporting her, shook his head. "It occurs to me that there are beginning to be an unusually large number of casualties connected with this operation."

Bruckner shrugged. "Just make sure one of them isn't you, old sport."

16 _____

THE FUNERAL WAS HELD on Friday, an overcast, humid, gray Paris day during which large drops of rain occasionally spattered down from leaden skies. The requiem mass was scheduled for ten o'clock that morning at the Sacré-Coeur Basilica on the Butte Montmartre. Toberts arrived at nine-thirty and loitered at the front steps of the famous white pilgrim church, smoking cigarettes and watching everyone who entered. It would have been difficult to say what he was watching *for* exactly, except that he felt certain he would recognize it when and if he saw it.

He had tried to get Jessie to come along with him, to show her sympathy for a business associate whom Toberts respected, but mostly, he admitted to himself, because he feared that no one else would attend the service. But Jessie had begged off.

At five minutes before the hour a hearse drew up before the door, from which eventually emerged the body of Henri Joubert. Toberts himself had arranged for the hearse, in fact had made nearly all the funeral arrangements out of a sense of frustration and guilt. He waited until the casket had passed into the church, then followed it in without having seen anyone or anything at all suspicious.

The interior of the basilica was highly decorated with mosaics and gave Toberts a feeling of centuries-old religious sentiment. In fact, the Sacré-Coeur, though begun in 1876, had not been completed until 1910, which, as Parisian architecture went, was not old at all. Toberts had learned these facts by idly reading a plaque attached to the wall of the vestibule while he was waiting for the mass to begin. He entered the sanctuary and took a seat in a

186

rear pew, where again he could watch without being watched. Mme. Joubert was sitting with an older woman whom he took to be the aunt she had mentioned to him; all of the other relatives, she had told him, were either too old or too poor, but in any case lived too far away from Paris to attend the funeral. Most of the people in the church were vaguely known to Toberts, by face if not by name, because most of them were employed at the embassy and were Mme. Joubert's friends.

The tall, cadaverous-looking priest conducted the mass and eulogy in a deep-voiced monotone that was difficult for Toberts to hear, until finally he admitted to himself that he wasn't really interested in the words and so stopped straining to listen. He knew, in general, what was being said: homely·praise for a man who had never done anything special or unusual in his life and whom the priest had probably never met until the man's flesh was cold.

Finally, after an unseen voice had lugubriously sung two or three hymns and the priest had sprinkled the last drop of holy water, the small crowd of spectators filed out of the church and headed for cars parked nearby to drive the ten blocks in procession to Montmartre Cemetery. Toberts, like everyone else, drove the short distance but ended by berating himself for not walking; the exercise would have done all these overweight American and French civil servants a world of good. On the way to the cemetery the rain began again, this time more in earnest, and Toberts once again made a mental note to get the noisy and inefficient right-hand windshield wiper repaired before the next rain effectively opaqued that side of the Peugeot.

They entered the cemetery off the Rue Caulaincourt and drove along narrow hedged roads until the procession halted behind the hearse and two limousines. All the drivers simultaneously abandoned their cars and began straggling across the grass. The group at the graveside service was considerably smaller than the one inside the church, which, since the rain showed no signs of stopping, was understandable. Toberts pulled up the collar of his raincoat and moved a little closer to the rear of the small contingent of mourners. He could hear nothing that was being said beside the freshly dug grave, and let his attention wander to the other inhabitants of this lovely old cemetery, whose gravestones he and sometimes Jessie had discovered, in awe, on Sunday afternoon walks that seemed years in the past: Zola, Berlioz, Heine, Fragonard, Dumas, Degas, Delibes, Stendahl, Offenbach. And soon Joubert, who died perhaps a little before his time for a cause he would not have understood no matter how carefully it might have been explained to him.

Toberts looked to see whether Brian Jamison, at least, had made it to the cemetery, since he hadn't been present for the requiem mass; but his nominal superior was apparently not in attendance here, either. As his eyes swept the crowd something caught his attention, and he turned back to the left side of the grave, far back along the hedge bordering this particular section of the cemetery. What he saw through the pelting rain was a couple, a man and a woman, staring out over the crowd as Toberts had been doing and apparently for the same reason—searching for someone. The woman wore a scarf on her head that did not quite cover the reddish bangs, and the man was an obvious brute, with whom Toberts had exchanged unpleasantries in the past. The woman—the one Bruckner had called Ilsa—was the same one who had been holding Henri Joubert prisoner in the back seat of the car at the children's amusement park.

He turned his face away, though without any real hope that they hadn't spotted him, and saw that the officiating parties were lowering the old man's casket into the ground. Feeling a sudden chill, he huddled lower into the damp raincoat and stared across the wet grass directly into the penetrating eyes of Colonel Balachov's red-haired surrogate, admitting to himself for the first time just how badly she was beginning to get on his nerves.

17

THE NEXT TIME HE saw Solange Cordier, the day following the funeral, Paris was bright and sunny and warm, and it seemed to Toberts that maybe spring was really here at last and that shortly it would be warming into summer. Most Parisians disliked their summers and, if at all possible, managed to slip away into the cooler countryside for part of July and August. The really fortunate ones traveled to Deauville on the English Channel, to Nice and Cannes on the Côte d'Azur, or to the lakes region of Switzerland. Although Toberts had nothing against the famous resort areas, he saw nothing terribly wrong with Paris in the summer, either, except that it was hot and at times appeared to be nearly shut down.

They met, as usual, in the basement storage area of the Sorbonne library. Solange wore a beige sweater and camel pants of some soft material that fit the contours of her long body in a way that stirred an almost forgotten sexual excitement in Toberts. Jessie never seemed to care lately whether they had sex or not, and when they did it was invariably, for him, like screwing a slab of warm clay. It became less and less possible for him to reach orgasm with her (he doubted if she ever did, either, and perhaps never had in their monotonously proper thirteen years together); the only way he achieved sporadic release these days was by masturbation, which left a good deal to be desired. The almost unbearable urge he now had to put his hand gently upon the soft material stretched across the curve of Solange's thigh as she sat at the worktable embarrassed him but excited him, too.

"Sometimes," he told her, noticing that she had gone through several new folders since the last time, "sometimes

189

I feel that you're the one who started this project and that I'm just along for the ride."

She smiled up at him and brushed a wisp of dark hair from her temple. "Do you mind?" she asked him. "I find this work terribly fascinating—though of course for me it is simply curiosity and pleasure. Research is pleasant work for me, Martin. In fact, research has consumed most of my life."

"Then I'm glad I talked you into it," he said. "And Solange . . ."

"Yes?"

"I don't know exactly how to tell you this, but I'm so glad you're . . . who you are. I'm so glad that we met, and that we've had a chance to talk, to discover something about each other. It's been a long time since I've enjoyed anything as much as I've enjoyed talking with you, about all kinds of things. And being with you . . . it's as though I've come through a long, dark, unpleasant tunnel into the middle of a glorious Paris spring day. Am I making any sense at all?"

"Not much," she said, her head bent toward her work, but then she raised her eyes and looked steadily at him for a long, silent moment—perhaps to question his sincerity, Toberts thought, or perhaps only to let him know indirectly that she felt somewhat the same. He wished he knew more about women so that he could tell absolutely what her motives were, what she thought about his obvious attention to her, whether, in fact, she considered him a potential lover or simply a very common, ordinary thing —a middle-aged married man with a biological urge to explore new territory.

Toberts removed his coat and draped it across the back of a chair, and put on the reading glasses that he used at the embassy. Scooping up a handful of the folders containing large parts of her great-grandfather's intellectual life, he began to go through them systematically, looking for something that he might not recognize even when and if he found it.

They worked quietly for almost two hours. Toberts had caught up with Solange and was now reading the original old manuscripts first, then passing them to her. He was halfway through the second box when he began to notice something peculiar about the material her great-grandfather had written all those years ago. Up until now the prose had been relatively straightforward, serviceable French of a kind Solange assured him would have been natural in the late nineteenth century. But suddenly the words, the syntax, even the form of the writing seemed to be quite different, and Toberts commented on this to Solange.

"It's almost like poetry," she said, studying one of the sheets he handed her. "Except that it doesn't rhyme, and the meter is far too irregular."

"That was my opinion, too," Toberts said. "What do you think it could be?"

"I don't know. When you read small segments of it there seems to be a kind of sense present, but the overall effect is one of . . . senselessness. Not like his other writing, certainly."

"I think," Toberts began, realizing that he was about to tell Solange something he had no business telling her, but immensely excited about sharing the news, "I think this is a kind of code that Professor Cordier used to hide his real meaning. I would almost stake my career on the fact that there's a hidden meaning to these words, if we can just decipher it."

Solange nodded. "I think you may be correct, Martin. But if so, what do we do now? And why would my great-grandfather write anything in code?"

"For the moment we'll skip the second question. What we do now is go through the remaining papers and pick out any with the same kind of obscure, poetic feel to the writing. After that, we'll have to become code-breakers, I suppose. I know a fellow who works with the embassy sometimes who's very good with codes."

Solange glanced at him. "I would not doubt that you do know such a person." She continued to look at him questioningly until, unnerved, he turned away and began again the slow, arduous task of reading through the pages of manuscript, one by one.

Now that he knew what to look for, however, or felt that he did, the work went much faster, and in an hour he accomplished more than he might have in five or six hours before. Eventually Solange admitted that she was unable to keep up with him, and he said that was all right, she should just put the papers aside or back into one end of the cardboard box to indicate material she would go over later at her leisure. Within another three hours Toberts had completed the job.

He handed the final page of manuscript across the table to Solange and, sighing wearily, rubbed the back of his neck. "I think that does it, unless you're holding out on me."

"I don't know what you mean—*holding out*."

"I mean, unless there are other papers here that I haven't seen. I was just making a bad joke."

"No, I do not believe so. If there are other papers of my great-grandfather's in this library, I have not been made aware of them. I am certain these boxes we have researched are the only papers he left."

"Good," Toberts said, stretching his neck back over the chair. "My muscles are screaming."

"Then let me help," Solange said, getting up from her side of the table and coming around behind his chair. Instantly Toberts's reflexes went on the defensive. He did not like having someone standing behind him at any time, and especially not when he was seated without a forward view into a mirror.

"Relax, Martin," Solange said, putting both hands around the sides of his neck, which caused him to jump. "You are so tense. The cords of your neck are like steel pipes. Try to relax them, if you please. I'm not going to hurt you."

Her hands and fingers were strong and cool as they pressed against the tendons of his neck and shoulders brutalized by fatigue. He started, from habit, to tell her he didn't like to have his neck rubbed, but in this case it would have been such a patent lie he didn't bother. Instead, miraculously, as she continued to knead the flesh and bone beneath her competent hands, he began to feel the tension draining away from his body. With one small part of his brain he knew that at this moment he was very much at her mercy, should she choose to hurt him. An accomplished assassin would know the correct spot to press on each carotid artery to stop the flow of blood to the brain, at first eliminating his will to resist and then, as the pressure continued, eliminating his need for anything, ever again.

But what she did to him merely made him feel as good as he had felt in days—weeks, perhaps—and when she finished he leaned his head back and smiled at her upside-down. "Marry me," he said.

"But you are married already," she said matter-of-factly.

He righted his head and nodded, then stood and put his arms around her and kissed her very gently in her hair, on her forehead, her eyes, her nose, her cheek. Her hands were on his arms at first, not stopping him from holding her close, but perhaps testing the water, preparing for imminent flight. And then she encircled him with her arms and moved her mouth under his so there could be no doubt about their intentions.

They kissed for a long time. Afterward she buried her face in the smooth material of his shirt and for a while would not look at him, even when she spoke.

"You must think terrible things about me," she said in a whisper. "I did not mean for us . . . for this . . . to happen."

"I know. I know," Toberts said, smoothing her lustrous dark hair with his hand and his cheek. He hadn't planned it either, obviously, and the effect on him was stronger than he would have believed it could be. Never had he felt this way with Jessie, not even at the beginning. She had been an exciting, sophisticated woman and it had pleased him to think she wanted him, Martin Toberts, of all the attractive men she could have had for the asking. But the blood had never pounded in his head this way; he had never felt as if his body were about to float away, as it did now. Maybe in college, with Laurie, it had been almost the same, but that was no doubt due as much to youth and inexperience as to any deeper emotion. Neither of those excuses worked now; he simply felt that he was holding in his arms a vastly attractive and intelligent woman with whom he wanted to spend the rest of his days on earth, or as many of them as she would grant him.

She turned her head up to him and there were tears in her eyes. "I did not think this would ever again happen to me with a man," she said. "I purposely avoided it; I built my defenses well, I thought. I must have been wrong."

"I know the feeling," he said. "It was as if I wanted that part of me to dry up and eventually blow away. But apparently it hasn't. I love you, Solange. I can't explain it in any rational way and I won't even try. We haven't known each other long enough for the rest of the world's rules to apply to us. It's as if . . . as if we operate in a different medium, breathe a different air from all the others. Do you feel that, too?"

"Yes. Oh, yes, Martin, I do! Every time we've come down the stairs into this hidden archive I've felt very strongly that we were entering a strange, magical world, one where only we belonged, and that no others should be allowed. I do love you, Martin. More than I can begin to tell you."

"And I love you," he said, kissing her again, hard, on the mouth as though this might be the magic that would keep her safe with him forever.

They sat on the edge of the worktable with their arms around each other's waists and talked the nonsensical talk of lovers. Each time it seemed they might run out of conversation it also seemed they were just beginning to converse, and that there was enough left to say to keep them busy talking for years. Finally Martin looked at his watch, and in a while Solange looked at *her* watch, and sadly they agreed to part for a while.

"Let's put the poetic segments of the manuscript in a special place," Toberts said. "I don't know how to let my talented embassy friend work on them, though. Any suggestions?"

She smiled at him. "Yes . . . one. Take them with you."

"But I thought you said—"

"It was against the Sorbonne's rules? Of course it is, and it's also against my better judgment, but what can I do? You have mesmerized me, Monsieur Toberts . . . I am at your command." She stretched her arms before her in the manner of movie robots. "Speak, master, and I obey!"

Toberts laughed at her stiff-legged walk around the room. "Come live with me, then, robot. I need someone to do my laundry."

She dropped the pose and the humor slipped from her face. "That is not very funny, Martin. And not very kind."

He took her in his arms again and held her to apologize, held her a long time rocking back and forth, neither of them speaking. Afterward when they left the basement room, the strangely elliptical writings of Professor Cordier were folded and tucked safely in the breast pocket of Toberts's jacket.

18

Toberts drove the ailing Peugeot into the underground parking lot beneath the embassy, and instead of taking the elevator to the fourth floor of B Building, as had always been his custom, he walked through the tunnel into A Building and up to the main floor, where he stopped in to say good morning to Mme. Joubert in the office where the personnel branch had found her a new job. Her eyes were red—from lack of sleep or overabundance of tears, he couldn't tell which—just as they had been ever since the funeral. She smiled and nodded when he asked how she was getting along and said she liked the job "as well as could be expected, under the circumstances." Not wanting her to see how sorry he was for her, he wished her well and made his way rapidly to his sanctuary on the fourth floor of B Building.

He went straight to the mammoth safe and removed his half of Professor Cordier's intriguing manuscript. Pell Bruckner had the other half, which in the privacy of his room at the Crillon he was attempting to decode with the help of a huge French-English dictionary. Toberts had issued clear instructions that Bruckner was to deposit his half of the manuscript in the hotel's safe whenever he left his room for any reason. There were also to be no photocopies made of any of the pages—Toberts had seen more than one operation blown sky-high by someone forgetting that each copy made of any secret document geometrically increased its chances of falling into the wrong hands.

When Toberts had first shown the manuscript to Bruckner, he had been prepared for Bruckner to take a quick, casual glance at the professor's cramped writing and ask what all the fuss was about. But Bruckner had

196

surprised him. After Toberts had explained what the rest of the manuscript was like, Bruckner had agreed that there was definitely something odd about the sections Mlle. Cordier had allowed Toberts to bring out of the Sorbonne. "My French isn't great," Bruckner said, studying the pages, "but even I can tell this is not straight narrative. And if it's supposed to be poetry, it's the worst poetry I've ever read—it doesn't seem to make any sense at all, just a jumble of words that aren't even related."

"My opinion exactly," Toberts said. "And since, from all the available evidence, the professor was certainly not the frivolous type, I'll bet the old gentleman has invented his own code, for whatever reasons. It's up to us to unscramble this mess. Which do you want—the first half or the last?"

"The first," Bruckner had said without even a slight pause. Probably, Toberts had thought, handing over half the pages, in the same way Bruckner would have said, if he were asked which cookie he wanted from a plate, "The largest." In Bruckner's profile sheet from Langley was a statement that the agent had an uncanny knack for spotting patterns in seemingly unpatterned material. It would have been embarrassing if Bruckner had called before Toberts could return to the embassy to say that he had the thing solved, but Toberts would have been willing to suffer large amounts of chagrin in order to be shown in plaintext what Professor Cordier had taken such pains to hide.

As Toberts sat in his embassy office struggling with the possibility of a simple letter-for-letter substitution cipher, he suddenly and distractingly thought of Solange and wondered what Bruckner would say if he knew that Toberts had shown her a part of the coded manuscript and had left several pages for her to study on her own. The idea had seemed strange to Toberts, too, when it had first occurred to him—contrary as it was to all the years of CIA training and all his own experience to voluntarily show a piece of an operation to an outsider. But the more he had thought about it, the more he had felt that the entire manuscript, code included (if indeed there was a code and not just the ramblings of a senile old man playing literary games), was the property of Solange Cordier, and that she had the right to do anything with it that she wished. By her own admission she had spent a good part of her life doing odd bits of research, and certainly she was an intelligent and perceptive person. Why not let her help track down the key to the mysterious passages written all those years ago by her great-grandfather? If, in fact, there was a key. As Toberts scratched out yet another combination that didn't seem to be going anywhere, he wondered whether they weren't all acting a little crazy.

The telephone rang and Toberts, still without a secretary, answered it. The voice on the other end belonged to Harold Sloan. Sloan said he had important news and asked Toberts to meet him as soon as possible at the usual place. "Usual," in this case, was only a code word between them to indicate one of their preset and continually changing rendezvous points in the city—the boat landing beside the Lower Lake in the Bois de Boulogne. Toberts said he would be there, and not to start without him.

In less than half an hour Toberts found Sloan loitering beside the boat landing. Toberts paid the attendant seven francs to hire a small rowboat and an additional thirty francs deposit, and he and Sloan awkwardly boarded the little craft and began to row slowly and inexpertly toward the larger of the two islands in the middle of the lake. The day was cloudy and a strong wind had come up; at the moment there were no other boats on the lake.

"I've been poking around like you asked me to," Sloan said when they were out of earshot of the attendant. "And I've come across what I think you may agree is a possible long shot. Remember hearing about Princess Yurievskaya, the Russian bimbo that set up housekeeping with Czar Alexander II in the last half of the nineteenth century? Well, the history books I looked at say she left St. Petersburg in a big hurry after Alexander was assassinated, came to Paris with a few traveling companions, and eventually drifted down to the social life on the Riviera. There was an obscure cross-reference in one of these books to a tiny newspaper article in an issue of the *Côte d'Azur Gazette* or whatever it's called, a few years back. I got a copy

—don't ask how. And I'm telling you there's a good possibility that an illegitimate son of the Princess is still alive in the little hill village of Mougins, up above Cannes. What do you think so far?"

Toberts nodded. "It sounds like the best break we've had, if it's true."

"I think so, too. Okay, the guy calls himself Prince Dimitri Youssipov—pretty obviously a phony title. Where the Youssipov comes from I don't know, since the princess's family name was Dolgoruka. The article didn't give his age, but I did a little figuring. Based on the fact that the princess was thirty-three when Alexander was assassinated in 1881, and assuming that he was born in secret sometime after she left Russia—since obviously someone would have known about him if it had happened while she was still the czar's plaything—I figure Prince Dimitri must be at least ninety-two years old, maybe older. He may be no help at all."

"Sure—senile, or worse," Toberts said. "But maybe not —that Côte d'Azur air is supposed to be very healthy and life-giving. I think it's worth a try."

"You want me to go down and check it out?" Sloan asked hopefully.

Toberts laughed. "You're too eager to get your hands on those skinny-dipping beauties on the beach, you dirty old man. No, we need you right here, and Bruckner needs to keep on with the work he's doing for me. I'll drive down in the next day or two and see if I can locate this elderly prince. I've been running up against brick walls lately — the break might do me good."

"Whatever you say," Sloan said, not bothering to hide his disappointment. They turned the little boat around and rowed slowly back to shore.

Toberts returned to the embassy to work on Professor Cordier's manuscript, but after only half an hour or so he discovered he could not concentrate on what he was doing because of the normal interruptions of the office. On impulse he called the number of Solange's little office at the Sorbonne and found her in. "*Bonjour,* Solange," he said. "This is Martin Toberts."

"Oui, Martin Toberts," she said. "I recognized your voice immediately. Why do you suppose that is?"

"Give me a little time to think about it," he said. "How are you coming with the poetry?"

"The poetry? Oh, I see what you mean—the manuscript. Well, I don't seem to have solved the puzzle, if there is one. Perhaps I would do better if I had more of it to read."

Exactly what any well-trained KGB agent would say under the circumstances, Toberts thought, and immediately felt guilty for having considered such a possibility. "It doesn't seem to be helping me," he told her. "I haven't heard anything from my friend the expert yet, either. I was thinking . . ."

"Yes?"

"That maybe if you and I got together and compared notes or thoughts about the manuscript, one of us might hit on something from the other's words that would shed some sunshine on this fairly dark mess. Does that sound reasonable to you?"

"Oh, yes, that sounds very reasonable," Solange said. There was a bright note in her voice that hadn't been there before.

"Good," Toberts said. "Do you have any free time this afternoon?"

"It so happens that I do. There was supposed to be a class later, but I felt the students needed more time to work individually on their term theses."

"And when did you cancel this class, Mademoiselle la Professeur?"

She giggled charmingly. "As soon as I am able to reach the classroom after this conversation. I will write across the blackboard, 'Professor Cordier is indisposed—continue independent study.' The students will be very happy."

"I don't see why," Toberts said, "missing a chance to spend an hour with you."

"An hour and fifteen minutes," she said. "And the several handsome male students in the class will not miss anything, since I often invite them to my little office for private discussions."

"You're awful," Toberts said, laughing only because he felt reasonably certain she was teasing him.

They arranged to meet in her office as soon as he could get there. He left Stanley in charge of things and drove across the river to the Sorbonne complex, stopping on the way in the Latin Quarter to pick up at one of the numerous bookstalls along the Seine a book Solange had mentioned wanting, and to buy a fistful of fresh flowers

When he arrived in her office and handed her these gifts, her eyes grew large and serious and he could see tears forming in them. "You spoil me, Martin," she said. "You shouldn't do these things."

"Yes, I think I should," he told her, "because, you see, I love you. And when a person loves someone as much as I love you, his greatest pleasure is in doing things that can cause the kind of expression I've just seen on your beautiful face. You *are* beautiful, Solange. Even flowers don't stand a chance around you."

She put the book down on her desk, and with the flowers still clutched in one hand she threw her arms around Toberts's neck and kissed him passionately. "I do love you, Martin, so very much," she breathed against his shoulder. "I hope I will not disappoint you."

Toberts smiled. "That isn't even within the realm of possibility. Shall we see what, if anything, we can make of those pages I gave you?"

In Solange's small office they discussed the confusing manuscript for almost two hours. If there was a code, Toberts maintained, then there had to be a key. He remembered that in the section of Professor Cordier's manuscript immediately preceding the apparently coded material there had been a reference to Shakespeare that, given the context, had seemed out of place. He asked Solange whether she, too, had noticed it.

"I remember it," she said, "but not for any special reason. I suppose I thought he was using the works of Monsieur Shakespeare as a literary reference point, just as a good many other authors have. Why? Do you think it was significant?"

"I don't know—maybe. Do you happen to know whether

there was a complete French translation of Shakespeare published before 1880 or so?"

Solange looked thoughtful. "I'm sure there was, but I could be mistaken about the date. If you want I'll go down to the main catalog in the library and find out for you."

"You're very sweet," Toberts said. "I'll miss you."

"For ten minutes?"

"Yes."

She blushed and left him alone in the office. While she was gone he stretched and roamed around the tiny room, looking at her books, her diplomas, *her* things. He noticed several delicately tinted glass figures of animals interspersed with the textbooks and folders on the shelves, and seeing her office this way made him feel closer to her, more a part of her real life. Using his emotions as justification, he pulled open the drawers of her desk and riffled through the filed papers and personal effects. He was vastly relieved when he found nothing more incriminating than a friendly letter from one of the student leftist groups headquartered at the Sorbonne.

Solange returned shortly after that carrying a huge old volume bound in faded red leather. "I found it," she said, sounding as excited as if she were working on her own research project. "The first translation of the complete works into French was a twenty-volume set by Pierre LeTourneur in 1782, but the set is so valuable the library administration has chained each volume to the wall in a metal binder. This translation of the plays, however, was completed in 1869 by Etienne Murat."

Toberts took the heavy book she handed him and thumbed through the gilt-edged pages. "I'm surprised this, too, wasn't under lock and key," he told her.

"You forget, monsieur," Solange teased him, "that I am *la professeur*—I have special privileges."

Toberts studied the Shakespeare and the coded manuscript, together and separately, but the magic key, assuming there was one, refused to appear. When he realized they were no further ahead than when they had started hours before, he suggested that they give it up for the moment. "I think I'm going to have to turn all this over to my resident expert," he said, putting all the manuscript pages back in a neat pile. "Anyway, I have to go out of town for a few days."

Solange looked unhappy. "Must you go?"

"I'm afraid so. Do you know the village of Mougins, down near the Côte d'Azur?"

"Oh, yes, I do. It's a lovely place, high on the cliffs back from the Mediterranean coast. I would love to go back there someday—I haven't seen it since I was a girl. It's very small though, Martin—are you sure that is the correct place?"

"Yes, I'm sure, though I'm not at all sure I'll find what I'm looking for." He paused, long enough to run over the familiar arguments in his mind, then reached for her hand and held it pressed tightly between his. "Solange, I hope you won't be offended by what I'm about to suggest."

"Yes, Martin?"

"Would you like to go to Mougins with me? There are excellent reasons—reasons you know nothing about and that don't involve you at all—why such a suggestion is very foolish of me. But the truth is, I find that I don't want to leave you even for a day. We could be together for a while, pretend that we were other people, normal people . . . I don't know, it just seems like a good idea."

Solange stared at him a long moment and took back her hand. She played with a glass paperweight on her desk as though she had never seen it before. "As you say, Martin . . . foolish. A week, two weeks ago, if you had suggested such a thing to me, I would have had quite harsh words for you and, I believe, would have refused to see you again. But there have been changes in me, changes that I can only attribute to your influence and to the fact that you say you love me. I hope with all my heart that is true."

"It's as true as anything I've ever said or thought or felt in my life," Toberts said. "Truer than most, in fact. Will you go with me?"

"Yes, Martin, I will," she said, and suddenly she smiled broadly. "Oh, it sounds like a *lovely* trip. How do we go?"

"We'll drive, I think—leave all that to me. I know this is short notice but I would like to leave in the morning, very early in the morning. What about your classes? And your mother?"

"The head of the German department owes me a favor, so classes shouldn't be a problem. And as for Mama, I know someone who would be delighted to stay with her —an old friend who will enjoy it immensely. Mama will be furious with me for a while, but she will get over it. Anyway, I've decided that for the first time in a long time I am going to do something nice for myself. And I cannot think of anything nicer than going off on a holiday with you!"

Toberts smiled at her, but then frowned as a new thought came to him. "Solange, I don't know exactly how to say this, but if you wish it, I will of course get us separate rooms wherever we stay. I didn't want you to think—"

"Martin," Solange interrupted, "that's an awful idea and would be a terrible waste of money. We must think of your expense account."

"True, very true," Toberts said, taking the radiantly smiling Solange in his arms and very nearly crushing her with his love. When they left the office, he was carrying both the manuscript and the Gallic volume of Shakespeare.

The following morning at five o'clock Toberts picked up the sports car he had contracted for—a white English Morgan that looked something like the old square MG-TD, but with a rounded hood—at a Paris car rental agency, and after being given a cursory checkout on the controls, he drove straight to the address Solange had given him. He was worrying slightly about a possible confrontation with an angry mother, but Solange had thoughtfully solved that problem by being ready to go when he arrived and was actually sitting on her suitcase in the middle of the walk in front of the flat. She looked cold but happy.

After loading her gear into the inadequate trunk, they headed for the southern edge of Paris, where they picked up highway A6. After they had passed through the congestion near Orly Airport, they hit more or less open country and good roads. Except around the few towns that the road mostly skirted, there was surprisingly little traffic, for which Toberts was grateful. Although the distance was at least five hundred miles according to the map, he felt almost a compulsion to make it in one day's driving.

The sun came out eventually, turning the fields of bright May flowers into a picture postcard. They stopped in a wood on the outskirts of Lyon and opened the picnic basket Solange had packed for the trip. There were sausages, two kinds of cheese, a delicious rabbit pâté, a long baguette of good French bread, apples, and a bottle of red *vin ordinaire*. They spread all these things on a blanket Toberts had brought along and sat among the wild flowers eating hungrily, laughing at nothing and everything, drinking the wine, and occasionally kissing tenderly as though these were perhaps the last kisses either of them would ever enjoy.

Finally, as they gathered up the remains of their fine picnic and prepared to go, Toberts saw a large car speed past the Morgan parked beside the road. The driver of the large car hit the brakes and slowed perceptibly, as though interested in the Morgan, then drove on, but at a much slower rate than before. "That's odd," Toberts said. "I wonder what they wanted?"

"It's a cute little car," Solange said. "Perhaps they would like to buy it."

"No, I don't think so," he said, wondering if there wasn't something familiar about the other car.

"I meant to ask you, Martin—why did you rent a car instead of driving your own?"

"What? Oh, that—it's safer, I guess," he said cryptically. In fact it usually was safer, when the opposition knew your own car, to rent a different one for a particular operation. Not that this guaranteed any sort of anonymity —any agent who believed it did was a fool—but a car rented under false identification, as the Morgan had been, was simply harder to trace. Toberts felt foolish answering Solange's question as he had, and knew that it was only a matter of time until he would tell her about himself in some detail, even though there was no reason to think she desired or would welcome such esoteric information.

They reloaded the car and Toberts drove, anxious now to be in the little town of Mougins which was their destination. While Solange rested her bare arm on the back of his seat and stroked the hair on his neck, he kept his attention on the road ahead, darting around the slower traffic and trying to anticipate poorly marked curves and other hazards. Now and then his thoughts drifted back to Paris, specifically to Bruckner, who had not been at all happy when Toberts, handing him the other half of the manuscript and the Shakespeare volume, had told him to stay in the hotel working on the code, while incidentally guarding the manuscript with his life. He had debated with himself about the wisdom of telling Bruckner exactly where he was going and, especially, with whom he was going, but in the end had decided it was better that Bruckner know. The excuse he gave for taking Solange along was her supposedly intimate knowledge of the town and surrounding area, but he was sure Bruckner hadn't bought a word of it. Given the same but reversed circumstances, Toberts wouldn't have believed it either.

Up ahead Toberts saw a car parked on the right shoulder with its warning lights blinking. He slowed automatically, recognizing the other car as the one he had seen earlier inspecting the Morgan. The driver, a man Toberts did not recognize, was the only person in the car. As Toberts drove on past and speeded up, he saw in his rearview mirror that the other car had pulled out onto the roadway behind him and was gathering speed. He watched the car for a while, then lost it when other traffic separated them. Though he glanced in the mirror throughout the rest of the trip he never saw the other car again; but he knew it was back there somewhere, following them steadily, watching their every move.

Since they had beat the tourist season by several weeks, they were able, by asking questions of several locals, to find a charming stucco *pension,* a former villa subdivided into small, neat apartments, each with its own outside entrance, bath, and kitchen nook. Roses climbed up the walls of the building and clung to century-old cracks, and many varieties of flowers grew in riotous profusion under the low-set windows. "Oh, Martin, it is so beautiful!"

Solange exclaimed after they had arranged for the apartment. "It is made for a bride, I think."

She looked at Toberts and looked away, embarrassed. "I didn't mean . . ."

He cradled her in his arms. "It is beautiful—I know what you meant. Is it like you remembered, I mean the town?"

"That was a long time ago."

They walked out onto the tiny balcony off their bedroom window. Lights were coming on down below them toward the sea, and the headlights of cars moving along the coast road twisted like fireflies in the rosy dusk. "I remember being able to see the harbor at Nice, and the town of Grasse, over there, where they grow the flowers to make all the famous perfumes," Solange said. "And of course the Alps, behind us. Yes, when I close my eyes I see it is the same as then. More people now, more cars, more shops—but the town is the same."

They both seemed subdued by their arrival and by the wonderfully soft evening air. A tear rolled down her cheek unheeded; Toberts kissed it, tasting the salt, and kissed her on the lips, letting her taste her own tear. They clung to each other for a while, not speaking, feeling the warmth and desire flowing between their bodies.

Toberts turned off the room light behind them. Slowly, as excited as a boy, he began undressing Solange, pausing now and then to kiss her lightly perfumed bare skin. She returned the compliment by helping him undress, and when they both stood amid the fallen mound of clothes, she ran her hands over his body, as though to discover each hill and valley, each flaw, each perfection. He felt himself harden against her. Bending close enough to trace the sweet contours of her neck and breast with the tip of his nose, he took one dark nipple into his mouth and warmed it with his tongue until she sagged, moaning slightly, against him. Gently he lifted her in his arms and carried her back into the room to the quaintly old-fashioned brass bed, where for a long time they made love and called each other love-names and in exuberant whispers declared that there had never been anything like this for either of them.

Finally they grew hungry, and though they were reluctant to separate themselves from each other by clothes, they bowed to custom. Afterward they hurried down the street hand in hand to a small restaurant they had passed on the way in.

"I read an article in a gourmet magazine I subscribe to that mentioned Mougins," Solange said after they had ordered enough food for ten people. "There are apparently at least three restaurants in this tiny town, with a population of no more than four hundred, that have received one star in the Michelin guide, and one restaurant with a three-star rating—did you know there are only twelve of those in all of France?"

"No, I didn't," Toberts said. "Tell me, is this one of the famous restaurants?"

"No," Solange said, giggling like a schoolgirl. "The chef is fat and sick and blows his nose over the meats!"

"Then I'll eat your share," he said, laughing, and leaning close, he clamped his teeth over her tiny earlobe and shook it like a playful terrier.

"Martin, the other people!" Solange protested, frowning, but suddenly she burst into a grin. "I will get even with you later, monsieur!" she whispered.

"I hope so," he said. "Otherwise, being in bed with you is so boring that I may wish we had stopped off for a newspaper."

She kicked him hard under the table, causing him a considerable amount of pain. As he bent to massage the bruised spot on his shin, the waiter appeared with their soup course and stared at Toberts, whose head was resting on the tablecloth. "Is something the matter, monsieur?" the waiter asked, a worried frown on his doleful face.

"My great-aunt," Toberts said, tilting his head toward Solange. "When she becomes hungry before the food arrives she sometimes bites people in the leg. It's all right, though, she's had her inoculations."

The poor waiter hastily deposited their soup bowls on the table and backed away fast enough for it to be called a run. He was followed by the explosion of Solange's stored-up laughter and the uneasy glances of diners at nearby tables.

After the meal and two bottles of a dry rosé wine they left the restaurant and strolled through the town square with its statue of some local hero, water fountains, flower garden, and sweet-smelling olive and cypress trees. They passed a few people, all of whom looked like tourists—that is, like themselves, out for an evening's stroll. Toberts thought he would remember the face of the man who had been driving the car they passed on the highway, but though he paid close attention as they walked, just as he had in the restaurant even while he and Solange had been playing games, he saw no one whom he recognized. That fact alone did not relieve his mind, however; you never saw the best ones until it was too late.

Solange saw his look of concentration and asked him what was wrong. He smiled down at her, held her more closely in his arm, but did not answer. They were here primarily to work, starting tomorrow morning, and although he might have been able to keep his mission a secret from her, he had to face the truth sooner or later that he *wanted* to tell her, he *wanted* her to know about him and about his work. And even though he had decided some time ago that he would tell her, actually doing it was no easier than he had thought it would be. There ought to be a proper time for telling secrets, he thought; and there probably was, if only someone would issue him a written guarantee that no harm would come from it.

He stared down at her as they walked, trying to read her mind. If Solange was a plant, a provocateur for the KGB, then he was ready to pack it in anyway, because his emotions and all his sense of human actions and re-actions would have been proved fatally unreliable and he would never again be able to trust his own judgment. He felt that he desperately needed someone to confide in, and there was no one with whom he was that close except Solange. Certainly not Jessie, who had never been trust-worthy with confidences.

He was amazed to find that, thinking of his wife just now, he felt not the slightest guilt.

"What is it, Martin?" Solange asked him, a tiny frown pulling at her eyebrows.

He smiled at her. "Nothing. I was just thinking that

there's something I've been keeping from you that mustn't remain a secret any longer. I would trust you with my life, if need be—did you know that, Solange?"

"I am glad, for that, too, is a form of love."

"Yes. And I do love you, you know. I'm so tired of being forced by circumstances to distrust everyone all the time."

"Even me, Martin?"

"Yes, God forgive me, even you. Secrecy is a terrible thing, Solange, it can easily become an entire way of living. Or *not* living. A person with terrible secrets is necessarily a person without friends or love or much of any reason for living except to protect the secrets. I think I've found something better." And he hugged her closer to him and brushed her hair with his lips, wanting her more than he had wanted anything in a long, long time.

They returned to the little apartment and made love again in the soft luxury of the brass bed. Afterward, propped up against the headboard with Solange's cheek resting against his naked chest, Toberts smoked a cigarette and decided that now, if ever, was the time. "I told you a small lie, I'm afraid," he began.

She raised her head from his chest. "You don't love me, and you enticed me to travel with you only for the amazingly good sex I provide?"

"No, you crazy girl," he said, running his hand over the silky curve of her bare flank. Unbelievably, desire for sex ran through his body again so strongly that he had to force his mind away from that possibility for the moment. "I do work at the American Embassy, but press work takes up only about ten percent of my time, and then only because it diverts people's attention from the other things I do."

"Martin, you're not a criminal?"

He pushed her head down against his chest again. "No, no, although in the course of our work we sometimes end up committing a good many illegal acts. I work for the CIA, Solange. I take it you know what that is?"

"Spies," she said, her voice muffled in his skin.

"Intelligence-gathering is probably a better term. That coded material of your great-grandfather's contains information that we believe the Russians are eager to get

210

before we do. It has something to do with a very old and
very large treasure, and a surprising number of people are
apparently willing to kill for it. I have no doubt that my
life is in fairly constant danger, which means, unfortunately, that the lives of people around me are also in danger.
Yours, for instance."

Solange rolled over and lay on her back beside him,
staring at the glow of his cigarette in the darkness. "Me?
Why would anyone want to kill me?"

"Oh, they wouldn't, not unless they thought you had
information that was dangerous to them. I just thought I
ought to . . . prepare you, I guess. So that it won't be such
a shock if someone tries to hurt me."

Solange sat upright and threw her arms around Toberts.
"Oh, no, Martin, they wouldn't . . . they mustn't! You
mean here, in Mougins?"

"Here, in Paris, anywhere. The KGB gets around."

Solange hopped out of bed and rushed barefoot to
the front door of the apartment, checking to see whether
they had remembered to lock it. Toberts, lying in bed,
knew he had locked it but didn't say anything to her about
that, or about the fact that the poor lock and flimsy door
would not have stopped even the most amateur assassin.

Solange returned to bed but was obviously frightened.
"Tell me how you became a spy, Martin," she asked him.

"Intelligence agent," he corrected her. "About the same
way anyone does, I suppose. Every spring, when I was at
the university at Berkeley, all the big corporations would
send out professional headhunters to line up new talent
at graduation time. They would set up all these cardtables
out on the grass and sidewalks in front of Sproul Hall.
Each one would have a big sign with a slogan or a company logotype in bright colors, and the interviewers were
sharp people—they'd come on like friends trying to steer
you into the right choices for your life's work. I talked to
some of them and got a couple of offers, too—but that isn't
the way the CIA recruits their prospects. Not at all."

"How do they, then?"

Toberts lighted another cigarette and watched the smoke
drift lazily through the open balcony door out into the
Mediterranean night. He hadn't thought about his college

years in a long time, and telling Solange about them
brought back memories he had thought were so deeply
buried that they could never be resurrected, even during
enemy torture or interrogation under drugs. Now he was
speaking freely about them for the first time in twenty-
five years . . .

He had always suspected that the scholarship from
Berkeley was due more to the fact that he came from a
poor, sparsely populated state than that they thought he
was brilliant. But he didn't mind that. Without a scholarship, he had already been told by his father, there was
simply no money for a college education—and unless he
went into the Army and then, maybe years later, took advantage of the GI Bill, he ought to inquire about job
opportunities at the local electrical-products manufacturing
plant where his father worked. "They'll treat you right,
son," his father had said. "They've always treated me right
—food on the table and clothes on our backs, even during
the depression. I'll tell you something, son—I feel like I
owe 'em a lot."

But the scholarship had come through, and his father
had been so proud that Toberts was embarrassed. "The
boy's a scholar!" the father would proclaim when they
passed someone they knew on the streets of Albuquerque.
"He's gonna make his old dad proud of him out there
in California, I just know he is. I'm just sorry as can be
that his mother isn't alive to see it."

Toberts found that he took to the academic life quickly
and easily. He breezed through the required preliminary
courses as though he were still back in Albuquerque High,
and was delighted to discover that although economics
was possibly the most boring of all human endeavors,
political science might easily be the most fascinating.
Several professors seemed to take a special interest in his
progress through the upper-level courses, and one in particular, John Franklin Damian, became not only his upper-
class advisor, but also a very good friend. Damian was a
large, athletic man with a shock of iron-gray hair and the
most piercing eyes Toberts had ever seen. After they got
to know each other, Damian frequently took Toberts with

him on backcountry hikes into the Diablo Range, where they cooked and sometimes slept out under the California stars and talked of vastly important matters.

It had been on one of these outings during the spring quarter of his junior year that Toberts had first been made aware of Damian's "sideline." Sitting around a blazing campfire one evening after a delicious meal of steak and roast corn, which Damian had expertly prepared, and while they were peacefully working their way through a second liter of wine, the professor brought up again one of his favorite topics for discussion—what, precisely, did young Toberts plan to do with his life after university? They calmly talked about the uses of political science in the cold-war world of 1955, how Toberts's choices lay mostly in the academic or governmental arenas, the sort of salaries he might expect, the chances for promotion, etc. Damian seemed to know a lot about it, which, as a career counselor, he should have, but then the conversation took a turn that Toberts found unexpected and a little strange.

"Have you ever thought about a career in intelligence analysis?" Damian said, pouring out another measure of wine for both of them.

Toberts shook his head. "I don't know what you mean."

"Intelligence work for the U.S. government. I've been watching you for more than a year now, Martin, and I'm sure you have the potential to be a really fine political analyst, or if you'd prefer a more active role, there's always direct foreign fieldwork as an agent."

Toberts had taken a large gulp of wine and stared at Damian. "You're talking about being a spy, aren't you?" When Damian didn't immediately answer, Toberts repeated, "Aren't you?"

Damian shrugged. "Spies are what you read about in cheap novels, Martin. Supermen dashing around the globe with fantastic miniature weapons strapped to the insides of their legs, fighting off an army with one hand while they're making love to six gorgeous women with the other. That isn't the way it is in real life, not by a long shot. Have you heard of the Central Intelligence Agency?"

"Just barely. Why?"

"That's a branch of the government that gathers and assesses all sorts of information about this country's friends and enemies around the world. Some of the CIA's employees are out there gathering information on the spot, wherever they're needed; others, many others, literally never leave their desks back in Washington, D.C., or other places, where their job is to evaluate raw information collected from many sources and assess its importance. It's a huge job, Martin, and the CIA needs the brightest, most resourceful young people it can find to keep us on top of things. You've probably never even considered such a career, but I honestly think you'd fit comfortably into it and find it a real challenge where your particular talents wouldn't be wasted."

"I don't know," Toberts said. "I've never thought of myself in that kind of field. I mean, you know, stealing secrets from other countries and all."

Damian laughed. "Can't quite get over the hurdle of those paperback novels, can you? Well, it's just a thought, but I do think you ought not to rule it out quite yet. Tell you what—I'll bring you some literature I have in my office that might explain the possibilities a little better. You understand, it would be quite an honor to be interviewed by the CIA—they don't even *talk* to people they're not already pretty sure of."

Toberts stared into the campfire, thinking over Damian's words. Finally he said, "Are you implying that the CIA is already pretty sure of *me?*"

Damian smiled. "Let's just say that they're *aware* of you, Martin."

"And how did they become *aware* of me, Professor Damian?"

By a thing he did with his lower lip Damian indicated total innocence of any complicity in the matter, then rather abruptly changed the subject.

There were other occasions when the two of them had nearly the same discussion; Damian always introduced the possibility of intelligence work quite casually, and Toberts was nearly always surprised by it, mostly because he could never take the idea very seriously. Until one time, over drinks in a bar one evening, Damian admitted that he

214

believed the time had come to let Toberts in on a little secret—Damian's interest in recruiting Toberts and a few others for intelligence work was more than casual. In fact, Damian told him, he had been a rather high official in the Office of Strategic Services, or OSS, during World War II and had kept nearly all his old contacts in the organization, which had merged into the present-day CIA. "We're really quite interested in you, Martin," Damian told him seriously. "You're exactly the kind of person we're looking for. I can tell you that your background has already been checked out for things like relatives behind the Iron Curtain who could be used to put pressure on you, your personal habits—"

"My *what?*" Toberts fairly shouted.

"Calm down, Martin. Things like drinking or gambling to excess, sexual aberrations, anything that could be used against you or the organization by the enemy. I'm glad to report that you seem to have passed all their preliminary investigations with flying colors. The next step would be an appointment for a direct interview with a friend of mine in the CIA, then some special aptitude tests, and then a meeting with an assessment board. It's a little like going to work for IBM."

"But I've never said a word to you or anybody else that I might be even remotely interested in a job like that," Toberts said, afraid that his agitation was clearly evident in his voice.

Damian put his large hand on Toberts's shoulder and shook it slightly as though he were a friendly bear. "Are you, Martin? Are you interested?"

Toberts had taken a long, slow drink from his glass at the bar and had stared into Professor Damian's bright, inquisitive eyes. He had been looking for help, but this time got none. Finally he had heard himself say, "All right, let's say I'm interested," and had wondered at the time what he might be letting himself in for. It had taken him a good many years to find out.

The following morning Toberts insisted that Solange wander around the pretty little town on her own and perhaps do some shopping while he attempted to find out more about the mysterious Prince Dimitri Youssipov. Reluctantly she agreed.

He found a post office and began his questions there; the postmistress proved to be entirely too voluble, but apparently ignorant of the supposed remnant of czarist royalty reported to be living in their midst.

"But you must deliver mail to everyone who lives in Mougins—at least everyone who gets letters," Toberts insisted.

The postmistress explained that most people in the village picked up their mail from one of the boxes along the wall beside her counter, and that delivery was a very haphazard thing. She directed him to another official office, in which a sort of town clerk took care of things like tax records, births, deaths, and other civil matters. The clerk was very old and wore the boxlike speaker of a hearing aid clipped to his jacket pocket. He spoke a variety of French that Toberts had great difficulty understanding, but finally Toberts pieced together enough phrases to know that this old man had seen the newspaper article about the prince and didn't believe a word of it.

"*Imposteur!*" the clerk repeated several times, shaking his head violently. Toberts somehow finally calmed him down enough to let him know that he, Toberts, didn't really care whether the man claiming to be Prince Dimitri was an *imposteur* or not, he simply wanted to talk with him about a private matter.

The clerk rolled his eyes and, between consumptive-sounding fits of coughing, made it clear that he simply couldn't remember having ever heard where the fake prince lived. "Maybe in Nice, or one of the villas in Monte Carlo," he told Toberts, shrugging.

Exasperated, Toberts wanted to grab the old man's arm and shake him into remembering, but instead he reached into his pocket and pulled out a handful of francs, which he stuffed into the clerk's jacket pocket behind the hearing aid. The clerk asked whether Toberts was attempting to bribe a public official, and Toberts said he was, whereupon the clerk suddenly remembered that a very old and sickly man who put on airs and might very well be the phony prince lived in a small villa at the eastern edge of town with a housekeeper who was almost as old as he was. "Living in sin, if you ask me," the clerk volunteered, and Toberts, nearly choking with laughter, thanked the clerk and left the office.

On the way to find the villa Toberts turned a corner and almost collided with Solange, who was coming out of a hat shop. He nearly failed to recognize her because of the huge, seductively floppy straw hat that hid most of her face. "Is that you?" he asked her.

She tilted her head so that one eye became visible, winked at Toberts, and began walking slowly down the street swinging her hips. Laughing, he rushed up beside her and put his arm around her. "You're crazy, you know that?" he said.

"*Oui*, monsieur," she said with a saucy flip of her head. "Would you like a good time?"

"Yes, I would. Do you happen to know any girls that I might—"

She dug the point of her elbow into his ribs. "Do you know, I've been having the most marvelous time. There are all sorts of artisans' shops with jewelry, pottery, some lovely woven goods . . . I could have spent a fortune."

"Then I rescued you just in time," Toberts said. "Do you want to go with me to meet a Russian prince?"

"Oh yes, Martin! A real prince?"

"That you will have to decide for yourself."

By asking a good many questions along the way, they eventually found what had to be the villa the town clerk had referred to. It was a light pink, very old wooden structure that badly needed paint and a good many exterior repairs. They walked up the broad, sagging steps and knocked at the door. The housekeeper, a large and quite strong-looking old woman with flowing tendrils of once-red hair, answered their knock and, staring at them suspiciously, asked what they wanted.

"I am Mr. Toberts from the American Embassy and this is Mademoiselle la Professeur Cordier, from the Sorbonne in Paris," Toberts said. "We've come a long way to speak with Prince Youssipov about a most important matter. I wonder if we might see him?"

Still frowning, the housekeeper snapped, "I'll have to

ask him," and disappeared back into the house without inviting them inside.

Solange looked at Toberts. "Friendly old thing, isn't she?" Toberts shrugged.

The housekeeper reappeared and grumbled something to the effect that although he would see them for a moment, he was very old and tired and sick, and they were not to upset him in any way and were not to stay more than a few minutes. "His thoughts fade in and out of the real world these days," she said. "You're lucky, he doesn't see many people anymore. He must have liked your names."

The prince greeted them, if that was what it was, by slowly turning his head in their direction when they were shown into the sitting room. He was indeed very old; Toberts could easily believe Sloan's estimate of ninety-two. His wrinkled skin was so nearly transparent that every vein and ligament lay exposed like a medical school work-up. The prince wore no eyeglasses, but his blue eyes seemed to be filmed over with an opaque substance, and Toberts realized that he was almost blind. On the middle finger of his right hand was a huge gold ring, now many sizes too large for the shrunken finger, set with a clear blue stone the size of a grape.

He nodded once to Solange, once to Toberts, then seemed to settle back into the fabric of the lounging chair in which he was bundled from the waist down in a furry quilt. Toberts took a few steps toward the prince so that they might look at each other while they talked.

"Cordier," the prince said. "I once knew someone . . ." The voice, dry as the rustle of leaves in the wind, trailed off into a long sigh.

"Your Excellency, we have a few questions we would like to ask, if we may," Toberts said. When there was no response, he began very slowly and carefully to spell out the things they needed to know: Did he remember living in Paris as a young boy with his mother, Princess Yurievskaya, after she left Russia? Did he know anything of a rumored fortune in jewels that were stolen from the princess, or otherwise disappeared, in Paris? Did the name Cordier in fact mean something to him, and was it because of a Professor Maurice Cordier who taught at the Sorbonne those many years ago? In later years had he heard, from relatives or others, anything at all about the supposed fate of the family treasure, and why none of the jewels, some of which must have been magnificent, had ever appeared on any of the world markets?

Hard questions, prying questions, Toberts admitted to the old man. "But the answers are perhaps vitally important to the future relations of several world powers," he added. "Is there, please, anything you can tell us?"

The old man stared at Toberts with his wounded eyes a long time. "My mother," he said. There was a long pause. "Never liked me very well. I wanted a rubber ball, a red rubber ball with silver stars . . ."

He turned toward Solange and peered at her softly rounded bosom under the light blouse. Pressing his fingertips against the bones of his cheek, he made a clucking noise in his throat and turned back to Toberts. "Tell her," he whispered, "that I would like to kiss her nipples . . . rosy, pink, shining with sweat . . . like new apples . . ."

Solange blushed and Toberts shook his head impatiently. "Don't you remember anything about the things I asked you, Prince Youssipov? Are you," he said, taking a calculated risk, "really a prince, really the illegitimate son of Princess Yurievskaya? Or are you, as I suspect, just an old fake who's been living off an undeserved connection with royalty most of his life?"

If Toberts's words made any marked impression on the old man there was no outward sign. His face remained serenely impassive, like those of so many ancient and senile people. It was hard to tell whether he had even heard Toberts's questions, much less understood them. And even if he had both heard and understood, there might be many reasons why he neither would nor could answer.

As Toberts watched, Prince Youssipov blinked once, slowly, looking remarkably like an owl. "I have . . . no pleasures left," he whispered. "The doctor has even taken away my smoking, and allows only a single glass of wine before meals. But I do not eat . . . I wish only to die, soon."

219

The old eyes closed then, and it seemed apparent that the prince was taking a nap. As if on cue the housekeeper reappeared—Toberts suspected she had been lurking just outside the doorway the whole time—and scolded them roundly for tiring the prince unnecessarily. "You will have to leave now," she said brusquely. "Perhaps another time . . ." But the tone of her voice indicated that such an occurrence would be possible only over her dead body.

When they were outside the villa again, Solange admitted that she hadn't understood what most of the questioning had been about, and Toberts reluctantly told her that it had a great deal to do with the manuscript, but that he just could not tell her anything more about it right now.

"I hope you understand, dearest Solange," he said, "that this has nothing to do with you. It's simply that my job is so . . . strange, in so many ways. I've already told you enough of my secret world to get me shot for treason at least a dozen times. If, however, you are very patient, I'm sure I will eventually tell you everything that I've ever known or hope to know. Are you at all interested in the size of my underpants?"

"The last time I saw you," she said loudly for the benefit of two passing women, "you weren't wearing any undergarments at all. In fact, you were as naked as a baby, though of course with more hair."

Laughing at his discomfort, she slipped her arm through his. "Beautiful man," she said softly. "I want to buy you a present—may I buy you a present? Come with me, I saw just the thing this morning."

She led him to a little silversmith's shop where she bought him a solid silver cigarette case with heavy silver and gold filigree work on the cover. She slipped the case into his shirt pocket. "Wear it next to your heart, my darling," she told him, "and remember the love with which it was given."

He thanked her, then led her around the shop until he spotted a silver ring that she seemed to admire. The shop proprietor pulled it from the case on a tiny pillow of black velvet and slipped it onto Solange's finger, which it fit perfectly. "You make the ring beautiful, mademoiselle," he told her, and Toberts had to agree that it was true. Toberts paid the man, thankful that they were enlightened enough in Mougins to accept his American Express card.

They walked outside the shop and stood in the sun, enjoying the feel of it on their bodies. Solange lifted her hand so that the new ring caught the rays of sunlight. "I love it, *chéri*," she said.

Toberts smiled at her enthusiasm and thanked her again for the cigarette case. "It'll keep all those tobacco crumbs out of my shirt pocket from now on," he said. "I won't leave the house without it."

At the mention of his house in Paris, which he obviously shared with a wife whom he had not thought of in nearly forty-eight hours now, both he and Solange were somewhat sobered. "Well, what do we do now?" she asked him, a little too brightly.

"I don't know—try to enjoy ourselves a bit longer before we have to go back to the real world, I guess."

"I'm sorry this has been such a wild goose chase for you, Martin."

"Couldn't be helped. Besides, we found something else —something we hadn't been looking for."

"What is that?"

"Each other. I love you, Solange, more than I can possibly tell you."

Standing at the edge of the road in the sleepy central square of Mougins, they held on to each other and kissed hungrily, oblivious of the few passersby who stared. "Tonight I thought we might drive down to Cannes for dinner," Toberts said. "Would you like that?"

"Oh, yes, Martin, that would be lovely. But that still leaves us several hours with nothing to do . . ."

Toberts chuckled wickedly. "Come with me, my dear. I believe I know just the thing to kill a few otherwise useless hours."

He put his arm around her slender waist and they strolled back to the little *pension*, in no hurry because there was no longer anything they needed to prove to each other. He was amazed to rediscover the simple fact that, with someone you loved deeply and truly, just being together was often entirely enough.

19 _____

IN MID-AFTERNOON OF THE first day of Toberts's absence, in the elegant room at the Hotel Crillon in Paris, Bruckner discovered the code used in Professor Cordier's manuscript.

Immediately he began transliterating the coded French into plaintext French, and from there did his limited best to translate the French into a kind of elementary English. The book code that had been used was a relatively common and simple one—assuming the text on which it was keyed was known. And stodgy old Toberts had somehow happened on exactly the correct work—the complete plays of Shakespeare, in French. The fact that Toberts had handed Bruckner the key to the entire code, and had more than likely done it unwittingly, infuriated Bruckner unreasonably.

In the coded passages of the manuscript that had seemed poetic and nonsensical, Bruckner had discovered without much difficulty that the first coded word of the poem was the first word of a line in the first play in the book—which, since the plays were arranged in apparent chronological order, was *The Comedy of Errors*. The second coded word turned out to be the word preceding the word meant in that line. The third coded word was the first word of another of Shakespeare's lines further into the book, and so on. The complete plays of Shakespeare contained, apparently, all the words Professor Cordier had needed to tell his interesting tale, except for the proper names of people and places.

Working through most of the night and the following morning, Bruckner eventually finished the decoding and as much of the translation into English as he was capable of, considering his unfamiliarity with irregular French

222

verbs, usage, and grammar. His method of translating the text consisted of looking up each decoded French word in the big French-English dictionary and writing down the first meaning he came across in each case. This resulted in a confused syntax that, while he was working, had clouded the larger sense of Professor Cordier's meaning.

With not much else to do until Toberts returned, Bruckner took his version of the manuscript and sat in a large easy chair by the window overlooking the Rue Boissy-d'Anglas and the American Embassy, reading slowly enough so that he hoped the disjointed Pidgin English would begin to make sense. As he read further he became increasingly excited and began to read more hurriedly, rushing to the end so that he could go back and read it more carefully a second time.

The old professor's message could hardly be clearer, Bruckner thought; and even allowing for possible decoding errors or gross distortions in translation, he didn't see how there could be enough significant mistakes to change his conception of the text's meaning. No wonder people had been killed, he thought, the manuscript was absolute dynamite! The double agent in the metro station had been correct, the Russians had somehow known without knowing, and all the time the complete story had been under everyone's noses. Even Thornton Daniels's information—unconfirmed data that had doubtless been filtered through many heads and many languages into the Clandestine Operations Group at Langley—had been essentially on-target enough to have justified sending him, and Toberts, on this wild goose chase. And now they had the elusive Lamplighter, and the KGB didn't—at least, not yet.

Considering the possibilities, Bruckner decided to find a copying machine so that he could make a copy of the translated manuscript. He gazed out the window and saw the embassy across the street. Surely they had copying machines there—probably dozens of them—that were presumably safe from electronic tapping, or in any case safer than some unguarded machine in a dingy commercial shop. Toberts had warned him to stay well away from any contact with the embassy staff, but what the hell,

Bruckner thought, in a way he was working for them on this project, just as they in a different way were working for him in his capacity as tax-paying citizen.

He folded the original manuscript and his deciphered version and buttoned them inside his shirt. As he descended in the elevator, he was already, in his mind, buffing the rough edges off a cover story that had something to do with meeting a friend at the embassy cafeteria Toberts had mentioned. Satisfied with his inventiveness, Bruckner left the hotel and walked rapidly across the street toward the braced Marine guard beside the door of the American Embassy.

For the fourth day in a row Mme. Joubert left her office on the main floor of A Building at precisely eleven-thirty and walked down the long hallway that would take her to the basement cafeteria and another solitary, taste-less lunch. Now as she walked down the hall, she passed two women whom she knew and, nodding, attempted a friendly smile; but they were apparently busily engaged in destroying some mutual acquaintance's reputation and didn't even notice her. Shrugging, Mme. Joubert told herself that she would survive, that she came from a long line of survivors, and that if no one needed her at the moment, she certainly did not need them. The only person she really missed, besides her husband, was Mr. Toberts—and even he, nice as he was, had apparently been too busy the past few days to drop in and say hello to her. She wondered whether he would think her odd or too forward if she called his office someday and simply asked how he was getting along.

Just before she reached the stairs, she noticed that the door of the supplies and reproduction shop was closed, and this struck her as being so odd that she paused in the hallway to think about it. Most of the doors along the corridor were usually closed, of course—all except this one, which, because it was a central copying center for the building, had a kind of counter built into the Dutch door for walk-up business. As far as she knew this particular door was never closed except between the hours of about midnight and five A.M., and sometimes—during

224

state crises of one sort or another when the embassy staff tended to work around the clock—not even then.

Curious, she walked back a few paces and tried the door. Finding it unlocked, she quietly pushed it open an inch or two and peered inside. A man was standing in front of the new high-speed copier, feeding sheets of paper into it as fast as the machine would take them. He was dressed a great deal better than the people who worked in this shop usually dressed, subject as they were to ink spills and toner-fluid leaks and other kinds of grime present in a reproduction shop. But the oddest thing, besides the fact that no one else seemed to be around, was the fact that as the copier spit the reproduced copies out into a bin, the man would pluck them out and slip them inside his unbuttoned shirt.

She was about to close the door again and hurry to find a security guard when the man at the copier turned slightly so that she could see his face in profile. Surprisingly, she recognized him—it was the friend of Mr. Toberts's, the one who had been driving the car when they chased the horrible people who had kidnapped her husband. She didn't know his name—Toberts hadn't had time to introduce them—but she remembered not liking the man at all. Why she had felt that way she couldn't remember now.

In any case, she thought, if he was a friend of Mr. Toberts's, then he must be all right, and whatever he was doing was probably legitimate, or perhaps even being done at the specific orders of Mr. Toberts. Very odd, though. The fourth floor of B Building, which had been her home for so long, had its own reproduction center that was specially shielded from electromagnetic influence because of the highly classified material processed in it. Why hadn't Mr. Toberts sent his friend to use that machine?

Not quite sure why she was being so careful, she closed the door even more quietly than she had opened it and continued down the stairs to the crowded cafeteria, not at all looking forward to her daily fare of tasteless soup and a cardboard grilled cheese sandwich.

* * *

Bruckner arranged for the taxi to let him out three blocks from his destination. He paid the man, tipping exactly the correct amount so that there would be no reason, later, for the driver to remember him either for his generosity or his tightfistedness. He waited until the taxi had disappeared before he began to walk purposefully toward Martin Toberts's house.

After he had returned from the embassy with the set of copies and had assembled them correctly, laying them out on the bed in his room at the Crillon, he had begun to think about Toberts and how he was enjoying himself in the south of France with the woman from the Sorbonne while he, Bruckner, was left to do the difficult and potentially dangerous work alone. The more he thought about it the more he resented Toberts's smugness, his security in his job as CIA station chief, his tendency to order Bruckner around.

As he sat beside the incredible manuscript, he thought about Toberts's wife, Jessie—older than Bruckner by some ten years, probably, but still attractive in a harsh and dissipated way. She had taken an obvious interest in him at the Ghanaian reception, and later he had called her a couple of times when he knew Toberts wouldn't be in, mostly to keep all avenues open for possible future use —a policy that had saved his skin many times in the past. Suddenly he had an impulse to further this particular contact and had picked up the telephone to call her. Delighted to hear from him, she had invited him to come to dinner this evening—which, though it might have its perils, he had agreed to do.

Now he stood before the undistinguished small house and stared at the brass numbers beside the door. Debating only a moment, he walked quickly up to the door and rang the bell. No one answered and he rang again, twice. Finally Jessie opened the door narrowly, looked past him as though checking for curious neighbors, and took his hand to pull him inside.

"I'm so glad you came, Pell," she said, her face close enough to his that he could smell the whiskey on her breath.

"It was kind of you to invite me, Mrs. Toberts."

TAKING LIBERTY

"Jessie, remember? Aren't you going to kiss me?" And she put her arms around him and lifted her open mouth to him.

His response was quick and professionally enthusiastic enough that he doubted she could detect his indifference. She would not let him go, however, but insisted on rubbing her hand against the back of his neck and planting her wet lips on various parts of his face, until in desperation he told her that he was positively dying for a drink. It was the only thing he could think of that she might be willing to spend more time on than him, and as it turned out he had guessed correctly. She showed him where the liquor cabinet was and asked him please to make himself at home, to fix himself whatever he wanted and to make her a double of the same, she had had a trying day.

Probably so, he thought; trying to get drunk was sometimes a real chore for an alcoholic. He made both their drinks as strong as was possible—straight Scotch on the rocks with limited ice. As they sat in the living room talking and drinking, Bruckner having discreetly chosen to sit in a chair instead of on the sofa beside her, his mind wandered from her rambling description of diplomatic parties she had attended in half the countries of the world and the tacky manners, dress, and morals of most of the people in attendance. He began to enjoy the feeling of sitting in another man's house, alone with the other man's wife, drinking the other man's booze and about to consume his food as well, and the pleasure of it was heightened immensely for Bruckner by the fact that the other man was Toberts. Though he was hungry and would have liked to eat right away, Jessie apparently felt she had not drunk enough yet to make the party interesting and kept him busy refilling her glass with twelve-year-old Ambassador Scotch.

Supper, when it finally came, was about what he expected—a tasteless stew concoction drenched in wine that a true Parisian would have been reluctant to feed to a dog. But Bruckner cared very little; food was fuel for the body, and that, literally, was the extent of his interest in eating.

227

"Did I tell you how pretty you look tonight?" Bruckner said.

"My, my," she said, licking her lips with a moist pink tongue. "And you've only seen me all covered up . . . so far."

She took a partial mouthful of wine and leaned across the table toward him, the wine still in her mouth. Bruckner obligingly pressed his mouth against hers and, in the truly romantic gesture she had obviously expected of him, inserted his tongue between her lips to taste her wine.

In fact, the idea sickened him. He refilled her wineglass, after which he suggested that they return to the living room for more comfortable conversation. This she agreed to and, after quickly downing the freshly poured wine in her glass, suggested that they have a quickie double Scotch on the rocks—after which, she promised, she would just shower and slip into something a little more comfortable.

Like an old grade B-minus movie, Bruckner thought, pouring the Scotch for them and settling into the same easy chair he had occupied before dinner.

"I don't mean to be forward and aggressive, honey, but why don't you just come over here and sit beside me on the sofa," Jessie said, patting the small place she had left for him.

"I will, in a minute," he said. He lit a cigarette with an elegant engraved silver lighter, one he had bought himself for the panache it lent to an activity as mundane as smoking. He noticed that she was staring at him.

"What are you thinking, Jessie?"

"Umm . . . just how different you are from my husband. I don't see how you two could get along together at all."

"We don't, always. Business makes strange partners, sometimes."

"What do you think of him, Pell? No, don't look at me like that . . . I'm seriously interested in what you honestly think of Martin."

"I think," Bruckner said, aware of the deep waters she was perhaps unconsciously leading him into, "that Martin is a very capable fellow in his job at the embassy. Everyone speaks well of him. Of course, he doesn't give most people a chance to really get to know him—I haven't quite figured out whether it's shyness or an air of superiority."

"That's it—that's it exactly!" Jessie cried. "An air of superiority. You've said it exactly right, Pell. Oh, I could tell you things about that man that would curl your hair. They all think he's such a hard worker, such a paragon of virtue and morality. He's a bastard, though, you know that? A goddamn bastard, at least to me. Would you believe he never makes love to me anymore, never even lays a finger on me in bed? Swear to God, I think maybe he's one of those closet bisexuals you're always hearing about."

Breathing out slowly, Bruckner silently thanked her for taking his bait so nicely, almost before he had cast out his line. "Uh, Jessie," he said, "I don't quite know how to say this, but I think it's something you ought to know. It may hurt initially, but you're much too fine and decent a person to be . . . defrauded by a man like Martin. I'm just sorry that I have to be the one to tell you."

A frown worked its way across Jessie's forehead. "Tell me what?"

"Jessie, I don't know what Martin told you, I mean about where he is right now. The truth is, he went away with a girl."

"Oh, really? Where? And what girl?"

"The Mediterranean, somewhere around Nice, I believe. The girl is French . . . he's been seeing her here, in Paris, for some time. That's all I know."

Jessie drained her glass in one swallow. "That lying son of a bitch. I could *kill* him! Wait till he gets back here, comes crawling back to me . . ."

She glanced quickly at Bruckner and, turning away, exhaled a huge cloud of cigarette smoke. "Well, of course it isn't as though it were something serious, is it?" Her voice had turned blasé, sophisticated, but still her eyes gave her away.

"Jessie, you mustn't be too hard on him," Bruckner said. "After all, you don't know what pressures there may be on him in his job. Why don't you wait and see

229

what he has to say? He may very well deserve a second chance."

"Oh, Pell, you're so *good*," Jessie said, coming over to sit in his lap in the chair, her arms entwined about his neck. "A person like Martin doesn't hold a candle to you. Hey—what about fixing us another little drink?"

Bruckner reminded her that she had said something about taking a shower, and she laughed and asked if he wanted to join her. "Maybe a bath, with lots of bubbles . . . have you ever made love in a bathtub, Pell, darling?"

He declined, saying he would wait for her in the living room though the minutes would seem like hours. Such excess was corny but effective with oversexed, overly romantic matrons like Jessie. He knew exactly why he appealed to her—an attractive younger man whom, she must be thinking, she might be able to use eventually to hurt Toberts. And that was fine with Bruckner.

He heard the water running somewhere in the back part of the house and imagined Jessie taking off her clothes, standing nude in front of a steamy mirror, holding her sagging, slightly wrinkled breasts up in a position they must have occupied ten or fifteen years ago. Perhaps she was practicing smiling at him; perhaps she was already rubbing herself between her legs in anticipation.

Bruckner poured himself a full glass of Scotch and drank it down quickly, waiting for the alcohol to take away the distasteful image, waiting to become quietly, thoroughly drunk. It would be worth it, he supposed. Toberts might be keeping things from him, important things. It would be good to have Jessie as a permanent ally, a spy in the enemy camp to keep him informed of Toberts's movements from now on.

He finished the last puff of what must have been a pack of cigarettes he had smoked since coming to the house, splitting and rolling the paper of the butt into a tiny ball and scattering the unsmoked tobacco in the ashtray. He poured himself another drink. Perhaps Jessie, who despite her elegant exterior had something of the debauched about her, would think up several variations on the standard sexual practices, some of which might even be amusing. He fervently hoped so.

230

20

THE MORNING FOLLOWING THEIR visit to Prince Youssipov,
Toberts and Solange began packing their bags to return to
Paris. As he gathered up the scattered toilet articles in the
little *pension,* he thought about Bruckner, working back
in Paris to decode the manuscript, and hoped he was
having better luck than they had had in Mougins. Even
though he had reservations about Bruckner, serious reservations, he felt the other agent was probably more than
competent and was glad to have him helping out.

Solange, wearing only a half slip, stood before the mirror brushing her hair. Impressed by the simultaneous
beauty and sadness of this simple act, Toberts stopped
what he was doing and watched her for a long time, until
she saw him in the mirror and smiled, embarrassed. "Why
were you looking at me that way?" she asked him.

And Toberts, not trusting himself to speak just yet,
lifted his shoulders slightly in that most typical of Gallic
gestures, unable to explain his feelings in any satisfactory
way. "I love you," he said finally, and turned back to the
half-filled suitcase.

Through the open balcony door he heard a loud clanging sound from the direction of the town square. Almost
immediately there was a knock at the outside door, and
when Toberts opened it a small boy handed him a blue
envelope addressed simply to "L'Américain Monsieur Toberts." Wondering how the boy had found him, Toberts
gave him a few coins and asked him what all the racket
was about.

"It is the fire bell, monsieur," the boy said, and ran off
in the direction of the sound.

Toberts opened the envelope and unfolded what ap-

231

peared to be a hand-written note from Prince Youssipov; the words were scratchy and shaky almost to the point of illegibility. Since this was much different from the printed French Toberts was used to reading, he asked Solange to help him translate it.

The note had apparently been written sometime the previous day following their visit. Without salutation, it read: "I have remembered something that might be important. Please excuse this intrusion on your privacy—I await you at my villa. I must advise haste, before the others return. D. Youssipov."

"Martin, who are 'the others'?"

"I don't know—I don't even want to think about that. Are you coming with me?"

"Of course."

Solange hurriedly put on a dress and shoes and they left the *pension*, Toberts pulling her along by the hand. The day was bright, but there seemed to be a gray pall hanging over the sky to the east of town, almost like a layer of Los Angeles smog. Many children and adults were also hurrying in the same direction, a look of expectancy in their faces that Toberts might have associated with attendance at a circus or a street fair. But as they passed through the square and continued on the narrow road east of town, he began to notice the unmistakable odor of impure wood smoke, and from the excited chatter of the townspeople hurrying along behind them he eventually heard the one word he was most afraid to hear: "Youssipov!"

They arrived at the villa only a few minutes after the town's volunteer fire brigade with its single bright yellow pumping unit. For a while the stream of water jetting from the hose only seemed to make the flames leap higher from the windows and charred roof of the tinder-dry structure; even as they watched, a corner of the roof and supporting timbers gave way and crashed to the ground.

From the front door, which was not yet ablaze, three black-slickered firemen wearing oxygen masks emerged from the dense smoke carrying a blanket that sagged close to the ground. "Stay here!" Toberts shouted at Solange, and breaking away from her, he ran toward the firemen.

"Is anyone still inside?" he asked the nearest man wearing a helmet.

"They're cooked if they are," the fireman said. "Nobody can go back inside now."

"What's in the blanket?"

"We're not sure—it was hard to see in there," a second fireman said.

They set the blanket gently on the ground and a small crowd gathered around it. A gray-haired man who seemed to be in charge of the volunteers came up then and, pushing his way through the people, bent down over the blanket and unfolded the corners. As the fireman had said, it was difficult to tell exactly what was there, at first. But as Toberts forced himself to stare at the charred, smoldering mass of human flesh he eventually recognized the unmistakable shape of the housekeeper crouched over the prince's frail body, her arms bound around him protectively in what had become, for both of them, a loving death grip.

Toberts waited until the gray-haired man had re-covered the bodies and then approached him, using his most official tone of voice. "Pardon, monsieur. Do you know yet what caused the fire?"

The man shrugged. "Undoubtedly an accident of a most predictable type, monsieur. The old man was notorious for being careless with the ashes from his pipe—his housekeeper can attest to that."

"Could have, you mean."

"What? Oh—yes." And the man glanced down at the blanket, mounded over what seemed too small a lump to be two human beings.

The villa was burning out of control now, and even the firemen seemed to realize there was little use in continuing to pour water through the many gaping holes out of which bright orange flames leaped and swirled. Everything in the house would have been destroyed, Toberts thought. Any papers, notes, personal records—all gone now, their ashes curling up into the sooty sky, and no way at all to get at whatever it was the old man had wanted to talk about. Too bad, of course, but just one of those things that sometimes happened . . .

233

Except that Toberts remembered something the prince had said yesterday, about the doctor taking away his greatest pleasure, his smoking. This only confirmed what Toberts had already been thinking, that it was all too pat, the fire much too convenient to be a coincidence.

At that moment, through the smoky air on the opposite side of the small crowd still hovering gruesomely over the blanket, he saw the face of the girl Ilsa, her red hair plainly visible, and beside her the man who had been driving the car that had followed them on the highway coming down. The girl raised her eyes a moment and Toberts knew she had seen and recognized him. They had probably watched him many times—him and Solange—during the past two days, following him to the *pension,* following him to the villa yesterday after he had so conveniently found it for them. And he had no doubt at all that they had very carefully arranged for the old man's hideous death.

He found Solange again and led her out of the crowd. "Come on," he said, "we've overstayed our welcome in Mougins."

They packed the car hurriedly and drove down to Cannes, which had the nearest airport. There they turned in the car at a branch office of the rental agency and flew back to Paris on the noon flight in a mood of depression and, for Toberts, murderous rage.

21

THE AIRPLANE FROM CANNES was late and did not reach
Paris until almost two in the afternoon. Toberts and
Solange took a taxi in from Orly, and he would have
taken her on to her house, but she insisted that he let her
out with her baggage at a bus station on the Left Bank.
"I know you want to get back to your work, Martin,"
she said. "Don't worry about me, I'll be fine."

He did worry about her—especially now that Ilsa and
her friends had seen them together—but she was right
about his having to get back on the job. Of course, Mougins had not been all play, despite the exhilaration of
being with Solange. He couldn't help feeling that if he
had been better prepared, a better field agent, somehow
he might have prevented the untimely death of Prince
Youssipov and learned in the process a great deal of valuable information bearing on the Lamplighter project.

But there was nothing he could do about that now. "I
don't know when I'll see you again," he said, helping her
to dig her bags from the taxi's trunk. "What *is* today—
Thursday? I seem to have lost all track of time."

"I know," Solange said. "For me, also. It was a beautiful two and a half days, Martin. Call me when you
can . . ."

"I will, I promise. Soon."

"I do so love you," she whispered, burying her head
in his chest for an instant; then she hurried off with her
bags toward the bus station.

Toberts directed the taxi driver to the automobile rental
agency where he had picked up the Morgan on a Tuesday
morning that now seemed long ago. He transferred his
baggage from the taxi to his own car, which he had left

in the parking lot, and drove straight to the Paris *Times-Weekly* offices, where as he had hoped, he found Bruckner with Harold Sloan. "How did it go?" he asked Bruckner pointedly.

The other agent smiled and nodded. "I have it in the Hotel Crillon's vault, *as you suggested,* if you'd care to see."

"I would indeed," Toberts said, ignoring Bruckner's barbed remark.

They drove to the Crillon, where Toberts let Bruckner out and continued to drive in great circles around the perimeter of the Place de la Concorde. Eventually he returned to the Crillon entrance and pulled over to the curb so that Bruckner could hand him through the window the original manuscript, the decoded version, and the book of Shakespeare plays.

"Did Shakespeare help?" Toberts asked him.

"Yeah, that was the key, okay."

"And what's your opinion of the decoded manuscript —just off the top of your head?"

Bruckner shrugged. "Dynamite stuff, if it's true."

"If?"

"Yeah, if. Personally I doubt it. It seems too far-fetched, too many coincidences, just too neat and orderly, somehow."

"Well, I appreciate all your work on it. I'll want to study it pretty carefully myself, of course."

"Of course—*somebody* has to check my work."

"Don't be asinine, Bruckner. I'm not going to check your work, necessarily, but you know as well as I do that the more people we have coming in on a cryptanalysis and translation, the better the results are likely to be."

"No, I don't know that."

"It's true, regardless. I'll want to study it thoroughly, and then I'll get back to you and we'll talk about it and come up with some recommendations."

"As you wish," Bruckner said. "By the way, how was Mougins?"

"The prince, if he was a prince, died in a fire while we were there—before he could tell us anything. I'm not convinced there was anything to tell, but we'll never know

now. By the way, I saw your girl friend Ilsa down there—
she apparently knew about the prince, too. I think she
may have had something to do with the fire."

"And how was your girl friend?"

"Fine, thank you. Anything else happen while I was
gone?"

"I wouldn't know—I've been locked up in my hotel
room for four days straight now. Paris could have disintegrated and I wouldn't know about it."

"Well, as you can see, Paris is still here," Toberts said,
extending his arm out toward the magnificent city. "Paris
will always be here, I think. Look—go have a glass of
wine at a sidewalk cafe or something, Bruckner. Pick up
a girl, live a little. I'll be in touch shortly." And he drove
away before Bruckner could suggest that they double-date
with Solange.

The afternoon was more than half gone when he pulled
into the underground garage at the embassy across the
street from the hotel. For some reason he received a
fairly odd reception from Stanley, his round-faced, owl-
eyed, perpetually serious assistant in the office.

"It's a good thing you're back, Mr. Toberts," Stanley
said when Toberts first walked in. He had never been able
to break Stanley of the habit of calling him Mr. Toberts;
Stanley was the most proper, passionless automaton Toberts had ever known.

"I took the liberty of decoding your crypto cables,"
Stanley continued. "I handled the ones I could, but
several apparently require your personal action since
they pertain to subjects you have never seen fit to discuss
with me."

"We live in a secret world, Stanley," Toberts said with
a smile that he knew was not appreciated.

"And one other thing—or, rather, *two* other things. Mr.
Jamison called several times to say that no one had informed him you were going out of town, and he was
furious. I think you'd better call him right away."

"What was the other thing?"

"Oh, yes. A woman has been calling you for two days
. . . an older woman, by the sound of her voice. She
wouldn't leave her name, but she sounded positively

demented with the urgency of whatever it is she wants to say to you."

"My, I didn't know I was so popular," Toberts said. "Okay—thanks, Stanley, for keeping everything under control for me. If you'd like to bring me the cables I'll see what's been happening in the world of superspy."

Frowning at Toberts's flippancy, of which he undoubtedly disapproved, Stanley went off to collect the cables from the security vault.

But even surrounded by the very ordinary trappings of his trade—the overnight cables from Langley, the reports from field agents assigned to his control, the newspapers and magazines and technical journals that were the "white" or overt ways the CIA had of collecting information—Toberts could not forget the shape of the lumps under the blankets at Mougins, the smell of scorched flesh early that morning at Prince Youssipov's villa. And the look of utter disdain on the face of the agent Ilsa, who, it had to be admitted, had outsmarted him.

He grabbed a pad of cable forms, tore off the top one —having learned long ago never to write anything on pads of paper—and penciled in a draft of an urgent message to Thornton Daniels at Langley: "Finally making real progess on Lamplighter; however, cannot move freely because we're being smothered by attention from KGB. Request permission to arrange for the female agent Ilsa— documented in previous message 1080-C—to die of the measles."

Toberts coded the message himself, shredded the pencil draft for the burn bag, and sent the coded cable to the communications center for transmission. He might receive a reply by scrambled transatlantic telephone almost instantly, but chances were that the rather delicate matter would have to be discussed in a number of places within the Langley complex and perhaps outside. The answer would probably come by cable tomorrow.

As he returned to his other work Toberts thought about the terminology peculiar to the CIA and other intelligence agencies worldwide. "Dying of the measles" had a long history and was not even particularly arcane—it simply meant that someone arranged a death to look natural or accidental, especially the death of an opposing agent, because an outright killing would likely be politically dangerous for the side doing the killing. Of course, there were times when just the opposite sort of picture needed to be painted for your enemies—it all depended on the psychological analysis of the moment.

The telephone rang and Toberts, alone in the office, answered it. He recognized the voice instantly as that of Mme. Joubert.

"Mr. Toberts, is that you? I've been trying to get you since yesterday afternoon."

"I know, Stanley told me."

"That Stanley! I never liked him when I worked up there, did I tell you that? He's too suspicious of everybody, too distrustful, if you ask me."

"That's pretty much his job, though, Madame Joubert. What was it you wanted?"

"Do you have time for a cup of coffee in the cafeteria? Right now?"

"Well, I've got a lot of work to catch up on . . ."

"Please, Mr. Toberts. I think it's important, and I don't trust these phones."

"I don't blame you, I don't trust them either. Ten minutes okay?"

"Fine. Oh, and Mr. Toberts?"

"Yes?"

"I'm buying this round."

This late in the afternoon there were few people in the embassy cafeteria. Mme. Joubert was waiting for him just inside the door. She accompanied him through the serving line and he allowed her to buy the coffee as she had promised. "You may think I'm crazy," she said as they sat down at an isolated corner table, "but I had to tell you. Yesterday I saw that friend of yours, that Mr. Bruckner, here in the embassy."

Toberts frowned. "Are you sure? What was he doing?"

Mme. Joubert gave a little apologetic shrug. "I just happened to look in at the reproduction room, and I saw him in there by himself, running off copies of something."

"Was that all?"

"No. After he finished making the copies he . . . well, he stuffed them inside his shirt and buttoned up his jacket so they wouldn't show. That's when I left, and then I tried to call you but you weren't in."

"I appreciate your telling me," Toberts said thoughtfully. "But I'm sure that if it really was Mr. Bruckner he must have had a very good reason for doing what he did. We're on the same team, Madame Joubert. I'll ask him about it later, but I'm sure there's nothing for you to worry about."

Mme. Joubert looked skeptical. "You're a nice man, Mr. Toberts, and since I don't work for you any longer I guess I can tell you to your face—I think you let people take advantage of you, all the time. I always did think that. You're going to get in real trouble someday, just being nice and kind of easygoing like you usually are while somebody's sticking a knife in your back. I hope I'm wrong, but I don't think so."

Toberts reached across the table and patted Mme. Joubert's plump, wrinkled hand. "I appreciate your concern, I want you to know that. And now, if you'll excuse me, I really do have to get back to what they're paying me for."

He left her and returned to the fourth floor of B Building, thinking about what she had told him. She might have been mistaken about Bruckner, of course, but he doubted it; in all the time she had worked for him she had been most observant and had a knack for remembering faces. Which meant that Bruckner had probably been in the embassay yesterday, where he wasn't supposed to be for any reason, and had been making clandestine copies—of what, Toberts had no doubt.

But why? He couldn't believe that Bruckner, despite his unlikable qualities, was a double for the KGB or anyone else; there was far too much national, racial, and class chauvinism in his makeup for that. The only possibility was that he had decided to go into business for himself —it happened all the time, the temptation was always there in this business, and usually the opportunity as well. And it happened for a lot less money than seemed to be involved in this Lamplighter project. Christ, he thought, that's all I need now, a greedy agent.

He badly wanted to confront Bruckner with the evidence against him, but decided that he ought to wait and see what was in the manuscript first. It might even shed some light on Bruckner's irregular actions. He put the incident out of his mind and buckled down to the little mountain of paperwork overflowing his desk.

It was almost seven o'clock that evening when Toberts looked up from his desk, removed his glasses to rub his aching eyes, and realized that nearly everyone else had left hours ago. He started to pick up the phone to call Jessie and have her meet him in town for dinner, then decided he was just too tired for that. All he really wanted was to go home and go to bed.

Knowing that he wouldn't be working on them tonight, he left the original manuscript, the decoded version, and the Shakespeare book locked up in the office document safe and drove to his house in Montmartre.

There were no lights on to welcome him home after three days, and Jessie was not there. Not her fault, of course, since she hadn't known when he would return. She was probably out drinking with a friend, already becoming disgustingly flirtatious with whatever men she would have found in some high-class bistro. Or maybe she had a lover; maybe neither side of their bed had been slept in these last two nights.

Deciding that he really didn't care one way or the other, Toberts made himself a very strong martini and a pressed ham and Camembert sandwich on half a small loaf of French bread. The food tasted good, the drink even better. He made another triple martini and sat in the living room in his favorite soft chair, the dancing purplish shadows of the television set the only light in the room. All of his friends back in the States told him how bad American television was, but they had obviously never seen French TV. It was absolutely mind-numbing, but that was what he wanted just now.

After a while he began to think about Solange and how much he wanted her and missed her. He thought about calling her at her home, if he could find the number, but reluctantly admitted to himself that she very well might not appreciate that. Instead, he fixed himself another drink. As he walked back through the house from the kitchen to the living room he noticed something peculiar, not for most homes but for *his* home—the place had been cleaned and straightened thoroughly and almost professionally. Jessie detested housework of any kind and had done little of it in the last few years. He wondered at first whether she might have called in one of those house-cleaning services while he was gone, but it wasn't like Jessie even to notice the dirt and dust, much less to do anything about it. It struck him as so odd that his natural inquisitive instincts took over immediately and he began to search for a reason.

It didn't take him long to find it. In the garbage bag, which she had pushed under the kitchen sink but had not yet emptied, in among the egg shells and coffee grounds and butcher's paper, were the unmistakable remains of cigarettes that had been meticulously field stripped and shredded. And only one person that Toberts knew did that to his cigarette butts. Sighing heavily, he realized that there was no more running away from the fact that Pell Bruckner was his enemy.

He gulped down the tasteless martini, undressed and crawled into bed, and immediately sank into an exhausted, dreamless sleep.

22

WHEN HE WOKE EARLY the following morning, before the alarm could do its job, he saw that Jessie had returned sometime during the night and was dead asleep as usual, her pillow clamped tightly in the crook of one arm. As usual, he did not wake her, even to say hello or to piece together whatever information he could about her activities while he had been gone. He was a little surprised to find that her unfaithfulness with Bruckner did not upset him nearly as much as his unease about Bruckner's motives for the clandestine conquest.

He dressed hurriedly, scrawled a brief note to Jessie, and left for the embassy without stopping for breakfast. There was an overnight cable waiting for him in his office from Thornton Daniels at Langley. Quickly decoded, it read:

FM: CIA LANGLEY (DANIELS)
TO: AMEMBASSY PARIS///PRIORITY
    PRECEDENCE///TOBERTS EYES ONLY
TOP SECRET (ENCRYPT FOR TRANSMISSION)
CONCUR IN ILSA TERMINATION. MEASLES
NOT NECESSARY. FORWARD RESULTS OF
LAMPLIGHTER RESEARCH SOONEST.

Toberts was only momentarily surprised by the "measles" reference. Apparently Daniels and whomever else he coordinated the request with at Langley had decided that there was no point in keeping the CIA's involvement a secret from the Russians, and that, in fact, there might be valuable publicity spin-offs if the knowledge was not only made known to the KGB but was crammed down

243

their throats. Toberts did not agree. He had been following orders from Langley long enough to know when he could expect to win a skirmish and when he couldn't—and this point seemed more important to him than to Langley. He decided to handle it his own way.

With a strong feeling—unusual for him—that for the sake of his nervous system it was a good thing this was Friday, Toberts called Bruckner in his room at the Crillon across the street and asked him to meet him at the base of the Egyptian obelisk in the center of the Place de la Concorde—perhaps a half minute walk for each of them. The area was already so crowded with traffic and tourists that they could talk there, amid the fountains and flapping rectangles of the flags, with almost no danger of being overheard or recorded.

It irritated Toberts slightly that he had to wait almost fifteen minutes for Bruckner. "I hadn't brushed my teeth yet," Bruckner said when he strolled up to the obelisk. "Sorry."

"Never mind," Toberts said brusquely. "Remember the girl, Ilsa, the KGB agent who picked you up that first night in the Crillon lobby?"

"Sure. What about her—you want a date?"

"No, you do. Can you get in touch with her, casually, so she won't spook?"

"I think so. She gave me her telephone number right off the bat. I haven't tried it, but I assume it's legitimate. Probably wired, of course."

"Undoubtedly. I had a cable from Langley this morning. Here's what I want you to do—call the girl, get her up to your room—"

"Now how do you think I can manage that?"

"You'll think of something—something obscene, I'm sure. Once you get her in your room with the door locked, you are to dispose of her quietly. Is that clear?"

"You mean kill her?" Bruckner said, enjoying the effect the blunter language had on Toberts. "Should I ask why?"

"She's becoming a far greater menace to us than we can tolerate. They'll replace her, of course, but they'll have to stop and think about it awhile, and that will give us extra time. What sort of weapon do you prefer?"

"A Walther P38, nine millimeter, fitted with a silencer if you have it. Actually, it doesn't really matter—I've fired nearly every small arm in current use. I picked up a liking for the P38 from a Swedish Army captain in the Special Forces."

"I'll get you the silenced Walther and leave it in a brown paper bag at the drop in the Palais-Royal gardens," Tobert told him. "You might as well start walking over there now—it's ten or twelve blocks from here. I'll go requisition the weapon and drive over as soon as I can. When it's over, call me at the embassy and talk about a press assignment at the *Times-Weekly* or something. I know . . . mention the President's speech scheduled for next Thursday in the Chamber of Deputies. If anything has gone wrong, mention that the speech is not expected to be received well. Once you've called me, take a taxi to the Jardin des Plantes and leave the gun in our drop there. I'll pick it up tonight or tomorrow. After that, you have the weekend off."

Bruckner smiled. "You're thorough, I'll give you that. Sure you don't want to come along and watch the fun?"

"No, thank you. I'm leaving now, to talk supply out of a decent automatic. Good luck."

"I rely on skill, not luck, Toberts."

"Good skill, then, Bruckner. And be careful—she's dangerous."

"Aren't all women?"

"I don't know the women you know," Toberts said, thinking about Jessie and wondering whether they had both enjoyed whatever passed for physical love between them. He left Bruckner abruptly and walked back to the embassy.

Lying stretched out on the bed on his back, his feet crossed atop the low footboard, Bruckner took the card from his billfold and dialed the number on the room phone. He listened to it ring several times and was about to hang up when someone answered.

"Allo?"

"Ilsa?"

"Who is this?"

"Ilsa, this is the tall, thin gentleman you picked up in the bar of the Hotel Crillon several weeks ago. How've you been, sweetheart?"

"I don't remember . . ."

"Yes you do, Ilsa. You remember. There was an incident later, a little misunderstanding—you brought friends, remember?"

"Yes? So?"

"Nothing, sweetheart, I just wanted to tell you that I long ago forgot all about that unpleasantness. Tell you the truth, honey, I'm lonely as hell here in gay ol' Paree, and I thought maybe if you'd like to come over right away and keep me from being so lonely I'd make it worth your while."

"How much?"

"Why, same as last time, I reckon. Three hundred francs, wasn't it?"

"But, monsieur, there is the terrible inflation—the price of meat ascends, the price of caviar is unbelievable . . . My standard price is now four hundred francs, for no more than one hour."

"All right, it's high but I'll pay it."

"However," she added, her voice hard as nails, "I suddenly remember that you are the man with a desire for a disgusting, painful specialty. Unless you allow the use of grease there will be no Ilsa to play with. I must think of my health, monsieur."

Smiling, Bruckner reached across the bed to the heavy Walther lying snug in its black leather holster and pulled it loose, holding it above him to admire the sandblasted nonreflecting surface of the metal and the short, fat silencer screwed into the barrel. "We must all think of your health, my dear," he said into the phone. "Very well, you may bring grease if it pleases you. But hurry—I am growing impatient talking with you. And very, very horny."

"Ah, horny," she said. "I like that in a man."

"Say a half hour? Come directly to my room—I assume you remember which one it is."

"Fourth floor west. Yes, I remember. Ciao, my horny American!"

He hung up the phone and continued to hold the

246

Walther that Toberts had left for him in the Palais-Royal gardens drop. He stared at the dull machined surface of the gun and hefted it in his right hand; the look and feel of it gave him an almost sexual satisfaction. He had killed at least six men with such a gun, but never yet a woman. But there was, as the saying went, a first time for everything, and this was to be something special.

He cocked the pistol by ramming the slide back with his left hand and was almost able to hear the first of eight cartridges click into place in the firing chamber, so well did he know the workings of the weapon. Gingerly he released the thumb safety and laid the pistol on its side on the bed, covering it with a corner of the blanket. He reached for the French pornographic magazine he had bought downstairs, which featured both naked women and naked men, and lay back down on the bed to await the charming Ilsa.

She was late, but not enough to have made him impatient. "Come in, the door's open," he called when she knocked lightly. She pushed open his door and stood just outside in the hallway a moment, quickly and professionally surveying everything in the room. Then she nodded slightly and a huge ugly man wearing an ill-fitting brown suit pushed past her into the room, pointing a small pistol toward the bed where Bruckner was sprawled.

"You're late," Bruckner said, and under the blanket his index finger pumped the trigger of the silenced automatic twice in rapid succession, burning a large hole through the blanket. The man clutched his chest and fell backward with a thud, his eyes wide and already dead.

Even before the man's body hit the floor Bruckner leaped from the bed and caught Ilsa's wrist as she was starting down the hall. One hand over her mouth and the other bending her arm up between her shoulder blades, he wrestled her back into the room and threw her onto the bed, kicking the door shut behind him.

"The walls are very thick—no one will hear you scream," he told her. "Take your clothes off."

When she raised her eyebrows in surprise he explained, "I'm hornier than ever now."

"But . . ." she started, pointing toward her partner lying dead on the floor, his eyes still staring.

Bruckner ripped the blanket from the bed and tossed it over the body. "I wouldn't have thought you'd be that squeamish."

Silently she removed her clothes and handed him a tube of some kind of jelly. "Afterward," she said in a subdued voice, "perhaps we can talk."

Bruckner smiled and said, "Maybe." He undressed, laid the Walther automatic on a chair beside the bed, and turned Ilsa over on her knees with her head bowed down against the pillow. After applying the grease he entered her, the warmth and tightness beginning to stir erotic daydreams in his mind that had nothing to do with the girl Ilsa whose firm buttocks he now gripped tightly in his hands. He was remembering instead the young girl on the Algarve coast of Portugal, and how her downy skin had felt beneath his weight, and how she had been only eleven years old.

With his right hand he reached across to the bedside chair and without breaking the rhythm of his strokes slipped the Walther from its resting place. He held the tip of the silencer an inch from the back of Ilsa's head, aiming at the base of her brain. At the exact moment of his climax he pulled the trigger, and his simultaneous orgasm and the death convulsions of the girl's body provided him with the most exquisite sexual sensation he had ever experienced.

But the ecstasy lasted only a moment. Compounding his spent energy, he remembered vividly how the little Portuguese girl had run screaming from him after he had violated her, shouting that she was going to tell what he had done. He had known instantly that she would ruin him, ruin his career with her blabbering. And so he had run after her on that deserted strip of bright beach, his hands finding her small throat almost with a will of their own, and when she no longer struggled to breathe, her tiny heart stilled beneath the unformed buds of her breasts, he had dug a shallow grave in the sand, buried her, and covered her over with a marker of seaweed branches.

Shaking his head violently to rid it of these persistent images, Bruckner returned the still-warm pistol to its holster and, sitting beside Ilsa's body on the bed, picked up the telephone to call Toberts. After reporting in, he dressed hurriedly and left the room carrying the Walther and its holster in a paper sack, which he shortly returned to the drop in the Jardin des Plantes. When he returned to the hotel room sometime later, both bodies were gone, as were the bloodstained sheets, with no sign that they had ever existed.

Toberts, alone in his office at the embassy, took the call from Bruckner himself. "The *Times-Weekly* plans excellent coverage of the President's speech next Thursday in the Chamber of Deputies," Bruckner said as soon as they had established that it was official embassy press business. "Dual coverage, in fact—a bit unexpected."

They talked a minute or two, discussing other possible news stories that the embassy might be interested in, and then Toberts cut the connection and dialed another number. "Yes, Maillot, we have a special laundry pickup for you at the Hotel Crillon, room 423. The laundry needs special processing. Try the Bois de Vincennes area."

Toberts hung up and sat slumped in his desk chair, thinking what a dirty profession he was in and how much he would like to get out of it for good. In his mind he could see Maillot's people pulling up to the service dock of the Crillon in a marked laundry truck, later bringing down a large unwieldy bundle of supposedly soiled bedclothes. The bundle, of course, would contain Ilsa's body, as well as some other body that he hadn't counted on. Because of Toberts's phone reference to "special processing," Maillot's highly trained professionals would remove all but a couple of pieces of positive identification from the deceased, hold the rest for Toberts's later inspection, and take the bodies to the Bois de Vincennes and surreptitiously leave them where they would easily be discovered by the Paris police. "Two more unsolved murders in the park" was the way it would be reported in the newspapers.

Wondering why Professor Damian, the CIA recruiter back in his college days at Berkeley, hadn't told him the bad parts—the really terrible parts—about working for anybody's intelligence agency, Toberts shook himself out of his depression and glanced at his watch. Five-thirty, time to go home; he was dead tired, the tiredness less physical than from somewhere deep within his spirit. He opened the security safe and removed the original Cordier manuscript, Bruckner's attempt at decoding it, and the book containing the complete plays of Shakespeare. He rode down to the basement in the elevator, got into his car, and drove home to Montmartre, stopping along the way to pick up the Walther P38 that Bruckner had left at the dead drop in a crumpled paper sack.

Jessie was in the kitchen drinking sherry when he arrived, and from the slurred sound of her speech she had probably been hitting it all afternoon. "It's about god-damned time you got home," she greeted him, and he knew without question what shape their evening together would take.

"Hello, Jessie," he said. "I'm glad you're so glad to see me." He made himself a large martini, and when he found an empty jar in the refrigerator that had formerly held Spanish olives he threw the jar into the kitchen garbage pail, where it shattered against some other jar. "I suppose you forgot to go to the market again," he said testily.

"Well, lord and master of the manor, you're wrong again, as usual. Matter of fact, I've been to the market every day since you've been gone, seeing that there was nothing else to do. Thing is, *I* don't *like* martinis, with or without olives. So you can just damn well get your own special groceries from now on!"

"Thanks, Jessie, I'll do that," he said, rather than continue the argument. He took the martini into the living room with a newspaper and sat down to read before dinner, hoping that whatever it was he had smelled cooking or burning in the kitchen would turn out to be at least edible.

It was only marginally edible, he discovered much later after Jessie had filled and emptied her sherry glass several more times. They sat, silent and tense, across from each other at the small table where they shared all their meals, lifting forkfuls of badly overcooked roasted pork to their mouths automatically. Midway through the meal Toberts decided he could stand the silence no longer.

"How were things around here while I was gone?" he asked her, as pleasantly as possible under the circumstances, he thought.

But apparently she had been waiting for him to speak first so that she could then release all the venom she had been storing up for this homecoming occasion. "How *could* you!" she shouted. "You sick, philandering old man —oh, yes, I know all about the little French whore you took along with you on that manufactured business trip. Did you think it would stay a secret, Martin? The people in your office know all about it—they're laughing behind your back, if you only knew it. You're a pathetic laughingstock, and you don't even have sense enough to realize how ridiculous you make yourself appear. How old is she —eighteen? Nineteen? I'll bet she has pointed little tits and a cute ass, though. Did you teach her all you know about love and sex, Martin? That should have taken about three minutes, tops. So what did you find to do the rest of the time?"

"You're drunk, Jessie, stone drunk out of your mind, or you wouldn't be saying these things."

"And what do you think makes me get drunk and stay that way? It's you, you adulterous son of a bitch! If you'd stay home with me where you belong instead of sneaking around dipping your tiny little cock in some rancid piece of hooker's meat—."

"That's enough!" Toberts shouted. He hadn't meant to raise his voice to her, to lose control to that extent, but it felt good for a change and he found that he enjoyed it. "You've never been a help or a comfort to me, Jessie, not in a long, long time. Even when you're here you're not here, because you're down at the bottom of some bottle. And that isn't my fault, regardless of what you think."

"Whose fault is it? You don't give me any sort of life at all, Martin Toberts. A frigging *frog* has a better home life than I do."

"Is that another of your racial slurs, Jessie?"

"Oh, don't act so superior with me. You hate the French as much as I do—I've heard you yelling about

251

how they're always hamstringing you in your work because they're so suspicious of what you do. I could sure as hell tell them a few things!"

"Don't be stupid, Jessie. You know you can't say anything about my work, even what you've picked up around here. There's a lot more you don't understand . . ."

"You think I don't know you're some kind of big deal spy or something? Please, Martin, give me credit for a little intelligence."

"Whatever you know, or think you know, it would be very dangerous for both of us if you let something slip at the wrong time. Why do you think I worry so much about your drinking?"

"I guess it wasn't because you cared anything about me. No—you care about your precious contacts, your buddies in the department. Well, listen to me, mister big shot, I know a few things and I'll damn well talk to anybody I want and tell them anything I want. Is that clear enough for you?"

Toberts could feel the heat and color rising in his face and his fingernails cutting into the palm of his clenched fist. "The company would take a dim view of that, Jessie," he said with murderous quiet. "People have been known to disappear, permanently, for saying things like what you just said."

"And I'll bet you could arrange it, couldn't you?"

"If I had to, yes," Toberts said, and suddenly he realized that they were actually sitting here, in his own dining room, talking about the possibility that someday he might have to have his wife killed. The thought was so shocking to him that he forgot what the argument had been about. He stood suddenly, and went into the living room, his head spinning with the realization that things could have gotten this bad between Jessie and him. What were his options? Think now, he told himself, that's what they pay you so well for, your ability to think fast and accurately in crisis situations involving the destinies of whole sovereign nations. Surely you can come up with a simple solution for a little domestic crisis like this one. Can't you?

There was at least one option to continuing this farce,

and he took it boldly. "I'm moving out, Jessie," he said calmly.

"You mean now? Tonight?"

"Yes, at least until we're both thinking more clearly about things. I can't take any more of this, Jessie. I don't know whether it's mostly my fault or mostly your fault, but it doesn't matter. We rub each other raw, and I guess I'm tired of bleeding."

From the corner of his eye he saw Jessie pick up her water glass, and from some instinct he ducked just as the glass sailed past his head and crashed in fragments against the fireplace brick. "I'll get you, you son of a bitch!" she screamed at him. "If you move out on me, so help me God I'll go to my good friend the ambassador—you remember Walter Fitzgerald, don't you, Martin?—and I'll get him to have you recalled immediately to the good ol' U.S. of A. as a persona non grata. And you know he can do it, too. What do you think of that?"

Toberts took a deep breath. "I think you're crazy, Jessie, I think the alcohol has destroyed part of your mind."

"And you needn't think you can run to your floozy, either, you bastard! I'll never give you a divorce, you hear me? Never!"

Toberts picked up the two manuscripts and the Shakespeare book he had brought home, slung a jacket over his shoulder, and walked out the front door, not bothering to close it behind him. It was a little thing, not pulling the door to as he had always done, but it was surprising how refreshing that could be. He got into the car and drove off in the direction he took every morning going to work, and it was a good five minutes later before he realized he had no place to go.

He slowed the car, thinking about it, knowing that he probably should return to his office in the embassy and get started on his study of the manuscripts. And if worst came to worst he could always sleep on a cot that was maintained in the embassy's twenty-four-hour emergency center. But even as he was thinking this out he was also aware that it was not what he wanted to do. What he really wanted to do—the *only* thing he wanted to do—

was to see Solange. He pointed the car in a new direction and felt his life simultaneously slip into an exciting new gear.

There were problems at Solange's house—meeting her mother for the first time under less than ideal conditions, for one thing, and the fact that Solange had to find someone to stay with the old woman on short notice. But these things were accomplished almost painlessly, it seemed, and their real luck lay in this being Friday evening, which meant that neither Toberts nor Solange were expected at their jobs for two whole days.

They went to a small, quaint, but clean hotel off the Boulevard Saint-Michel that Toberts knew about from having occasionally met an out-of-town contact there. Solange teased him about taking his "other girls" there, and the teasing was fun for both of them because they were so completely wrapped up in their love for each other. The elderly room clerk was apparently affected by their efforts to appear serious and married, because the inexpensive room he assigned to them was large and well-situated, having both an elegant quietness about it and a magnificent view of the Eiffel Tower bathed in light. On the way up the stairs the clerk pressed a bottle of wine into Toberts's hand, the cost of which, Toberts knew, would be added to their bill. Nevertheless, it was a thoughtful gesture.

They made love hungrily and breathlessly, as though it had been years since the last time instead of only a day and a half. "I never seem to get enough of you," Solange breathed into his ear, and he kissed her and thanked his nameless gods for having brought her into his life.

Afterward, propped up in bed side by side against huge pillows, with the two manuscripts and the Shakespeare spread out across their laps, they began to study together the fantastic legacy of Solange's great-grandfather, Professor Maurice Cordier, whose notes from nineteenth-century Paris formed the basis of weighty twentieth-century intelligence files called, depending upon their ownership, *Fonarshchik* or Lamplighter.

TWO_____

23 _____

Owing to a personal predilection for neatness and order that amounts to compulsiveness, and because I cannot, in good conscience, go to my grave clutching such a magnificent secret to my cadaverous bosom, I, Maurice Cordier, have set forth the following description of a most extraordinary sequence of events, of which I not only have an intimate knowledge but also participated as one of the principal characters of the dramatis personae, as it were. I have taken some pains to preserve this information, because of its delicate and potentially explosive nature, from the prying eyes of casual readers of this manuscript by encoding my words in a cipher of my own devising. I trust that those who may, in future years and perhaps long after my passing, have prior knowledge of the subject matter treated here, because it is within the realm of their responsibilities to have such knowledge, will recognize my feeble attempts at literary deception as merely a device to disguise the information so presented, not to inter it in a crypt of eternal mystery. To you, then, faithful burrower in obscure works of French pedantry, my felicitations and congratulations; for if you have but reached this point in your deciphering, then surely your comprehension of the whole is only a matter of time and some little effort. And I say to you in all sincerity, may your efforts be rewarded a thousandfold, and may you richly deserve the fruits of your labors.

Bon appétit!

Mother Russia was changing, in a manner so gradual that only those foreigners who infrequently visited within her vast borders had an opportunity to remark upon the obvious differences each time they returned. And nowhere were the changes more pronounced, yet outwardly unremarked, than in the glorious capital city of St. Petersburg.

Designed by French and Italian architects, the buildings of St. Petersburg were constructed entirely of stone on a grand scale, and none was larger or grander than the Winter Palace, which stretched magnificently along the Neva for more than half a mile at the terminus of the broad and celebrated Nevsky Prospect. Already, in the fall of 1880, it had served as the principal residence of the czars for nearly one hundred and twenty years, although Alexander II, its current occupant, took no particular pleasure in that fact. His domestic life, as were his foreign affairs, was complicated immensely by the fact that his wife, Marie of Hess-Darmstadt, who had borne him six children over the years, was a wife in name only. It was common knowledge within the court circle (and among the servants, naturally) that his one true, life-sustaining love was the beautiful Catherine Dolgoruka, thirty years his junior, who was known at court as Princess Yurievskaya.

The emperor found a pleasant apartment for his young Catherine—so close by the Winter Palace that no one with two eyes could have overlooked his intentions. In time the beautiful Catherine, a direct descendant of the Grand-Duke of Kiev, bore Alexander a son and two daughters whose existence and heritage were the subject of much whispering in the halls and inner apartments of the Winter Palace.

Jealousy and resentment of Catherine, or Princess Yurievskaya, was not confined to her rival, Empress Marie, but was widespread among the members of the imperial court, particularly the female half. These women, for some of whom gossip was their only entertainment, accused the princess of everything from shadowy, near-illegal real estate dealings to hypnotizing Alexander into secretly bestowing upon her various pieces from the fabulous Romanov crown jewels. In fact, the latter accusation was not even within the realm of possibility; for the Diamond Room in the Winter Palace—the *Brillyantovaya Komnata*—which housed most of the Romanov crown

258

treasures, was guarded night and day by two sentinels and could only be entered by two people: the Keeper of His Imperial Majesty's Wardrobe, and the Chamberlain of Her Majesty the Czarina.

These strict regulations, designed to protect the Russian nation from the accidental or premeditated loss of its national treasure, did not prevent Alexander from expressing his pleasure with his beloved Catherine in tangible ways. She adored emeralds and over the years he arranged to present her with a fortune in jewels, both mounted and unmounted, which he largely acquired through the services of the court jeweler Bolin. The superbly mounted pieces themselves were rumored to be valued at more than twenty million gold rubles (ten million dollars), and the loose diamonds, emeralds, sapphires, rubies, and pearls must have equaled at least half that amount.

Among other specialized pieces was an ivory jewel case shaped like an egg, with an emerald clasp and containing an emerald parure or matched set, given to Princess Yurievskaya as an Easter present by the infatuated emperor. On other occasions he presented her with a jade snuffbox worked with sapphires and diamonds, a golden egg encrusted with diamonds and lined inside with rubies, and at least three rope necklaces of huge matched pearls. Perhaps the most fabulous gift of all was what came to be known as the "Catherine" necklace, made unique by the placement of an enormous perfect emerald of nearly two hundred carats within an array of smaller emeralds and diamonds. Alexander had purchased the central stone for his beloved from an Indian raja, who had acquired it from Spanish adventurers, who had stolen it years before from the shrine of a South American native tribe that had worshiped it as the healing Green Eye of one of their gods.

But despite the grandeur and carefree elegance of Alexander's court, Mother Russia was changing in a way and to a degree that few of those involved understood. The winds of revolution were in the air; the strictures of the ruling social order could, it seemed, only be countered by total anarchy of thought and action. Alexander II had freed the serfs, or so it was said, but no one was made

happy by his well-publicized deed, least of all those desperately poor families who had for centuries been bound
inescapably to the land. Now they were free to escape
—but to what? There was no other employment for them.
Most remained where they had always been—tied to
someone else's land through back-breaking labor—and a
few, the bitterest, escaped into their desperation and
dreamed of heroic acts in the name of The People. Ultimately, the failure of the agrarian populist movement
led to the formation of radical terrorist groups, and nowhere were these groups more active than in St. Petersburg.

The reason, quite simply, was the terrorists' unreason-
ing hatred of the emperor. The writer Dostoevski felt
strongly that the idea of regicide was in the air, and
shortly before his death he informed the editor of *Novoye
Vremia:* "You said that there was some clairvoyance in
my Brothers Karamazov . . . Wait till you have the sequel
. . . I shall make my pure Aliosha join the terrorists and
kill the Tsar."

There was a nearly successful attempt to do just that
in February 1880. An explosion timed for the beginning
of Alexander's dinner in the Winter Palace—loud enough
to be heard on the far bank of the Neva—completely
wrecked the dining room and killed twenty-nine butlers,
footmen, and Finnish Guards. Alexander had been entertaining his nephew in another part of the palace and had
forgotten all about dinner.

The executive committee of the terrorist organization
known as *Narodnaya Volya*—"The Will of the People"—
took credit for the destruction and near miss, as well it
might. For this most radical of revolutionary groups,
organized in 1879 with the publication of a manifesto ex-
tolling the people's will and the people's welfare, soon
came to assert that their ends justified any means of accomplishment, including destructive and terrorist activity.
The leaders of *Narodnaya Volya*'s executive committee
were a fanatic named Zhelyabov and his mistress, Sophie
Perovskaya, who was known to be more ruthless than her
lover. The czar's secret police had been busy for more
than a year nipping at the heels of suspects, obtaining

confessions through torture, banishing suspected or even rumored sympathizers to the outermost reaches of Siberia. By late 1880 the hard-core remnants of *Narodnaya Volyu* decided to concentrate all their efforts in St. Petersburg, with the sole objective of murdering the emperor. Their dedication was matched perfectly by their youth and resourcefulness; surprise was their secret weapon. The vast capital city of Russia was literally at their mercy.

That winter ice had come early to the Neva River, but on the evening of the last day of 1880 the atmosphere inside the grand ballroom of the Winter Palace was warm and gay. Beautiful, laughing women and handsomely uniformed men talked of court intrigues, ate tons of beluga caviar brought from the Black Sea, and drank copious amounts of vodka from small silver goblets. Magnificent clusters of jewels sparkled on every woman's bosom, the brilliant radiance of the multihued gems enhanced by the incandescent lights recently installed in the enormous chandeliers overhead.

From the vantage point of a small balcony inset high in the east wall of the ballroom, Ilya Kozlov stared down at the dancers and tried to identify his pretty, dark-haired young sister, Tatiana. He should not have been there, watching unobserved as the cream of Russian royalty immersed themselves in the traditional pleasures of the court. If a guard had seen him, however, the guard would not have been surprised, since Ilya Kozlov, although only a common laborer in the palace, was a well-known and well-liked young man and had become great friends with most of the gendarmes who protected the czar. But there were things about him they did not know.

Every citizen of troubled St. Petersburg was required to carry a passport as well as a work-card at all times, and to show them upon official request many times a day. The passport that Ilya Kozlov carried with him at this very moment bore the name Khaltourin, and though Tatiana Kozlov, the principal lady-in-waiting to Princess Yurievskaya, was indeed his younger sister, he pretended to the winking guards and court ladies that he was court-

261

ing her favor and that they were in no way related. Tatiana, for her part, despised this deceitfulness and allowed it only because her brother had convinced her that it was somehow important, not only to him but to all the people of Russia as well. She had no idea what he meant by this, and he did not explain further; but she trusted him now as she had always trusted him, because he was older, undoubtedly wiser, and most of all because he was her only living close relative since their parents' death several years before.

At the stroke of midnight sounding from the golden clock set into a marble column along one wall of the ballroom, Czar Alexander suddenly appeared at the far end of the room, and on his arm was the beautiful Princess Yurievskaya. The crowd instantly hushed, the dancers stopped in their tracks, and the orchestra switched almost in mid-note from the lively mazurka they had been playing to the traditional royal salute. Ilya stared at the couple from his aerie and felt nothing but hatred, though in truth he was not so much concerned about the princess.

Upon the death several months earlier of Alexander's wife, Empress Marie, Alexander had secretly married the Princess in shocking haste. Those few among the court who knew about the morganatic marriage spoke in disgust about how the two ceremonies—funeral and marriage—occurred nearly simultaneously. Ilya knew, as did nearly everyone in St. Petersburg, that the princess had been Alexander's mistress for at least fifteen years, and a good many citizens also knew about the three illegitimate children she had borne.

Such matters were of little concern to Ilya Kozlov. As Alexander and his lady passed beneath the opening high in the wall, Ilya wished for a gun with which to shatter the Czar's proud head, or a bomb to hurl at his feet, or even a poisoned glass of tea to be served with proper ceremony on a silver platter. Someone had to accomplish it. Ilya had worked hard to become accepted in a position where it might be possible, and now he was certain that soon that distinct honor would be his.

*   *   *

On a bitterly cold night late in February 1881, Ilya Kozlov slipped through the heavily guarded streets of the capital toward a rendezvous with the executive committee of *Narodnaya Volya*. Upon reaching the safety of the house, he was greeted by his revolutionary comrades in the organization, including the young radicals Rysakov and Grinevetsky, the eminent chemist Kibaltchitch, and, of course, the leaders Zhelyabov and Sophie Perovskaya. Because of the extreme danger to those inside the meeting place if their presence were to be discovered by the *Okhrana*, the Czar's dread secret police, the planning session was kept as short as possible.

"Comrade Kozlov," Zhelyabov said, even before Ilya had shaken the loose snow from his high boots, "the committee has been discussing the need for immediate and direct action against the Czar. We have waited long enough for the perfect opportunity to present itself; now we must stop talking and act. There have been rumors of a new official edict by the Czar which would consolidate his position of authority over the people while leading them to believe that he was acting in their best interests. We have tentatively decided to concentrate all our efforts on one particular day, the sooner the better. Do you have a suggestion along these lines?"

Ilya nodded. "I do. And, yes, I agree wholeheartedly with your plans." He accepted a glass of tea from Rysakov's wife. "Alexander goes every Sunday to pass his troops in review at the Mikhail cavalry school. Through my sister I have learned that, although Princess Yurievskaya has begged the Czar to stay within the walls of the Winter Palace, Alexander has refused to give up his Sunday ritual. I suggest this would be a perfect opportunity, if Kibaltchitch can manufacture sufficient bombs by March first."

"Do not worry about me." The voice, high and humorless, came from a small gray man huddled inside a lamb's-wool coat in the corner by himself. "My chemical toys will be ready before you need them."

Sophie Perovskaya jumped up from a bench and unrolled a large hand-drawn map of St. Petersburg. "Show us the route, Kozlov," she barked, and there was no doubt of the command in her voice.

Ilya went to the map and pointed. "Here," he said, "and here. Along Malaya-Sadovaya and Gorokhovaya streets."

Sophie nodded. "Then we will mine those streets by digging trenches beneath them and wait for the carriage to pass."

"But what if there's a change of plans at the last minute?" Zhelyabov asked, asserting himself over his mistress in an attempt to retain his supremacy on the committee. "Or what if the *Okhrana* discover the trenches before they can be put to use? I say that as many of us as possible should be stationed along the probable routes, with inconspicuously packaged bombs hidden beneath our coats."

"But that means almost certain capture and death for the one who throws the bomb," Ilya protested.

"Of course, you fool!" Sophie shouted. "If you are not prepared to risk suicide in the furtherance of our goals, then you do not belong in this organization. Agreed?"

"Agreed," he consented.

"There is a letter from our friend in Paris, just recently smuggled in by a comrade returning from a visit with his mother," Zhelyabov said. Ilya recognized this as a reference to Professor Maurice Cordier, a scholar and linguist at the renowned Sorbonne who had been one of the most eloquent spokesmen for the Paris Commune ten years before, in 1871, when Paris had been under siege by the Prussians. Somehow, word of *Narodnaya Volya* had reached the professor in Paris shortly after its formation in 1879, and his letters of encouragement and practical information had been arriving in St. Petersburg irregularly ever since. "He says he is in full accord with our stated goals," Zhelyabov continued, "that terrorism is perhaps the only way to accomplish those goals, and that we are not to be dissuaded from our purpose by rhetoric or lassitude."

"He is a good friend," Ilya agreed. "He will perhaps help us even more in the future, when we will need the support of world opinion to see us realize our goals."

Sophie Perovskaya banged the table with her fist. "We

have only one goal at the moment, Comrade Kozlov, and that is to kill the Czar!" And with that pronouncement the meeting of the executive committee was adjourned.

A few days later, on Saturday, 28 February, the head of the secret police announced to Alexander that his men had captured the feared Zhelyabov, leader of *Narodnaya Volya*, but that others equally dangerous remained at large. Princess Yurievskaya and others at the Winter Palace urged Alexander to keep to the palace and forgo his usual Sunday ride to the Mikhail academy. But the Czar, unusually optimistic, decided that with his escort of six cossacks, in addition to two sledges carrying a senior police official and an equerry, his carriage would be perfectly safe in the streets of St. Petersburg.

On Sunday, just before Alexander left the palace, Princess Yurievskaya received word from an informer that Malaya-Sadovaya street would be extremely dangerous and convinced her husband to use another route. Ilya Kozlov, through his sister, Tatiana, had received and passed along to Sophie Perovskaya and others the word that Alexander's ride would take place as usual; the change in route, however, was decided too late for him to act upon.

The streets of the capital were nearly deserted as the Czar's carriage and retinue traveled silently through the deep snow to the Mikhail cavalry school, then to his cousin's palace for a visit, all without incident. But on the return trip to the Winter Palace, when told to hurry because Alexander had an appointment, the coachman chose a quicker route that had not been given to the plainclothes police officers scattered along the original route. And no one noticed that an old herring woman, who was in reality the disguised Sophie Perovskaya, saw the change of plans and signaled to Rysakov nearby.

As the carriage, sledges, and cossacks' horses hurried down the broad Ekaterinskaya Canal quay, Rysakov suddenly stepped out from a corner and hurled a package in front of the carriage. The explosion killed two cossacks, an unfortunate errand boy who happened to be passing by, and several horses, and blew the carriage apart. Miraculously, Alexander was only shaken by the powerful blast and emerged from the wreckage to confront the conspirator. People ran toward the explosion from all directions. A police officer attempted to persuade Alexander to get in one of the sledges and hasten back to the palace. As he nodded and turned to step into the nearest sledge, a second conspirator, Grinevetsky, calmly came forward from the crowd and tossed another bomb at the Czar's feet.

When the smoke and powdered snow cleared, it could be seen that more than twenty people were dead, including Grinevetsky. Alexander, his legs shattered and blood streaming down his face, sagged against the canal railing and feebly asked that he be taken back to the Winter Palace to die. As he was helped into the sledge he lost consciousness. Doctors were summoned to the palace, but when Alexander arrived they were as helpless to save him as were the other assembled members of his family. As he lay on a sofa in his study, Princess Yurievskaya knelt beside him and kissed his unfeeling hands. In less than an hour he died without having regained consciousness.

With the passing of Czar Alexander II an era of reform in Russia's history came to an abrupt end. Alexander's son, Alexander III, assumed the throne and very soon instituted a series of harsh controls on nearly every facet of Russian life. So much power was given to the secret police that there was no chance for the few remaining members of *Narodnaya Volya*'s executive committee to carry out further revolutionary plans, at least for the time being. What was needed, they decided, was a period of regrouping, of lying low to lull the present sense of danger, and most of all to add somehow to their pitifully small supply of operating capital. To that end Ilya Kozlov had a plan.

At a clandestine meeting shortly after the assassination Ilya proposed to Sophie Perovskaya and others that, without a great deal of trouble, he could arrange for the theft of Princess Yurievskaya's fabulous collection of jewels. "The princess, I have learned, is leaving Russia within the month," he told his comrades. "She is despised equally by the court and the common people. Already she has

266

made arrangements for travel by rail to France, where she proposes to lead a splendid life financed by the handsome trinkets given her by the Czar. The former Czar. The princess will take only a few servants and her three children with her. Did I ever tell you that my mother was French?"

"What has that to do with anything, Kozlov?"

"Simply that because my sister, Tatiana, can speak enough French to communicate with that country's workmen, food vendors, officials, and so forth, the princess has decided to take her along to Paris. I think I can convince her to relieve the princess of most of her ill-gotten wealth, and to put it into the hands of those who know better how to use it for the good of the people."

Sophie Perovskaya paused to consider the possibilities of Ilya's plan. "It might work, at that," she said. "And the beautiful princess would have no recourse to the officials here if she discovered the theft before she left Russia."

"That's true. Of course, the theft may have to be arranged along the way, or even in France. And she might very well report the theft to the French police, thus endangering Tatiana. The jewels will have to be smuggled out of France—I believe they are probably too well known in most of Europe to allow their being converted readily into cash. For several reasons I believe the United States of America is the most fertile ground for conversion."

"And," Sophie added, "with the proper contacts in that country we could perhaps use the money obtained to finance the formation of a group in America sympathetic to our own goals. Such a transhemispheric organization would lend new meaning to 'The Will of the People.' "

"I assume we can expect a certain amount of assistance from this Professor Cordier in Paris with whom we have been corresponding?"

"I should think so," Sophie agreed. "He is the only man in France I would trust not to appropriate the jewels for his own gain. Do you wish me to contact him?"

"Not yet," Ilya said. "I must first make certain arrangements with my sister. I will, however, need the professor's address."

Nodding, Sophie took a small black book from beneath her petticoat and copied from it an address at the Sorbonne. Ilya took the slip of paper, folded it twice, and slipped it into a secret pocket in the top of his left boot.

That evening Ilya approached his sister, Tatiana, with the barest rudiments of the plan to steal Princess Yurievskaya's jewels. Horrified by what she saw as her brother's turning toward barbarism, and having never understood the lure of anarchism in any case, she flatly refused to take any part in Ilya's plan. "I respect the princess," she told him. "She has become my friend as well as my employer. She's offered me the chance of a lifetime to see something of the world by accompanying her on this trip to France, and now you want to spoil it all. I won't let you, Ilya, I won't!"

"Now, now," Ilya said soothingly, stroking his sister's lustrous black hair. "It was simply a proposal, nothing more. Now that I see how you feel about the matter, I shall have no more to say. Your well-being is my uppermost concern, dear Tatiana. Besides, I assume the princess's jewel collection has already been packed for the trip, so that even you would not have access to it. Isn't that true?"

"Oh, no, not yet. She still wears a piece now and then, but of course only in her private chambers. A few of the more ordinary pieces she will probably carry with her in her personal toilet on the trip, but the rest she expects to have sealed in a strongbox and then crated for shipment. In fact, I wouldn't be surprised if you were asked to help with the crating. I shall have to watch you closely, dear brother."

"Nonsense, Tatiana, I haven't the nerves for stealing. But I am an excellent carpenter, as you know. Tell the princess that I am at her service should she need me."

Within a fortnight it was known throughout St. Petersburg that Princess Yurievskaya was traveling to France with several railroad cars of personal possessions, and that she had been all but told by the new Czar's family that she would never again be welcome inside Russian borders. As Ilya had intended, Tatiana passed along word of his skills in cabinetmaking, and on the day before the princess and her small party were to leave for Paris he was summoned to her quarters to help with the crating. Anticipating what he would need for the job, he brought along an extraordinarily large toolbox. Unknown to anyone but himself, only the top layer of the stout box contained tools.

The princess was taking no special precautions with her precious gems except to watch them closely while supervising the other packing. Ilya worked around the strongbox, awaiting his chance; when it came, Tatiana was unwittingly the catalyst, for she called to the princess from another room. In the brief period of her absence Ilya managed to secrete the strongbox in the hollow space beneath his tools; then he hastily sealed a crate he had put to one side for that purpose.

When the princess returned, she casually inquired about a small but heavy box—had it been packed? Ilya assured her it now rested comfortably within the crate he had just finished nailing shut.

Every minute he stayed in the room now, Ilya thought, brought him a minute closer to being caught with the jewels in his possession, but of course he was committed to finishing the job of crating the princess's possessions. Finally they were finished. Ilya put his tools away carefully in the immense toolbox and had to restrain himself from running back to the small staff room he shared with several other workmen in the basement of the palace. Passing through one of the long east-west corridors, he rounded a corner and felt a hand grasp his shoulder.

"Your passport and work card!" a guard unknown to Ilya barked in his ear.

Ilya fumbled in his blouse for the identification that, even as he searched in vain, he knew he had not brought with him, for no one on the palace staff had asked him to identify himself in a long time. Just as he was about to admit that he had left the cards in his quarters and would be happy to get them, one of the older guards approached and vouched for Ilya's identity and right to be where he was. "It's all right this time, Ilya Khaltourin," the friendly guard said. "But times are changing in the palace—in fact, all over St. Petersburg. You will have to

269

carry your identity cards with you at all times from now on."

When they let him go, Ilya hurried down to his room and was glad to see that no one else was around. So that he would not forget again and call attention to himself, he immediately opened the small cabinet where he kept the passport and work card. But the cards were not there and, indeed, were nowhere to be found in the room. A cold chill ran through Ilya's body as he contemplated what the officials would do to him if they somehow discovered that his credentials were false, or had been issued in a false name. In reality, both the name Khaltourin and the identity cards were genuine; only Ilya Kozlov was not genuine.

The following morning Ilya received permission from his employer at the palace to accompany his supposed lover, Tatiana, to the rail terminal and kiss her good-bye. As Princess Yurievskaya and her party were about to board the train, Ilya handed his sister a small tin of sweets and a letter addressed to her. "You are to open neither the sweets nor the letter until you have crossed over the Russian frontier," he commanded her, and made her promise that she would read the letter first.

"I shall miss you, brother Ilya," Tatiana said, tears welling up in her violet eyes. "Promise that you will write to me often."

"Of course, little Tatiana," he said, knowing that almost certainly he would not. "Go with God, my sister."

Somewhat wistfully Ilya turned to make his way back to the palace and to try to obtain replacements for the missing identity cards, but he found his way blocked by two men who were strangers to him. One of the men took his arm.

"Ilya Kozlov?"

Ilya looked from one to the other. "No, no . . . Khaltourin, my name is Khaltourin . . ."

"Ilya Kozlov?" the second man repeated, in such a way that the question was more like an answer, a very final answer. "You will come with us, Ilya Kozlov, to give us information about several things."

"What things?" Ilya stammered. "I know nothing of any value . . ."

"*Narodnaya Volya,*" the man explained. "Sophié Perovskaya. The assassination of Czar Alexander II. These and other things. You will tell us what you know."

"I will tell you nothing!" Ilya spat out, knowing that nothing could save him now and determined not to end his days on earth as a coward.

"You will tell us everything, Ilya Kozlov," the first man said with deadly quiet. "In the end you will beg us to allow you to tell more than we have a need to know. Death, for you, will be a long time coming, Ilya Kozlov."

On the second day the train from St. Petersburg passed across the Russian border into Poland, and Tatiana Kozlov, alone and bored in her tiny suite, remembered the strange promise she had made to her brother. She took the box of sweets and the letter from beneath the seat, where she had put them for safekeeping, and opened the letter first as instructed. The message was brief and eloquently straightforward:

Dearest Little Tatiana: You must not show this letter to anyone else, and you must destroy it immediately upon reading it. I have not been quite honest with you, my sister. Since you would not agree to steal the jewels of Princess Yurievskaya, I have stolen them myself during the crating, and now I have given them to you. The tin I gave you as a gift contains, I am afraid, no sweets but only a princess's fortune in perfect gems. There is no way you will be able to return them to the princess without casting a large amount of suspicion on yourself, if only as my accomplice. And, in fact, I do thank you for your help. In Paris you are to contact Professor Maurice Cordier, of the Department of Comparative History at the Sorbonne. Explain that you have the jewels intended for transport to the United States of America—he has already been made aware of their ultimate purpose and will guide you in what further actions to take. I am sorry to put this burden on you, little Tatiana, and do so reluctantly. But there was no other way. Please know that in my own strange way I love you and wish you well. Ilya.

271

Dumbfounded, Tatiana slowly reached for the sweets tin. With some difficulty she pried open the cover. Inside she found a purple velvet bag, closed with a woven drawstring. It was a bag that she had seen before. Looking about her to make certain she was alone, she pulled open the gathers of the velvet bag and peered inside; and though she had been nearly sure of what she would find, the splendor of the jewels dazzled her so that she gasped and pulled the drawstring tight again. For a long time she sat with the closed bag on her lap and stared straight ahead at the wall, her slight body trembling violently in counterpoint to the clacking of the wheels as the train sped westward across Poland toward the City of Light.

"Oh, that poor girl!" Solange said, raising her head from Toberts's shoulder in the hotel bed where they had been reading the professor's manuscript together.

Toberts smiled and kissed her hair. "It has been my experience, mademoiselle, that women's purpose on earth is to be used—badly, if at all possible."

"Chauvinist!" Solange yelled, playfully pummeling his bare arm. To protect himself Toberts laid the manuscript aside and took her in both arms, kissing her tenderly.

"I always wondered whether eyeglasses would get in the way of a really good kiss," Solange said.

"And?"

"They do—but it doesn't matter."

Toberts removed the glasses and laid them on the lamp table beside the bed. Thoughtfully, he rubbed his eyes and picked up the manuscript again.

"Please, Martin," Solange said, "let us wait until tomorrow for the remainder of the story—your poor eyes are nearly bleeding."

"What? Oh—well, maybe I'll just rest them for a minute. Forty winks might do me a world of good, actually."

He closed his eyes and slipped down lower in the bed so that his head was on the pillow, his feet hanging an inch or two over the end of the mattress. Soon Solange, watching him, heard his breathing flatten out into long, deep, regular exhalations and she knew that he was asleep. She pulled up a corner of the thin blanket and covered his naked body, then turned off the lamp and lay beside him, her arm resting protectively across his chest.

Frowning, she pressed her face against his shoulder. She loved him so much that she thought she would probably die if anything bad happened to him; and yet, now that she knew the kind of work he did and the kind of people he must be associating with, she had to accept that as a real possibility. Shuddering with sudden fear, she clasped his sweet body closer to hers, and that movement, or some unknown dream, made him groan deeply in his sleep.

24

LAZILY, TOBERTS AND SOLANGE lay in the too-short bed in the small old hotel for more than an hour after they had awakened. They had made love earlier, and now they were entwined so completely in each other's arms that it was difficult for them to move.

They lay very still, each listening to the rhythmic miracle of the other's breathing, until Toberts changed the mood by glancing at his watch.

"I forgot to ask," Solange said. "Must you go so soon?"

Toberts smiled at her. "Not today. This is Saturday, a day of leisure. I plan to spend the entire day convincing you to fall in love with me."

"Starting, I hope, with breakfast," she said. "I'm starved."

They dressed casually—which for Toberts meant leaving off his tie—and walked out of the hotel into a gorgeous Parisian spring morning. Somehow the smog of this city was unlike the smog in Pittsburgh or Los Angeles, in that it was colored as though from within by the delicate pastel colors of Paris itself—grays and mauves and lavenders and pinks and steel-blues. Two blocks from the hotel they found a sidewalk café where they ordered cappuccino from a complicated brass machine resembling a steam engine, and accompanied the sweet espresso with deliciously light croissants.

"How well do you know Paris, Martin?"

Toberts shrugged. "I've been here five years, as I told you. My work takes me around and about, here and there."

"*Oui,* but you never see anything except what you are

274

looking for," Solange said. "That is no way to treat a lady like Paris."

"You're right, absolutely right. What do you suggest?"

"Oh, simply that I take you on a short tour of the city, some of the more interesting parts, and that whether or not you've been there before, you let me explain things to you, in the manner of a native speaking to a tourist."

"Well . . ." Toberts put his hand inside his jacket and felt the folded pages of the manuscript. "We still have work to do—at least, *I* do."

"I know that, Martin. But there is an expression that all work with no time for pleasure—"

"Makes Jacques a dull fellow. Or, in this case, Martin. Okay, you temptress, lead the way."

And lead she did. For the next several hours Solange showed Toberts things he had either never seen or never taken the time to notice before, but mostly they walked and talked and held hands and managed almost entirely to forget the pressing problems of the real world.

From the Eiffel Tower they walked the mile and a half or so to one of the entrances to the huge, forested Bois de Boulogne. This reminded Toberts of business that had sometimes been less than pleasant, but the Bois was so large that each part of it was like a separate park. They passed by the deserted Auteuil racetrack. Solange described a thrilling steeplechase race there on which she had won five hundred francs the previous autumn, and Toberts remembered meeting an Algerian informer in the stands, perhaps on the same day, and remembered that the man had later been murdered in an alley in Montparnasse, which he did not tell Solange.

After a lengthy tour of the Père-Lachaise Cemetery on the opposite side of the city, Toberts finally admitted that he was bone tired.

"Poor darling man," Solange said. "I forgot how much older you are. I will take you to one of my favorite places in all of Paris for sitting and resting."

The place she had in mind was the Vert-Gallant Square at the extreme western tip of the Ile de la Cité, in the middle of the Seine. The large triangular-shaped square was actually a park, with long rows of benches along both sides separated by huge trees from the river and the rest of the city. In the middle of the square there were gardens with many flowers in bloom. They chose one of the benches and sat close together, feeling enclosed by the little green world of this quiet, peaceful setting, yet aware that they were literally surrounded by the bustling city. Through the trees they could make out one of the parapets of the Louvre.

"I like it here," Toberts said. "I'm glad we came."

"I thought you would," Solange said, resting her head on his shoulder.

After a while Toberts remembered the manuscript in his pocket and opened it on his lap at the place where they had stopped reading the night before. Solange smiled at him, understanding his need to continue the work whether she agreed with his timing or not—which was one of the things he liked best about her. Checking Bruckner's translation together, they slipped easily back into the 1880's world and language of her great-grandfather, Professor Maurice Cordier.

I first became acquainted with the young Russian woman Tatiana Kozlov on a cold, rainy evening early in May 1881. Having just alighted from a carriage still standing in the street before my humble lodgings near the Sorbonne, this fetching young woman—hardly more than a girl—appeared utterly dazed and lost, so that my heart went out to her immediately; and though the rain had soaked her clothing and drenched her dark curls, her beauty was no less obvious for the unobliging weather.

"Monsieur le Professeur Cordier?" she asked me in acceptable French, her eyes wide and somewhat fearful.

"Yes, that is who I am," I answered, and attempting to put her at ease, I invited her to step inside out of the rain where we could talk more conveniently. At first, understandably, she was quite reluctant to do so, until my mention of brewing the both of us a pot of chamomile tea, which I find relaxes me marvelously of an evening, seemed to sway her. After telling the carriage driver to wait for her, she accompanied me into my very small but adequate parlor, where, by her words of admiration for those per-

sonal items of furnishing that I have collected over the years, she proved beyond doubt her gentle breeding.

As we sat quietly sipping our tea, the lovely Tatiana Kozlov related to me in great detail the story I have set down in an earlier part of this manuscript, although some of my information was derived from other sources of which she was not at this time aware. The simplicity and sadness with which she sketched out for me these dramatic incidents nearly brought tears to my eyes. The Narodnaya Volya organization of St. Petersburg was of course no stranger to me, as I had corresponded regularly with members of its executive committee for several years. And Tatiana was indeed surprised to learn that I had known of her brother Ilya Kozlov by reputation. The story of the theft and secret transport of the jewels formerly belonging to Princess Yurievskaya was nearly unbelievable to me, I must admit, until this raven-haired young angel slipped a small velvet bag from beneath her petticoats and handed it to me, telling me to open it. When I did so, the brilliance of the gems inside the velvet dazzled my eyes, and upon pouring out into my palm only a small portion of the fabulous jewelry, I knew immediately, even with only the understanding of an amateur, that the contents of the bag would be worth many millions of francs, probably tens of millions.

For a moment I could not speak, and then my words rushed and ran together, so eager was I to learn every detail of the bold action. Tatiana, for her part, seemed strangely subdued and apart from both the gems and the situation in which she found herself—rightly assuming, as I imagined, that none of this had much to do with her, that she was merely an unfortunate vehicle by which others carried out their grandiose plans. I sympathized with her and felt somewhat disgusted with her at the same time, the latter because of her utter indifference to the radical socialist aspirations of her brother and his friends and, indeed, of myself. And I determined at that moment to do everything in my power to bring about a change in this young lady's thinking by directly involving her in the scheme in connection with which, until now, she had been only an innocent bystander. And the way to accomplish *that end, I quickly saw, would be through the power of love and devotion—if not to a cause, then to an individual with a cause. My choice for her partner in this adventure would be my young and fiery radical friend, M. Alain Picot.*

It was, however, nearly a fortnight before I could arrange this happy meeting of the two young people— again, in my own poor chambers. The occasion was Alain's need to practice before an audience the speech he had written and was to deliver soon to one of the ubiquitous socialist groups to which he belonged. I asked Tatiana to come and serve as hostess. Alain's rhetoric, alas, was far less enjoyable than the meal; nevertheless, even a blind man could have seen that Alain and Tatiana, outwardly so different, were, in fact, fascinated with each other from the beginning.

"At which trade do you earn your living, Monsieur Picot?" Tatiana asked him.

Alain shrugged. "It is not important work, Mademoiselle Kozlov. I am a worker in iron and copper, a fashioner and riveter of metals for structures both large and small."

"Rather large, at the moment," I added, and when Tatiana appeared puzzled I went on to explain. "One of the largest and most complex wastes of the people's resources since the extravagances of the Louis regimes. You see, my dear, Alain is very good at what he does, which is why he was selected by the celebrated Alsatian sculptor, M. Auguste Bartholdi, to participate in the erection of a colossal statue to be called, I believe, 'Liberty Enlightening the World.' This statue, to be donated to the people of the United States of America upon its completion—though no one can say when that will be—has already cost the poor people of France a million francs, and the final cost may be half again as much. Think of the waste! Think of the ways in which that sum could have been spent for the betterment of mankind, instead of the personal glorification of one Alsatian. Eh, Alain? But of course you do not agree with me."

"Not completely, Monsieur le Professeur. Mademoiselle," Alain said, turning again toward the young girl from whom he had not been able to take his eyes all eve-

ning, "*would you be so kind as to tell us a little about yourself?*"

Blushing prettily, Tatiana looked at me as if to ask permission, and I nodded. "*Monsieur Picot must know all about it, Tatiana, since he is ultimately to be an integral part of the plan, although he is not yet aware of this.*"

Tatiana then explained to Alain about her former position as lady-in-waiting and wardrobe mistress to Princess Yurievskaya, to whom she was now more than anything else a companion and friend in a strange land. Tatiana hesitated, then went on to explain about the jewels and how they had come to be in her possession.

"*And where are they now?*" *Alain asked, sensibly enough.*

I left the room and fetched the jewels in their velvet bag from a small sealed compartment at the back of my wardrobe closet. We had decided upon Tatiana's first visit that it was much too dangerous for her to keep the gems herself, and we could trust no one else. Reluctantly, I had accepted the awesome responsibility.

Alain's reaction, upon seeing the jewels laid out in all their splendor, was much the same as mine had been. When he had recovered his power of speech, he inquired of me how he was to become involved with these marvelously valuable stones.

"*I have been doing a great deal of thinking since Mademoiselle Kozlov appeared at my doorstep,*" *I told them.* "*The original plan, as constructed by the Narodnaya Volya executive committee, was to see that the jewels in some fashion eventually reached the United States of America, where they were to be used to recruit people to our cause. I believe that is still the best possible use of the money to be gained from sale of the gems. In any case, Tatiana has informed me that Princess Yurievskaya went immediately to the French police upon discovery that a large portion of her wealth was missing. Of course, she probably assumed that the jewels had been stolen before she departed from Russia, which is fortunate since, otherwise, dear Tatiana would most certainly be under some suspicion. However, because the authorities are aware of the jewels and doubtless have a more or less complete description of them, it would be unwise and perhaps impossible to dispose of them anywhere in Europe. Which, again, argues well for their transport to the New World."*

"Yes, but I still do not see how I am involved," Alain said impatiently.

I smiled at him. "The statue, of course. Think, Alain —when the statue is completed and the time arrives to ship it to New York City, it will have to be disassembled and carefully crated for shipment, and you will certainly be present for that operation. The crates will not be subject to any customs check whatsoever, since their contents will be well-known worldwide. And then, Alain, you will go to America yourself, and at some appropriate time you will retrieve the jewels, arrange for their sale at the best possible price, and will then begin to do what you have done so well here in Paris—you will form a radical socialist organization so powerful and well-financed that it will startle the entire world! Think of it, Alain—you will head that organization. It is the opportunity of a lifetime, my young friend—virgin territory, yours nearly for the asking. How I envy you!"

Alain, thinking about all that I had said, slowly poured the gems back into the velvet bag. "They take up but a small space," he marveled. "They could be sealed inside a tiny iron box that could easily be welded to one of the statue's supporting rods. I alone would know the purpose of the box, and since I will surely be made a foreman within the next six months or so, according to Monsieur Bartholdi's promise to me, there would be no one to question the box, no one to argue that it was not a necessary part of the bracing construction for the statue's skeleton, so carefully designed by Monsieur Eiffel, the builder of bridges."

We drank a little more wine, and Alain offered to escort Tatiana to her lodgings with the princess in an apartment at the Hotel Ravignon. I urged her to accept Alain's offer, which she eventually did. They seemed terribly pleased that they were able to accommodate an old man's wishes in this way.

TAKING LIBERTY

After they had gone, I made several entries in my journal to remind me in the future of our conversation. I determined on the spot to keep an accurate, if sporadic, record of all important or illuminating aspects of our project as it progressed, and occasionally to dramatize scenes of which I had no firsthand knowledge. It seemed ironic that the vehicle leading to our success was to be the colossal bourgeois statue called, by its creator, the rather too self-important sculptor Frédéric Auguste Bartholdi, "La Liberté Eclairant le Monde"—"Liberty Enlightening the World."

6 May 1881

The carriage in which Alain Picot had brought Tatiana Kozlov back to her lodgings from the meeting at Professor Cordier's that evening drew up before the Hotel Ravignon. Alain took Tatiana's hand and helped her from the carriage. At the door of the hotel they stood close together, whispering for fear the bored driver would hear them, though what they said made very little sense.

"I . . . I feel that I have known you a long time," Alain said. "You are so very lovely—I think that you are a princess."

"Thank you, monsieur. You may kiss me now if you wish."

Alain was thankful for the dark so that she could not see him blush. "I . . . am sorry, mademoiselle, for being so clumsy. I have never kissed a girl before."

Tatiana smiled and boldly touched his arm. "But you are so handsome, Alain. Surely you must have had many girls, as many as you wanted."

"My free time is spent working for the cause. I have had no time for girls in my life."

"And now?" Tatiana asked coquettishly.

Alain bent forward and brushed his lips very properly against her cheek. "May I see you again, Mademoiselle Kozlov?"

"Only if you call me by my Christian name."

"Tatiana, then. Will you accompany me to Père-Lachaise Cemetery on 28 May? Afterward we shall eat supper at a café and celebrate our good fortune."

281

Tatiana seemed puzzled. "A cemetery is good fortune in your country?"

"No, silly girl. Sympathizers from all over Paris plan to gather at the cemetery to pay their respects to the loyal dead of the Paris Commune fighting. Our meeting tonight was good fortune—don't you think so?"

Tatiana was silent for a moment, not because she did not know the answer, but because the intensity of her emotion kept her from speaking. "Yes, dear Alain, I do think so," she said eventually.

This time Alain had no trouble finding her lips.

10 June 1881

At my invitation, the three of us—Alain, Tatiana, and myself—met late in the afternoon at the southern end of the Pont Saint-Michel and together walked slowly downstream along the bank of the river. I discussed the lecture I had just completed at the Sorbonne, which was doubtless dull fare for the two young lovers, but I had sad news to deliver later and my mind refused to invent pleasant trivialities. Tatiana discussed her day serving the increasingly irritable Princess Yurievskaya, while Alain gave us a verbal portrait of M. Eiffel's iron skeleton for the gigantic statue rising in the courtyard of the largest atelier in Paris, that of Gaget, Gauthier & Cie. at 25 Rue de Chazelles, near the Arc de Triomphe.

Near the Rond Point we stopped to watch the various Punch and Judy shows, each competing more industriously for our attention than the last. Later we chose a pleasant café where I insisted on treating us all to a light supper of eels in a cheese pie. It was here that I chose, wisely or not, as we sat watching the happy citizens of Paris stream past our table, to deliver my sad news.

"Dear little Tatiana," I said, reaching for her delicate hand across the table, "I have had word from my contacts in St. Petersburg . . . about your brother, Ilya Kozlov."

Her eyes, always large, grew saucer-sized and overflowed with fear. "What is it? What has happened to him?"

"I am sorry to be the bearer of these tidings, Tatiana, but it cannot be helped. It has been over two months ago

now—he was arrested at the railroad station following your departure, was found to have been using forged identity cards, and was hanged in public two days later. You cannot know how difficult this is for me."

Alain jumped up and slammed the table with his fist. *"Czarist butchers!"* he shouted.

"I must go to St. Petersburg," Tatiana said, her eyes glazed and staring. *"I must go to my brother Ilya."*

"But he is gone, Tatiana," I said, *"dead and buried these two months. There is nothing you or anyone can do for him now, except to pray that his soul finds peace. In any event, you must never return to Russia—the Czar's secret police would undoubtedly consider you an accomplice of your brother's and would at the very least imprison you."*

Tatiana sat playing with her wineglass, staring at the crimson liquid as though it were blood, and then asked to be taken to her lodgings. I nodded to Alain, who rose on cue and escorted her away from the table. As he passed me, I slipped a twenty-franc gold coin into his palm, which, as I knew, his pride made him resent but which he accepted nonetheless. I ordered a liqueur and continued to sit at the café table, contemplating how my life had taken a melodramatic turn, much as in M. Zola's book Nana, published to much acclaim last year. I must be getting old and sentimental.

21 June 1881

The odd sights to be seen in the workshops at 25 Rue de Chazelles were beginning to draw larger crowds of Parisians than any circus sideshow ever did. All day long now the men and boys who worked on the huge, disjointed parts of the statue were shouting to each other happily above the constant din of the carpenters, copper workers, and bricklayers, who were busy in the courtyard of the studios constructing a hundred-foot-square brick and concrete block on which the completed statue would ultimately stand.

Alain had been promising to show Tatiana the statue for some time. Having asked permission to bring her, he took Tatiana by the hand and led her into the dusty,

283

noisy interior of the cavernous atelier, which had been enlarged by the owners just to accommodate the statue. Her eyes grew wide with wonder at the marvelous, unearthly things she saw, and she had to ask Alain to explain everything to her.

"It must look frightening to you," he said. "The first part we completed was the arm and torch, which Monsieur Bartholdi had us crate in about twenty parts and send to the Philadelphia Exposition a little over five years ago, in 1876. After the Exposition the arm and torch were moved to Madison Square in New York City, where they remain to this day. Sooner or later they will be brought back to Paris to rejoin the rest of Liberty; but for the time being Monsieur Bartholdi says the exhibit may influence some of the thousands of visitors—who climb through the arm on a ladder to the torch—to contribute to the fund for construction of the pedestal."

"But if the Americans do not contribute enough to build the pedestal?" Tatiana asked.

"Do not even suggest such a thing—Monsieur Bartholdi acts completely confident, but I believe he is quite worried. If the Americans do not raise the money to construct the pedestal on Bedloe's Island in the harbor of New York City, we will keep Liberty in Paris."

"And France is paying the total cost of the statue itself?"

"The *people* of France, Tatiana, not the government. All the money has not yet been raised, but Monsieur Bartholdi is confident it will become available soon."

Tatiana looked around the huge shops and shook her head in amazement. "What am I seeing, Alain? All those wooden forms, plaster pieces with wires running to other plaster pieces—it seems like a giant's toy puzzle."

Alain laughed. "I am sure it must. That part over there that looks like four crooked tunnels is Liberty's left hand, which will one day be cupped around a tablet of law bearing the Roman numerals for the date July 4, 1776. That is the date of independence for the Americans."

The giant, curved fingers of the statue, lying off in one corner by themselves, were each taller than a man; the thumbnail itself was one-third of a meter long. In another part of the workshop was a foot, so huge that it dwarfed the men in dusty smocks who scurried about the studio, measuring with wires, hammering copper onto wooden forms, chipping away the initial plaster casts.

"But I still do not understand," Tatiana said, "how you or Monsieur Bartholdi or anyone could possibly know what the statue will look like when it is assembled from all these bits and pieces."

Alain smiled. "I could tell you, but perhaps it would be better if the sculptor and creator himself explained it to you." And he led her by the hand toward a scaffolding upon which several men stood; they were using carpentry and metal-working tools on a section of the statue that Alain said was a single layer of one of the folds in Liberty's copper gown. One of the men looked up from a stack of drawings and notations clipped on a board in his hand and, smiling down at Alain, descended from the scaffolding. He was dressed like all the other workmen in a long, dusty smock; his full beard was gray from the plaster dust swirling through the air, and when Alain introduced him to Tatiana he smiled even wider and kissed her hand.

"Monsieur Picot has told me about you, Mademoiselle Kozlov," M. Bartholdi said, for it was he who held her hand. "But he failed to adequately describe your beauty. Come, let me show you some of the wonderful things taking place within and outside the walls."

Bartholdi led them around the workshop, pointing out where various unrecognizable pieces of copper would fit into the general pattern of the finished statue. He took Tatiana to a raised place in the center of the largest part of the studio and showed her the original clay model of "Liberty Enlightening the World." It was one and a quarter meters high.

"We enlarged this model three times in plaster," Bartholdi said. "First to nearly three meters, then to about eleven meters, and finally four times again to the full size of the projected completed statue. We divided the eleven-meter model into about three hundred sections, measured each point of each section at least three times, and gradually constructed the parts of the full-size plaster model in this way. We constructed intricate wooden frames over the plaster, following each tiny bend and curve of Liberty's features, and as you can see, we are still working on the wooden frames for some parts of her gown. The next step was to hammer very thin sheets of pure copper over the wooden forms, then gradually work the copper smooth and perfect. As each piece of copper is completed, we store it outside in the courtyard—come, I will show you."

Bartholdi led Alain and Tatiana outside where, beside the brick and concrete pedestal for the statue's framework, there were piles of irregularly shaped burnished metal. "It doesn't look like much at the moment, of course, but soon it will be magnificent!" he said confidently. "Come inspect the head and shoulders with me—we exhibited Liberty's head at the 1878 Paris Exposition and, I must say, it was the most spectacular attraction of the show."

Because of its colossal size Tatiana had not even recognized the head of the statue rising magnificently off in a corner of the courtyard. Bartholdi led them through a door in the temporary base upon which the head rested and up a ladder inside to the cavernous interior room of the crown. "At times during the Exposition no less than forty persons were able to stand inside her head at once, looking out through the twenty-five windows at their friends on the ground below," he said proudly. "Imagine what it will be like, when Liberty stands her full height atop a proper pedestal in the entrance to New York Harbor, to look out these same windows and view the world!"

25

"HAVE YOU EVER SEEN *our* Statue of Liberty?" Solange asked Toberts, interrupting their study of her great-grandfather's manuscript.

"What do you mean?" Toberts asked her.

Solange playfully snapped her fingers in front of Toberts's face. "I simply asked whether you knew Paris has her own Liberty. Back in 1883 Monsieur Bartholdi offered us his original eleven-meter plaster working model of Liberty if someone wanted to cast a statue in bronze for the city of Paris. I suppose the money was raised easily enough, and now we have a statue, too. Would you like to see it?"

"Sure," Toberts said, removing his glasses and rubbing his eyes. "I need a rest anyway."

They walked to the nearest river landing and boarded a *bateau-mouche*. At a landing near the Grenelle Bridge they left the boat and walked out to the little island half-way across. "It's called *Allée des Cygnes*," Solange said. "Swans' Walk." There on a point of land stood the quarter-scale version of perhaps the most famous statue in the world—though in its reduced size it seemed less than properly significant, Toberts thought, remembering all the times he had flown past the full-size statue in New York Harbor and had felt a twinge of pride or patriotism or some other indescribable emotion.

"You don't like it, do you?" Solange said, reading the expression on his face.

"No, no . . . it isn't that," Toberts said, but he found that he could not explain his mood.

Leaving the statue they found a metro station and caught the next train to Place Charles de Gaulle where, through the Arc de Triomphe, they watched the sun set behind the huge triangular C.N.I.T. building. Hand in hand they wandered back toward the center of Paris along the Champs Elysées. They stopped in at a small restaurant that neither of them had ever heard of. It appeared uncrowded, and they soon discovered why there were not more customers—the prices were high and the food was awful, served lukewarm by the slowest and most supercilious waiters on earth.

After the poor meal they continued walking down the Champs, and eventually they came to the quieter section of the avenue that ended at the Place de la Concorde. Toberts looked across the wide plaza toward the American Embassy, his eyes automatically tracking up to the fourth floor although, where his office was, there were no windows.

"Planning to do a little office work tonight?" Solange asked him.

Toberts shook his head. "I would invite you up to see where I spend my days, but I can't. You know why."

"Yes," she said, gripping his hand a little tighter. "I know why."

"Let's go back to the hotel," he said suddenly. "I want to read a bit more of Professor Cordier's manuscript."

"That is not what I would prefer to do," Solange said coyly, "but if you insist . . ."

Toberts smiled at her. "Work before pleasure. Didn't your mother teach you anything?"

"Oh, yes. She taught me that to please a man you must . . . please him, which means doing what *he* wants. And that to please yourself you must do what *you* want. Which means there is no possible way two people can be happy together."

"I don't believe that," Toberts said.

She considered it a moment. "Neither do I."

They returned to their hotel room, undressed, and crawled under the covers with the manuscript, resuming —where Toberts had turned down the corner of a page —the documented lives and pursuits of Alain Picot, Tatiana Kozlov, and Professor Maurice Cordier.

"You look like an owl," Solange said as Toberts pushed the heavy horn-rimmed glasses up on his nose.

He looked at her over the top rim of the glasses, his nose less than an inch from her delicate pink nipple, and sighed. "You drive me wild," he said, and turned back to the manuscript in time to avoid the look of disappointment on her face.

24 October 1881

On this sunny, crisp autumn day fifty distinguished gentlemen in frock coats and top hats stood silently in the courtyard of 25 Rue de Chazelles while Levi P. Morton, American envoy to France, slowly raised a large hammer and drove the first rivet into the first piece of the copper skin to be mounted to the iron framework—the big toe of Liberty's left foot. Morton spoke with feeling about the statue and the United States' preparations to accept it.

"May the statue stand at the entrance of the great harbor of the New World," he said, "as an illuminated emblem of the friendship between the two republics which will last for all time."

Reporters from *Le Petit Journal* dutifully recorded his words, while photographers went out into the street to take photographs that would adequately show off the name of the newspaper on its offices nearby.

2 June 1883

"Princess Yurievskaya asked about you the other day," Tatiana said to Alain as they walked close together along the boulevards toward Montmartre.

"What did she say about me?" Alain asked, frowning slightly. He did not altogether trust the princess or her views, since he considered her as much a part of Russian nobility as the czar had been. And now word was coming out of St. Petersburg that her assassinated husband's son, Alexander III, had instigated massive pogroms against the peasants, particularly the Jews.

"She thinks that I ought to know more about you—which means that she thinks she should know more about you. But she understands about two people, such as we, being in love and loving each other despite the problems. Really, she is quite sympathetic."

Alain shrugged. "It doesn't matter to me very much whether she is sympathetic or not. Is she still very depressed about the loss of her jewels?"

"Not often. Occasionally she says something, but I think she has finally accepted the fact that she will never see the gems again. From what she has told me of her conversations with the prefect of police, they are amazed that no one has been caught trying to smuggle or sell the jewels by now. In any case, I believe the princess will be leaving Paris shortly, perhaps to take up residence in the south of France."

As they sauntered along the Boulevard des Italiens, the overhead rings of gas lights threw their shadows at odd angles on the broad sidewalks lined with overhanging trees. They passed many little shops and cafes, and from many of the street lamp poles hung gaily colored posters advertising this or that cabaret or theater. Some of the posters were boldly signed by their creators—Toulouse-Lautrec, Bonnard, Chéret, occasionally Pissarro and Degas and other famous, or beginning to be famous, Impressionist painters.

"The statue is going well," Alain said. "We have so many visitors now that we can hardly get our work done, but still Monsieur Bartholdi is reluctant to turn them away. His pride will yet be our undoing, I am afraid."

"And when do you expect to complete her?" Tatiana asked. She had taken up the habit of Alain and the other workmen of referring to Liberty as though she were a real woman—which, in a way, she was, her features having been modeled quite closely on those of Bartholdi's mother.

"I am not sure," Alain answered. "There is some talk that there is no work being done on the pedestal for her in New York, and that, in fact, even the ground has not yet been prepared. They say there is a lack of interest on the part of the American people, and therefore a lack of funds."

Later, on the Boulevard Montmartre, the two young people joined a crowd of dancers in an open square. Alain held Tatiana as close as he dared and breathed in her perfume. "If Princess Yurievskaya does leave Paris to take up residence in Nice, as you said she might, what would you do?" he asked her.

She looked up at him and, smiling, shook her head. "What do you think, you madman? I would stay here, in Paris, because I love you with all my heart and could not bear to be parted from you. Didn't you know that?"

Alain's face was grim. "You know what sort of life I lead, the constant possibility of trouble, of arrest by the police. You know that I can offer you almost nothing in the way of a stable home life, a place to raise a family—"

"Sh-h-h!" Tatiana said, placing her finger against his lips. "For now, we need not talk of marriage—I can see that it pains you, and it is my only wish to make you happy. If the princess departs, I shall find a job of some kind to support myself. As a seamstress, perhaps—I used to be a rather good one, did you know that? Things will work themselves out in the end, dear Alain. We must be content in the knowledge that we belong to each other, forever, and that our love will never die."

18 May 1884

As the last rivet was driven into the torch's copper flame, the workmen at 25 Rue de Chazelles let out an enormous cheer and literally danced with each other around the completed statue. Auguste Bartholdi stood off to one side and gazed up at his creation, thankful that nothing had prevented him, during all these years, from seeing its completion. A few days later a prominent American businessman in Paris, Henry F. Gillig, gave a lavish banquet in Bartholdi's honor, which was attended by many well-known French and American diplomats and citizens of Paris, as well as contingents of the press. When it was suggested that Paris, too, should have its own statue of "Liberty Enlightening the World," Bartholdi offered his quarter-scale plaster studio model to be cast in bronze. Later, when he heard about Bartholdi's generous offer, Alain Picot was very happy.

LAWRENCE DUNNING

11 June 1884
Levi Morton, U.S. envoy to France, gave another banquet in honor of the completion of the statue, at which Bartholdi was praised for having given ten years of his life to this single idea. Among the dinner guests were the premier of France, Jules Ferry, and Vice-Admiral Peyron of the French Navy, who solved one of M. Bartholdi's last problems concerning the statue by offering to transport it to New York aboard the French naval vessel *Isere*.

4 July 1884
Although the presentation ceremony was not scheduled to begin until eleven o'clock, at Alain's suggestion he, Tatiana, and I appeared at the foot of the completed Liberty in the courtyard of Gaget, Gauthier & Cie. early that morning and were thus able to secure a seat on one of the many benches that had been set up before the large ceremonial platform.

Eventually, after the band had played a suitable number of stirring musical tributes, including the national anthems of both the United States and France, Count Ferdinand de Lesseps, builder of the Suez Canal and present chairman of the Franco-American Union, rose from his place on the platform and gave a ringing tribute to the work of Bartholdi and the vision and perseverance of all those involved in the massive undertaking. With the American envoy, Levi Morton, standing beside him, Count de Lesseps then officially presented "Liberty Enlightening the World" to the United States of America. A great cheer went up from the assembled dignitaries as well as the hundreds of common workmen standing in the street outside the courtyard. It was somewhat ironic that, although no one present knew it at the time, it was to be more than two years before the statue stood erect and in place in New York Harbor.

As M. Bartholdi led a large group of guests up inside the statue through a door in the sole of Liberty's sandal, a question occurred to me that I had been meaning to have answered for some time, and leaning out to speak across Tatiana's fair bosom, I caught Alain's attention.

"Yes, Professor Cordier?"

"What will happen now—in the coming days and weeks?"

"The statue will remain on exhibition for several months, probably—Monsieur Bartholdi says the funds for the American pedestal project have not yet been sufficiently subscribed. Then we shall dismantle the statue piece by piece, crate the pieces individually, and put them on the steamship for America."

I motioned to Alain and he followed me away from the benches, out of Tatiana's range of hearing. "And have you decided where the jewels are to be secreted, and when?"

He glanced about us furtively. "I have. I shall choose my opportunity carefully before the dismantling and crating begins. Presently I shall seal the gems inside a small metal box that I have already fashioned from scraps. Since the crates will probably be sealed immediately upon being filled, I plan to go inside the statue on one of my many routine inspections. On the pretext of taking measurements for the crating, I shall crawl out on the temporary interior scaffolding and fasten the box by welding it to an iron strut that I have already selected, a strut beneath the left breast and toward the cavity made by the tablet of law—which is, I might add, conveniently far enough away from the central staircase up through the statue that no one going up or down would ever notice the box. In fact, once in place I expect the box full of gems to look remarkably like a genuine part of the ironwork, strengthening that particular joint in the skeleton. I am certain no one, with the possible exception of Monsieur Eiffel or Monsieur Bartholdi, would ever suspect a thing."

We returned to Tatiana, who was beginning to look worried at our absence. Alain took her hand and kissed it gallantly, saying, "This is indeed a glorious day. And in honor of the occasion, Tatiana and I have something to tell you, Monsieur le Professeur." He looked down into her glistening eyes. "Tatiana and I plan to be married, exactly one month from today. We would both like you to be present for the ceremonies, and Tatiana has a most important question for you."

293

"Yes, I do," Tatiana said. "Would you, dear Professor Cordier, act in my parents' stead and officially give me away to Alain?"

I looked at the two young and handsome people so obviously in love, and though I had grave misgivings about such a move as marriage for a radical and politically active person like Alain, whose life was necessarily filled with extraordinary uncertainties and danger, I gave my consent. After all, what real choice did I have in the face of Cupid's barrage of arrows? None whatsoever.

29 November 1884

On this cold winter day a slow-moving old gentleman with white hair, accompanied by his daughter and grand-daughter, visited the statue of "Liberty Enlightening the World." Although he was eighty-two years old and in frail health, he would have climbed to the very top of the colossal monument if his daughter had not stopped him. Still playing the role of proud parent, Auguste Bartholdi presented the old man in the frock coat with a suitably inscribed fragment of Liberty's copper skin. The old man, a renowned French author, was one of the last to see the statue erect and in place in Paris. His name was Victor Hugo.

3 February 1885

Late on this bitterly cold night Alain Picot let himself into the atelier of Gaget, Gauthier & Cie. with his passkey and lit a single gas lamp. The huge studio was eerie in the inadequate fluttering light; Picot could imagine less pragmatic individuals than he being frightened of ghosts in a place such as this. And even he was not eager to spend more time here than necessary.

The statue was gone from the courtyard. In its place, and throughout the interior studio, were huge, many-shaped wooden crates filled with the dismantled pieces of the statue and its steel skeleton. To help with the construction and reassembly of the statue at its final resting place in New York Harbor, Bartholdi himself had written a number or figure on each individual packing crate and had also noted on a large sheet of paper how each piece fit together with its adjoining pieces. Since Picot had not been present for most of the actual crating and marking, he had come here tonight to find the paper "key" to the Liberty puzzle.

The workshop was still filled with odd pieces of lumber, crating screws and nails, copper, iron strapping, and even plaster, and blueprints and other papers lay strewn about many of the working spaces. Picot knew, though, that Bartholdi was a methodical man—who else would have designed a statue that ultimately required more than twenty-seven thousand precise measurements?—and this led Picot to believe that the "key" would be kept in a rather more special place. Surely he hasn't taken it home with him, Picot thought, worrying that, in fact, that had been the case.

But luck was with him this evening. He found the intricately notated and diagramed sheet of paper in an unlocked cabinet in the partitioned cubicle Bartholdi sometimes used as a little office. Picot brought the paper out under the flame and searched eagerly over the details for the one joint in that innumerable maze of joints in Liberty's skeleton that held more than mere iron and steel and copper and the necessary rivets. And when he located the place on Bartholdi's list where he had secreted the metal box of jewels, he carefully wrote down the corresponding number of the crate in which it was packed: 183. Of all the 214 crates it had taken to pack Liberty's skin and bones, only one now meant anything at all to him.

15 May 1885

"But of course we both want you to come, Professor Cordier," Alain and Tatiana had said earlier, which is why, although I felt very much in the way, I had accompanied the young married lovers to the huge Gare de l'Ouest to see Alain off on the night train to Le Havre. Tomorrow he would board a steamship for the United States of America, and it would have been ridiculous for me to have denied that I envied him greatly.

"Where is your famous statue now?" I asked him as we stood together waiting for the dispatcher's signal to board the train.

LAWRENCE DUNNING

"At Rouen, since ten days ago. That is where the Isere is tied up. I understand it may take another week before Liberty is entirely loaded into the hold."

"Then you should have no trouble arriving in New York before her."

"Unless the ship I am on capsizes," Alain said with a sigh, then laughed to let Tatiana know he was joking. But it was not the sort of joke his bride of nine months wished to hear at the moment.

"Please don't tease me in that horrible way," she begged him. *"I can hardly bear to think of being without you, even for a little while. Tell me again how long it will be before we are together again."*

Alain smiled and put his arm around her shoulders. *"If all goes well, a very few months—seven or eight at the most. I must not only retrieve the jewels from their hiding place, but also find a buyer and make the transaction. Another month, say, to organize the nucleus of a working group to further our ideals. I will either return to Paris or send money for you to join me in America. Which reminds me, Monsieur le Professeur—thank you again, more than words can tell, for lending me part of the steamship fare. I shall repay you at my earliest convenience, have no fear!"*

"Nonsense," I said. *"Consider it a gift for a worthy cause. And now I shall say good-bye, my dear Alain, and let you two have a moment alone."*

We shook hands heartily, and I must admit there were tears in my eyes as I moved away from them down the platform. Tatiana hung onto his arm until the last minute, then released him and covered her mouth with her gloved hand. He waved from the step into the compartment, and both Tatiana and I waved helplessly as the train swallowed him up. Tatiana was crying openly now. *"Oh, Professor Cordier!"* she sobbed. *"I have the most awful feeling that I shall never see my dearest Alain again. I cannot bear the thought."*

I put my arm across her delicate shoulders, as Alain had done earlier, and tried to comfort her as best I could. *"Alain is a bold and resourceful young man,"* I told her. *"I am certain he will do what he must in good speed and

296

will return to you before you have had time to miss him properly."

"Oh, I do hope so," Tatiana said, staring where the tracks led out across the nighttime French countryside as though she might still be able to see the smoke from the train or hear its lonely whistle.

There was an obvious breaking point in the manuscript here, and Toberts laid it aside on the bed and took off his glasses. "What do you think so far, Solange?" he asked her, rubbing his eyes with his knuckles.

She turned toward him in the bed and put her hand gently against the back of his neck. "I think it a beautiful and very sad love story, and I see great similarity here and there between us—you and I—and the two young lovers Alain and Tatiana."

"How so? I fail to see the connection."

"But think about it a moment. Both you and Alain are all business—you both have your causes that assume more importance in your lives than anything else ever could. And then, on the sidelines, there are these two pathetically weak women—Tatiana and I—who can hardly function at all because of our love for this lout of a man who only thinks about his 'cause,' his ultimate importance in the world of political affairs."

"Ah, but you are missing one important point, I believe, in your little analogy."

"And what is that, pray tell me?"

"Simply that I, unlike poor Alain, am not planning to go anywhere in the near future," he said, smiling as though he had won a point in a college debate.

Frowning, Solange rubbed Toberts's shoulder for a while, then reached across his chest and turned out the light. "Hold me, please, very close," she whispered, and he felt her comfortable body tremble in his arms.

26

EARLY THE NEXT MORNING, Sunday, the first light of dawn slipping past the edges of the worn hotel curtains woke Toberts and he could not go back to sleep. After tossing in bed a quarter of an hour, he crept out from the covers, trying not to wake Solange, and went to the window. Naked, shivering slightly, he stood for a while gazing out at the slumbering city of Paris. The rooftops were all pink and purple, there were flowers hanging in baskets from almost every conceivable place where a basket could be hung, and he knew that it was going to be a beautiful, sunny June day.

"Is it time to get up so soon?" Solange's sleepy voice asked from behind him.

He watched with pleasure as she stretched her slender arms toward the ceiling and yawned. "Only if you want to," he said. "It's Sunday, remember?"

"Yes, I remember . . . vaguely. Time seems to have slowed down in some lovely way for me. Does that ever happen to you?"

He shrugged and came over to stand by the bed. "I've never had much luck with mystical experiences of any kind."

"And what about erotic experiences, especially in the morning?" she asked him, half rising in bed and staring closely at his penis.

"What do you mean?"

"Breakfast!" she cried, and giggling like a schoolgirl, she took him into her mouth and bathed his hardness with the warm slippery juices of her tongue.

They made love wildly, dozed off for a while, and awoke ravenously hungry. "What does one do for a very special

298

Sunday morning breakfast in Paris?" Toberts asked her, and seeing the look on her face added, "I mean, besides that lovely, lovely thing you did just now."

"Ah, *food*," she said. "On a beautiful Sunday morning the best place in Paris for café au lait and croissants is the Dôme. Do you know it?"

"By reputation," Toberts said.

They dressed and left the hotel, deciding to walk to the cafe. The terrace of the Dôme was already beginning to be crowded, but they managed to find a table set back from the street and out of the main bustle of the place. Their order was slow in coming, but they didn't mind because it was so pleasant sitting out there in the early morning sun, smiling fatuously at each other because of their good fortune at being in love. The only thing that Toberts felt he lacked at the moment was a Sunday newspaper, which Parisians somehow did without.

"I wonder what the poor people are doing this morning?" he said, knowing that Solange understood that his comment had nothing to do with economics.

After the harried waiter finally found them, they ate slowly and drank their creamed coffee like misers. Toberts took the silver cigarette case that Solange had given him from his shirt pocket, where he had gotten in the habit of carrying it, and extracted a cigarette, which he held lovingly between his lips for a moment before putting a match to it. "How long do they let you sit here?" he asked, and she assured him that as long as they bought an occasional cup of coffee, they could probably stay all day.

He took the ubiquitous manuscript from his inside jacket pocket and moved his chair around closer to Solange's so that they could both study the pages that he spread out before them. "It's almost like a mystery story," Solange commented about her great-grandfather's revelations, and Toberts nodded, thinking that it was indeed a real mystery and that, unknown to Solange, it involved real assassins and real death. But there was no use frightening her unnecessarily with specific details, he told himself, as he turned to the part of Professor Cordier's narrative where they had stopped reading the previous night.

*   *   *

Following the departure of Alain and the statue for America, my life assumed a somewhat lonely and brittle air. I discovered that my involvement with the lives and affairs of the young lovers had consumed more of my thoughts than I had been aware of, and that now, where there had been almost constant news and activity, there was merely a large void.

For what meager and sporadic news there was I remained a kind of central clearinghouse, for while I both spoke and read Russian fluently by virtue of my long-standing association with the revolutionary groups of St. Petersburg, Alain's few letters were written in street French—which Tatiana had never learned to read, although she spoke it well enough—and hers to him were written in cultured Russian, of which Alain had no knowledge at all. And so it was that I began to perform a translation service for each of them, receiving, translating, and sending on to the other these missives of love that periodically crossed the ocean separating my young friends.

I have included here copies of several of Picot's letters to me and to Tatiana, pertinent information from which I subsequently passed on to his radical friends here in Paris and also to the Narodnaya Volya remnant in St. Petersburg.

10 June 1885, New York City

Dearest Tatiana:

I promised to write to you as soon as my ship landed safely on these foreign shores. We docked day before yesterday, and since that time I have done nothing but walk the streets of New York, looking at the buildings and the people, listening to the harsh, flat language of the Americans, and trying to keep my poor head from spinning off my shoulders. Everything is so new here.

The Atlantic Ocean crossing was uneventful, fortunately, as even on the relatively calm seas my stomach longed for dry land. As we came up through what is called The Narrows between the states of New York and New Jersey, just before docking, I was surprised as I stared out from the deck where all the passengers had gone for the view. The land is green and wooded, and the countryside that rolls down to the shore is dotted with huge mansions and clean-looking farms with cows grazing peacefully near the water. On the tongue of land that is called Manhattan there are clusters of low houses that all look alike, with here and there a common church spire sprouting above them.

We passed Bedloe's Island very close by on the ship's left side and were told by some of the crew that it was the future site of the statue of "Liberty Enlightening the World." We could see that there has been a considerable amount of work done on the foundation for the statue, but the pedestal itself has risen only about three meters thus far, and as I remember from the information given to M. Bartholdi, the finished pedestal is projected at twenty-seven meters—or eighty-nine feet in the system of measurement used by the Americans.

My thoughts are of you, dearest Tatiana, in this far-away land. Oh, how I wish that you could join me here —together we could discover America! That last evening in Paris at the Gare de l'Ouest, as the train began to pull away from the station, I saw you crying and my heart nearly burst with sadness at the thought of not seeing you again for many months. I can only tell you to be brave, little Tatiana, and know that I love only you, and that I shall forever.

I must go now to find a more permanent place to live. I have stayed in a hotel two nights, but the rates are much too expensive for my limited funds. Perhaps other accommodations can be found nearby. I am attempting to stay in the area toward the southern tip of Manhattan Island because that is where the *Isere* will eventually dock and unload her precious cargo. Just how precious, no one imagines. If you have the opportunity, please tell Professor Cordier that the latest esimate for the *Isere*'s arrival is 17 June. I shall write him immediately when I have further news.

Until next time, your loving Alain.

14 July 1885, New York City
My Dear Professor Cordier:
I regret that I must greet you from the New World in this fashion, but my news is not good.

301

The *Isere* dropped anchor off a place called Sandy Hook on the night of 17 June. The engineer on the pedestal project, General Charles Stone, and others went out to the ship and conducted some sort of ceremony, after which a contingent of more than ninety vessels accompanied the *Isere* to Bedloe's Island. Journalists were allowed to go below decks and view the crates in which Liberty crossed the ocean; one of these reporters was from the French-language daily newspaper *La Ville Française,* published in New York City, from which I get a great deal of my information about current events.

Immediately a crew of men began unloading the *Isere* by means of a huge crane, transferring the crates to a lighter which, when alongside the Bedloe's Island dock, was itself unloaded onto little rail cars and the crates moved across the island to the temporary sheds, where they will remain until construction begins. The job was not completed until the third of July. The emptied *Isere* set sail for France, leaving her cargo of 214 packing crates under tin roofs beside the unfinished pedestal.

My job was to have been relatively easy—rent a small boat to take me to the island and under cover of darkness locate the crate having the correct number and remove the "excess objects." There were, I discovered, only two watchmen on the island, which should have made my job all the easier. Alas, it was not to be!

Rowing to the island from the point of land at the lower tip of Manhattan known as the Battery was not very difficult, though somewhat exhausting. I tied up away from the dock and scampered up the rocky beach with the implements I had brought with me—a silent rubber mallet, two cold chisels, a pry bar, a small kerosene lantern, and a length of stout rope in case I should have to hoist myself some height to find the proper crate. The watchmen, as I had suspected, were useless; one was asleep and the other sat smoking a pipe and warming his hands at a fire fueled by wood scraps.

The sheds were not even locked, as no one expected a need for locks. Inside, with the aid of the lantern, I quickly found crate #183 stacked atop a row of larger crates, but easily accessible. Having witnessed and even helped with the crating in M. Bartholdi's atelier in Paris, I knew exactly what to do, and in no time a portion of the steel skeleton was revealed to my eyes. But, alas, it was the wrong portion, for there was no "excess material" fastened to the joint made by the iron straps.

I knew from the moment of breaking open the crate that the pieces were wrong. They probably fit off to one side of the location I had selected. Somehow, in those last mad days of disassembling and packing and attempting to identify by symbols each and every piece of Liberty, there had been some errors—errors that will only be discovered when the skeleton and the copper skin are erected and fastened together.

I thought briefly of attempting to open crates within my reach at random, but soon saw the foolishness of such an attempt. Each moment I remained on the island increased my chances of being caught by the inept guards and sentenced to months in prison, at the least, for attempted theft. And there was, of course, no way to know what number the crate containing the metal box now carried on its side.

As I slipped back to the boat and rowed for shore I was already aware of my only alternative: Be very patient, wait until the pedestal and then the statue is constructed, and as soon as possible thereafter return to the island—perhaps with a bonafide tour group—conceal myself inside the statue somehow, and locate the box from its actual position in the interior. The job will be more difficult this way, but certainly not impossible.

One further word. The best estimate now being made by the newspapers for official dedication of the statue of "Liberty Enlightening the World" is at least one year from today and perhaps longer. Completion of the pedestal will be the main hindrance, and that only recently seems possible, thanks to the promotional efforts of a New York newspaper called the *World* and its editor, M. Pulitzer. The pedestal cost had been only half subscribed as recently as this past March; now only a few thousand dollars are lacking and receipt of those seems only a matter of time.

If you have occasion to speak with Tatiana, please tell

her that I am well and that I shall write when I have the time. During this enforced interval I shall not be lazy. I will, of course, need to find a job paying enough wages to support myself, and shall attempt to make contact with persons and/or organizations of New York City supportive of our causes.

Thanking you once again for your monetary help, I remain yours truly, Alan Picot.

21 November 1885, New York City
Dearest Tatiana:

Thank you, my darling, for your many wonderful letters; they fill me with joy and sadness at the same time, for while they bring us close together for a little while, still they remind me each time how great the distance, in both days and kilometers, that presently separate us.

The big news of late was the visit to these shores of my old friend and mentor M. Auguste Bartholdi, to see for himself the progress on the Bedloe's Island pedestal for his Liberty. While he roamed the streets of New York, I must admit that I had a most powerful urge to seek out and greet him once again, though of course I restrained myself as I knew well the probable consequences of such a foolish act.

New York City now includes one and a half million people and is growing larger every day. Fifth Avenue is a street of millionaires, lined with mansions that resemble palaces and fabulous shops that rival any we have in Paris. Although it still crosses some open fields, Broadway is said to be the world's longest street, and the Brooklyn Bridge, completed two years ago, is said to be the world's largest. In what is called the midtown area they are constructing six-story buildings with shops along the ground level and famous, expensive restaurants on the landscaped roofs. Of course, I have not seen such places for myself, but the newspapers often run pictorial sections describing their splendor for the common people.

In order to save as much money as possible I have been living on a hay barge moored in the East River with several other men, two of them my closest friends, Mick Delaney (Irish) and Pauley Santella (Italian). They are both fine fellows who have taken me under their wing, so to speak, and are showing me around New York. Pauley knows a little French, from his mother's side, and they are teaching me English. Neither has any money at all, because they have spent whatever they had on the rising socialist movement in New York, and as their time is also taken up with this very worthwhile work they cannot very well hold ordinary jobs. So I have been sharing what I have with them.

I have been offered a job as an apprentice ironworker— since I have no proof of my journeyman, and even fore- man, status in Paris—and Mick and Pauley are helping me to fill out the proper official papers that will allow me to work. It will be good to get back to what I know, even though the methods and language of the work will be strange to me.

I must sleep now, dearest Tatiana. Each night my dreams are of you, particularly in that pink dress with the white lace that I liked so well. I miss you terribly, my love. These six months have been the longest of my life; I dare not even guess how much longer we must wait to be together again, as the statue's pedestal is only half com- pleted and work has nearly stopped for the winter.

I wish only happiness for you, my sweet. No other woman could ever take your place in my heart.

Your loving Alain.

3 August 1886, New York City

My Dear Professor Cordier:

This will be but a short note as I am very tired these days, from working twelve hours a day at my job and using what time is left to pursue the organizing chores which, I must confess, are not going as well as I had hoped. Of course, the lack of money is largely responsible, and I have only myself to blame for my own personal lack of funds, but more about that later.

The pedestal for the statue on Bedloe's Island was com- pleted in April and work on the statue itself began imme- diately. Within three months the skeleton was completely erected, and on 12 July the first two pieces of Liberty's copper skin were riveted into place. About one-third of the statue is now covered with copper; the work has been slowed, again, by obvious mismarking of sections and also, I suspect, by a certain amount of warping of the metal from such long storage in the crates. There are, as I may have mentioned to you or Tatiana at one time or another, more than 600,000 rivets in the entire structure. The inaugural ceremonies for the completed statue are now scheduled to be held on 28 October, providing nothing unforeseen further slows completion.

I mentioned previously a lack of personal funds. I can hardly believe that two such good friends and loyal socialists as Mick Delaney and Pauley Santella would deliberately take money from me for their own personal gain with no thought of returning it; yet that is what has happened, it appears, for after I lent the two of them nearly everything I had been able to bank since obtaining this job, they simply disappeared from sight, and I have not seen or heard of them since. That was three weeks ago. I still believe they may turn up in a day or two with some plausible reason for their actions, for I believe them to be honorable men and true comrades. Still, I worry.

Give my love to Tatiana when next you see her, and assure her that, if all goes well, our time of separation should be growing short indeed. I have made discreet inquiries about a possible "buyer" for our wares, and have several leads in that direction. As soon as the goal is within reach I shall send for my beautiful Tatiana so that we may properly live together as man and wife.

Yours truly, Alain Picot.

**Friday, 29 October 1886, New York City
(clipping from New York World):**

"Yesterday New York celebrated Bartholdi Day, in honor of the French sculptor and principal architect of our new lady in the harbor, the statue of "Liberty Enlightening the World." Over one million of our citizens stood side by side along the five-mile route to watch the spectacular Bartholdi Day parade and to cheer mightily as the various military and civilian groups marched past displaying French and American flags. Outside our own *World* building was a sixty-foot-high evergreen-covered arch spanning the street through which the more than twenty thousand paraders passed for two and a half hours.

"Inside the reviewing stand at Madison Square were many French and American notables, including, besides Auguste Bartholdi and Count de Lesseps, President Grover Cleveland, Secretary of State Bayard, Secretary of War Endicott, Secretary of the Navy Whitney, Secretary of the Interior Lamar, and New York Governor David Hill. The parade, which crossed City Hall Park and continued down Park Row and Broadway to the Battery, was so long that the dignitaries had no time for lunch before they boarded the U.S.S. *Despatch* at West Twenty-third Street. The little ship led nearly three hundred other vessels down the North River and into the Upper Bay. Shortly the twenty-one-gun presidential salute from the warships and harbor fortifications filled the air with smoke and thunder.

"At three-fifteen in the afternoon the ceremonies at Bedloe's Island got under way with a prayer invoked by the Reverend Storrs from the speakers' platform at the foot of the pedestal within the ramparts of the eleven-pointed star. Count de Lesseps, the first orator, spoke in French and was wildly applauded. Then Senator Evarts, former secretary of state, rose to give the principal address and to present the statue to President Cleveland. During an unfortunate pause in his speech, which was taken by a spotter in the crowd to be the conclusion of the presentation, the signal was given to Bartholdi, high up in the statue's torch, to pull the cord releasing the tri-colored veil from Liberty's face. Near bedlam ensued; Senator Evarts sat down, overwhelmed by a cannon salute that lasted all of fifteen minutes, accompanied by screeching whistles, clanging bells, and wildly cheering spectators.

"Later there was a short, dignified oration by the President, who concluded with these words: 'We will not forget that Liberty has here made her home; nor shall her chosen altar be neglected. Willing votaries will constantly keep alive its fires, and these shall gleam upon the shores of our sister Republic in the East. Reflected thence, and joined with answering rays, a stream of light shall pierce the darkness of ignorance and man's oppression, until liberty enlightens the world.'

"There were other speakers, including the French envoy to the United States, W. A. LeFaivre, and Chauncey Depew, counsel for the New York Central and other railroads. Assistant Bishop Henry Potter gave the benediction, after which the President and his party again boarded the *Despatch* and headed upstream. Because of the cold rain, the scheduled fireworks display and official lighting of Liberty's torch were postponed until the first dry opportunity.

"The *World* has learned of two incidents that took place during the Bartholdi Day parade down Manhattan's avenues, one tragic and the other with its humorous aspects. The tragedy occurred when a French citizen, employed in New York City for the past several months as an iron-worker, bolted from the sidelines of the parade route directly toward the carriage conveying, among others, Auguste Bartholdi, the statue's sculptor. Apparently frightened by the man's sudden appearance, the horses reared and caused the carriage to swerve into the man, flinging him aside and inflicting massive head injuries that killed him instantly. The carriage did not slow down, and the occupants apparently were unaware of the man's approach or his death. There was no known connection between the Frenchman, whose name was Alain Picot, and Bartholdi.

"In a lighter vein, two professional pickpockets and con artists, known to the New York police and underworld as Michael (Mick) Delaney and Paolo (Pauley) Santella, were arrested immediately upon attempting to steal the wallet of a prosperous-looking gentleman who appeared to be deeply engrossed in the passing parade. The well-dressed dandy, unfortunately for the two crooks, turned out to be Detective Sergeant Rory McQuaig, who was assigned to work the parade route in plain clothes for just such purpose. Once again, the *World* offers living proof that CRIME DOES NOT PAY!"

30 September 1917

It seems more than likely that this will be my last occasion to mention the priceless jewels that once belonged to Princess Yurievskaya. In the thirty-one years since the last sad entry concerning the death of young

Alain Picot my plans to have someone else retrieve the gems from inside the statue never materialized. There are complications; for one, no one except Alain ever knew exactly where the jewels were hidden, though I have no doubt a well-organized search party could find them soon enough. Alas, I am eighty-three years old and will, I trust, soon go to my grave, though I am loath to leave this one matter unsettled. Tatiana, my blessed wife of thirty years who consented to marry me after her young husband and my friend was so stupidly killed in New York City, says that I mustn't talk as if I will be dead tomorrow, but in truth I know that I have not long to live. I regret that I must leave Tatiana to settle the affairs, but it is fortunate that she will have the aid and comfort of our two fine children, Alain and Solange, whose physical beauty has been matched by their superior intelligence and a striking ability to get along in the world.

These present papers, which I have taken the time and effort to encode from prying eyes, should keep the secret of the jewels safe for many years, possibly forever. I must, however, take that chance. Times are very bad in Russia. The assassination of Czar Nicholas II and the royal family left me singularly unmoved—he was not only a despot, he was also a stupid and ineffectual man. But the provisional government of Alexander Kerensky, formed in July, offers little alternative and no hope of success. The extremist wing of the Russian Social Democratic Party, known as Bolsheviks, are everywhere gathering strength and intend, I believe, to foment revolution and chaos. I do not know what may have happened to my correspondence with the Narodnaya Volya remnant in St. Petersburg concerning the disposition of the jewels, but the internal disruption of the country precludes my obtaining any reliable information at the moment. I can but hope that, should this correspondence eventually surface from its burial site in some Russian state archive, its discoverer will be a person worthy of the information. But that, clearly, would be too much to wish for.

Toberts took off his glasses and shuffled the papers of the manuscript, straightening the edges. "Quite a document," he said casually to Solange. They had each finished a third cup of café au lait in their pleasant corner of the Dôme terrace, and Toberts, at least, felt an urge to stretch his legs.

"Imagine!" Solange cried. "My grandmother Solange was in the manuscript—and Tatiana Kozlov was my great-grandmother. I knew we had things in common! But I never knew she had been married previously, even if it was only for a short time. I don't believe they ever mentioned that to the family, or if they did the information never filtered its way down to my level. Are you a big family man, Martin?"

"Not in the least."

"It's strange," she said, "reading about members of your family in an old manuscript that way, as though it were all happening right now. I keep thinking I ought to be able to go find a telephone and call Tatiana up and invite myself over for a visit. But she's been dead nearly forty years."

"You might try a medium," Toberts said, only half joking. It was, he thought, something that Solange might enjoy—the obverse of the staid Sorbonne intellectual.

"Would you go with me?"

He shook his head, his thoughts turning bleak. "At least, not now . . . Solange, I have a great deal of work to do, based on the information in this manuscript, and there are all sorts of people who'd like to beat us to the prize."

"By 'us' I assume you mean the United States of America?"

"Well, yes. I'm not sure who the jewels, if they still exist, legally belong to, but it damned sure isn't the KGB."

"And so you go on playing cops and robbers," Solange said gravely. "Cowboys and Indians. Those are the American terms, aren't they?"

"You know it's more important than that. Don't you?"

"Yes, I guess I do. What about us?"

"You mean now?" He saw the way she was playing with the large opal locket around her neck, carefully avoiding looking at him. "Solange, I have to go back to my wife, to Jessie, at least for a while. There are social obligations . . . the embassy expects it, the CIA expects it, *Jessie* expects it . . ."

Solange shrugged with Gallic expressiveness. "We wouldn't want to disappoint anyone, would we?"

"Just until I can turn this project over to someone else. Then I have several very serious things I want to say to you, things like—"

She put her finger across his lips. "Hush, dearest Martin. There will be time enough to say these things when you are ready. You would only confuse me now, and I expect confuse yourself. I trust you. And that is because I love you as I have never loved any man before, nor ever shall again."

Toberts slipped the folded manuscript into his jacket pocket and stood to go. "We have to check out of the hotel soon," he said. "Do you think we might . . ."

"Enjoy the bed once more before we must give it back? I think that would be a lovely thing to do."

Arm in arm they walked hurriedly back to the little hotel and up to their room, where they undressed and made love a final time with a special sweet sadness that threatened to engulf them both in a welter of tears.

27 _____

HAVING ARRANGED EARLIER A time and place to meet, Toberts and Pell Bruckner strolled casually beside the Pompidou Art Center in Beaubourg and attempted to pass for tourists.

"How was your weekend?" asked Toberts.

"Interesting," Bruckner said. "I flew to Tangier for a short holiday. There's something about Morocco this time of year . . ."

"The heat, mostly," Toberts said. "Don't you think you might have let me know you were leaving the country?"

"For God's sake, Toberts! It's like flying from D.C. to New York on the shuttle. Being out of the country was only a technicality."

"Uh-huh. That kind of technicality can get you killed."

They stopped on the street to watch a puppet show, which was soon joined by an itinerant fire-eater and a woman with three trained poodles. The small crowd of spectators, including Toberts and Bruckner, threw coins to the impromptu performers and moved on through the Plateau de Beaubourg toward other amusements. Speaking to some invisible person directly in front of him, Toberts said quietly, "You were seen in the embassy last Wednesday, Bruckner."

"Which embassy?"

"Don't be cute. You were seen making copies of a document on one of our photocopy machines. Explain, please, what the hell you were doing."

"Making a copy of the Cordier manuscript, as you must have guessed. I just had a feeling that one copy wasn't enough—I've seen too many 'only' copies lost or

312

destroyed, leaving everybody up shit creek. If you want it back you can have it."

"You bet your ass I want it back. We don't need a thing like that floating around uncontrolled."

"*Not* uncontrolled, Toberts."

"Anyway, you were supposed to stay out of the embassy, for obvious reasons."

"I know. But it was handy and I knew they'd have a copier that was a hell of a lot more secure than anything I could have found on the street."

"Don't do it again without asking me," Toberts said. "By the way, that was an extremely interesting manuscript. I agree with you that there are questions about its authenticity—at least I'd like to see corroborating proof of some of the main points."

"Yeah. The letters could have been written by almost anyone. The only thing in the manuscript that couldn't have been faked was the newspaper clipping, and it didn't have much hard data on the guy who supposedly hid the stuff—what was his name? Picot. At least, not anything definitely tying him to the Statue of Liberty when it was being built."

"That gives me an idea," Toberts said. "I'll check it out and get back to you, probably later today. If I call Sloan's number at the *Times-Weekly* and mention that our planned fishing party for this weekend has to be called off, I want you to meet me on the steps of the National Library within ten minutes. That's right across the street from the Palais-Royal gardens. You got that?"

"I've got it," Bruckner said. By the time the words were out of his mouth Toberts had disappeared.

Later that afternoon Toberts made the appropriate telephone call, and Bruckner met him in the courtyard of the Bibliothèque Nationale off the Rue de Richelieu. Toberts led him inside to the main reading room where, on a long table, he had spread out some materials about Auguste Bartholdi and the fabrication of the statue he had earlier dug out of the archives.

"What do you think?" he said, pointing to a photographic reproduction from a Paris newspaper bearing the date October 24, 1881. The photograph had been taken at the studio where Liberty was being assembled, upon the occasion of the driving of the first rivet into the big toe of Liberty's left foot. The accompanying explanatory text listed the names of those prominently shown in the photograph, including the American envoy to France, Levi Morton, holding a large hammer, Gustave Eiffel admiring his naked iron skeleton soaring into the sky, Auguste Bartholdi standing beside Morton beaming, and next to him one of the chief metalworkers, a young man in a long white smock who was identified as Alain Picot.

"I think," Bruckner said, "that we've got hold of the genuine article."

"No question about it," Toberts agreed. He looked around at the nearly empty room to make sure they wouldn't be overheard. "I was followed over here this afternoon by the KGB goon—you know the one, Ilsa's friend. And Solange said there was a guy parked near where she parks at the Sorbonne this morning, like he was waiting for her to come to work. He started to get out of his car when she did, and she ran into the building and told the guard. They're only about half a step behind us, I'm afraid."

Without blinking, Bruckner said, "You want me to dust a couple more of them?"

"Jesus Christ, Bruckner!" Toberts whispered. "We can't just go on indefinitely killing their agents without expecting some kind of massive retaliation. And I don't know about you, but I'm not ready to die yet."

"One doesn't necessarily follow from the other. I've been in business quite a while now. See? Not even a scratch." And he held out his arms toward Toberts as if for inspection.

"You've been damned lucky, and don't forget it. No, I've got a much better idea to get them off our necks for a while. We're going to have to rewrite the professor's manuscript—all the coded parts—except that we substitute gibberish. We'll split the manuscript in two; you do one half, I'll do the other. Don't worry about neatness. I know a man here in Paris who specializes in forgery."

"What about the paper? It's almost a hundred years old. And the ink."

"No problem," Toberts said. "My friend also knows how to process papers and inks to make them appear old and genuine. He once did a Seal of Napoleon for me that fooled three different art experts."

"And then?"

"Then we get Solange to return the phonied-up document to the Sorbonne library storeroom where we found the original. And if Colonel Balachov's people manage to steal or copy it, as I suspect they will, it should take them a good long while to discover that what looks like a code is simply meaningless French words."

"About Solange-baby," Bruckner said, deliberately watching Toberts's eyes. "It seems to me she must know more by now than is healthy for anybody. Even if you haven't told her anything significant about Lamplighter, you've asked her to do favors that must have seemed strange to her, and I assume she's not the kind of dumb broad you could snow with some asinine excuse."

Toberts studied Bruckner's placid expression for signs of trouble. "You're correct, to a point. Solange knows in general what Lamplighter is about and what we're after —I had to let her in on that much in order to double-check the reliability of her great-grandfather's story."

"Has she seen any part of the decoded manuscript?"

"Yes."

"All of it?"

"Yes. I told you—"

"I know, you had to."

There was an arrogant look on Bruckner's face, as though he had suspected it all along and was now considering the consequences. "Look, Bruckner," Toberts said, "I had Langley run a complete file check on her. She's as clean as anyone living in the second half of the twentieth century could be."

Bruckner smiled. "I'm sure we all hope so."

Four days later Toberts met Solange for lunch at one of the nondescript little brasseries near the Sorbonne that catered primarily to insolvent students. Before they were served, Toberts handed Solange a rolled wad of papers held together with a rubber band. "I'd appreciate it if you

315

would return these to the proper place," he said. "I don't think I ought to go back there again if I can help it."

"Of course," Solange said. She laid the papers on the table and they talked of other things, mostly of the previous weekend and how incomparably beautiful it had been for both of them. "My mother suspects something, Martin," she said. "I had to tell her that I was seeing a man and that she was not to worry about me."

"And what did you tell her about me?"

"Just that you work at the American Embassy. She wanted to know if you were married."

"And?"

"I told her that you were. Unhappily. She abruptly changed the subject."

Toberts smiled forlornly. "I'm sorry that I complicate your life."

"I'm not," Solange said, reaching for his hand across the table.

When they had finished the *choucroute* and the beer, Solange picked up the rolled papers and removed the rubber band. Toberts watched her closely but said nothing. She scanned the first few pages, the ones that had first given them a clue to her great-grandfather's coded adventure. A frown gradually clouded her face and she looked up at Toberts. "There's something wrong here, Martin. I can't exactly explain it, but I am sure the words are different."

Pretending innocence, Toberts shrugged off her doubts. "That's your great-grandfather's handwriting, isn't it?"

"As nearly as I can remember, yes. The same ink and paper, too. But still, I think this is a different set of papers."

Toberts smiled. "My God, I'm glad you're not a foreign agent! You're right, of course—those papers are different. They were done by an expert."

"You know all sorts of experts, don't you?"

"It helps."

"And now you want me to replace these papers in the Sorbonne library, just as though they were genuine?"

"That is exactly what I'm asking you to do, Solange. I know you have rigid academic beliefs about honesty, integrity, and all that. But I'm still asking you to pretend that those papers are genuine. The originals won't be destroyed—they'll merely be *elsewhere* for a while, in my safekeeping."

"I see." Solange rolled the papers as before and replaced the rubber band. "Well, I am certain you knew I would do this, for you, and of course I will. But I think you ought to know that I do not like being made a part of your secret games, that, in fact, I don't even like *your* being a part of them. I realize that I have no right to ask you to give up your way of life."

"But you do have that right. Please, Solange, just a little longer. I must finish what I have begun here, don't you see that?"

"If it does not finish you first. Be careful, Martin. I worry so about you, never knowing what danger you may be in, who may be trying to hurt you . . ."

"I'm *very* careful," Toberts said, holding her hand between both of his. He saw no reason to tell her that the short, slight man sitting at a table by himself in a corner of the brasserie had followed him here from the embassy and would doubtless follow them again when Toberts walked Solange back to the Sorbonne. At least, he thought, for the moment no one was shooting. Perhaps his luck would hold.

After reminding Bruckner a second time about returning the copy of Professor Cordier's manuscript that he had made on the embassy machine, Toberts finally collected the copy from the prearranged drop in the Bois de Boulogne and took it back to the embassy. At his desk he studied the manuscript to make sure it was complete and even compared it page by page with the original. Then he selected three random pages of the original and carried them down to the first-floor reproduction center in A Building, where, after filling out the proper form, he asked the operator on duty to run off a single copy of each page.

"Do you always use the same type and weight of paper in that photocopier?" Toberts asked him.

"Yeah, it's always the same," the operator said. "See, it

comes off these big rolls. There's a little knife inside there that cuts 'em to page size."

The operator glanced at the request form. "You're from the fourth floor of B Building?"

Toberts nodded.

"How come you don't use the photocopier up there? It'd be a lot handier for you."

"It was, ah, shut down for maintenance, at least a while ago."

"Oh, I see. Well, here's your copies, and here's the originals."

"Thank you," Toberts said.

He took the papers back to his office and compared the new copies with the copies Bruckner had given him. The paper stock was slightly different; that from the machine downstairs where Mme. Joubert had said she had seen Bruckner making copies was slicker and thinner. There were also slightly different markings in the photographic reproductions themselves, as each individual photocopier produces its own "signature" of imperfections. There was no doubt about it—Bruckner had made at least one additional copy of the original manuscript, or a copy of the first copy, on another machine, and had given Toberts the second copy by mistake or, what was more likely, hadn't thought about the possibility that Toberts might check it against the output from the embassy machine. Bruckner, of course, would deny the whole thing.

He struck a match and touched the flame to a corner of the first page of Bruckner's copy, holding it over the wastebasket until the ashes floated down and disintegrated in little piles of carbon. One by one he burned all the pages, including the three extras he had made from the original. As the final page turned crisp and brown, then black, Stanley poked his head in the doorway and sniffed the air. "We smelled something burning," he said, turning up his nose and thus raising his owlish glasses. "What on earth are you doing in here?"

"Burning the evidence, my boy," Toberts said, smiling cryptically.

"What's wrong with using the regular burn bag?"

"Nothing. I just had a desire to witness my own flames this time."

"It's highly irregular," Stanley said. "The building safety people would hemorrhage if they found out about it."

"Then," Toberts said, "let's see that they don't. Right, Stanley?"

Unsmiling, Stanley left the office, and Toberts wondered briefly whether, if the chips were ever down, Stanley would defend him or cheerfully throw him to the wolves. It was a question Toberts was not eager to have answered.

He drafted a cable to Thornton Daniels at Langley, requesting permission to act as his own special courier to hand-carry the complete verified file on Lamplighter back to Langley as soon as possible. He also discussed Bruckner's actions from the beginning and asked for further instructions, though in his own mind he had already decided that a free Bruckner was entirely too dangerous to the success of the project, and that he either ought to be locked up immediately or perhaps disposed of in some more permanent way.

What to do with Bruckner *now* was the question. Toberts would have preferred to keep Bruckner with him around the clock until he received a reply from Langley, but besides not being very practical that would tell Bruckner too much about what Toberts suspected. But maybe, Toberts thought, just maybe there was a way to force Bruckner's hand; it was an old agent's trick to make your adversary act before he was quite prepared.

Toberts picked up the phone and dialed the *Times-Weekly* number, and when Harold Sloan answered, he asked for Bruckner.

"Bruckner," Bruckner said, coming on the line.

"Yeah," Toberts said, "I just wanted to let you know I think the time has come to send off the entire file back to the States. It's a hell of a good story—I think our facts check out across the board now. Do you agree?"

"When did you plan to send the stuff?"

"I'm getting confirmation to fly it in myself—you know, add the personal touch, the eyewitness account."

"Sounds good," Bruckner said. "There's one more thing I ran into just this morning that I'd like to check out quickly before you move the file, if you can hang on a day or so."

"Sure, no problem if it'll help make a more complete file. You want to meet me downtown in half an hour to run over what you've got?"

"Right—half an hour," Bruckner said and hung up.

"Downtown" was their word for a meeting place on the second platform level of the Eiffel Tower—377 feet above the base—the special elevator to which cost eight francs. Toberts arrived early and stood looking out at the Bois de Boulogne spread out west of the tower and, to the northwest, the skyscrapers of La Défense. But although he waited for nearly three-quarters of an hour, Bruckner did not appear. With a final glance at his watch, Toberts brushed past the tourists and entered the open latticework elevator for the slow descent to the ground, thinking that Bruckner had better have a damned good excuse for his absence.

28 _____

AFTER TOBERTS'S TELEPHONE CALL to the *Times-Weekly* office, Bruckner realized that time was running out, and immediately went to Harold Sloan's private office and closed the door behind him. "That was Toberts," he said.

"Yeah, I recognized his voice," Sloan said.

"He's got something special going—we discussed it earlier, that call was just the confirmation—and he wants you to find him some special equipment."

"Like what?"

"Like a Russian-made machine pistol with a noise suppressor and a couple of magazines of Russian-made bullets. Any problem, do you think?"

"Probably not," Sloan said. He wrote down an address on a slip of paper and handed it to Bruckner. "This guy has it if anybody in Paris does, and if not he knows where to get it. Tell him I sent you. He'll no doubt call me back to check you out."

Having previously located the street on Sloan's large wall map of Paris, Bruckner had little trouble finding the address. It was not far from the *Times-Weekly* offices, on a block of jumbled business establishments off the Rue d'Alexandrie; the specific address was a jeweler's shop.

Bruckner entered the shop and approached a fat, well-dressed little man who was standing behind a glass-topped counter filled with diamond-studded wristwatches. "What can I do for you, monsieur?" the man asked him in French.

"Harold Sloan sent me, about some special merchandise," Bruckner answered in English.

"Please wait one moment, monsieur," the fat man said, this time in English. He disappeared into a back room and

321

Bruckner could hear him talking to someone, probably on the telephone. In a minute he returned and asked what, specifically, the gentleman required. Bruckner gave his order somewhat skeptically, because, in fact, the man looked exactly like a diamond merchant and not at all like an arms dealer.

"The, ah, Russians do not make a machine pistol that I am aware of," the man said. "If the necessity arose, I believe they would use the Vz61 *Skorpion,* of Czechoslovak manufacture."

"I'm familiar with the weapon," Bruckner said, surprised at the man's knowledgeability. "Do you have one, with silencer and shells?"

The man bent low behind the case full of watches and unlocked a drawer in which, Bruckner saw, there were several wooden boxes with small labels stenciled across the tops. The man removed one and handed it to Bruckner. "Will you be needing a shoulder holster for that?" he asked him.

Bruckner shook his head no.

"Then everything else you require is in the box."

"What about the purchase price?" Bruckner asked him. "And how do I pay?"

The man shook his head. "No purchase price—we rent only, and expect return of the merchandise after its use, in the same condition in which it left this shop. Monsieur Sloan has an account with us."

"Thank you," Bruckner said.

"Good day," the man said, and Bruckner would not have been surprised if he had added, *Good hunting.*

The more Harold Sloan thought about Bruckner's request, the more he wondered about its legitimacy. After the arms dealer had called him, Sloan dialed Toberts's number at the embassy. It was probably a stupid question and not really any of his business, but Sloan couldn't help thinking that Toberts would have asked him directly about the special weapon, instead of relaying the request through Bruckner.

A man with an officious voice answered Toberts's telephone and said that Mr. Toberts was not in the office.

When Sloan asked him when Toberts might return, the man said he really couldn't say and asked if Sloan would like to leave his name and number. Sloan said no, he would try again later, and hung up, feeling even more helpless than usual to shape or alter the events bubbling up all around him.

From his hotel room at the Crillon Bruckner telephoned Jessie Toberts and asked her to tell Toberts when he returned that evening to call him at the hotel because he had important and rather urgent news.

"Yes, of course," Jessie said, her voice already thick with alcohol. "But Pell, honey, you haven't been over to see me in a *long* time. Couldn't you slip away right now for a little while and come see your Jessie baby? I've missed you terribly, sugar—I'd be very, *very* nice to you. Remember what fun we had that last time you were here?"

Bruckner remembered; the pathetic woman had been insatiable. "It'll have to wait a little while, Jessie," he said. "I'm sorry—business before pleasure."

"Awww," Jessie moaned, "that's the trouble with you men. A girl's practically gotta beg you to fuck her."

Bruckner pushed the plunger on the phone to break the connection, then looked up Solange Cordier's number at the Sorbonne and dialed her office.

"Mademoiselle Cordier, my name is Pell Bruckner," he said when she came on the line.

"Yes?"

"Martin Toberts asked me to call and tell you to meet him as soon as possible in the Bois de Vincennes, in front of the restaurant on the island in Lake Daumesnil, close to the zoo. Do you know where that is?"

"Yes, I do," Solange said, "but tell me, why did not Martin himself call to ask me this?"

"I'm sorry, Mademoiselle Cordier, it was impossible at the moment. He told me that he would not be near a telephone for an hour or so, but that he would appreciate it if I would call you instead. He and I work together, you see. Although I have not had the pleasure of meeting you in person, I have heard a great deal about you from Martin. I don't know exactly what it was he wanted you to meet him for, but it sounded urgent. I'm sorry I don't have more information for you."

"No, that is all right if Martin wishes it. The restaurant on Lake Daumesnil, you said?"

"Yes, that's what he told me. As soon as you can get there. And please take a taxi—Martin wants to drive you home himself."

"All right, Monsieur . . . Bruckner? It will be nearly an hour though—I must arrange for someone to take over my class, and then the traffic . . . Do you think that will be soon enough?"

"I'm sure it will. Thank you, and I'm sorry to have bothered you this way."

"Not at all, monsieur."

Smiling at the receiver, Bruckner carefully hung up and lay back on the bed, his arms behind his head, staring at the ceiling. The plan was simple enough, and simplicity had everything going for it, as long as you thought of everything.

He went to the closet and took out the wooden box he had obtained from the diamond merchant, opened it carefully, and stared at the contents. The *Skorpion* machine pistol was truly a work of art. Designed for use by armored vehicle crews or anyone forced to operate in a confined setting, it was only eleven inches long with the wire stock folded over the barrel—scarcely longer than many ordinary pistols. The effective range was only about fifty yards but that was plenty for his purposes. He lifted out the three-inch silencer from its little velvet nest and screwed it slowly onto the threads encircling the short barrel. In a separate compartment he found three box magazines, each spring-loaded with ten 7.65 mm shells— the equivalent of .30 caliber American rounds. He slammed one of the magazines into the receptacle beneath the barrel, pushed the selector lever to full automatic, and sighted along the top of the barrel. Standing up he raised the tail of his jacket and slipped the *Skorpion* into the hollow of his back beneath his belt. In front of the full-length mirror on the closet door, he practiced reaching behind his back beneath the jacket and drawing the pistol as rapidly as possible. When he was satisfied, he removed the magazine

324

and silencer from the gun, switched the lever to safety, put everything back in the box in the closet, then left the room.

He remembered a pharmacy along one of the hallways radiating from the lobby of the hotel; luckily it was arranged somewhat like an American drugstore. He bought a bottle of eyewash preparation that came with a rubber-tipped glass dropper, and as soon as he was out on the street he emptied the contents of the bottle into the gutter and put the empty bottle and dropper into his pocket. Ignoring the taxis standing in a row by the curb, he walked a couple of blocks north of the hotel and only then hailed a taxi off the street to take him back to the *Times-Weekly* offices. There he borrowed Sloan's car and drove straight to the Bois de Vincennes, a trip lasting exactly thirty-five minutes.

He parked on the access road close enough to the footbridge across to the island that he would have a clear view of anyone arriving. Ten minutes later a taxi drew up at the edge of the lake and a woman got out, paid the driver, and after looking around her walked slowly across the bridge. As soon as the taxi left, Bruckner got out of the car and rapidly crossed the bridge behind the woman, who seemed to match Toberts's brief description accurately enough. "Mademoiselle Cordier?" he said when he was directly behind her, and was pleased to see that she gave a frightened little jump.

"I'm sorry to have frightened you," he said. "My name is Pell Bruckner." And he shook hands with her.

"Where is Martin?" she asked him immediately, looking around again as though he might suddenly appear from the tree- and bush-lined walkways that honeycombed the little island.

"He's here," Bruckner said, "right over this way." Without waiting to see how she might react to this news, he began to walk along a path that, he had noticed earlier, led back away from the restaurant through a densely wooded area toward the far side of the island. She hesitated a moment, then hurried to catch up with him.

As the woods grew deeper Bruckner commented on the good weather while casually checking the path ahead of

325

and behind them. There was no one else in sight. "In here," he said, taking her arm and propelling her through a break in the high bushes lining the path.

"*Mon Dieu!*" she gasped. "What—"

But Bruckner's powerful thumbs and fingers closed around her neck, shutting off the air and the sound. Her startled eyes bulged, the color in her face quickly changing from deep mottled red to bluish-purple. Eventually, when he released the pressure on her neck, there was a muffled gurgle from her throat, and he allowed her lifeless body to slump to the ground.

Stooping over her body, he carefully ripped open her blouse, popping off several buttons, and slipping his fingers under the front of her bra, he tore it loose from her breasts. He lifted her skirt, pulled down her pantyhose, and carefully tore away her thin flowered bikini panties. He stared down at her a moment, feeling himself grow hard, and understood why Toberts had become so infatuated.

Standing against a nearby tree where he could still see her bare thighs and breasts, he quickly masturbated into the eyewash bottle. After cleaning himself with his handkerchief, he inserted the dropper into the bottle and drew out a quantity of semen, which he then deposited into the dead woman's vagina, careful to let a bit of the sticky fluid trail out onto the surrounding region of pubic hair as well. It was a useful trick, to make it appear that she had been the victim of a sex murder—common enough in the parks and alleyways of Paris, though not nearly so common as in New York City or Washington. If the police were looking for a sex criminal, they would be much less likely to happen upon the real reason for the murder.

Bruckner screwed the dropper back into the bottle and dropped it into his pocket to be disposed of later, far away. He stood and surveyed the scene, taking in all the details as though he were an architect appraising his latest creation. The woods were so deep here that her body might not be found for some time if left where it was, and it would suit his purposes better if she was discovered quickly. He started to drag her toward the pathway by her foot, but then, realizing that the police would think it strange if the murderer left drag marks toward the open path, he lifted the body in his arms and carried it nearer the path. He carefully arranged one bare leg so that it protruded slightly from the bushes; that would certainly attract some attention the next time anyone used this path.

With a final look around he walked back the way he had come, passing no one. The few people around the entrance to the restaurant paid no particular attention to him. He returned across the bridge to Sloan's car and drove steadily away from the area in the direction of his hotel. Just before he left the park he rolled down his window and tossed the eyewash bottle into the bushes along the road, where it would no doubt remain for years to come.

Back in his room at the Crillon Bruckner telephoned Sloan at the *Times-Weekly*. "Something's come up, Sloan. I have to do a special job for Toberts and I need to keep your car a while longer. Any problem?"

"No, I guess not," Sloan said. "I plan to leave shortly, but I can probably get a ride with one of the other guys here. Where *is* Toberts, by the way?"

"I thought you knew you weren't supposed to ask questions like that," Bruckner said, and hung up before Sloan could give him an argument.

After a while he got the machine pistol from the closet and reassembled it. The two extra loaded magazines he dropped into his pocket. He switched the selector lever to full automatic and slipped the pistol under his belt next to his back. In the full-length mirror he satisfied himself that the outlines of the weapon didn't noticeably bulge his jacket, even when he bent over. Then he sat down on the edge of the bed to wait for Toberts's call.

It came a few minutes past six-thirty. "What's up?" Toberts asked first. "And where the hell were you earlier?"

"Sorry about that," Bruckner said, "but it couldn't be helped. I think you'll understand when I tell you what I've got. Can you meet me at the main post office in half an hour?"

The "main post office" was their term for the principal

dead drop near the Pré Catelan in the Bois de Boulogne. "Too soon," Toberts said, "it'll take me at least forty-five minutes from here. Couldn't it wait until after I've had dinner?"

"No, I promise you it can't. Forty-five minutes, okay? Oh, and bring the papers with you, original and copy—I want to show you something strange that may be important."

"I don't much like the idea of doing that."

"I know, and I agree," Bruckner said. "But in this case I think it's worth the risk. I believe you will, too."

"All right," Toberts said. "Jessie's going to be madder than hell, though—I think she fixed something special for dinner."

"That's too bad," Bruckner said, with visions of something awful burning in Jessie's oven. "See you there."

He hung up the phone and left the room. On the way down in the elevator he went over all the details in his mind and couldn't think of anything he had left out. Knowing that he had plenty of time, he stopped off in the bar and gulped down a double Scotch on the rocks, then went outside, got into Sloan's car, and drove as fast as he dared to the rendezvous point in the Bois. By the time he reached the Pré Catelan the sun had dropped below the horizon and the evening air was beginning to soften in pale blue and lavender tones as the park took on the enchantment of a Paris summer evening. It was ironic, he thought, that seven or eight miles across the city, in another large park, the body of a lovely young woman might even now be attracting official attention while her lover hurried in the opposite direction.

Shortly he saw Toberts's Peugeot pull up and stop some distance behind his car, and he waited until Toberts had gotten out and started walking toward the gatepost of the château where their drop was located before he, too, left the car and joined Toberts. "Let's walk," he said, noticing that a wad of folded papers protruded slightly from the inside breast pocket of Toberts's jacket.

They walked along the pathways a short distance until Toberts said, "Where *were* you this afternoon when you were supposed to meet me?"

Bruckner looked at him. "You may not want to believe what I'm going to tell you, Toberts, but it's the truth. I went out to the Sorbonne to check on what you told me about some KGB type hanging around the parking lot waiting for your friend, Mademoiselle Cordier. I checked around without turning up anything, and I was just sitting there in the car about to leave when this woman comes out of the building and walks toward a little car parked in the lot. A big guy with a messed-up face came out of nowhere, but he wasn't rushing her, you know? It was like they knew each other, or at least expected each other. He called her by name so I knew it was her. They walked over to her car and he leaned in the window and they talked for a while, too low for me to hear, and then she slips him a big envelope full of something and he shoves it inside his coat and takes off. A minute later a big black car comes barreling around the corner and stops just long enough for the goon to hop in, then takes off like something's chasing them. Your friend drove on off then. I flipped a mental coin and decided to chase the bad guys, but they knew more about the streets than I did and I lost them. What do you make of it?"

A frown settled over Toberts's face. "Damned if I know. It could have been some school business, I suppose—you know, she might have been giving him an envelope of perfectly innocent stuff pertaining to next semester's curriculum or something."

"You don't really believe that, do you? I mean, the way I explained it is the way it happened, big black car and all."

Toberts shrugged, but the frown remained. "I don't know. I guess I'll have to ask her about it."

"If it's what I think it is, she'll deny it, of course," Bruckner said.

"What? Oh, yeah, sure, I suppose you're right," Toberts said. They walked a bit farther along the wooded pathway. "Where did you get the car?"

"The car? Oh, it was Sloan's—he's been pretty good about letting me borrow it."

"Yeah. Sloan's a good man, believe it or not."

329

"Well, I wouldn't trust him with my life, if that's what you mean."

"That is what I mean," Toberts said, "and I would trust him even with my life."

Bruckner snorted. "It's your life. By the way, did you bring the manuscript and the decoded copy?"

Toberts took them out of his pocket and held them in his hand, an obvious question in his eyes.

"Let me show you something interesting," Bruckner said.

He took the papers from Toberts and held them in his left hand. There was no one on the path ahead of them, and behind them there was only a man walking a very small dog on a leash and dreaming of the supper his wife was even now preparing. The park was beginning to be blanketed in deep shadows, and although there were electric lamps along the walkways, they were scattered and the light from them was romantically dim.

"You know that stuff I was just telling you about seeing the Cordier broad at the Sorbonne?" Bruckner said. "It was all bullshit—pure, unadulterated bullshit."

While he talked Bruckner had nonchalantly reached for the machine pistol in the hollow of his back, and now he held it pointed unwaveringly at Toberts, the silenced muzzle only a foot or two from Toberts's chest. "Sorry old sport," Bruckner said lightly.

Toberts instinctively stepped back toward the bushes lining the sidewalk. "It's the manuscript, isn't it?" he asked Bruckner. "All those jewels just sitting there, or even the possibility that they *might* be there . . . and you got greedy. But it won't do you any good—too many people know about the Lamplighter project, about the manuscript, and that kind of news gets around. They know you were working on it with me—you'll be the only likely suspect if I'm found murdered."

Bruckner smiled. "Wrong on several counts. I've gone to some little trouble to obtain this sterling example of the Eastern bloc's arms manufacturers, and I understand the bullets it fires are quite recognizable. Everybody in the company—the French cops too, for that matter—will believe it was just another East-West shootout among

330

Paris's itinerant intelligence agents. I, of course, will be suitably helpful with descriptions of the goons who've been seen following you."

"Listen, Bruckner, maybe we can work something—"

"Shut up, Toberts. The other error in your statement a minute ago was that, in fact, nobody knows about what's in this manuscript except you, and me, and Mademoiselle Cordier. Too bad you had to blow your oath and tell her about it—the fact is, she has already been taken care of quite permanently."

Bruckner paused to let this news sink in, enjoying immensely the look of disbelief and then pain that distorted Toberts's face. "I have a bootleg copy of the decoded manuscript," he went on. "I'll simply destroy these two, and I will literally have the only one in the world. I've won, you see, Toberts. Efficiency always wins over ethics."

"You killed her?" Toberts murmured.

"I killed her. Given the circumstances, I had no other options."

"Oh, Jesus God!" Toberts said. His eyes were glazed over with more agony than Bruckner had ever seen before in the eyes of a victim. "How did you do it?"

Bruckner smiled. "Actually, you might have enjoyed it. You never told me how large and rosy her nipples were, or what a tight little cunt she had, almost like a virgin . . ."

In a blind rage Toberts lunged at Bruckner, who crooked his index finger around the trigger of the pistol and sprayed a fusillade of nearly silent bullets at the charging agent. The impact hurled Toberts back into the bushes. Aware that many of the bullets had probably missed their target because the light weapon's extreme rate of fire made it nearly uncontrollable, Bruckner wrenched the spent magazine from beneath the barrel and dug in his jacket pocket for one of the spares. But out of the corner of his eye he saw that the man with the little dog was much closer than he had realized, although still apparently unconcerned and unaware of what had happened.

Toberts had not moved, of that much Bruckner was certain; if he was not already dead, he was certainly dying. Weighing his alternatives quickly, Bruckner dropped the pistol into his pocket along with the unused magazines and walked rapidly in the opposite direction from the man with the dog. His confidence increased with every step, so that by the time he reached Sloan's car he was quite exhilarated with the knowledge that nothing on earth could stop him now.

29 _____

THE DARK-HAIRED MAN held the leash attached to the tiny dog's collar and watched Bruckner intently until he was out of sight. Then the man scooped up the miniature animal in one hand and placed it, along with its leash, in a huge pocket of his raincoat that might have been made for just such a purpose. Without seeming to run, he nevertheless sped along the sidewalk to the spot where Toberts had fallen only moments before.

Bending over the strangely contorted body half hidden by the bushes into which it had tumbled, the man probed the body in a professional manner for signs of life. His fingertips found a weak pulse beating under Toberts's jaw —which, given the bloody holes obvious in his clothing, seemed improbable at best. The man's hand touched something hard and flat in Toberts's shirt pocket; upon examination it was revealed to be a silver cigarette case with the tip of a bullet still embedded in its cover and two fresh dents beside the bullet. The assassin Bruckner had taken no chances, it seemed. But still, as sometimes happened, he had failed.

The man signaled across the park with his hand, and in a moment he was joined by a large brutish man. "Quickly, Fon," the first man said in Russian. Together they lifted Toberts's body upright between them and half-carried, half-dragged him to a waiting black sedan with only its parking lights on. The car sped out of the Bois and after crossing the river headed directly for the Russian Embassy on the Rue de Grenelle.

The man who had been walking his dog in the Bois and the man called Fon carried Toberts inside the building. The first secretary met them in the foyer and, upon seeing

333

the unconscious Toberts slung between them, his wounds openly bleeding now, rushed to find help. Almost immediately Colonel Alexis Balachov appeared, along with the deputy for information and two assistants. Colonel Balachov went straight to Toberts, a smile playing about his lips. "Well, well, what have we here?" he said, holding Toberts's head up by the hair. The painful tugging caused Toberts's right eye to open partway, though it was hard to tell whether he was able to focus on anything.

"Martin Toberts, my old friend," the colonel said. "So good of you to pay us an official visit after all this time. Feel free to stay as long as you wish."

Toberts opened his other eye and concentrated very hard on Colonel Balachov's face, but said nothing. The colonel opened Toberts's shirt, and with a gold penknife from his pocket he slit Toberts's undershirt down the middle of his chest and pulled it apart to view the wounds. There seemed to be three altogether—one, an obvious flesh wound, through the upper left arm, one in the left shoulder, and a third in the right side of his torso. "You've done well, Boris," he said to the dark, thin-lipped man who had been following Toberts in the Bois. "That fool Andrei has gone to get Dr. Litvinov. These wounds look rather serious to me—I should think Litvinov will want him transported in some haste to the clinic. Fon, see that the car stays ready, please."

Colonel Balachov noticed how Toberts's shirt hung to one side and found the silver cigarette case in the shirt pocket. He turned it over in his hand, studying the two deep depressions beside the embedded bullet. "I wonder whether our Mr. Toberts realizes he undoubtedly owes his life, what is left of it, to this little case?" the colonel said. Using his handkerchief he carefully plucked the bullet intact from the metal case and held it up to the light for examination. "Boris, would you say this looks like one of ours?"

Boris bent to study the bullet more carefully. As Colonel Balachov's deputy in the Paris KGB apparatus he was familiar with most of the world's hand weapons, and now he nodded at the colonel. "I believe without question that it is, Colonel. A 7.65 millimeter shell, fired through a noise suppressor—which I was aware of in any case because of the lack of sound in the Bois. Our ballistics team should be able to tell us from what sort of weapon it was fired."

"Definitely automatic?" the colonel asked.

"The entire episode was over in a second or two," Boris said. "Yes, definitely automatic, and as compact as a pistol. Perhaps something like a Czech *Skorpion*."

"I have seen them," the colonel said. "Very effective."

"Very," Boris agreed. "Do you suppose Bruckner possessed a motive, other than killing efficiency, for his choice of weapon?"

"You mean to implicate the KGB, as a rival intelligence faction? Yes, I am certain of it, Boris. His reasons for doing so elude me at the moment, however. Perhaps we shall be able to ask Mr. Toberts himself about it."

Andrei, the first secretary, brought Dr. Litvinov into the foyer. "There he is," he said to the doctor, pointing at Toberts, as though there could be some doubt about who in the room needed medical attention.

Dr. Litvinov, a small, gray-bearded, balding man whose remarkable physical resemblance to Lenin had stood him in good stead with the party for many years, took a stethoscope from his medical bag and bent over Toberts's body. With his thumb he held Toberts's eyelids back and peered through thick lenses into the glazed eyes. He took a chromed probe from his bag and poked into each of the wounds separately, causing Toberts's body to jerk each time he abused the nerves. Finally he placed the inflatable cuff of a blood pressure apparatus on Toberts's upper arm and squeezed the bulb several times, watching the dial closely as he released the air.

Colonel Balachov watched Dr. Litvinov replace the instruments in his bag. "Well, Litvinov?" he said impatiently.

"Oh, he will live," the doctor said. "The blood pressure is good, the pulse only slightly irregular. Fortunately for him the bullets made very small, neat holes in the flesh, so there was only minor structural or tissue damage. The one through his upper arm here missed the bone by a couple of centimeters and passed on through. This one through his side also passed through mostly fatty tissue and left the body—no particularly traumatic damage unless it caught his kidney on the way out. But here we may have trouble," he said, pointing to the wound in Toberts's left shoulder. "The bullet entered beneath the clavicle but did not exit the body. My guess is that it is lodged against the scapula, and will have to be probed for and removed before infection sets in."

"Then you will want him transported to the clinic?" Colonel Balachov asked.

The doctor considered the question. "Is, ah, *privacy* a consideration?"

The colonel nodded. "Most definitely."

"Then I believe there is no compelling reason to move this man from the embassy. Our dispensary has everything we need, and we can use one of the upstairs bedrooms. The surgical procedure is not particularly delicate."

Boris and Fon carried Toberts's limp body upstairs and down a long, gloomy hallway to an empty bedroom. They placed him on the bed, but when Dr. Litvinov arrived a few moments later, he asked them to move Toberts to a daybed in the center of the room. "It will be easier to work around, and the firmer surface makes it easier to operate," he told them. They moved several floor lamps around the head of the daybed. Dr. Litvinov scrubbed his hands in the adjoining bathroom and laid out his instruments on a small table beside the daybed. He broke open a sterile needle and inserted it into the rubber top of a bottle of sodium Pentothal, then pressed the needle into Toberts's vein and squeezed the plunger. "This should keep him quiet long enough to do the job," the doctor told Colonel Balachov.

"Fine," the colonel said. "I would like to stay and watch."

"Of course," the doctor said, though it was clear he would have preferred that they leave him alone with his patient.

With the woman who tended the dispensary acting as his nurse, Dr. Litvinov used various instruments to probe the flesh and open the wound further, without injuring good tissue, until finally he located the bullet deep in Toberts's shoulder under a layer of cartilage. He extracted the gray metallic mass with forceps and held it up for Colonel Balachov and Boris, seated in the corner of the room, to see and admire. "Save the bullet, please," the colonel told the doctor.

All during the probing operation Toberts had murmured unintelligible phrases; the sodium Pentothal, known for its other uses as "truth serum," had left him in a twilight state of semiconsciousness. At one point he had begun thrashing around so violently that the doctor had asked Boris to tie Toberts's hands and legs to the frame of the daybed. Now Dr. Litvinov dressed the wound with antiseptic and sewed the flap of ruptured skin, then attended to the more or less minor needs of the other two wounds.

When he had finished his work, Colonel Balachov came over to the daybed and stood looking down at Toberts. "Give him another injection of the Pentothal," he told the doctor.

"I'm not sure that is wise," the doctor said. "The amount I gave him was quite adequate."

"Not for my purposes," the colonel said grimly. "If you refuse to give the injection, we shall simply have to do it for you."

Without further argument, because he sensed that it would be useless, Dr. Litvinov did as he was told, injecting a second syringe of the clear liquid into Toberts's vein. "Thank you, Doctor," the colonel said. "You may leave us now."

When the doctor and nurse had taken their stained implements and soiled towels with them and left the bedroom, Colonel Balachov lifted Toberts's head by the hair and let it drop against the day-bed. He peered beneath the eyelids, then rolled Toberts's head from side to side repeatedly. "Can you hear me, Martin?" he asked in a loud voice. "We have been friends for a long time, Martin, and I want to help you. I know that you are in trouble and I want very much to help you. But you must *allow* me to help you, Martin. You must give me enough information so that I *can* help you. Do you understand what I am saying?"

Toberts's lips moved soundlessly for a while, and then a grunting noise issued from deep in his chest.

"What was that, Martin? I didn't quite understand you."

"Help . . . me . . ." Toberts whispered, his eyes closed tight. "Please . . ."

"Yes, Martin, we want to help you. You have been very badly hurt, by Mr. Bruckner, whom you believed to be your friend. Why did he try to kill you, Martin, do you know?"

"Bruckner . . ." Toberts said, pausing as though trying to remember where he had heard the name before. "Bruckner . . . hurt me. He cannot be . . . trusted."

"Why did he want you out of the way, Martin?"

"Not . . . my friend," Toberts whispered weakly.

Colonel Balachov saw that his captive was sinking back into total unconsciousness, which was always the trouble with the potent psychoactive drugs. He squeezed Toberts's cheek between thumb and forefinger until Toberts winced and tried to shake away the offending hand. "Martin," the colonel said reassuringly, "I won't let them hurt you again, you must believe that. You are safe now, here, with me. Try to relax and let us talk as one friend to another. Please tell me what you remember concerning *Fonarshchik* —Project Lamplighter. Just start at the beginning and tell me very slowly. Everything."

There was a long pause during which Toberts's eyelids fluttered and nearly opened several times. In the end he spoke only one word: "Solange!"

The colonel looked at Boris, who shrugged. They were both aware of who Solange was, of course, but while mention of her name assured them that Toberts's mind was reaching in the proper direction, they needed concrete facts from him—names, dates, places, intended courses of action.

Colonel Balachov tried again. "You were speaking of the Statue of Liberty, Martin . . . the Statue of Liberty. Think about it, about how important it is. Have you seen the Statue of Liberty, Martin?"

Toberts's eyes fluttered. "Statue? I saw the statue . . . dark, cool . . ."

"And what about the statue is so important?"

Still strapped to the daybed, Toberts's arms and hands strained to free themselves; his powerful fingers curled and uncurled in fist after fist. "Important . . ." he whispered. "Solange . . . important. Must tell . . . Solange . . . love her."

The colonel and Boris took turns questioning the drugged Toberts, but their pointed questions elicited only vague responses or more references to Solange and his love for her. "He has pulled an old trick," the colonel said after a while, wiping the sweat from his face—evidence of the effort involved in this sort of interrogation.

"Yes," Boris agreed. "He seems to have transferred all his intellectual machinery to a single emotional wavelength, involving his love for this woman Solange Cordier. No matter what we ask him, his response will be in terms of loving her. We cannot penetrate that defense."

"And it would necessarily be a genuine emotion that he feels toward Mademoiselle Cordier?" the colonel asked Boris.

"In my experience," Boris replied, "it has always been a genuine, powerful emotion—love, hate, fear—that would allow a drugged mind to block out the conscious knowledge that is being sought by the interrogator."

"That has also been my experience," Colonel Balachov said. "I believe we shall get nothing further from Mr. Toberts today. Let us leave him to rest and recuperate as best he can. Perhaps in the meantime, we can find this paragon, this Solange, and bring her here to see her beloved. Perhaps, Boris, we may even be able to think of some way to use the woman to make Mr. Toberts more cooperative. I should think he would not like to see her hurt."

They left the bedroom and closed and locked the door behind them. The colonel suggested to Boris that he post Fon outside the door as a twenty-four-hour guard. Inside the room, as the door clicked shut, Toberts's arms and legs relaxed inside their restraints and his head nodded comfortably off to one side against the hard surface of the daybed.

30 _____

THE MORNING AFTER SHOOTING Toberts, Bruckner composed and sent off to the Editor, International Economic Newsletter in Washington, D.C.—a prearranged address for a nonexistent publication—a memorandum to Thornton Daniels at Langley assuring him that the information in Professor Cordier's manuscript had been proved conclusively, by Toberts and himself, to be almost totally false.

Concerning the main points of the manuscript, in which the professor had stated that a valuable treasure might have been secreted inside the Statue of Liberty and never removed, there had been nothing at all that he or Toberts had been able to pin down through countless interviews and cross-checking of records and reports, but he was going ahead with one or two leads that Toberts had suggested even though neither of them had any hope they would produce concrete results. The most damaging evidence, Bruckner reported, was the total lack of evidence that two of the main characters in Professor Cordier's story had ever lived, plus an indication that the professor had been noted in academic circles of his time as something of a practical jokester, willing to go to great lengths to embarrass or mislead his friends with a well-designed literary hoax. Bruckner ended his communiqué by stating that Toberts would probably forward a copy of the manuscript to Langley in any case, mostly as a curiosity.

There were other things he could have told Thornton Daniels, of course—things that not only good old Thornton but everybody else at the huge CIA complex in Virginia would have been very interested in. Like, for instance, the strange disappearance of Martin Toberts. He knew there hadn't been time yet for Toberts's death to be reported in the newspapers (he had hurriedly checked this morning's *International Herald Tribune* anyway, just to be sure), but when the story finally did break in the Paris papers he would cable Langley, offering his own opinion that Toberts must have been blown away by the KGB in retaliation for the death of the agent Ilsa, which they would assume he had ordered. The fact that Russian ammunition had been used should be evidence enough for whatever investigating team would be assigned to the case by Daniels.

If he, Bruckner, were still around, he could expect to go through a rather thorough interrogation by the team, including a polygraph series that he might or might not be able to circumvent by lying convincingly. He had fooled them before, several times, but anyone who deliberately subjected himself to matching wits with the awesome machine was an utter fool. In any case, Bruckner thought, he would not be here to greet the gray little men from Langley with their suitcases containing portable lie detectors.

Toward the end, Bruckner paid a visit to Harold Sloan. "I need information in a hurry," he said. "I need to know a name, someone I can talk to about recruiting three or four men to do a specific technical job."

Sloan looked at him and frowned. "Will this be a dirty job, would you say?"

"Yes, maybe even black. Extreme danger, no questions, the only requirement being to follow orders implicitly and get paid well for doing that. There are other requirements of a physical nature that I'll discuss with the contact. Do you know such a man?"

"I know a man," Sloan said, "but you won't like him."

"Why not?"

"No one does."

"Is he efficient?"

"As far as I know or have heard."

"Then there's no need for me to like him. How do we arrange contact?"

Sloan scribbled an address on a slip of paper. "He hangs

out in this bar, near the waterfront. Ask for Gros-Jacques —that means 'Big Jack' and he lives up to his name. I ought to warn you, though—he can be a mean son of a bitch, especially if someone he doesn't know is asking around for him. But that seems to be what you want."

"We'll see," Bruckner said noncommittally.

"By the way," Sloan said, "have you talked to Toberts lately? I can't seem to locate him."

Bruckner pointedly ignored the editor's question. "One other thing, Sloan. I have to ask you for five thousand dollars in cash, right now. Half in francs, half U.S. I know you have it."

Sloan laughed. "Everybody thinks I'm a rich man . . ." The laugh faded away. "How do I know what you'll do with it?"

Bruckner shook his head. "You don't, and won't."

"I don't know," Sloan said. He seemed to be studying the wall behind Bruckner's head. "With Toberts not available to check these things out with . . . I just don't think I want to take the chance, Bruckner."

"The only chance you'll be taking is if you refuse my request. I'm warning you, Sloan, this is official U.S. government business. If you jack me around anymore, I promise you I'll file a formal memorandum to the effect that you were grossly uncooperative with me in a line-of-duty situation, and I will recommend that all CIA support be withdrawn from you and your operation. I think you know I can make it stick."

Sloan's complexion faded to that of a sickly old man. He sat very still in his wooden swivel chair, staring at Bruckner as though he had never seen him before. Finally he said, "You know I've always cooperated with you people—one hundred percent. Toberts knows it, even if you don't."

He got up from his chair and went to the wall safe near the floor in a corner of his cubicle. He twirled the dial back and forth, eventually pulled open the heavy door, and extracted a long metal cash box. He opened the box and fumbled among packages of bills secured by rubber bands. After a long time of counting and recounting, he tossed a handful of francs and dollars onto his desk, and watched while Bruckner counted them out himself.

Nodding at Sloan, Bruckner stuffed the bills in his pocket. "Thank you for being a cheerful giver," he said. "I'll be in touch." He left the office before Sloan could think of a suitably caustic reply.

It was late afternoon when Bruckner instructed the taxi driver to let him out in the tourist-infested Marais quarter of Paris. Bruckner had no desire to gawk at the beautifully restored sixteenth-century town houses that were the principal attraction of the area. Instead, he walked south toward the Seine until he reached the Quai de l'Hôtel de Ville. Eventually, more by accident than purpose, he found the bar Sloan had directed him to near the Marie Bridge landing from Ile Saint-Louis. He took the scrap of paper from his pocket once again and stared at the name Sloan had written—Le Barreau Plus Bas (The Bottom Rung) —and slowly raised his eyes to the shabby establishment attached like a canker to the end of a long row of disreputable-looking shops and alleyways. The bar, Bruckner thought, appeared to have been well named.

He pushed open the door on its one unbroken hinge and stepped into the long, dark, narrow room that contained nothing but the reason for its existence—the bar. No tables, no chairs, not even a railing for the tired drinker to rest his foot upon. The customers were uniformly scruffy-looking; Bruckner guessed that most were men who worked and lived on the river or the nearby docks and warehouses, and the other types who would find hanging around such a place profitable for one reason or another—loan sharks, deserters from the armed forces (not necessarily French), petty criminals. It was the sort of bar Humphrey Bogart films used to glamorize, but Bruckner knew there was nothing glamorous about this place or the hundreds of others like it he had been in all over the world, from Amsterdam to Port Said. It was the sort of place where human life was valued very little—much less than a glass of cheap whiskey—and it was possible to get yourself killed by nothing more threatening than raising your eyebrow at the wrong moment.

343

He had decided the second he walked in the door what he would do; in fact, it was less a decision than reflex action. He stood at the end of the bar nearest the door and motioned the bartender over. When the mean-eyed little man asked, in French, what he wanted, Bruckner said in very loud English, "Where do I find the filthy pig who calls himself Gros-Jacques?"

Several glasses stopped momentarily in midair, just as they sometimes did in Hollywood films. Bruckner stared at the row of potential killers along the length of the bar, each one of whom looked at him to see just what kind of fool he might be.

"What you want weeth eem?" the bartender said, that much English obviously a struggle for him.

"I'm going to take his balls off and make him eat them," Bruckner said, more to the crowd than to the bartender. "Except that I understand he probably has no more balls than a woman."

The bartender shrugged, lost in the intricacies of a language he knew little about. But one customer at the bar had not only heard and understood Bruckner's insult, he was somehow personally suffering from it. The man separated himself from the others, and Bruckner saw now that he was huge—taller than the other men, thicker in the arms and chest, with a black scraggly beard that had probably never been combed or trimmed. The man walked toward Bruckner very slowly, obviously expecting the much thinner man to seek an immediate hiding place. He advanced to within a foot of Bruckner's face, so close that Bruckner smelled the foulness of his breath.

"If you're looking for Gros-Jacques, you're looking for me," the man said in quite passable English. "Would you like to repeat those fucking words?"

"Outside," Bruckner said, not waiting to see what the other man did or said about it. He was through the door and heading around the corner of the building into the alley when he heard the same door crash behind him and knew that the man had taken his bait.

When Gros-Jacques stepped into the alley, Bruckner waited only that split second it took the larger man to see whom he was facing. Then Bruckner grabbed the man's

344

beard with both hands and jerked downward with all his strength, at the same time propelling his knee upward with tremendous force. There was a satisfying crunch as the top of the knee crushed the nose.

Bruckner released the man's beard and hopped back out of reach in case there was to be a second contest, but it was apparent Gros-Jacques was dazed and only remained standing out of habit. Bruckner knew the pain had to be fierce. The man held his hand cupped around his ballooning nose as blood gushed through his fingers and down his cheeks. Bruckner reached in his pocket and handed the man a fresh white handkerchief.

"I'm sorry but it was quite necessary," Bruckner began, with Gros-Jacques watching him warily. "It was necessary that I establish from the beginning that I will be the boss in any future relationship between us. Oh, and don't think that the next time I turn my head you'll even the score by taking me apart . . . I want you to understand that I am not bragging, but that I could quite easily kill you with my bare hands, or feet, or elbows, or—but you see what I mean, don't you? I've killed a good many men, I've been carefully trained for the job. And the truth is, killing doesn't bother me in the least; in fact, I rather enjoy it. So let's be friends, shall we? And not enemies?"

Bruckner smiled and extended his hand in the customary greeting. Gros-Jacques looked at the hand, then looked in Bruckner's eyes and shifted his weight slightly, like a boxer about to feint and go for the kill. The smile disappeared entirely from Bruckner's lips. "Take my hand and shake it, politely, or I'll break your arm in three separate places, punk," he said so murderously quietly that Gros-Jacques's eyes grew wide. Still holding the handkerchief to his nose, Gros-Jacques slowly held out his right hand and the two men clasped each other's palms.

"Good," Bruckner said. "Now, can we go somewhere and talk business?"

Gros-Jacques looked toward the bar they had just left. "Not back there," he said.

Bruckner nodded. "Yes, it would be slightly embarrassing for you. So you lead—I'm sure you know the area better than I do."

Within less than a block there was another bar that looked almost as disreputable as *Le Barreau Plus Bas*. They went inside, stopped first at the bar to pick up two glasses of beer apiece, and carried them to a table in the very back of the room where they would not be disturbed.

"I should have introduced myself earlier," Bruckner said. "My name is Bruckner and I'm American—that's all you need to know."

Gros-Jacques flicked a matchhead with his thumbnail and lit a large black cigar. "Who put you onto me?"

"Someone who's heard of you, obviously. The person said you were the man for the job, you and some of your acquaintances. I do hope he was right."

"Depends on the job," the goon, as Bruckner had come to think of him, said. He spat brown juice from the cigar onto the floor, reminding Bruckner of all the grade B Westerns he had seen as a boy.

"These are the requirements for the job, so listen carefully," Bruckner said. He took a large gulp of beer from his glass. "I'll need four men—including you or not, that's up to you. There are certain attributes that I require of each member of the team. First, they must be able to speak English well; I speak some French but I don't want to have to be bothered with it on top of everything else. Second, they must be willing and able to leave the country legitimately on a commercial airliner traveling to the United States, for a stay of no more than two weeks or so. Third, they must have had some experience—preferably, considerable experience—in making technical rope climbs under adverse conditions, including darkness. Fourth, they must be skilled in the use of a wide variety of weapons and explosives of a military grade, and should know something about the operation of small boats. Any questions so far?"

"Yes. Let's talk about the pay."

"Of course. But first, there's a fifth requirement, and a very important one it is—they must not be squeamish men."

"Pardonnez-moi?" Gros-Jacques frowned over his beer glass, not understanding the peculiar American word.

"Squeamish," Bruckner repeated. "Oh, I don't *expect*

the need for any killing, but it may become necessary due to unforeseen events. And if it does, the men you select must be able to do it quietly and professionally. As for the money, each man will be paid the equivalent of twenty-five thousand U.S. dollars on completion of the job. I leave it to you to figure out what that might be in francs."

"Approximately one hundred and nine thousand, at the official rate," Gros-Jacques said nearly instantly. "But there is a flaw in your reasoning, Monsieur Bruckner. I myself intend to be one of the four men on the job, and since I must recruit the others and take, shall we say, certain unusual risks, I demand to be paid at a substantially higher rate than the other three."

Bruckner had, in fact, expected this. "Agreed," he said. "How does fifty thousand U.S. dollars sound to you?"

Gros-Jacques nodded once. "That sum will not, however, repair the damage you have done to my nose."

"Or, especially, to your wounded pride," Bruckner said. "But it will certainly help. Do the requirements I have spoken of present too specialized a problem for you in your recruiting, do you think?"

"Special, *oui*. But not impossible, I think. How soon do you need these 'special' men?"

"By the morning of day after tomorrow."

Gros-Jacques slammed his beer glass down on the table. "*Merde!* It is impossible!"

"Nothing is impossible, Gros-Jacques. I cannot give you details, but there is a reason it must be done as quickly as possible."

The huge man across the table raised his eyebrows and looked at Bruckner with interest. "Are you perhaps being . . . pursued, monsieur?"

"Not yet, but soon," Bruckner answered honestly.

"So." Gros-Jacques started on his second glass of beer. "It may mean that we must accept one or two men with whom I am not personally acquainted. If so, I shall verify their qualifications with someone trustworthy, one way or another."

"Good." Bruckner took from his pocket a list that he had carefully written out in his hotel room the previous evening and handed it across the table. "That is a list of equipment we'll need and which you must provide before we leave Paris. Every item is *mandatory*—I will accept no more and no less than *exactly* what's on the list. Understood? The items will have to be crated and smuggled on board a cargo ship going to New York City, to arrive in a week's time. Do you foresee any problems there?"

Gros-Jacques studied the list for several minutes. "Interesting," he said. "I will need operating capital—money to purchase the supplies and to hire the boat and the captain's silence. Cash only, of course."

"Of course." Bruckner took Sloan's five thousand dollars from his pocket and flipped through the bills. "Do you prefer all French money?"

"Excuse me—yes, monsieur, French money. There was a time when American dollars were to be preferred almost everywhere, but these days . . ."

"I understand. Here's ten thousand francs."

Bruckner peeled off the bills and handed them to Gros-Jacques, who sat looking at the money disdainfully. "That is not enough."

Bruckner, watching the big man across from him, tensed his body to leap up and push the table in his face should it become necessary. "That is quite enough," he said. "I am not an amateur in these matters, Jacques. I purposely did not give you enough to make a handsome profit for yourself—the profits for all of us come when the job is done. Please do not waste any more of my time or yours treating me like a fool. If you do your part of the job properly you will be amply rewarded."

Gros-Jacques stared at Bruckner. "What is it that we are seeking in New York, monsieur?"

"A small metal box that is somewhat inaccessible. There is no need for you or the others to know what it is—it would mean nothing to anyone but me."

"Ah," Gros-Jacques said, raising his dark bushy eyebrows. "A sentimental trinket, perhaps?"

"Precisely," Bruckner said, and though it was obvious the other man did not for a minute believe him, he didn't elaborate.

"I can't guarantee what kind of scum will sell military

348

assault materials or put a decent boat in the water for this pitiful sum of money," Gros-Jacques said, pocketing the handful of francs. Muttering to himself, he got up from the table and left the bar. Bruckner finished his beer and left soon after.

The following morning Bruckner left the hotel early and went to the nearest newspaper kiosk in the Place de la Concorde, where he purchased copies of every morning paper he could find, as well as leftover copies of *Le Monde* and *France-Soir* from the previous evening. He took them all back to his room in the Crillon and spread them out on the bed and across the floor.

There was nothing of interest in either evening paper. The first of the morning papers he checked—the *International Herald Tribune*—carried a small story about the police finding the body of a female Sorbonne professor in the Bois de Vincennes; it was assumed she had been raped and strangled. *Le Parisien Libéré*, *Le Figaro*, *L'Aurore*, and *Le Matin de Paris* all carried stories on the unfortunate sex slaying of Mademoiselle Solange Cordier with accompanying photographs, and two of these newspapers ran associated editorials pointing out the need for greater community concern about the lack of police patrols and proper lighting in the city's parks. The peculiar thing, though, was that not one of the seven daily newspapers had printed one word about the finding of another body in a park, the body of Martin Toberts, prominent member of the American diplomatic corps in Paris. Not one word.

Bruckner picked up the telephone and dialed the *Times-Weekly* offices. "This is Bruckner," he said when Sloan came on the line. "Have you seen or heard anything of Toberts? I was supposed to meet him yesterday morning but he never showed. I'm a little worried about him."

"No, I haven't talked to him in the last two or three days," Sloan said thoughtfully. "You might try the embassy."

"Yeah, I guess that's what I'll do," Bruckner said, wondering whether Sloan might be lying to him. He pressed the plunger to break the connection and dialed Toberts's home number. His luck held; Jessie answered on the third ring.

"I just wanted to talk to Martin a minute," he told her. "Is he there?"

"Why, no," Jessie said. "Isn't he at the embassy?"

"No, I just tried there and they said he went home."

"That miserable son of a bitch!" Jessie shouted into the phone. "He's probably with that little French cunt, then. I hope he gets syphilis and his *thing* falls off."

"Would you please call me at the Hotel Crillon if you hear from him, Jessie? I'll probably be here most of the day."

There was a sound at the other end of the line, a sound like the tinkling of ice cubes in a whiskey glass. "How 'bout, since Martin isn't here, how 'bout you come on over, lover, and we'll practice some new tricks in my nice, empty bed?"

"Later, maybe—yeah, that sounds fine, Jessie. I'll talk to you later." And he hung up quickly before she could really begin to work on him.

He leaned back on the bed with his head propped against two pillows and stared out the window at the gray day. The forecast was for rain this afternoon. He thought about the possibilities; there weren't many ways to go on the problem, and only one direct way of verifying a central fact—*too* direct for safety, probably, but it seemed to be his only option at the moment.

He put on a dark raincoat and thought about taking an umbrella but decided against it. He left the hotel and took a taxi to the Racing Club of France, the headquarters of which were in the Bois de Boulogne in a building not far from Pré Catelan. When the taxi had disappeared he walked toward the west, along the path where, two evenings ago, he had last seen Martin Toberts.

He was a good hundred yards or so from the spot where Toberts's body had fallen half hidden by the bushes along the walkway, but already he could see that nothing was there. There shouldn't have been anything there, of course —not after two days with people passing by constantly. Still, as he drew even with the exact spot, or as close to it as he could remember, he peered carefully into the bordering shrubbery while trying not to appear to, for there was good reason to suspect that somewhere out of sight two men in an unmarked police sedan might very well have binoculars trained on him at this very minute. Knowing better than to slow his pace noticeably, he kept walking past the spot and continued on other paths for another three quarters of an hour, eventually leaving the Bois at Porte de Passy, where he caught a taxi back to the hotel.

He knew now that something was very wrong, and because he didn't know exactly what it was, he worried. Back in his hotel room, he called Toberts's number at the American Embassy, which he would have preferred not doing, and asked to speak to Martin Toberts. The person who answered, a man with a somewhat prissy voice, told him that Mr. Toberts was no longer employed by the International Communication Agency and that his present whereabouts were unknown. "In case we hear from Mr. Toberts in the near future," the prissy-voiced man said, "whom shall I say called him?"

Bruckner broke the connection immediately and sat holding the dead receiver in his hand, a cold chill settling into his neck and shoulders. Toberts was dead, there could be no doubt of that—no one who was human could take a full clip from a machine pistol in the upper torso and live. Which left two other possibilities. Either the CIA had found Toberts's body somehow and didn't want that fact publicized, for reasons of their own, or else the KGB had been following one of them, had seen the action in the Bois, and had snatched Toberts's body. But why? The only reason that made sense was that they thought Toberts might have had the old professor's manuscript hidden on his body somewhere, perhaps as a microdot. Bruckner visualized the way the park had looked that evening, just before he killed Toberts, and how certain he had been that no one was close enough to see anything incriminating. Except a man with a small dog—the bloody dog walker!

Bruckner looked at his watch. It was time for dinner but he wasn't in the least hungry. He went downstairs to the Crillon bar and began to drink straight Scotches, one after the other, to calm his nerves. At one point he imagined that he saw Ilsa circulating among the men patrons of the bar, soliciting business for the evening ahead. But he was dead certain that he had killed her, too, and the image unnerved him so much that he returned to his room, took three barbiturate capsules that he kept for the purpose, and stretched out in a cold sweat on the unmade bed, willing himself into the luxury of unconsciousness.

31

TOBERTS TURNED OVER IN bed and concentrated on the various parts of his mistreated body, trying to pick up distinct sensory impressions from the most distant territories first—the feet, the hands, the arms, and legs—gradually moving up to the chest and, particularly, the head. For the first time in three days since they had brought him here he was aware that he did *not* have a pounding pain in the back of his head, and that he could, miraculously, draw a deep breath without the accompanying sensation of a red-hot meat cleaver being drawn through his lungs.

Moving slowly and quietly, with an eye on the locked door into the hallway, he swung his legs heavily over the edge of the bed and sat up, then carefully, holding onto the headboard, stood up on legs that felt remarkably like soft plastic. But he didn't pass out, in fact, did not even feel particularly light-headed, and that was important. Because he intended to leave this place, and he had to be able to move under his own power.

He knew that it was probably foolish to try too much before his wounds had had more time to heal, but there was a particular urgency about his plans now. The previous evening he had overheard Colonel Balachov discussing with someone the fact that their guest Mr. Toberts seemed to be recuperating well enough that they could begin to try more physical means of persuading him to tell them what they wanted to know without risking his dying on them first. Toberts knew from many sources that Colonel Balachov was an expert torturer, and that it would only be a matter of a few excruciatingly painful hours of interrogation before he would tell them anything and everything he knew or had ever known. The best thing he would have to look forward to after that would be his own merciful death.

He took stock of his situation. They had dressed him in a pair of loose-fitting white pajamas. There was a window beside the bed, but it was permanently and opaquely sealed. From things he had overheard he knew, though, that he was on a floor above the ground floor—probably the second. There was a closet in one corner of the room; crossing his fingers for luck as he moved toward it, he discovered that someone had stored inside it the clothes and shoes he had been wearing that evening with Bruckner in the Bois. The shirt was a bloody mess, and wasn't usable at all, but the jacket would do even with several bullet holes it in. He left the pajama shirt on and quickly donned the jacket, pants, shoes and socks, grimacing each time he bent or twisted as pressure was exerted on the stitches in his chest.

They had been careful and there was nothing in the room that could be used as a weapon. The bedside lamp was far too heavy and unwieldy, the plastic water pitcher far too light. His own physical condition was such that a schoolgirl could have beaten him in any hand-to-hand situation. Clearly brains, not muscle, would have to be employed.

He turned off the lamp and, with only the dim ceiling light to work by, stood on the plug end of the cord and ripped the wires loose from inside the lamp. He separated the two wires down to the plug, attached one bare end to the metal doorknob, and shoved the other end under the carpet about two feet inside the room. Next he saturated the carpet area over the stripped wire with water from the bedside pitcher. Finally he inserted the plug into an electrical outlet in the wall close to the door, turned off the ceiling light, and sitting on the edge of the bed began to moan and groan as loudly as he dared.

The brute they called Fon, the one Toberts had fought that night outside the Hotel Crillon, had been assigned to guard the room from the hallway outside. Toberts heard a key turn in the lock and watched the door swing inward as Fon peered cautiously into the darkened room. Risking it, Toberts groaned again from the bed.

One hand still on the doorknob, the other holding a pistol, Fon took a couple of steps into the room and let out a surprised grunt as the electrical shock jolted his massive body. His eyes popped wide open as he tried, and failed, to will the muscles of his hand to release the metal knob. The useless pistol jerked up and down in his other hand as more than two hundred volts of electricity coursed through thousands of nerve synapses in his body, rendering his muscles as helpless as if they had been made of jelly. In a matter of seconds the largest muscle, the heart, faltered and then stopped, and Fon's huge body sagged to the floor, his hand still glued to the doorknob. Only when Toberts crept to the wall socket and pulled the plug did Fon's twitching arm fall lifeless upon the rest of his crumpled body.

With great effort Toberts managed to free the pistol from Fon's grip; it would be better to have it than not, and it might give him added confidence, but he prayed that he would not have to use it. He stepped over the body and peered around the edge of the door into the hallway. There was no one in sight, and no noises indicating where in the building other people might be. He took a few steps into the hall and then crept to the banister of the stairway. It seemed a long way down through unprotected space, but in fact he could see now that it was only one flight to the main floor. Clutching the pistol in his right hand, he began descending the stairs, slowly at first out of fear, then faster and faster, until at the bottom of the staircase he was nearly running.

He pulled up short against the wall and looked around, listening through the sound of his own painfully heaving chest for those other sounds that would indicate immediate danger. Somewhere he heard a metallic banging that he could not for a while identify, but in time he associated the sound with a kitchen—the sound of pots and pans and silverware being washed and put away or readied for another meal. The kitchen, if he could find it, would do nicely for his purposes, as a kitchen nearly always had an opening to the outside. He had already discarded the only other way he knew of to get outside the embassy—through the front door—as being impossibly dangerous. Even if he were lucky enough to make it out that way without drawing attention to himself, there were always at least two armed and uniformed Russians standing guard just outside the front door, and he would never make it to the massive iron gate alive.

He followed the sound through what appeared to be a formal dining room and into an alcove behind it. He was about to open another door when he heard the unmistakable sound of a door on the far side of the next room being opened and boxes being thrown or dropped roughly on the floor. He cracked the near door a fraction of an inch and put his eye to the crack; a man wearing French workman's clothing with a red cloth tied around his neck was opening a cardboard box with a large knife and counting the contents—large cans of baby peas—to himself in French. He was obviously here from the market delivering foodstuffs to the embassy's pantry.

Holding the pistol by its barrel behind his back, Toberts pushed the door open a bit farther and said, *"Bonjour,"* pleasantly to the man, hoping that no one else would hear him. The man looked up and automatically spoke the same words just as Toberts's hand and the pistol butt came down hard on his head. The man grunted softly and collapsed. Instantly Toberts unbuttoned the man's dirty white smock and put it on over his own clothes, then tied the red cloth bandanna around his own neck and pulled it up to partially cover his face. Hiding the pistol in his pocket and picking up an empty carton, Toberts peeked through the far door directly into the kitchen. There were several cooks and dishwashers milling about the huge sinks and ovens, as well as servants in uniform and at least one chef with the traditional high white hat. Across the kitchen there was a door standing open to the outside, and with any luck at all there would be a truck from the market parked at the curb with the key in the ignition.

With the kind of calm that descends on a man when he knows he has no choice but to go forward, Toberts ducked his head toward the empty box in his hands and walked briskly into the middle of the bustling kitchen activities, his eyes never wavering from the open door. He heard a question in Russian from behind him; no doubt it was directed at him. Then someone spoke in French, quite close by, but he looked only straight ahead and increased his pace. Rounding the corner of a huge cast-iron oven, he nearly collided with a second chef and was rewarded with a string of what he took to be Russian expletives, though the words themselves were lost on him. The chef stopped abruptly in the middle of his tirade and suddenly pointed a finger at Toberts, a puzzled look of surprise on his beefy face. The kitchen was deathly quiet for an instant, and Toberts, recognizing the signal for evasive action, threw the cardboard carton into the air as high as he could for the sake of distraction and raced flat out for the door. A cook stepped into his path and he stiff-armed him with the heel of his hand just under the nose, in a move that would have gotten any NFL running back benched for the rest of the season.

Outside now, aware of the beating pain in his chest, he fumbled with the pocket of the smock as he ran, searching for the pistol, which seemed to have disappeared. There was a truck parked near the rear entrance and he ran to it and jumped inside. His luck held; the keys dangled invitingly from the ignition. Feeling an instant of remorse about having hurt the innocent deliveryman, he started the engine of the truck and spun off down the gravel path that led to a closed and guarded rear gate. He could hear the cooks and other kitchen workers shouting after him now, the noise loud enough that the two guards popped out of their stone gatehouse and slipped the straps from their submachine guns. Without even thinking about what he was doing, Toberts aimed the truck at full throttle directly at the center of the gate and crashed into and through it before the guards could fire a decent shot.

Once outside the Russian compound and out on the French street he felt relatively safe, at least for the moment. He slowed the truck to a reasonable speed and entered the flow of traffic, trying to look as much like a market deliveryman as possible for the benefit of the passing drivers.

Now there were certain decisions to be made. He would

357

have to ditch the truck as soon as possible because the French police, at least, would be after him in a matter of minutes. *Finding* him, of course, would be another matter, since the vehicle he was driving resembled all the other delivery trucks in the city, and not even the police would have the nerve to stop them all.

He dug in the pockets of his pants for the first time to see what the Russians had left him: a few coins, a handkerchief, a package of chewing gum with three sticks left in it, and a comb. That was all. There were two different sets of keys missing, and of course his billfold, which had contained less than a hundred dollars in cash, his passport, and all the cards and scraps of paper that could prove, or disprove, that he was who he said he was. If a policeman stopped him at this moment, there was absolutely no way for him to prove that he was an American citizen named Martin Toberts, or indeed that he was any other living human being.

He stopped the truck beside a tobacco shop where he knew there was a telephone and used most of the change remaining in his pocket to call his number at the American Embassy. Stanley answered on the first ring, and when Toberts identified himself there was an odd pause at the other end. "We've been expecting you to call in," Stanley finally said.

"Well, I ran into a little trouble," Toberts said. "I'm out here in the cold, so to speak."

"All right, Toberts, tell me where you are so we can send a car to pick you up."

There was something funny about Stanley's voice, or what he said. It was a few seconds before Toberts realized that it was the first time Stanley had ever called him Toberts without preceding the name with Mister. It gave Toberts a distinctly uncomfortable feeling, as though something between his assistant and him had just now changed in a subtle but vastly important way that Toberts did not quite understand.

"Where are you now?" Stanley repeated.

On one of those impulses that intelligence agents develop instinctively as a means of survival in whatever political jungle they find themselves, Toberts gave Stanley an address that was miles across Paris from where he was right now, and also from where he expected to be in the next few hours.

"Don't move," Stanley ordered, with more authority in his voice than Toberts had ever heard before. "We'll be right there for you, in a gray Simca sedan—I've already ordered it. But while you're on the line, tell me what sort of trouble you've been in, will you? We've all been quite worried about you, as you might imagine. Even old Fitzgerald called down to inquire about you."

Toberts had a sudden vision of the comm section people on the fourth floor hastily checking out circuits and tracing the location of his call in. He pressed the disconnect lever and hung up the receiver; he could always claim later that the connection had been broken somewhere else.

With the last bit of change in his pocket he placed another call to the embassy, this time to the general number. He told the receptionist who answered to get Mme. Joubert on the line, and in a moment he heard the familiar voice of his former secretary and den mother saying, "Yes? This is Madame Joubert."

"Please don't act surprised or anything, Madame Joubert. This is Martin Toberts. I don't have much time but I need a bit of information, and you always did seem to know more about what was going on in the embassy than everybody else put together. What are they saying about Martin Toberts, Madame Joubert?"

There was a pause at the other end. "There is very strange talk here lately. The scuttlebutt is that the gentleman in question has gone bad—defected to the other side—and there are lots of people out in the streets of Paris looking for him."

"You mean to bring him in and question him?"

"No, I do not believe so. The word 'termination' comes to mind. The fear is that he will tell the other side all he knows, if he hasn't already."

"Well, I haven't, Madame Joubert, and I haven't gone bad. The trouble is, there's no way for me to prove that right now."

"I'm . . . terribly sorry, monsieur. Is there anything I can do to help?"

"No, nothing, thank you. You must not get involved, dear lady. I appreciate your information more than I can tell you. And now I must go."

"Take care of yourself, then. I shall pray for you."

"You do that. Someday we'll both laugh about all this, I promise you."

For one insane instant Toberts wanted to put his head in Mme. Joubert's comfortable lap and let her soothe him and nurse him back to health. Shaking off the image, he quietly replaced the pay phone receiver and returned to the stolen market truck, which by now had to be getting undesirably conspicuous on the streets.

He drove as fast as he dared, keeping to the busiest streets. Regardless of the danger, he had a terrible errand to run—ever since he had regained enough consciousness in the Russian Embassy to remember what Bruckner had said about having killed Solange, he knew he would have to find out if it was true.

Without knowing exactly how he would handle asking such a question, he drove slowly down the street where Solange lived with her mother. When he saw the large black wreath on the front door of the little house, the pain of certainty nearly overcame him, but he drove past without stopping; there was nothing he could do for her now, and never would be again.

He crossed the river to the Right Bank where a doctor he knew who had done special favors for him in the past kept a small private office. There were two people in the waiting room, but Toberts simply walked through to the back office. Dr. Kells, a short, round man, was seeing another patient but excused himself and hustled Toberts off into an examining room.

"What the hell have you gotten yourself into this time?" the doctor asked him, as he helped Toberts take off his shirt. After a quick but thorough examination Dr. Kells swabbed antibiotic liquid on the wounds and redressed them with fresh bandages. "Don't do any pole-vaulting for a couple of weeks, but I think you'll pull through," he told Toberts. "You've had remarkably good surgery, wherever you got it done—Russia, I should think, by the look of the stitches. You wouldn't want to tell me how you acquired those bullet holes?"

"That's right, I wouldn't. Can I travel?"

"Not for at least a week."

"Too bad. Are there any exercises I can do so that when I do travel, or go pole-vaulting, for that matter, I won't split myself open?"

The doctor gave him a booklet of printed instructions, a vial of thirty antibiotic capsules, and a small box of tiny round white pills. "Capsules four times a day, and do the exercises. The white ones are for pain, and you'll probably need them; take more than three at one time, though, and you'll never tap-dance again. Two days from now you'll have to snip out the stitches yourself—straight down the middle and tweeze out the thread ends from the sides. Think you can handle it?"

"I think so."

"Good. Call me if complications set in."

Toberts shook his head. "That might be one hell of an expensive call. Send the bill to my office at the embassy, please. Someone will pay it eventually."

"I'll live without it," Dr. Kells said. He extended his hand. "Good luck, Martin."

Toberts shook the pudgy, talented hand. "I'd just as soon you didn't report this to the embassy or anybody else who might ask," he said, knowing Kells might be forced to do so anyway. He was certain he would never see the little doctor again.

His next stop was Harold Sloan's office at the *Times-Weekly*. When he saw the look of surprise on Sloan's homely face, he shook his head and laughed. "I'm not a ghost, if that's what you're thinking."

"No, it isn't that," Sloan said. "I just . . ."

"Never mind. First, there's a market truck double-parked right outside your front door. Tell somebody to take it, if it's still there, and drive it out by the Bois de Vincennes, leave it, and take public transportation back. It's dangerous—the truck's hotter than hell about now with every *flic* in Paris looking for it—so pick somebody with a brain. Here are the keys."

While Sloan disappeared with the keys, Toberts sat down

361

across from the editor's desk and rested his head against the back of the chair. Things were moving too fast for him, and there was no way to slow them down. The one thing he knew was that, for a while anyway, he had to keep moving. The police, the KGB, and the CIA were all after him with a vengeance—it would have made a lurid and entirely unbelievable script if it hadn't been true. If I have a choice of who gets me, he thought, I'll certainly take the police. But of course, no one was going to give him a choice like that.

When Sloan returned, Toberts's eyes were closed and he nearly couldn't force himself to open them. "You want news?" Sloan asked him.

"Yeah, sure."

"Your friend Bruckner asked me for a lead on a special 'work crew'—and he took five thousand dollars. U.S. and French mixed. I also put him onto a guy who deals in illegal arms."

"Who, Fawzi?"

"That's the one. Bruckner wanted very badly to get hold of a Russian-made machine pistol, for some reason."

"Well, he found one," Toberts said, opening his shirt so Sloan could see the bandages. "The bastard suckered me, Sloan, even after I knew I couldn't trust him. And now everybody and their dog is after me—my buddies at the CIA think I've defected because the KGB picked me up and kindly took me to their embassy for a little combined surgery and interrogation. The KGB probably passed the word to the CIA clandestinely that I had, in fact, defected. People from both sides were probably standing there in the park admiring the trees when Bruckner blasted me."

Sloan whistled. "What if Bruckner pops in again?"

"He may. He's definitely about to be on his way out of town, but he may stop by. If you see him or talk to him again, don't tell him anything about seeing me. In fact, ask him about me, to throw him off. Did you take care of the truck?"

"Yeah, Barney's a good man. I think he used to steal cars back in the States, when he was younger."

"Thanks, Sloan. I need a couple of things out of that wonderful safe of yours."

"Money? You can have whatever's left after Bruckner's haul."

"Money, and that passport I left here for just such an emergency."

"Yeah, I remember—it's in a white envelope with 'Lesley' written across the front of it."

Sloan opened the safe and gave Toberts the passport. "You want francs, or what?"

"A few francs, the rest dollars."

"Oh?" Sloan said. "You going home?"

"Better you don't know, Sloan."

Sloan handed him the money, and although he didn't say anything, he looked as though he wanted very much to ask Toberts a question.

"What is it, Sloan?"

"I was just wondering about something," Sloan said hesitantly. "I mean, you're pretty obviously splitting, no matter where it is you're headed, and I just wondered about our . . . cash arrangement."

Toberts sighed and shook his head. "I'm not the CIA, Sloan—just one of its innumerable minions. The agency will probably continue to take care of you financially in the same manner as always, if that's what you want. But let me tell you something—you were once a damned good newspaperman, which is, of course, why we set you up here in the first place. I happen to think you still are a damned good newspaperman, or could be. I honestly believe you could make the *Times-Weekly* a legitimate, profitable operation if you wanted to, instead of this whoring for the U.S. government."

Sloan shook his head, thinking about it. "I don't know, Martin, I'm too old to get out there and hustle for a buck in competition with all these smart young studs. Too frigging old . . ."

"Come off it, Harold," Toberts said. "For once in your life do something for the right reasons."

"Yeah, maybe you're right. Well, good luck, Martin, and thanks for everything. I don't really know what kind of life you lead, but in my book you're a prince. I just wanted you to know that."

"You're not a bad guy yourself, Sloan. By the way, the

CIA locals will no doubt question you, but just play it cool. If they get tough, tell them the truth, or what you think is the truth. You don't have to be a martyr—I'll be long gone by then anyway."

"Do you need anything else?"

"Yes—an uncommon amount of luck." He reached in his pocket for the Russian Fon's pistol that he'd picked up in the embassy. "Lose this for me, will you? The Seine's not a bad place for it."

"It's done," Sloan said, and Toberts knew he could count on that.

The main thing, Toberts thought, was to get out of Paris alive; after that, things would pretty much take care of themselves. He took a taxi to the Gare du Nord train station and, feeling that unfriendly eyes were on him the entire time, booked passage on the night ferry—the still elegant relic of European railway travel at the turn of the century. Now it was simply a tourist attraction—an old-fashioned, romantic way to travel between Paris and London and, as such, about the last place anyone would look for an intelligence agent on the run. He got the ticket without incident, though the ticket-seller looked at him rather strangely when he pulled the loose bills from his pocket. Because of this, when he left the station he stopped in the first little shop he found and bought a cheap billfold. Since he knew he had to stay off the streets for the next five hours or so until the train left at ten that night, he bought a copy of *Le Monde* at a news kiosk, found a small but busy café, and settled down with a glass of wine for the long hours of waiting.

To pass the time he glanced at the newspaper to see if there might be something in it about him. There wasn't, of course, but as he idly turned the pages, he nearly cried out when he suddenly found himself staring at a photograph of Solange, wearing a suit with a ruffled blouse. The story was straightforward, making the lurid details seem less so by a conscious restraint in the language—the way newspapers ought to be, he thought, and almost never were. The article mentioned that her body was still being held at the police morgue on the Ile de la Cité, pending further laboratory tests. Although he dreaded going that far and risking discovery and capture, or worse, on the streets, he nevertheless could not sit there in the café knowing that her body was lying on some cold metal slab in the basement of the Préfecture de Police.

He took the metro from the Gare du Nord station to the Cité and, claiming to be a cousin of the deceased, was taken down to view the body by a disinterested attendant. There were ugly purple bruises around her lovely neck; otherwise, except for the pallor of death, she looked remarkably peaceful and beautiful and much as he remembered her the last time he had seen her alive. He touched her face with trembling fingers. As the attendant pushed the refrigerated case back into the wall, Toberts felt cold tears rolling down his cheeks though he had not been aware that he was crying. To himself he swore that he would make Bruckner pay for her death if it was the last thing he ever accomplished.

The night ferry left the Gare du Nord on time. In his spacious compartment on one of the ten sleeping cars making up the train Toberts tried to sleep, but during the four-hour run from Paris to Dunkerque he managed no more than about fifteen minutes at a stretch.

At Dunkerque he raised the window shutter a few inches to watch as the sleeping cars were uncoupled from the engine and shunted into the cavernous interior of the ferry boat on tracks fixed to the deck. After the cars were chained to the deck, the huge gangplanks were pulled up and the ferry began its three-and-a-half-hour crossing of the English Channel. Toberts had made this trip twice before—both times with Jessie—and he knew that the customary gentle pitching caused by the waves made this the best time for sleeping. He closed his eyes and settled into the soft pillow, and though he did fall asleep, his dreams were so terrible that at the first slight jolt as the cars were reattached to an engine on the Dover side of the Channel, he sat bolt upright in the bunk and for a moment could not remember where he was. He remained awake during the hour and a half it took the train to reach Victoria Station in London. As he handed the phony passport to the British customs agent, he glanced at the huge station clock and saw that it was a little after six o'clock, London time.

The passport check was only a formality, as he had hoped. He took a limousine bus from Victoria Station to Heathrow Airport, hoping that they wouldn't have anyone watching there yet. Certainly Orly and de Gaulle in Paris would be crawling with agents and police by now; it was the main reason he had decided to take the ferry train and try for a plane from London instead.

"Mr. Lesley?" the ticket agent at Heathrow asked, staring at the passport photograph that looked remarkably like the man standing in front of his window.

Toberts nodded, remembering, Mr. Lesley had been an American tourist in Paris several years ago who had unfortunately had his passport stolen; the American Embassy had issued him a new one. Toberts knew it would be several weeks before the name Lesley could be run through a computer check by the State Department's Consular Service Bureau, and by then he would have disappeared into the middle of New York City.

"There is a flight departing for John F. Kennedy Airport at ten-thirty," the ticket agent was saying. "Do you wish me to book passage for you, sir?"

Toberts thought about where in the United States of America an agent on the run from Europe would be likely to head. New York City, of course—certainly as a first stop. "Do you have anything earlier going to another city in the eastern U.S.?" he asked the man.

"Let's see, sir, . . . no, not earlier, but there's a noon flight to Logan Airport in Boston. Would that do?"

"Yes, please. One way, tourist, an aisle seat, please, in the smoking section if you have it."

The ticket agent was beginning to write out Toberts's ticket to Boston when Toberts noticed a man in a brown business suit standing against a wall holding a newspaper as though he might be reading it. There was nothing unusual looking about the man—indeed, perhaps it was his extreme ordinariness that attracted Toberts's attention to him—but for whatever reason Toberts would have bet his last dime that the man was an intelligence agent for *somebody's* service.

He had the ticket agent change his ticket to the earlier flight to Kennedy. He had to chance it, because the longer he stayed here the more danger there was that someone, like the man in the brown suit, would try to stop him from leaving. He took the ticket and poor Mr. Lesley's passport to a small out-of-the-way alcove off the passenger lobby, where he would have a clear view of anyone attempting to follow him, and waited the longest half hour of his life to board the BOAC flight to New York City. The man in the brown suit, he was glad to see, was not a passenger.

32

WITH A DECIDED SENSE of urgency, as though he were living in a frail house of cards that might come tumbling down around him at any moment, Bruckner moved about the room at the Crillon gathering up all his belongings that he had brought with him when he was first assigned to Paris on the Lamplighter project two months ago. When the suitcases were all packed and standing beside the door, he called down for a porter and told the desk to hold the bags in the lobby and that he would be needing a taxi to de Gaulle Airport shortly.

From his breast pocket he took the folded papers—which were the only remaining translated copy of Professor Cordier's remarkable manuscript—and glanced over them hurriedly a final time, then replaced them in his pocket, where they would be as safe as anywhere he could imagine. He had studied the papers repeatedly during the past couple of days until, now, he thought he knew them nearly by heart.

There was a brisk knock on the door. Bruckner opened it, saw that it was only the porter, and allowed him to take the bags away. Then he closed and locked the door, went to the telephone, and dialed Toberts's number at the embassy from memory. An assistant who spoke in a bureaucratic monotone—the same person Bruckner had spoken with several times before, although the man had never identified himself—answered by repeating the number Bruckner had dialed.

"Is Martin Toberts in?" Bruckner casually asked.

"No, I'm afraid not," the voice said. "Who's calling, please?"

"Pell Bruckner, from the *Times-Weekly*. When you see

Toberts, would you tell him that I'll be out of town for a few days, in North Africa, on that special matter we discussed?"

The assistant paused, then said, "Perhaps you should come in to the embassy now to discuss this *special matter* with us, instead. Mr. Toberts may be tied up indefinitely."

"No, I think not," Bruckner said. "It was a purely personal, private matter between Martin and me—wouldn't mean a thing to anyone else, I'm sure. Just tell him I'll be back in a week or so and will call him again."

"I believe Mr. Toberts would have wanted us to make personal contact before you—"

Bruckner hung up before the officious assistant could explain what it was Mr. Toberts would have wanted. The call should at least establish that he, Bruckner, had no knowledge of Toberts's present whereabouts, and certainly not that he was dead.

Carrying a raincoat over his arm against the possible bad weather that he fully expected in New York, Bruckner went down to the lobby and checked out of the hotel. The porter who had taken his baggage hailed a taxi from the ranks standing at the door and told the driver where Bruckner wanted to go. "What airline?" the driver asked in French, and Bruckner told him, "Air France, flight 403 to New York City." Gros-Jacques and the three men he had selected for the job were to board the same flight —separately, individually, as though they were totally ignorant of the others. There was always the possibility that someone might be watching, though who it would be Bruckner could not imagine. Silently, as the taxi raced toward the sprawling airport complex north of Paris, Bruckner congratulated himself on having covered his tracks completely.

Another porter at the airport took his suitcases and disappeared with them; Bruckner would not see them again until they appeared on the moving baggage distributor at Kennedy. At the Air France ticket counter he confirmed his reservation and loitered in the area long enough for the four others to spot him, as they had agreed he would do. He saw Gros-Jacques almost immediately —the man would stand out in any crowd, which was a decided drawback for a person in his line of work. Still, he must have been good at it to have survived the number of years Sloan had said he had. At the meeting Gros-Jacques had arranged last night, he assured Bruckner that the equipment and supplies Bruckner had ordered had been crated and sent off on a freighter without a hitch, and that they would be off-loaded and stored in a dockside warehouse exactly six days from today, where they would remain for forty-eight hours and then, unless claimed in the meantime, would be removed from the warehouse and destroyed.

Hoping he would remember the other three well enough to spot them in the airport crowd, Bruckner searched the area near the ticket counter, then wandered off toward a newsstand, where he pawed idly through the French magazines with their nonpornographic photo layouts of young French girls with bare breasts, somehow much more sexually stimulating than the glazed-eyed hookers the American girlie magazines seemed to prefer. It was nearly two hours until departure time for his flight.

A slender, dark-haired, wiry-looking man with thin, humorless lips peered over the top of the newspaper rack just opposite where Bruckner stood, then walked away in another direction. But in those few seconds Bruckner had recognized another of his "team," the one Gros-Jacques had introduced as Kummel. "He comes highly recommended," Gros-Jacques had said, indicating that he did not know the man personally. "A mountain climber, tough as they come, apparently been involved in his share of black-bag jobs in various parts of Europe. He doesn't talk much, about himself or anything else."

Deciding to use the direct approach, Bruckner had pulled his chair over beside the man known as Kummel in the waterfront bar where they had all met last night—a different bar from Gros-Jacques's hangout—and had simply said to him, "I understand you're a climber. Do you know the southwest face of the Jungfrau?"

The man had stared at him in nearly the same penetrating, unfriendly way as he had just now at the airport, and had finally said to Bruckner, "There *is* no southwest face of the Jungfrau. Please do not bother me again with such

370

childish *testing*—I know my job and I do it as well as anyone could." His accent, which Bruckner had assumed from the name would be somewhat Germanic, had something else in it instead, perhaps Slavic overtones. Names, of course, were easily assumed and just as easily discarded.

Bruckner found the third man in one of the airport cafés, sitting at a small table by himself eating a huge ice cream and cake dessert that he seemed to be washing down with red wine. Only a terribly uncivilized palate could have done such a thing, Bruckner thought, as he ordered coffee at his own table across the room. But it seemed to fit the man, a small, mean-looking Sicilian named Paolo who had a terrible scar across the right side of his face. At some point during the previous evening Kummel had made a remark about Paolo's size, or lack of it, and his ability to do whatever would be required of them, whereupon the Sicilian flicked open a knife from somewhere beneath his coat and threatened to cut various parts from Kummel's body and make him eat them. No finesse, Bruckner had thought at the time, but a certain bravura style that he had to admire in so short a man.

Bruckner thought he saw Paolo glance at him across the horrible dessert concoction just now, but at least it was quite subtle; the man obviously knew his business. Though Gros-Jacques had not worked with him before, he knew his reputation, and as for Paolo's agility, Gros-Jacques had it on good authority that the little man had once worked for an Italian circus on the high wire until he had had to flee after slashing a fellow performer's throat with a razor.

Bruckner finished his coffee and left Paolo sitting in the café. There was still an hour until flight time, which meant he had another half hour to roam the airport looking for the fourth member of the team, a tall, nervous Frenchman with a mop of red hair named Luc. Gros-Jacques knew him personally and had worked with him on a number of occasions. He was supposed to be an excellent rope man, having learned his trade as a smuggler in the French Alps, but if there was one trait Bruckner distrusted more than any other in a man he had to work with, it was nervousness. The man who was sure of himself, even if dead wrong, could usually bluff his way through nearly any situation; but the man with an airtight story who told it as though he had something to hide was sooner or later sure to get caught and bring destruction to those around him. Bruckner would have turned Luc down flat if there had been time to look for a replacement, but in this case he had decided to trust Gros-Jacques's judgment—the kind of thing Bruckner had carefully avoided doing all his life.

Bruckner made a large circle tour of the airport's lobbies and waiting rooms and baggage rooms and restrooms, checking out the many newsstands, cafés, flower and gift shops, even the barbershop. He was going down toward a lower level in one of the futuristic escalators encased in serpentine coils of clear plastic when he suddenly saw, in the adjacent plastic coils of the escalator going up, the unmistakable red hair of the fourth man. Luc turned just in time to look across at Bruckner watching him, and for a dreadful moment Bruckner thought Luc might yell or wave or perhaps run away. As it was, the manner in which Luc violently turned away from Bruckner's gaze was far too obvious, and Bruckner was sorrier than ever that he hadn't followed his own first impulse.

But at least now he knew that the team was assembled, and he felt as he imagined the World War II Allied generals must have felt the day before D-day. Already he was beginning to think of himself as an ex-CIA agent; the reality was a step he needed to take care of. If the operation went well, as he fully expected it to, he would have enough money to stay permanently out of Langley's reach and live well, even elaborately, for the rest of his life. There was no way a CIA agent could simply disappear for a while, stringing his control along with some cock-and-bull story; there was also no way to remain an active agent and still enjoy the vastly increased wealth he expected to have shortly without arousing Langley's suspicions. No, the only thing that made sense now was to leave the agency, permanently.

He took an unsealed but stamped white envelope from his pocket and read the address he had written on it: The Editor, International Economic Newsletter, Washington,

D.C.—the prearranged way to contact Thornton Daniels at Langley. Standing beside one of the terminal mailboxes, he took out his carefully composed letter and read it over again. Essentially, it was a letter of resignation from the agency. Oh, they wouldn't *like* it—Langley invariably wanted to go through their standard and very elaborate debriefing procedure with any resigning or retiring agent. But Bruckner knew where too many of their most putrid corpses were buried for them to risk raising too much of a fuss—and, in any case, there was a neatly typed piece of paper in his central file stating that, due to the rather unusual nature of his work for the agency, he would be eligible for reduced early retirement after only ten years of continuous employment, if he lived that long. He had reached that point a year ago with no thought of exercising his unique privilege anytime in the near future. That, however, had been before Lamplighter and the prospect of ten million dollars or so in gems waiting to be collected.

The letter ended by telling Daniels that he, Bruckner, was heading for a much-needed vacation in North Africa, that he might not be using his own name for a while, and that he knew Daniels would understand why that might be necessary. He hinted that his nerves might have finally given way, which the paper in his file had anticipated. He asked Daniels to set up whatever annuity was coming to him so that the money was forwarded to account number 771-34068-3 at the Chase Manhattan Bank in New York City. He indicated that arrangements had been made with an officer at that bank not only to make deposits in his name, but also to hold and periodically forward mail to their client Mr. Bruckner, wherever he might be. Bruckner, of course, had no intention of going near the Chase Manhattan Bank or trying to put his hands on the pitifully small annuity; he felt sure someone would be waiting for him to do exactly that, and no institution had a longer memory or was more patient in the pursuit of its goals than the CIA.

Bruckner licked the envelope and sealed it, then casually dropped it in the mail slot. As he did so the loudspeaker above his head announced his flight number and asked all passengers to queue up for boarding at gate 27. The announcement was made in four languages.

He walked to the boarding area but deliberately hung back from joining the queue until the other four team members were ahead of him. He watched as Paolo, then Kummel, then Luc joined the line, each separating himself from the others by several passengers. Gros-Jacques queued up in his turn, and Bruckner let three nuns, a businessman, and a large family group intervene before he, too, joined the line.

He watched Paolo and Kummel move past the ticket checkers and out toward the waiting airplane, but as Luc stepped forward and presented his documents, there was a mild commotion and suddenly two uniformed security policemen pulled the hapless Luc from the line and led him away pressed between them like a piece of bologna between two substantial slices of French bread. Gros-Jacques merely turned and stared for a moment in the general direction of Bruckner, and that, Bruckner thought, was certainly to his credit.

There was no further incident as Gros-Jacques and then Bruckner boarded the plane and took their separate seats. Bruckner was aware of where each of the other three were sitting, yet he did not see any of them look directly at him as he stowed his raincoat in the overhead compartment and strapped himself into his seat. It was too bad about Luc, but maybe it was for the best; the operation Bruckner had tentatively sketched out in his mind would have been safer with the extra man but could certainly survive quite well without him. And, fortunately, no one but Bruckner yet knew anything concrete about the operation, so there was literally no chance that Luc could give them away.

As he sat waiting for takeoff, Bruckner plucked a magazine from the seat pocket in front of him and, staring in disbelief, almost smiled to himself at the coincidental irony of what he saw. For there on the cover, obviously taken from a helicopter circling at about crown level to illustrate an article about vacations in the Big Apple, was a glorious full-color photograph of the guardian of New York Harbor, the Statue of Liberty.

THREE

33

Malcolm Williams rolled over in bed and punched off the alarm buzzer. With his eyes still closed he reached over to the other side of the bed and felt for the soft, sweet body of Lucy, his wife of eighteen years. But when his hand touched only the rumpled sheets he sat straight up and rubbed the sleep from his tired eyes, only then remembering where Lucy was and why she wasn't beside him. Shaking his head at the prospect of another day of coping with tourists, he climbed out of bed and padded into the adjacent room to see if Bobby was up yet, but his son was nowhere to be found. It was all right, of course, because there was really no place here for even an adventurous ten-year-old like Bobby to get into serious trouble or to disappear for very long.

Malcolm dressed in a freshly pressed two-tone green uniform of the National Park Service—one of seven or eight he owned—and prepared and ate his usual hearty breakfast of juice, cereal, eggs, toast, and coffee. He was a large, beefy man, the athletic outdoor life of his early years with the Park Service having given him a well-developed upper torso on a base of muscular thighs. In the past few years, though, his abdominal muscles had not been able to keep up their end of the bargain, so that a certain amount of paunch rolled over the top of his service belt and served as a kind of end table for the lower tip of his regulation tie.

After breakfast he affixed a badge above his left breast pocket and removed the stiff-brimmed Smokey the Bear hat from the wooden press where it was kept during off-duty hours. With the hat squarely on his head he walked out the front door of the house and looked up at the sky

—a ritual he had been following every morning for the past twenty-six years. When, eight months ago, he had been assigned to Liberty Island for what was usually considered the hardship post of superintendent of the Statue of Liberty National Monument, he had seen no reason to change this habit.

Nodding his hat toward the soaring green back of Miss Liberty at the opposite end of the tiny island—which had also become habit—he walked slowly around the outside of the house to the small beach area and seawall behind it. It was still too early for the first Circle Line ferry over from the Battery in lower Manhattan, but one of the staff boats—the small *Liberty II*—was tied up in its berth, and beside it he saw Bobby and old Willie Teal down in the little motorboat puttering with the outboard engine.

He walked past the Park Police day barracks, in which Willie—as handyman and general caretaker of the island —maintained a permanent room, and continued along the path to the dock. It was still too early for the guards to be stationed at the gates across the tourist ramp up from the ferry mooring, or in the little gatehouse across the way. He walked out to the second slip and stood watching the top of Bobby's blond head buried almost beneath the large outboard motor.

"Hi, Dad," Bobby shouted up, waving. "I'm helping Willie fix this old outboard motor—aren't I, Willie? He says maybe this afternoon or tomorrow he'll let me pilot the number two staff boat over to Ellis Island. You want to come with us, Dad?"

Malcolm smiled and shook his head. "Sorry, son, I have to work. Your old dad doesn't get summers off like you do."

When Bobby went back to discussing the engine's problems with Willie, Malcolm left the dock and walked along the main tourist thoroughfare that led past the snack bar and souvenir shop toward the entrance to the statue. Across from the concessions was the two-story administration building where Malcolm spent his working days on the island and where he now turned in.

"Morning, George," he said to the ranger at the desk by the door and continued back to his own office. "Morning, Susan," he said to his secretary, who was also in uniform. He removed his hat and sailed it toward the stand between her desk and his; it would have missed the peg by several inches if Susan hadn't leaped up to snatch it by the brim and lower it gently onto the peg, as though they went through this ritual, too, every morning of the world.

"Morning, chief," Susan said, smiling brightly. "You're getting worse. I think you ought to stand closer."

"Never!" he boomed. "It's an old Park Service tradition —ten feet and not an inch less. If my predecessor could do it, so can I."

Susan laughed out loud—a nice girlish laugh, like Lucy's used to be, Malcolm thought sadly. "Is that what they told you?" she asked him. "Poindexter could never even hit the stand."

Malcolm looked at her and saw the nice way she rounded out the uniform. "And did you catch *his* hat for him, too?"

Seeing that it was somehow important to him, Susan shook her head. "I've never caught anyone's hat but yours, chief."

"Good," Malcolm said, and with a smile on his face he sat down at his desk to go over the day's schedule.

After a while he leaned back in his government-issue swivel chair and folded his hands behind his head. "Hey, Susan—I'm scheduled to be a superstar today, did you know that?"

"That's *right!* I'd forgotten all about it. He's from the *Times,* isn't he?"

"Yeah—a Mr. William Johnson, ace reporter for *The New York Times,* along with a photographer. You should have reminded me yesterday afternoon so I could look especially presentable this morning."

"What were you going to do—wear a feather in your hat?"

"Never mind the smart remarks, young lady. They're supposed to be out on the first boat over. It's been my experience that reporters aren't too dependable, though."

"I suppose they'll want pictures of Bobby, too," Susan said. "He's sure a cute little guy."

"Yeah, I guess he is," Malcolm said, thinking about the reporter who was coming and the questions he'd probably ask. It was supposed to be a feature article on the superintendent and his family, and the strange way they lived beside one of the most famous landmarks in the world. That was going to be tough, the family angle, with Lucy gone. How could he explain to a million or so readers that his wife had just up and moved out of the house one day almost four months ago, moved off the island and into a crummy little third-floor walkup apartment in Greenwich Village so she could study art at the New School, live like a hippie, and *find herself,* whatever that meant? No, there was no way he could do that—he would have to lie about it, that's all there was to it. The National Park Service would never countenance anything but a nice wholesome family image for its senior employees, and besides, if he kept his nose clean he still might have a shot at Yosemite before he retired.

Arch Delbert, the newest ranger on the island, stepped in to tell Malcolm that the morning's first Circle Line ferry from the Battery was just pulling up alongside the dock. "It's loaded, chief," he said. "Looks like a bunch of school kids on it."

"Right. They're from a summer day school in Brooklyn —about sixty of 'em, supposed to be. I'd like for you to go meet the chaperones and give them a deluxe tour, Arch, if you would."

"Sure, chief. Oh, by the way, I saw your son Bobby and Willie Teal down by the docks, thick as thieves. They looked like they were cooking up World War III. I hope someday I'll have a son like Bobby—I really mean that."

"I'll give him to you," Malcolm said, to hide his embarrassment and pride at one more example of the constant attention all the rangers and concession people gave his son. Bobby *was* kind of special, there was no doubt of that; Malcolm was already missing him for the time when, at the end of the week, he would have to return Bobby to Lucy's incredible way of life in the Village. He was no longer sure they had made a wise decision when they had agreed to share Bobby, a week at a time, during the summer vacation.

When the reporter and photographer showed up, Malcolm let them come to him inside the administration building. "William Johnson," the reporter introduced himself, shaking Malcolm's hand. "What do I call you—superintendent?"

"Mr. Williams will do fine," Malcolm said.

"And this is Mike, our photographer," the reporter said. "He'll be taking pictures of just about everything on the island so we'll be sure to end up with plenty of usable shots. Just try to act natural and don't pay any attention to him at all—we never like to take posed shots if we can help it."

The man with the notebook and ballpoint pen in his hand was very much like all the other reporters Malcolm had come in professional contact with over the years. It was the photographer who threw him off a bit—the man was huge, dwarfing the tiny 35-millimeter camera in his hands, and in a dimly lighted room he could easily have passed for something that had escaped from the simian house at the zoo. Malcolm led them around the administration building, handing the reporter maps and charts and promotional brochures filled with photographs and historical facts about the statue. "You can keep that material for reference, if you like," he told the reporter.

They walked outside the building while the photographer finished clicking away inside. Along the walk toward the main entrance at the back of the statue, they passed under tall, scaly-barked trees with large leaves and the reporter asked him what they were. "Sycamores," Malcolm told him. "Transplanted, of course—they're not native to the island. Nothing here is, including the grass."

"You have nice lawns," the reporter said.

They waited for the photographer to catch up, then passed through the double glass doors into a passageway that led to the central information lobby directly beneath the statue at the base of the pedestal. "We're entering what used to be Fort Wood," Malcolm told them. "It was a real fort protecting the harbor—you can still see the gun emplacements. Walls twenty feet thick at the base. Have you gentlemen visited the statue before?"

The photographer only grunted and the reporter said he

had been once, a long time ago, but had forgotten everything he'd seen. "I suppose you lock those doors at night?" the reporter said.

"Oh, yes, we have quite adequate security. That glass is thicker than it looks." The girl at the information counter nodded and he waved back to her. "We'll go on up the stairs to the balcony level and I'll show you the American Museum of Immigration, which is the most recent addition to the pedestal area—President Nixon dedicated it in 1972."

They toured the museum quickly, as the reporting team seemed less than excited by the photographs and text on the walls. Malcolm showed them the bronze plaque set into one wall that was inscribed with the famous poem "The New Colossus" written by Emma Lazarus for the dedication of the statue, the last few lines of which Malcolm knew by heart:

> *"Keep, ancient lands, your storied pomp!" cries she*
> *With silent lips. "Give me your tired, your poor,*
> *Your huddled masses yearning to breathe free,*
> *The wretched refuse of your teeming shore.*
> *Send these, the homeless, tempest-tost to me,*
> *I lift my lamp beside the golden door!"*

"Most people think that plaque's been here since the statue was erected, but it hasn't," Malcolm said. "Not till twenty years after she wrote it." The reporter shook his head in amazement but didn't write anything in his notebook.

Malcolm led them through the Statue of Liberty Story Room. Again the *Times* reporter and photographer seemed less than enthusiastic about what they were being shown, but Malcolm could understand that—the Story Room wasn't exactly a news-making place. As they headed toward the statue, Malcolm told them they could either climb 167 steps up through the pedestal to the base of the statue proper, or they could ride up in the elevator, which usually cost a dime but which he would give them free. "Personally, I'm going to climb the stairs," he said, "even though there are another one hundred and seventy-one steps inside the statue itself and no elevator up there. I'm not as young as I used to be, but I hate to admit that to any-body."

"You look like you're in pretty good shape," the reporter said.

"Well, I've lived a fairly rugged outdoor life most of my life, at least until I was assigned here," Malcolm said. "Are you an outdoorsman, Mr. Johnson?"

The reporter looked at him strangely and said no, he wasn't.

Before they climbed the pedestal stairs Malcolm took them out through a set of glass doors resembling the double set on the lower level, out onto a concrete terrace that was also accessible from the ground level by outside stairs. They stood for a moment watching the tourists walking up to the entrance below them. "We get almost three thousand visitors to the statue every day, rain or shine," Malcolm bragged. "Of course, we get more in good weath-er. But the crowds never stop."

"What time does the first ferry leave Manhattan for the island?" the reporter asked him.

"You were on it this morning."

"And what about the last one at night?"

"I believe the last one leaves here at five-fifteen in the afternoon—you can check with the Circle Line people when you get back."

"No night tours, then?"

"No."

"Why not?"

"There'd be too many problems," Malcolm said quickly. "We'd have to set up lighting all over the island, and that would spoil the floodlighting of Liberty herself, and the way it looks at night from the harbor. If you gentlemen are ready we'll climb the statue now."

They passed by the elevator and climbed the stairs up through the pedestal. To rest for the second ascent, Mal-colm led them out onto the balcony where they could view the surrounding water and land areas of New York and New Jersey. "That way is north," Malcolm told them, pointing toward the skyscrapers of Manhattan he knew they had left less than an hour ago. "You can see the George Washington Bridge over the Hudson, and on the other side all the bridges over the East River. That's Governors Island over there, almost due east of us. There's a big Coast Guard base there. It's where my son goes to elementary school in the winter, and where the people living here on Liberty Island do their basic shopping for groceries and anything else the commissary carries. To the south there is the Verrazano Narrows Bridge—the longest suspension bridge in the world—and, of course, Staten Island. And then west of us is Jersey City and one of the largest oil-refining areas in the United States."

The reporter was making notes as Malcolm talked, and the photographer was hopping around from one place to another, getting shots of everything in the harbor as well as everything surrounding the statue that was visible from the balcony. "Well, are you gentlemen ready to begin climbing again?" Malcolm asked, leading them back inside to the base of the spiral stairway to the crown. People were coming down one side and waiting to start up on the other. "Sometimes it gets a little stacked up here—we get a few people who take a few steps up these narrow old pie-shaped stairs and then start to wonder whether they'll ever make it all the way up."

"What happens if they don't?" the reporter asked.

"Well, there are two rest platforms, one-third and two-thirds of the way up, where you can cross over to the down side of the stairs. A good number of older people do just that. If they get stuck between levels, though, everybody behind them just has to wait. We try to tell everybody beforehand that people with bad hearts or dizzy spells shouldn't attempt it."

As they began the climb inside the wire cages surrounding the tight spiral of steps, the reporter asked Malcolm why it seemed so gloomy inside the vast cavernous interior of the statue.

"We don't really attempt to provide a lot of lighting down here," Malcolm told him. "Just enough to see to climb by. Look through there—see all those points of bright light near the copper skin? That's daylight shining through rivet holes."

"Almost like stars," the reporter said, writing something in his notebook.

Here and there beside the stairway was a floodlight trained on some particularly interesting aspect of the statue's interior construction and framework—the iron strapwork holding the copper skin, in sections, to heavier iron rods, which were in turn fastened to gigantic steel girders that disappeared up into the perpetual dusk of the statue's upper reaches. Once they passed a grilled metal doorway off the staircase leading to a kind of catwalk away from the central spiral core. "Where does that go?" the reporter wanted to know.

"Toward the arm holding the torch," Malcolm said. "There's a ladder up to the torch but we haven't let the public climb it for thirty or forty years—it simply made for too much congestion around the torch. Our maintenance staff uses it to check and repair the torch's lighting system."

"What about lighting?" the reporter asked. "Torch and statue?"

"Hang on till the next rest stop," Malcolm said, puffing hard now. When they reached the place where a metal landing had been built out from the stairs with a bench on it, he and the reporter sat down. The photographer continued to pace across the narrow space like a caged cat, now and then pointing the camera at something and clicking the shutter.

"Most of the statistical stuff is in the brochures I gave you," Malcolm said. "I won't repeat it, except to say that when Liberty was erected in 1886 and for a good many years afterward, the lighting was abominable. I've heard that it was nearly impossible to see the torch at night unless you were almost standing on top of it. The electrical lighting system has been upgraded several times since then, and now it includes transformers, switch panels, and automatic clock controls to turn the whole works on at dusk and off at sunrise. Basically, in the floodlighting system around the eleven star points of the old fort we're standing above right now, there are ninety-six thousand-watt incandescent lamps and sixteen high-intensity four-hundred-watt mercury-vapor lamps. In the torch itself we've got ten thousand-watt incandescent, three two-hundred-watt incandescent, and six four-hundred-watt mercury-vapor lamps—gives it more the look of a real flame. They say the entire floodlighting system is equal to twenty-five hundred times the effect of full moonlight."

"Has anything else changed since the original conception?" the reporter asked.

"About the only thing that's been changed on the statue itself since old Bartholdi created it was when, shortly after the First World War, Gutzon Borglum—the sculptor who later did the presidents' faces on Mount Rushmore—climbed up into the torch and cut away a lot of the solid copper, leaving open spaces that were covered over with yellow and amber glass. Too bad we can't go up and see it."

"Yeah, that *is* too bad," the reporter said.

When they finally reached the last step of the spiral staircase and stepped out into Liberty's crown, they found that the reporter, who was a couple of inches over six feet tall, had to bend over slightly to keep from hitting his head on the ridged copper plates. There were a series of twenty-five windows in the crown, most of them rather small and covered with metal grillwork. "To keep people from accidentally breaking them or trying to throw things out," Malcolm explained when he saw the question on the reporter's face. "Come over here—you can look down at the law tablet in her left hand and see the date July 4, 1776, inscribed on it in Roman numerals."

The reporter and photographer both looked, but neither seemed terribly impressed. "Hasn't there been some trouble up here from time to time?" the reporter asked.

"What sort of trouble?"

"Oh, you know, people trying to take over the statue—terrorists, that sort of thing."

"Nothing very serious," Malcolm said. The question made him uneasy; he personally had been very lucky so far. "Back around 1965 three black extremists were caught with a load of dynamite smuggled in from Canada, but they never got near the statue with it, even though they said they planned to damage it. In 1971 a group of veterans occupied the statue for several days in a peaceful but highly visible protest against the Vietnam War. More recently, in October of 1977, a group of about thirty

Puerto Rican nationalists occupied the crown here for nine hours or so and strung a flag across her forehead and once in a while there's a bomb threat. But these things are all just bids for attention by some pressure group or another. Once they get their publicity—which, I don't mind telling you, I think the newspapers are wrong to give them so freely—they usually come down peacefully and go their way."

"Into prison, you mean?"

"Well, that depends. Yeah, usually they go to jail, but that's publicity, too."

After they had all looked through the various windows, from some of which they could see the right arm holding the torch and from others the harbor and the boat dock on the south side of the island, Malcolm led them to the head of the descending stairway. The reporter noticed two electrical junction boxes on the wall and asked about them.

"Just fuses and such for the lights in the crown," Malcolm said.

"I noticed a generator down by the dock," the reporter said. "Do you generate all your own electricity or is it supplied from the mainland somewhere?"

"I'm afraid that's classified information," Malcolm said. "You understand, I hope—there are lots of crazy people around these days. We just can't afford to give out that kind of vital data to strangers."

"I understand," the reporter said. The photographer took a picture of the junction boxes.

When they had climbed down the dizzying spiral of stairs—the equivalent of twelve stories—Malcolm was panting heavily and was surprised that the reporter and photographer were not. Nevertheless, he suggested that they ride the elevator down the rest of the way and was glad when they accepted his offer.

On the ground level they wandered slowly back through the lobby, watching the tourists who were busy buying slides and postcards. "What else can I show you, gentlemen?" Malcolm asked, somewhat less than enthusiastically. He was growing tired of the interview and wanted to get back to his office and the work waiting for him.

"You've been most kind, superintendent," the reporter said. "But we're really after the more personal touch, about you and your family and the way you live on the island. Could we see where you live, for instance?"

"Yes, of course—though it's in an area of the island that's off limits to the public. Come on, we'll talk as we walk over."

"Are there any vehicles on the island, by the way?"

Malcolm looked at the reporter. "Vehicles for what? There's no place to go here—the biggest thing we've got is a couple of riding lawn mowers. We have races on them every Fourth of July." The laugh this got, Malcolm thought, was just barely adequate.

"How many people live on the island full-time?" the reporter asked.

"Three," Malcolm said without thinking, then caught himself. "Actually, four—myself, my wife and son, and a caretaker-handyman. My wife is staying over in Manhattan for . . . a while."

"Doesn't it get lonely for your family?" the reporter wanted to know. "You'd think they wouldn't allow dependents to live here."

"It's better with them than without them, as far as I'm concerned," Malcolm said and meant it. "I think I mentioned the public school on Governors Island that Bobby goes to, and the commissary—we're allowed to use the staff boat pretty much any time and any way we want to. Trouble is, of course, if you go over to Manhattan for a night at the theater or something that lasts past ten-thirty, when the staff boat quits running, then you have to stay till morning. Sometimes Bobby and I go over in the outboard, but they don't like us to—the cross-channel currents can be pretty tricky in a small, light boat."

The reporter was making notes steadily now. "Just how far is it from the mainland?"

"You mean Liberty Island? About a mile and five-eighths from the Battery at the southern tip of Manhattan, and only about three-eighths of a mile offshore from Jersey City. Geographically, we're in the territorial waters of New Jersey, but because of an interstate agreement a long time ago, the island itself above the mean low-water mark is part of New York State. The part underwater still belongs to New Jersey, though, and every once in a while some wiseacre politician over there suggests that they tow their part back and attach it to the mainland. They just hate to see twelve acres of real estate as valuable as this not be used for something profitable, like another oil refinery tank farm."

It was a joke he had used before with good results, but neither the reporter nor the apelike photographer even cracked a smile. Malcolm began to wonder where the *Times* had dug up these two barrels of fun.

He led them past the paved walkway between the concessions building and the administration building, nodded to a guard that it was all right for them to go back into the posted off-limits area, and took them to the pleasant three-bedroom house that he and Bobby—and Lucy, at the beginning—had called home for eight months now. He took a key from his pocket and unlocked the front door, and when the reporter asked him why he bothered to lock it, given the low population of the neighborhood, Malcolm said he guessed it was just plain habit.

He took them around the house, showing them how you could see the back of the statue from the master bedroom window. When the reporter spotted the telephone beside the bed, he asked Malcolm what it was connected to.

"The mainland, obviously, but I can't even tell you *which* mainland. It's another of those classified bits of data we can't discuss."

"Your water source is classified too, I suppose," the reporter said.

"That's right. I'm sorry, but you understand."

"Not really," the reporter said. "What happens if your telephone goes out and tidal waves start washing over the island—how would you ask for help?"

"Oh, there's a radio transmitter in the administration building. We're in continual contact with people like the Coast Guard and the New York Police Department Harbor Unit. They'd just send over a helicopter and rescue us, I imagine. Except that there aren't any tidal waves here."

Malcolm took them outside and they walked along the planted lawns and pathways lined with trees. In the center of the area surrounded by the house, other living-quarters buildings, and the back of the administration building was an oval of grass edged by low hedges and containing an elegant assortment of playground equipment—a high spiral slide, a candy-striped swing set, and a merry-go-round. A battered rowboat leaned on its side against the swings. "My Bobby's getting almost too big for this stuff now," Malcolm said, "and there aren't any other kids living here to use it. Sometimes on warm nights, I come out here and sit in one of the swings myself."

"And no one else lives in those other four or five buildings?" the reporter asked, pointing to the connected row of institutional-looking brick apartments.

"Just the caretaker," Malcolm said, getting edgy again over the reporter's pointed questions. "Willie Teal is his name—he pilots the staff boat most of the time. Used to be an East River tugboat pilot before he retired. And we have a guard barracks, too, but I'd just as soon you didn't say anything about that in your article."

"How many guards do you need here?"

Malcolm looked at the reporter and shook his head.

"More classified information, I suppose," the reporter said then. "You're beginning to sound like the CIA."

"Unfortunately, that's necessary," Malcolm said.

They passed an archery target standing on a tripod beside the playground and the reporter asked about it. "It's mine," Malcolm said, adding proudly, "I'm pretty good at it, too. It's been a hobby of mine for a long time."

"Ever do any bow hunting?" the reporter asked.

"Sure—all over the States, and I've hunted game in Africa several times. Nothing on the endangered list, you understand."

The reported nodded. "What kind of bow do you use?"

"Hang on a minute, I'll show you," Malcolm said and went into the house. He came out carrying an elaborate fiberglass compound bow and a quiver of steel-tipped arrows. "I'm kind of proud of this equipment," he told the reporter. "My wife never could understand how, for the same money, she could have bought a new refrigerator."

Carefully Malcolm fitted the nock of an arrow into a

390

certain spot on one of the bowstrings, slowly drew back the arrow, aimed using the special attachment on the bow, and released the arrow. It entered the target at the edge of the bull's-eye with a satisfying *thock*.

"What draw weight is your bow?" the reporter asked.

"Adjustable up to sixty-five pounds. You sound like you might be a bow hunter, too."

"Not lately," the reporter said, as though he wanted to drop the subject.

"Here—take a shot," Malcolm urged, handing him the bow and quiver. "Just for fun."

The reporter fitted an arrow to the bowstring and glanced at the target, then pulled and released the string as though he might have known what he was doing. The arrow was low and to the left. A second shot was slightly better, but this time was above the bull's-eye and to the right.

The reporter turned away from the target and shrugged at Malcolm. "I'm not used to the bow."

"Sure," Malcolm said, grinning good-naturedly. "For a minute there it looked like you might be trying to sight in a rifle."

"Really?" the reporter said. He took another arrow from the quiver, held it up to his eye to check its trueness, and after settling it against the string, he flexed the bow several times, watching Malcolm. Suddenly he whirled around toward the target, the pull and release of the arrow so quick that Malcolm didn't even see it. The arrow struck the bull's-eye dead center.

The photographer, who had been watching the action, laughed hoarsely. Amazed, Malcolm took the bow and quiver from the reporter and congratulated him, but the reporter seemed to have lost all interest in his remarkable accomplishment.

"We can tour the perimeter of the island now, if you'd like," Malcolm said. "I really have to get back to my office pretty soon."

He led them to the well-kept lawn areas surrounding the pedestal of the statue, and from there walked with them around the broad tourist walkway that served as a seawall, around the front of the statue, past the boat dock, and back up to the island's central crosswalk. They stopped beside the unused wooden pier on the Manhattan side, and while the photographer took pictures of the grass growing up in the middle of the rotting trestles of the pier, the reporter lighted a cigarette and offered one to Malcolm, who turned him down. "I quit years ago—don't miss 'em a bit now, except once in a while with coffee."

The reporter asked a few more questions—almost, it seemed to Malcolm, out of politeness—and the photographer scurried around taking a few more shots of nothing in particular. Then, seeing that the reporter had finished his cigarette, Malcolm asked him please not to litter the grounds, there were butt cans placed all around the island for that purpose.

"I wasn't going to," the reporter said rather testily. He wet his thumb and forefinger with saliva and pinched out the glowing ember of burning tobacco. Then, carefully, he began to field strip the cigarette and scatter the tobacco crumbs into the grass, after which he rolled the paper remnant into an almost invisible ball and flicked it with his thumb into the wind.

Malcolm shook his head and smiled. "I haven't seen anybody do that to a cigarette since Army basic, years ago."

The reporter stuck out his hand and shook Malcolm's hand, thanking him for the tour. "We've got to get back as soon as possible," he said. "Is there another ferry returning to Manhattan soon?"

Malcolm checked his watch. "In about ten minutes. You can make it."

As the reporter and the photographer hurried off toward the boat dock, Malcolm called out after them, "When will the *Times* print the article?"

The reporter looked back at Malcolm over his shoulder. "Soon, very soon!" he shouted. "I'll let you know."

34

MARTIN TOBERTS LOOKED UP from the classified section of *The New York Times* in his hand to the weathered old brownstone building directly across West Eleventh Street from where he stood. *Furnished room, single, light cooking, no bath. $35/week. Half block off Fifth Ave. bus line.* The ad was simple and direct, a no-nonsense appeal to the person with little money to spend on rent and a total lack of fastidiousness.

Toberts had decided to try this place because of its location in the nicer part of the West Village, an area he had found charming on his first visit to New York more than twenty years ago. It seemed to him that the Village —at least the old houses, the broad sidewalks, the tree-lined streets—had changed very little in all those years. West Eleventh Street reminded him of parts of Paris; standing here on the sidewalk now, looking aross at the row of tall and narrow soot-blemished stone houses, the hazy sunlight filtering through the leaves of a plane tree, he felt almost at home for the first time since the flight from Paris two days ago.

He crossed the street and rang the doorbell, and was eventually met by a round, frizzy-haired woman who, in Paris, would have been called the *concierge*. She showed him the room—a surprisingly light, high-ceilinged cubicle whose single window opened onto West Eleventh Street three floors below. The furnishings consisted of a narrow bed, one chair, a low unpainted table with a broken leg, a two-burner hotplate atop a half-size refrigerator, and a wash basin. Toilet and bath, for those who needed them, were down the hall.

"I like it," Toberts said almost immediately, and pulled enough money from his billfold for the first two weeks.

"You're a real spender," the frizzy-haired woman said, but she was smiling at him. "Ain't *nobody* here pays me more than a week at a time."

"I like the feeling of permanence it gives me," Toberts said, smiling back at her. "Tell me, is there a phone I can use?"

"Down at the end of the hall, pay phone. You can get calls on it, too—I answer the fool thing when I hear it, or else one of the other tenants does."

"My name's Peter Owens," Toberts said, "in case I do get any calls."

"Okay," the woman said. "You *look* like a Peter Owens, come to think of it."

Toberts gave her a Peter Owens–type smile. "What about bedding?"

"There's a linen supply room downstairs. You get fresh sheets every other Tuesday, 'cept when the laundry fucks up. Say, Mr. Owens, do you drink?"

Toberts frowned. "Not to excess, I assure you."

"Oh, shit, I don't care about that, long as you don't bust up the furniture," the woman said. "I was just thinking you looked like you needed a drink, and I got me a bottle of Gilbey's gin downstairs ain't hardly been cracked yet. What do you say?"

"Thanks," Toberts said and started to add, maybe next time. But he caught himself; the woman was just being friendly, he hadn't heard a single friendly voice in at least a week, and chances were she could be useful to him if he was going to live here awhile. "That's the best offer I've had all day," he said. "Lead the way."

"You're on!" she said. "And I won't even ask how come you ain't got no suitcases with you."

"Good," Toberts said. He put the key to the room in his pocket and followed her down the dimly lit uncarpeted stairs.

In the days that followed Toberts took the Circle Line ferry across to the Statue of Liberty five separate times, staying for several hours each time. He hauled himself up

394

the spiral staircase to the room inside the crown and was forced to hang onto the grating in front of the windows while the pain from the wounds in his side and shoulder subsided. But he knew he was getting stronger every day, and that he was going to be all right; he had realized he was going to make it that first night in New York when, in the hotel room, he had managed to remove his own stitches without passing out.

On his second visit to the statue he found himself absolutely alone inside. About halfway up the spiral stairs he suddenly stopped climbing and sat down on the next pie-shaped step, and for a good ten minutes he studied the girders and beams and cross-bars of the immense dark interior of the statue, hoping for a miracle. But of course there was no more reason to think he would spot Alain Picot's small metal box than that any one of the millions of other visitors to Liberty should have discovered it over the years. And no one had yet—if, in fact, it was still here, or ever had been.

"Pardon!"

The voice was close to Toberts's ear; the unexpectedness of it caused him to jump to his feet and nearly topple from the step. A chunky older man wearing a furry green Tyrolean hat with a yellow feather in its band pushed Toberts aside and continued up the spiral staircase. The man was wearing lederhosen and had fat legs and large buttocks, but what Toberts noticed most was the hat—he remembered having seen one like it somewhere in Paris under less than ideal circumstances. Not being able to remember disturbed him greatly, though, in fact, he realized that men all over the world—particularly, it seemed, fat little men—wore hats exactly like the one he had just seen. Nevertheless, his hand was somewhat unsteady on the staircase railing as he descended on the wrong side, until he could cross over to the down spiral and put as much distance between himself and the fat man as possible.

The trouble was, he realized, that he could sit somewhere out on Liberty Island forever without ever seeing Pell Bruckner. Because while he was sure Bruckner would sooner or later head for the place where the jewels were supposed to be, there was no reason to think he would do it immediately, and no real reason to think he would necessarily do it himself instead of hiring a mercenary crew. On the other hand, if Bruckner came to the island in person and spotted Toberts before Toberts spotted *him*, Bruckner would either be alerted to keep out of sight for a while or—a very real possibility—would simply kill Toberts all over again.

There was, of course, another alternative, and that was for Toberts somehow to conduct a full-scale search of the statue's interior and find the jewels himself before anyone else could. He had considered the idea but, finally, had rejected it for two reasons. His examination of the statue and all his instincts told him that such a thorough search in the short period of time that would be available would require a highly organized special team, and all of his contacts with men who could pull off this kind of operation were back in Europe. The second reason was his knowledge of how such black-bag jobs usually went and his fear that innocent people—such as security guards—would necessarily be hurt or even killed. No more, he had thought, there had been far too much killing for the jewels already.

One day after he had returned from the statue, Toberts went back to his room on West Eleventh Street and sat down on his bed with a Manhattan telephone directory that he had taken from beside the hall phone. The listings under "New York, City of" were less than helpful, and the jurisdictional maze surrounding the statue and Liberty Island were nearly impenetrable, or so it seemed.

Finally, after half a dozen calls that ended up being blind alleys, Toberts was accidentally put in touch with a very helpful man in the New York Port Authority office who explained that while they themselves had no police powers in the port they supervised, the New York City Police Department maintained a special Harbor Unit with boats, helicopters, and men on call twenty-four hours a day who did nothing but police the harbor. A Captain Nick Shaner ran things in the Harbor Unit, the Port Authority man told Toberts. "He's a gruff old sonofabitch, but one hell of a good cop."

Toberts thanked the man and hung up, then dialed the Harbor Unit number and after a slight delay was put in touch with Captain Shaner himself.

"My name is Peter Owens," Toberts began, "which won't mean a thing to you. I'm sure you're a busy man, Captain, but I have reason to believe that I possess certain information that could have a large impact on your jurisdictional area."

"And what would that be, Mr. Owens?" the captain said wearily, sounding as though he had heard it all before.

"My information concerns the Statue of Liberty and what may well be an attempt to destroy it."

"Tell me about it."

"I would rather come down and talk to you directly, if that would be possible," Toberts said. "This afternoon, preferably."

"You don't trust the telephone company, is that it, Mr. Owens?"

"The *company's* okay—it's their equipment I don't trust," Toberts said. "There's really no way for us to know, for instance, how many other people are listening to this conversation at this moment."

There was a pause at the other end of the line, then Shaner said, "I'll be here all afternoon, Mr. Owens. Suit yourself as to time."

Forty-five minutes and a short subway ride later, Toberts was sitting across from Captain Shaner's desk in the Harbor Unit headquarters. The captain, puffing on a plump, foul-smelling cigar, had a pad of lined yellow paper in front of him on which he had written the nonexistent Peter Owens's name and telephone number and the single word "statue." He had added nothing further during the past fifteen minutes of Toberts's admittedly involved and somewhat unbelievable explanation.

"I don't blame you for being skeptical, Captain," Toberts said. "I didn't believe a lot of it while it was happening, either. But I guarantee that Pell Bruckner is a killer and an extremely dangerous man in all kinds of ways."

Shaner nodded. "And you say you have no documents to verify any of these . . . accusations?"

"They were stolen, as I told you. Until I have time to replace a few personal papers, I can't even prove that I'm who I say I am."

"Peter Owens," the captain said, glancing down at his notation on the yellow lined paper. "That's your real name, I take it?"

"It is."

"Mr. Owens, you still haven't explained how you happen to be personally involved in all this *secret* stuff—information being searched for by several nations, spies, Mata Hari–type females, nonstandard weapons . . . Are you implying that you're some kind of spy yourself?"

"I am in the intelligence field, Captain Shaner. *U.S.* intelligence. Beyond that I really can't speak openly about my role."

"Why can't your own agency or department or whatever vouch for you?"

Toberts shook his head, knowing that anything he said about his present relationship with the CIA would sound foolish, if not actually incriminating. "There was a, ah, problem—purely a misunderstanding. It will be straightened out shortly, I can assure you."

"Fine," Captain Shaner said. "Meanwhile, I have your number here in case anything comes up where we need to get in touch with you."

"But aren't you going to take some positive action right now to stop Bruckner and any others he may bring with him?"

"How, Mr. Owens? You want us to close up the Statue of Liberty, tell all those school kids and servicemen and foreign visitors that the lady's out of order indefinitely? Based on something you *think* might happen?"

Toberts stood up abruptly. "It *will* happen, Captain. I can't tell you exactly when or how, but I'd bet my life on it!"

Shaner nodded. "Tell you what—I'll call the superintendent out at Liberty Island and pass along your information. They maintain their own security out there and they're pretty good at it. That's about the best we can do."

Toberts sighed and shook his head wearily. "I'm afraid it won't be nearly good enough, Captain Shaner. But thanks for hearing me out anyway."

"That's what we're here for," Shaner said, nodding as Toberts left the room. He ripped the note from the lined yellow pad and threw it into the tray on the edge of his desk, fully intending to call the National Park Service people when he had a spare minute.

But other, more urgent work was subsequently dumped into the tray on top of the note about the statue, and when Captain Shaner found it there several days later, the matter seemed to have lost its urgency. He filed the name "Peter Owens" and a telephone number in a card file in his bottom drawer and tossed the slip of yellow paper into the nearest wastebasket.

35

AFTER PELL BRUCKNER AND Gros-Jacques returned from Liberty Island, where they had posed as both halves of a reporter-photographer team from *The New York Times,* they met with Kummel and Paolo to pass along the news. Their meeting place was a small, dingy coffee shop near the north side of Battery Park.

Following a thorough discussion of what the two had learned from Superintendent Williams on the island, Bruckner laid out a plan of action that involved independent reconnaissance by each member of the assault team, as they had come to think of themselves. Over the next several days all four men individually took the ferry across to the island, behaved as the tourists behaved except for the copious notes they took in small identical notebooks, took a certain number of photographs—mostly of National Park Service personnel this time—and carefully noted times of arrival and departure for both themselves and for those who worked on the island. They talked to guards at the statue, they talked to the pleasantly helpful rangers, they talked to the people who worked in the concessions building behind the snack bar and the gift counters, who in some ways were the most helpful of all. And gradually, as they met back at the coffee shop to compare notes and impressions of the system surrounding the Statue of Liberty, certain definable patterns began to emerge.

They found, for instance, that although there was no essential difference in the uniforms worn by the Park Police and those worn by the rangers, the police could be spotted rather easily by their physical characteristics— tough, brawny, most of them black, as opposed to the usual assortment of guides and rangers who tended to be

400

smaller and rather soft-spoken. The police were a great deal less friendly toward people who asked specific questions about the island, and were not very well informed about the nonsecurity aspects of their assignment. (In a test, Bruckner had asked two obvious guards what sort of trees those were with the scaly bark and large leaves; neither had any idea and had acted as though the question were pointless.) One real help to Bruckner and his comrades was the fact that nearly all of the uniformed employees wore name tags above their right shirt pockets. The important question was, how many guards remained on the island at night?

With Bruckner's help, it was Kummel—the least talkative of the group—who devised a method of finding out. During the following day Bruckner, Gros-Jacques, and Kummel went across on the ferry and made notes on all the guards they could find anywhere on the island, leaving Paolo sitting on a bench in Battery Park with a pair of binoculars trained on the island and all the traffic to and from it. Then the three returned on the last public ferry back, which left the island at five-fifteen and docked a few feet from Paolo's bench at five-thirty. There they waited together for the arrival of the staff boat. They knew from experience that it would dock approximately forty-five minutes after the last ferry, at a Park Service slip next to the Circle Line pier, bringing home for the night all the Liberty Island employees except those who were, presumably, not planning to leave.

Using their two pairs of binoculars to closely view the employees as they stepped from the boat, and then spreading out nonchalantly to mingle with the uniformed men and women as they chatted and walked to their cars parked in a parking lot a short distance away, the four men were able to identify everyone they had seen on the island earlier, both by name tag and by physical characteristics. Everyone, they agreed at a meeting later, except for three large, uncommunicative men who, if they were not cops, had certainly been trained to act the part. A check by Bruckner the following morning, beginning with a watch from the Battery Park bench at five A.M., proved what they had already assumed—the Park Police guards worked on rotational eight-hour shifts from eight to four, four to midnight, midnight to eight the next morning.

Two additional days of detailed checking by the assault team showed that their first information was correct: three guards were always left on the island overnight, along with the old man who piloted the staff boat and returned in it each evening after his run to deposit the other employees on the mainland. In addition, all Park Police were accounted for each day, which meant that none of them lived on the island in the barrackslike buildings. On one of the days Bruckner and Gros-Jacques each spent twenty dollars for a twelve-minute commercial flight with the Big Apple Helicopter Service from a concrete landing circle at the foot of East Twenty-third Street and the East River. Both took fully loaded 35-millimeter cameras and pulled off as many shots as possible during the brief overflight of the statue and the back part of Liberty Island; the rolls were back for study the following day from a twelve-hour developing shop Kummel had located near Times Square.

Over mugs of terrible black coffee at the coffee shop near the Battery, the four men looked at each other and discussed things they had all heard before, detail by detail. "Tell me again about the intrusion alarm at the statue itself," Bruckner said to Kummel.

Kummel nodded. "It is a rather primitive system. There is a photoelectric cell—an electric eye—by each of the two main outside doors. These are used primarily to count the tourists automatically during the day, and only incidentally are they used as a kind of alarm at night. It is obvious that the National Park Service is equipped to handle tourists, not terrorists."

"I noticed the same thing," Bruckner said. "All right. Gros-Jacques and I have an errand to run early tomorrow morning. Paolo has found us an abandoned school building awaiting destruction at Eleventh Avenue and West Twenty-ninth Street. We'll meet there at ten o'clock sharp with the van and go over the final preparations. No one in that neighborhood will pay any attention to you unless you give them trouble, in which case you may get knifed

402

for the gold in your teeth. And at this point, so close to our objective, that would be too bad."

Early the next morning, with Gros-Jacques as copilot, Bruckner drove the light green Chevrolet van they had rented to a dingy, run-down-looking warehouse beside the docks at the western end of West Fifty-fourth Street. Gros-Jacques had the name and partial description of a guard who could be bought; they found the guard, the sum of money offered was agreeable, and the crated supplies and equipment that had been transported clandestinely from Paris were quickly and discreetly loaded into the back of the van from a loading dock inside the warehouse.

Not more than three blocks away was a man who had agreed to sell them a small rowboat fitted with a used outboard motor and four oars. "She'll be fine for trolling on a small, calm lake," the man assured them, accepting their one hundred and fifty dollars. "Though why you'd want all them oars I can't imagine." He looked expectantly at Bruckner, then at Gros-Jacques, for an answer to his perfectly logical question, but none was forthcoming. They loaded boat, motor, and oars into the back of the van beside the six wooden crates, and without having asked for or received a receipt for the boat, they drove the van to the abandoned school building on West Twenty-ninth Street.

With the help of the waiting Kummel and Paolo, they removed the crates from the van and carried them inside the school building through a door not easily visible from the street and that, thanks to Paolo's knife, was no longer locked. On the dusty wooden floor of a large room that had once been a gymnasium they opened the crates and spread out their contents in a circle that corresponded roughly to the former basketball center court. It was the first time any of them except Gros-Jacques had seen the equipment, and like schoolboys at an automobile show they walked and stooped among the piles of supplies and gadgets, eagerly examining each piece of gear and commenting on it to themselves and each other.

A large portion of the equipment was of a type that could have been found in a well-stocked hardware or sporting goods store catering to mountain climbers. This included complicated patterns of ropes, slings, pulleys, and body harnesses, as well as several lengths of flexible aluminum cable with preformed loop ends. There was a slightly different group of items that included assault gear and outdoor or camping gear—combat-type canned or foil-packaged food with high protein and carbohydrate value, as well as water and flavored dextrose liquids; propane floodlights; miner's battery-powered headlamps; a large, heavy multichannel radio transceiver field unit with fifteen-foot whip antenna; and personal walkie-talkies, one per man, which would be preset to the same frequency.

A third group of items included a wide assortment of small and large tools, many of them duplicates to allow simultaneous use by two or more members of the team—pliers, vise wrenches, several types of adjustable wrenches including various-sized pipe wrenches, screwdrivers, wire and bolt cutters, electric saws and drills that operated off current from portable power packs, and an acetylene cutting torch.

The last group of items comprised a selection of sophisticated weapons that would have made many a small revolutionary army envious. These items understandably drew the most attention from the assault team members; among other things there were individual automatic pistols fitted with silencers, an assortment of smoke, tear gas, and fragmentation grenades, four Uzi submachine guns with two dozen preloaded thirty-two-round magazines, several knives and garrotes, half a dozen U.S.-made M72 disposable rocket launchers, various explosive and incendiary charges, reels of electrical wiring, and a detonator switch box. Spread out beneath the entire cache was a large black vinyl waterproof tarpaulin in which to wrap the crates for the journey to their destination.

"Any questions?" Bruckner asked, looking at the other three men the way a teacher might look at pupils he fears may not pass the final examination.

Paolo nodded. "We go across in the little boat, at night, the four of us and all of *this?*"

"That's right," Bruckner said. "We'll make it, Paolo—just remember not to stand up."

"We know there will be guards—at least three," Kummel said.

"Only three," Bruckner assured him. "We've checked it, remember?"

"Yes. How do we dispose of these guards?"

"Well, we could try to capture them, tie them up and gag them."

"Is that feasible, do you think?"

"No. Unfortunately, we will have to kill them. It is the only way. Is there anyone who disagrees with that assessment?"

No one disagreed.

"The superintendent and his son may or may not be on the island," Bruckner continued. "They could become useful as hostages, so we will try very hard not to kill them."

Gros-Jacques fidgeted about the edge of the group; finally he pulled his great hands from his pants pockets, as though he found it too difficult to speak without using them. "Tell us again what it is we will be searching for, Bruckner," he blurted out.

"Of course, Gros-Jacques. It is a small metal box—I should think about six by nine inches, three inches deep. That would be about fifteen by twenty-three by eight centimeters. It will be old-looking, with a dull, somewhat corroded finish, and will be sealed shut, probably welded at the seams. It will be welded in place against one of the beams of the statue's supporting skeleton, either in a pocket along one of the main vertical struts or, more likely, hanging below one of the angles made by several iron rods coming together. This joining may be close to the copper skin of the statue, or close to the spiral stairway, or hanging in midair. And if it is still in place after remaining undetected for nearly one hundred years, I suspect it is neither readily visible nor easily accessible. The job will not be easy, particularly since we will be working under the pressure of time; but then if it were simple to find it, I would have no need of you fine gentlemen."

Bruckner smiled and Gros-Jacques frowned. "I ask again, Bruckner, what is in the box?"

"And I tell you again, my inquisitive friend, that is none of your business. You are being paid, all of you, to do a specific job. If you do it well, you will have earned the pay; if you do it poorly, you will probably die in the process, one way or another. Do I make myself clear?"

One by one the three other men answered Bruckner in the affirmative.

"All right," Bruckner said. "Let's repack the gear in these crates and load everything back into the van—I think it will be safest there. Go to your hotels and stay out of trouble. Get as much sleep as possible between now and tomorrow evening, because once we start there won't be any way to stop until the job is completed. Tomorrow night we assemble at precisely eleven-forty-five at the designated spot off Battery Park, load the boat, abandon the van, and at fifteen minutes after midnight—when the guard shift has changed and the harbor traffic is as light as it ever gets—we four will quietly cross a little bit of water and visit one of America's favorite shrines. We will have almost six hours until daylight and about eight hours until the first staff boat of rangers and guards arrives for the new day. If all goes well, that should be plenty of time to find the box and leave the island the same way we came to it."

"And if not?" little Paolo asked, his bushy eyebrows arched.

"There will be time," Bruckner said calmly.

"But if not?" Gros-Jacques persisted.

Bruckner shrugged. "Then, *mon ami,* we bargain."

36

THE FOLLOWING DAY WAS heavily overcast from noon on, and during the afternoon and early evening the clouds periodically spit huge drops of rain. The forecast for the New York metropolitan area was for possible light rain throughout the night with high winds off Montauk and consequent small craft warnings.

Wearing waterproof jackets with the collars pulled up around their ears, Bruckner and Gros-Jacques brought the loaded van to the rendezvous point and found that Kummel and Paolo, similarly attired, were waiting for them.

"Hell of a night," Paolo said, spitting into the wind.

"I don't like it," Gros-Jacques agreed. "I think we should wait until the weather clears."

Bruckner looked at him and shook his head. "I find it hard to believe you're afraid of boats."

"I don't like them, that's all. Not little ones like the dingy we've got in the van. In this kind of sea they become swamped if you lean over to tie your shoe."

"Then leave your shoe untied," Kummel said.

Bruckner frowned at Kummel's feistiness toward the much larger Frenchman; such internal bickering could be dangerous. "We cannot wait," he told Gros-Jacques, "because everything is ready *now,* and the longer we put it off the more chance there is for someone to discover our plans. In any case, the weather works to our advantage— it will help to hide both our crossing and our activities on the island."

"I still don't like it," Gros-Jacques muttered, but he began passing the crates of supplies and equipment from the van to Kummel and Paolo. Bruckner, meanwhile, wrestled the dingy from the van and with Kummel's help carried both it and the heavy outboard motor to the edge of the water.

When the boat with motor attached had been lowered into the water and loaded with the vinyl-wrapped gear, the four men carefully squeezed down into the little boat and glanced back toward the twin spires of the World Trade Center, aware that there was at least some chance they would never see land again. Farther along the shore, toward the lights of the Coast Guard Administration building and the Circle Line pier, an old couple—their arms around each other's waists—stood staring out across the water at the hazy illumination of Governors Island, Staten Island, and the southern end of Jersey City. The Statue of Liberty's torch could not be seen at all.

The motor started easily on the second pull but sounded much louder than Bruckner had thought it would. Other than his worrying that the noise might give them away, however, the fifteen-minute crossing to Liberty Island was uneventful. Halfway across it began to rain harder and the men huddled even lower in the boat, raising only their previously blackened faces from time to time to fix on their destination.

A quarter of a mile from the island, with the brightly lighted statue glowing green through the sheets of rain, Bruckner cut the outboard motor and the four men began to row silently with the oars. Even if one of the tugboats they had seen had passed within yards of them now, it was unlikely anyone on the tug would notice, so well did the black-clad men and the silent boat blend into the rain-swept waters.

According to the prearranged plan, Bruckner and the others guided the boat directly under the front of the statue and around to the left, past the boat docks and all the way to the back or Jersey side of the island close to the mostly empty buildings. There, they had noted, the island sloped gently down to the water and would provide easy access for the little rowboat.

Carefully, so as not to scrape the bottom of the boat over the rocky beach, they felt the bottom of the channel with their oars and slowly let the prow drift up against the shore. Gros-Jacques hopped out first to fasten the line to a convenient rock, and was followed by Paolo. Kummel and Bruckner, remaining in the boat, opened one of the crates and handed out the garrotes, knives, and the silenced pistols, after which they re-covered the crates with the black vinyl. Crouching low, the four men started toward the nearest building. A sudden flash of lightning froze them in their tracks as the ensuing thunder rolled across the wet island.

"Who's there?" a voice shouted at them from farther down the shore.

"Jesus!" Bruckner whispered. "All right, Paolo, see what you can find. The rest of us will stay right here."

Before Bruckner had finished speaking, little Paolo had disappeared into the rain farther inland. The other three melted into the sand and pointed their weapons in the direction of the voice.

"Who is it, I said!" the voice came again, this time much nearer.

Bruckner could barely make out the shape of a man standing partly hidden behind a bush. "I'm going over," he told Gros-Jacques and Kummel.

Keeping as low to the ground as he could, he scurried up the beach until he was near enough to make out quite distinctly the grizzled features of the old man who sometimes piloted the staff boat, the one Superintendent Williams had called Willie Teal. Teal saw him now, too, but as far as Bruckner could tell he had no weapon. Casually Bruckner sighted along the top of his pistol, but then the old man turned to someone in the shadows beside him and asked calmly, "Who *are* you people and what do you want?"

"We want to visit the Statue of Liberty," a voice Bruckner recognized as Paolo's said.

"Well, it's closed—you'll have to come back tomorrow," Willie Teal said reasonably. He might have said more, but suddenly he made a quick sucking noise and clutched at his throat. Bruckner saw the dark blood spurting from between the old man's fingers as he toppled to the ground; the falling body made hardly any noise. Paolo stepped out of the shadows, wiping the blade of his knife clean with a

409

practiced thumb and forefinger. "Stupid old man," he said to Bruckner. "He thought we were lost."

"Not at all," Bruckner said. "He knew approximately who we were—he simply had no choice."

"Yah, well, he's dead just the same," Paolo said and spat contemptuously.

The four members of the team crept toward the superintendent's house. They had guessed that one of the three guards would stay in the housing area at the back of the island, one would probably circle the outside of the statue's base, and one would almost certainly be stationed inside the statue itself, or at least in the lobby of the pedestal. "Spread out," Bruckner whispered. "Check out each building, inside and out. Move in a line toward the back of the statue."

They went off in four different directions. Bruckner headed directly for the superintendent's house, which looked exactly like thousands of other ranch-style houses in the suburbs—even the front porch light was on. Bruckner stayed in the shadows as much as possible until he was directly beneath one of the windows of the house. There was a light on inside, the sort of light that people leave on in their houses when they are not at home. Bruckner walked around the back corner of the house to check a different window and nearly collided with a uniformed park policeman. The man, a huge black in a rain slicker, was fumbling for the revolver at his hip when Bruckner pulled the trigger of his own silenced pistol, twice, hearing the insignificant little *fftt-fftt!* that caused the guard to double over and sag headfirst into the mud beside the house.

The house, as Bruckner had thought, turned out to be empty.

The four men met on the broad walkway between the concessions building and the administration building, both of which were dark and locked. The other buildings on the back part of the island had all been empty. Keeping close to the low box hedges bordering the walks behind the statue, they worried about the fact that the green copper surface of the statue floodlighted by more than a hundred thousand watts of electricity reflected a good bit of light

410

into the area through which they were now moving. "I wish somebody'd turn off that fucking light," Gros-Jacques whispered to Bruckner. The idea was almost funny.

Suddenly Gros-Jacques squatted and pulled the others down with him. "Another *flic!*" he whispered, pointing to the sidewalk parallel to the one they were crouching on, but separated from it by a double row of hedges and a broad expanse of lawn.

"I think we need him alive," Bruckner whispered.

Nodding agreement, Gros-Jacques slipped along behind the hedge to an intersection at the end of the walkway, toward which the guard was walking slowly. When the guard passed the spot, Gros-Jacques leaped up behind him, covered his mouth, and pulled his head back with one huge hand, and with the other he held the point of a knife to the startled man's throat. "One word and you die," Gros-Jacques promised. The guard showed no signs of wishing to fight it out.

Immediately the other three surrounded the guard. "There's one more inside the base of the statue, is that correct?" Bruckner asked him.

The man's eyes were wild with fright as he nodded the answer. "All right," Bruckner said, "when the big man takes his hand off your mouth, you will use your walkie-talkie and ask your friend to come outside. Say you want to show him something. Is that clear? Do as we say and you won't be harmed, but if you fuck up, the big man will drive that knife straight through your throat into your spine."

The guard nearly fainted but managed to nod again. Gros-Jacques took his hand away, Kummel walked up toward the entrance to the statue, and the guard used his walkie-talkie as instructed. His voice was not as steady as it might have been, but he made no attempt to warn anyone.

The three members of the team and the frightened guard watched the entrance to the pedestal from behind the hedge. The inside guard eventually came through the second of the double glass doors, and Kummel was instantly behind him, a garrote twisted around the man's neck before he was aware he wasn't alone. After a feeble struggle his arms collapsed at his sides, and in a moment Kummel released the wire noose and allowed the body to sag to the ground of its own weight.

"You said we wouldn't be harmed!" the first guard moaned, twisting slightly in Gros-Jacques's grip.

"But we lied, *mon petit chou*," Gros-Jacques said contemptuously and plunged the knife deep into the tendons and flesh and arteries of the guard's unprotected neck. The amount of blood that spurted from the wound would have surprised someone not used to seeing such things.

Kummel and Gros-Jacques cleaned the blood from their weapons, and leaving the bodies where they lay, the four men entered the pedestal through the doors the guard had conveniently opened for them. They searched the lobby, the offices behind the service desks, and the next several floors, which housed the Immigration Museum and the pictorial history gallery. Satisfied that they were now alone on the island, they left the statue and returned to the rowboat tied up behind the housing area, where they hoisted the crates of equipment onto their backs and carried them back to the base of the statue. When the gear had all been moved safely inside, they piled it into the elevator and rode up with it the ten stories to the balcony level of the pedestal. When the elevator door opened, Paolo and Kummel experienced their first glimpse of the inside of the Statue of Liberty itself.

Standing beside the bottom step of the twelve-story spiral staircase leading to the crown, Paolo shook his head in wonder. "Mother of God, she's a giant!" he said in awe, staring up into the dark upper reaches of the dimly lighted interior. Even the normally reserved Kummel was obviously impressed; only Gros-Jacques began to complain about the tactical problems they faced. "There's a hell of a lot more iron up there than you might think," he told the others. "That box or whatever it is we're looking for could be in any one of a thousand damn places."

"Ten thousand is more like it," Bruckner said, "which is why we can't afford to waste any more time. Paolo and Gros-Jacques, you two begin carrying some of this stuff to the crown, which is where we'll base our ropes. Kummel and I have to do a little wire-cutting."

They removed the crates from the elevator and broke open the one containing the walkie-talkies. Bruckner took one, leaving the rest to be carried up into the statue, and he and Kummel rode back down in the elevator to conserve their strength. Outside they went first to the administration building and shot through the lock on the front door. After locating the radio transmitter Superintendent Williams had told Bruckner about, they put bullets through the tubes and transistors and ripped a great deal of the wiring apart; it would take someone weeks to repair it.

Next they went out to the back part of the island and began searching with a flashlight at the edge of the water near the dock and the emergency gasoline generator. It didn't take them long to find the bundle of waterproofed electric power and telephone cables that disappeared into the murky water and emerged somewhere on the Jersey shore three-eighths of a mile away. "For God's sake, don't get the power lines," Bruckner warned Kummel. "If the lights on the statue go out we'll have every security unit in the harbor on our necks. It's got to look completely natural while we're working inside."

Kummel, Bruckner had been told, was an expert communications technician. He quickly found the right bundle and cut the cables neatly with his knife. "I do not believe these other wires power the statue lights," he told Bruckner. "Perhaps they are only for the emergency generator. Last week I noticed a switch box with automatic timers inside the pedestal building. I searched the base of the building but found nothing; therefore, I assume the main power lines exit beneath the statue, enter the water at some point below the surface, and continue to their source on the mainland."

He looked at Bruckner and came as close to smiling as he ever seemed to. "For the moment, at least," he said, "Liberty Island would seem to be ours."

They went back to the statue, where Bruckner left Kummel on guard with the walkie-talkie on the second level. So that Kummel would have a quick entrance and exit from the observation deck into the statue, they broke the glass in the heavy metal-framed door and shattered the lock with two bullets from Kummel's gun. "Let us know if you hear anything," Bruckner said. "There's a good chance the superintendent will be returning for the night in his small motorboat. As soon as he's accounted for you come up and help us in the search."

"I would not think of missing that pleasure," Kummel said, and something about the set of his jaw, or the inflection in his voice, made Bruckner think that perhaps he had seen this man Kummel before; though where, or under what circumstances, he could not imagine.

Malcolm Williams tilted the glass of California port wine toward the low ceiling of his wife Lucy's apartment. The one-room apartment was on Jane Street in Greenwich Village, not far from the New School, where she was taking two courses in nonrepresentational graphic art and was presumably "finding herself." He finished the wine, poured himself more after offering Lucy another glass, and saw that his son Bobby was rubbing his eyes sleepily as he paged through one of his mother's fashion magazines.

"It's terrible weather out there, Lucy," he said. "The boat motor was acting up on the way over from the island—ask Bobby. I don't see what it would hurt if I stayed over—I can sleep right there on the sofa and nobody would even know I was here."

Lucy ran her fingers through her short dark hair and shook her head. *"I'd* know, and that's the difference." She had a habit of looking at him over the tops of her glasses when she was angry or exasperated with him, a habit that annoyed him unreasonably. She was looking that way at him now.

"Lucy, baby, we can work it out—*together.* You know I can ask for a transfer in a little over a year. And you know they've practically promised me Yosemite before I retire. If you'll just come back to the island and stay with me and Bobby—all three of us, like a family ought to —for the next year, then you can do whatever you want in California, even set up your own art studio."

"There's nothing sure about Yosemite, Malcolm. You've said so yourself. I hope you don't have your hopes set too high—about that or . . . other things."

"What other things?"

"Us. You know. Whatever."

"And that's why you won't even let me sleep here tonight, with my own wife and son—and not even in the same bed?"

Lucy glanced sharply at Bobby. "I'm happy right now with the way things are. I'm really into this art thing, you know. The teacher says I have definite talent, that I ought to continue with it, and really, I feel better about myself than I have in years. I mean I'm *doing* something, Malcolm, something that you didn't arrange for me, and I like that feeling of independence."

"Damn it, Lucy!" Malcolm said. "I'm sure the New School has art classes during the day, or early evening, whenever you wanted them, but you could still live on the island with me and commute on the staff boat. You know you could."

Lucy shook her head slowly. "It wouldn't be the same."

"No, I'll just bet it wouldn't—you couldn't very well entertain men out on the island like you can here."

"That wasn't fair. You know I don't entertain men here. I'm still married to you, after all, and I have scruples about that sort of thing."

"Then come back, Lucy. Please."

"When the time's right I expect I will. But not now, Malcolm, and most especially not when *you* decide I should."

"Damn, you're a stubborn woman! I never knew how stubborn."

"You never knew a lot of things about me."

Staring angrily at her, Malcolm gulped down the remaining wine and went over to Bobby and picked him up in his arms. "Come on, sleepyhead, we're going back to Aunt Liberty. I need you to guide me straight through this awful weather."

"No, Malcolm! It's too late to be taking him anywhere tonight. He can come over tomorrow in the staff boat and start his week with you then."

"He's coming tonight, Lucy. He's got to be a man, doesn't he?"

"Jesus!" Lucy said. "That's what's wrong with men

these days, always telling their sons they have to be big strong men. Why don't you let him be a child for a while? He's got all the rest of his life to be like you."

"Starting now," Malcolm said, and before there could be any more senseless argument, he pushed Bobby higher up on his shoulder and stormed out of the apartment, slamming the door behind him. He had seen that Lucy had tears in her eyes, and even now, angry as he was with her, he wanted her so badly that it amounted to a deep physical ache. As he walked down the almost deserted streets of the Village looking for a taxi, Bobby squirmed in his arms and asked to be put down. "Don't you and Mommy love each other anymore?" he asked his father, and Malcolm took the small ten-year-old hand in his and nearly cried.

"Of course we still love each other, son," he said. "Basically. It's just that we don't seem to know how to live together anymore."

"That shouldn't be so hard," Bobby said. "You just *do* it."

He was right of course, Malcolm thought, as he flagged down a taxi to take them back to the National Park Service dock at the Battery. The trouble was, sometimes the simplest things were the most complicated.

From their base of operations in the crown of the statue—large enough to accommodate about thirty people at one time—Bruckner, Paolo, and Gros-Jacques unpacked their gear and surveyed the vast dark spaces below them. One of their first achievements was to set up powerful battery-operated floodlights in such a way that they illuminated both sides of the central stairway. Able to study their objective much more clearly now, they arbitrarily divided the irregular space inside the statue into four quadrants for simultaneous search, including one for Kummel who was serving as lookout some twenty-two stories below. To keep in constant contact with him yet avoid tying up their own walkie-talkie units, they had devised a system whereby the large field radio was set to receive a warning signal from Kummel and emit a loud electronic tone—loud enough to be audible throughout the cavernous interior of the statue—whereupon one of the other three team members would contact *him* on their small hand-held units.

The next step was the rigging up of the ropes and cables and harnesses from which the men would eventually begin to swing down into the void beneath them—a void, however, filled with a great deal of unpredictably angled iron bars, as Gros-Jacques had earlier observed. These would be both a help and a hindrance to the searchers, for while they would occasionally provide a convenient sort of stepping-stone in space, they could also knock a man senseless if he happened to swing back into a part of the framework he didn't know was there. "It won't be like ice-climbing, or loose shale cliffs, or anything else you've ever attempted," Bruckner warned them again. "Keep your wits about you and you won't get hurt. That box is here somewhere, and I intend to find it within the next seven hours."

As they knotted ropes and lowered them from the platform, brilliant light from jagged bolts of lightning flashed through the windows in the crown and fierce peals of thunder rattled the metal skeleton of the statue. Gros-Jacques, holding a length of rope motionless in his hands, stared wild-eyed out the windows. "That whore-mongering lightning is going to hit this structure sooner or later!" he yelled to Bruckner over the thunder. "There'll be a million volts of electricity bouncing around off the iron framework—where we'll be hanging by our thumbs!"

"My God, you're a baby," Bruckner chided him. "When they designed this thing, they insulated all the rivets between the iron skeleton and the copper skin with pieces of asbestos, to keep it from turning into a giant battery. Williams, the superintendent, told me about it. So just keep your hands off the copper and you'll be all right."

"But what if that's where the box is?" Paolo wanted to know.

Bruckner shook his head. "It isn't."

The large transceiver beeped loudly beside them, and Bruckner immediately called Kummel on his walkie-talkie.

"What is it, Kummel?"

"A noise, like an outboard motor, over by the docks. I

can't see anything but I'm sure that's what it is. You'd better get down here."

Bruckner and the other two lost no time descending the dizzying spiral and then taking the elevator to the lower part of the pedestal. They joined Kummel, who was waiting for them just outside the statue, and now they, too, heard the outboard sputtering.

Keeping close to the shrubs and sides of buildings, they raced through the rain and shadows to the side of the dock used by the Park Service employees. In the bluish light from a single floodlamp mounted on a pole beside the pier they watched Malcolm Williams and his son, Bobby, climb up onto the pier out of their small motorboat. Bruckner and his team stepped into the circle of light and pointed their silent weapons at the superintendent and the boy. "Good evening, Mr. Williams," Bruckner said with exaggerated politeness. "Isn't it rather a wicked night to be out for a pleasure cruise?"

Malcolm looked into Bruckner's face and it was obvious that he suddenly recognized him. "You aren't really a reporter for the *Times*, are you?" Malcolm said.

"Afraid not, old sport."

"All those questions, all that in-depth probing . . . but then I don't suppose you know the jargon, either."

"Enough to get by," Bruckner said, motioning with his pistol for Malcolm and Bobby to precede him off the pier.

"I say we kill them," Gros-Jacques said, and Paolo, holding one of his beloved knives instead of a gun, nodded his agreement.

"Search him," Bruckner said to Kummel.

Sticking his own pistol in his belt, Kummel thoroughly patted down Malcolm's jeans and waterproof orange jacket. "Nothing," he reported to Bruckner.

"It is still possible that we'll need hostages at some point," Bruckner explained to the two dissidents. "The superintendent for stature, and the boy for the emotional response. We will use them as a tool, nothing more nor less, but it's too early to burn all our bridges behind us. Let's visit the superintendent's house."

They forced Malcolm and Bobby to walk at gunpoint

418

to the house, unlock the front door, and lead the men inside. "What are they gonna do to us, Daddy?" Bobby asked, and Malcolm patted his son on the shoulder and shook his head. "Nothing, we'll be all right—just do as they say."

"Sit down on the couch there, both of you," Bruckner said to Malcolm. "Search the entire house for weapons!" he ordered the others.

He glanced at Malcolm and the boy. "We've destroyed the radio and the telephones so you needn't hope to become a hero."

At one point while the search was going on, Malcolm started to say something, but Bruckner shut him up with a threatening motion of his gun. "This is not a social call, old sport," Bruckner reminded the superintendent.

Paolo, Kummel, and Gros-Jacques eventually returned. "No radios or other communications media," Kummel said, "but we did find this in a closet." And he held up Malcolm's competition-class compound bow and a quiver of arrows.

Bruckner took the bow from Kummel. "Sorry, Superintendent—I know how fond you are of it." He grasped both ends of the bow and brought it down sharply across his uplifted knee, snapping it in two pieces which, still attached to the strings and pulleys, he tossed into a corner of the room. Suddenly he grabbed Bobby's arm and jerked him up off the couch, holding him securely with an arm under his chin. Malcolm lunged for Bruckner and was batted down by Gros-Jacques for his trouble. "Leave Bobby alone!" he shouted. "What kind of monsters are you?"

"He comes with us—insurance, you know. Gag the superintendent and tie his arms and legs securely," he told Gros-Jacques. "We've wasted too much time already."

When Malcolm was tied and gagged, Bruckner looked around the living room once more, then shoved Bobby out the front door. Kummel, Gros-Jacques, and Paolo followed in single file, Paolo kicking the door shut behind him.

*　　*　　*

When he was certain they were gone, Malcolm swung his bound legs off the couch and tried standing up. Finding that he could manage that fairly easily, he hobbled and jumped his way to the southeast window that looked out on the lighted but nearly formless green mass that was the back of the towering statue. He watched as the dark, rain-obscured figures of the four men, one of whom was dragging the reluctant Bobby, disappeared into the pedestal of the statue.

There should be a guard there somewhere, he thought; two guards, in fact, one inside the statue and one making an irregular route around the base. But then, staring harder, he thought he could make out the shapes of the two guards' bodies lying in the middle of the hedge-bordered sidewalk behind the pedestal, and his heart sank as he realized that the third guard was no doubt also dead. These men, wherever they had come from, were efficient monsters who apparently killed as easily as some men drew a breath. And with terrifying impact he understood now that Bobby's young, vulnerable life was balanced on the knife edge of their sadistic whim.

37

THE IMPORTANT THING NOW, Malcolm knew, was somehow to get himself untied so that he could move about freely. The ropes were good and were knotted securely; it would take days to work them loose, if that was even possible. He thought of all the ways of getting untied that he had seen on television, most of them involving handy pieces of broken glass. But there was no broken glass in his house, and even if there had been, he thought, he would probably have just managed to slash his wrists.

Then he thought of another way. He hobbled into the kitchen, leaned over the sink, and turned on the hot water faucet with his mouth, then made his way into the back hallway where the water heater stood beside the furnace. Turning on the hot water had made the burner at the base of the heater spring into life. Malcolm squatted on the floor, his back to the heater, and by touch, because he couldn't see what he was doing, lifted the trapdoor in front of the burner and gingerly stuck his wrists back into the flame. There was no way to keep from getting burned, but by weaving his hands in and out of the flame, he managed to keep the ropes directly in the flame long enough to burn through them eventually.

Once his hands were free the rest was easy. He cut the ropes on his legs with a small paring knife and put salve on his wrist burns. Earlier he had been thinking about what he could do if he did get free, and it had seemed to him that since there was no way he could hope to overpower four professional killers, his only alternative was to attract help to the island from outside. The radio in the administration building and the phone lines to the mainland had been destroyed—the reporter who was not a reporter had told him so, and he believed him. Still, Malcolm picked up the telephone in the bedroom and listened for a moment, but there was only the absence of sound of a totally dead line.

He had already considered and rejected the possibility of intercepting or controlling the statue's lighting system. The control switches were inside the statue, so there was no possibility of blinking out a message in Morse code. And the electrical lines went from beneath the statue underground into the water and across to the power source in Jersey City, making them effectively tamperproof.

He crashed helplessly through the house, picking up things and throwing them down, hoping an inspiration would leap out at him from some unexpected place. In Bobby's room he glanced at the debris of toys, clothes, and books scattered everywhere and thought how much his son needed a mother again—how much they both needed Lucy. It was probably a good thing she wasn't here now, he thought, shuddering as he considered what the four men might have done to a young attractive woman like Lucy.

Pawing desperately through the large toy box he had made for Bobby two years ago, he came across the toy walkie-talkie set that, when he turned the switches, emitted no sound to indicate that they worked. But by dismantling two flashlights from other parts of the house he installed enough batteries to make one of the handsets operative. Not much good it would do him, though, as the toy CBs were supposed to have a maximum range of only an eighth of a mile—far too little to reach either Jersey City or Manhattan. Still, it was all he had; it was worth trying, if only to keep his mind off the hopelessness of the situation.

He went outside the house, hoping to get more range, and discovered that the rain had temporarily stopped. Extending the tiny aerial its full length, he began to shout into the speaker, "Mayday! Mayday!" asking and then begging for help. But the only sound he heard when he released the talk button was a faint electronic crackle from the dark void outside the island. He tried again several times with the same results, and was about to give up when he thought he heard the faint echoes of a man's voice. He turned the receiver volume up as far as it would go and heard the voice more clearly this time—a man calmly replying to Malcolm's weak signal: "Say again, Mayday, and give your location."

Hardly able to believe his good luck, Malcolm pressed the talk button and gave his name and title, his location, and briefly explained the trouble he was in. He asked the man if he had received all of that, and to tell him who he was and where.

"Loud and clear, good buddy," the man's voice came back. "Clear, anyway. Right now my rig is about halfway across the Brooklyn Bridge, heading for Manhattan. What do you want me to do?"

"Try to contact the chief of security at the National Park Service regional office—it's at 15 Pine Street, I don't know the number. If you can't raise anyone there, and you probably can't at this hour, get in touch with the New York Police Department Harbor Unit, or else the Coast Guard unit on Governors Island. However they want to handle it is okay, but please, *please* make sure they understand that the four men are holding my ten-year-old son hostage inside the statue, and that they have already killed at least three park policemen. Do you understand?"

"Roger, I'll do the best I can. Sit tight and don't worry —I'm about to lose you now."

"This was just a freak occurrence, my making contact with you on this toy walkie-talkie—I'm afraid there won't be any way for anyone else to reach me, or me to reach them. Can you still hear me?"

Malcolm released the talk button, but there was only the same faint electronic crackle as before. And although he tried not to think about it, he knew that his life and Bobby's life almost certainly depended now on the actions of some unknown truck driver who had just crossed the Brooklyn Bridge into lower Manhattan—and who, for all Malcolm knew, might at this moment be stopping for coffee at some all-night coffee shop, where he would entertain the customers by telling them about this cuckoo on the CB network pretending to be the superintendent at the Statue of Liberty.

Malcolm went inside the house and put the toy away. He looked out the window again at the back of the statue, but there was not much to see. He couldn't just sit and do nothing while the killers had his son, yet nothing he could think of would do either of them the slightest bit of good. Still, some sort of action, no matter how useless, might keep him from going out of his mind with worry.

He left the house, leaving the door unlocked for the first time since he had come to the island, and walked over to the statue. The door into the pedestal lobby was open, and crouching down, he went through into the familiar surroundings that now seemed strange and frightening. He had thought one of the four men might have been left as a guard inside the lobby, but of course that would have been ridiculous—there was nothing left to guard against. Distrustful of what they might have done to the elevator mechanism, he began the slow climb up to the top of the pedestal and the base of the statue itself.

The first thing he noticed was the bright floodlights pointing down into the interior from about the level of the crown platform. By shading his eyes he could barely make out several dark shapes moving about, one of which might have been Bobby. As he tried to think what move to make next, one of the men stepped out of the shadows beside him and stuck a gun in his ribs.

"I have the superintendent down here!" the man shouted up into the statue. "He was sneaking around. What should I do with him?"

The phony reporter, the one the others had called Bruckner and who was obviously the leader of the group, shouted down for the man to hold Malcolm.

Malcolm could stand it no longer. "Where's my son?" he yelled up into the void.

"Your kid can't talk just now," Bruckner yelled back. "We taped his mouth just in case. But he's all right for the moment. How long he stays that way depends on you, Williams."

Someone had pointed a strong spotlight at Malcolm while Bruckner was talking, and he now stood in a circle of light. "I want to see my son," Malcolm shouted up into the blinding glare of lights.

"Sure—if you promise to go back to your house like a good fellow and wait for us there."

"I promise," Malcolm said, not believing that any of this was happening.

Bruckner ordered the floodlights cut and then directed a spotlight across to a vertical beam. Malcolm saw his son half crouched on a projecting shelf of metal, his arms tied behind him to the upright beam and his mouth taped shut. His eyes, Malcolm thought, looked like those of a frightened animal in the forest at night.

"It's all right, son," Malcolm yelled up, trying to soothe Bobby's fears. "Be a brave Indian, like we used to talk about. Those men don't want to hurt you—they're after something else, and when they find it they'll go away and leave us alone."

"He's right, Bobby," Malcolm heard Bruckner say. "Paolo! Come back up here and leave Mr. Williams—I have a job for you." They turned the floodlights back on up in the statue. Malcolm remained where he was for a while, wondering why they had let him go. But shortly he understood. The man who had caught him, the small one named Paolo, had reached the top where Bruckner was, and Malcolm saw Bruckner say something to him in a low voice. Malcolm also saw Paolo take the pistol from his belt, cock it, and head for the spiral staircase back down to the level where Malcolm stood. It didn't take a genius to figure out what Bruckner had told him to do, and the only reason Malcolm could think of why they hadn't done it earlier was perhaps they thought Bobby would be less cooperative if he heard them order his father killed.

This time Malcolm took the elevator down to the ground, his mind racing through the short list of options available to him. The one thing in his favor was that he knew the island better than Paolo did—knew it better, in fact, than anyone else possible could, because it was his home. He ran from the pedestal lobby out through the door and toward his house, keeping in the shadows as much as possible. Now he was glad he hadn't locked his front door; he burst through and grabbed up the bow that Bruckner

425

had broken and the quiver of hunting arrows, along with
the paring knife he had used earlier to cut his ropes.

In the yard behind the house he went directly to a
young sycamore and broke off a lower branch that was
relatively straight and pliable. With the knife he quickly
stripped the leaves and shoots from the branch, notched
the ends, and after cutting the proper length of bowstring
away from the shattered bow, he attached it to the sapling
branch with an archer's knot at each end. Testing the
draw of the makeshift bow, he went around the corner
of the house to where the archery target was set up, inserted one of the excellent arrows, and from thirty yards
out put the arrow into a spot two rings from the bull's-
eye.

He was drawing back the bowstring for a second practice shot when something moved into the corner of his
field of vision, and when he turned his head slightly, he
saw a shadow slip closer to the children's slide on the playground. It was too far away for any sort of accuracy with
this makeshift bow, but not too far for a bullet. He ducked
away into the nearest shadow, and although he had heard
no shot, the unmistakable sound of a bullet whizzing
through the air close by his ear scared him badly. He
had never considered the possibility that their guns were
silenced, and while the fact didn't affect their deadliness
one way or the other, somehow it made them more men-
acing.

He managed to slip behind the house into a row of trees
beside a path that led along the seawall back to the statue.
There he waited behind a large tree, the seated arrow pointing up and ready. In a moment he saw Paolo dart behind
a bush close to the far corner of the house, and since he
was certain Paolo did not know exactly where *he* was, the
game had been nicely turned around so that now Malcolm
was the hunter, Paolo the hunted. Little picture memories
of the hundreds of times he had stalked wild animals
crowded into Malcolm's head and gave him confidence.
It was a game he knew how to play; perhaps Paolo didn't.

Paolo moved away and Malcolm, knowing he would
have to expose himself to danger in order to trap his
quarry, rushed headlong beneath the row of trees until he

was opposite Paolo, then deliberately rustled the branches of a low bush. Sure that Paolo had heard the sound, he burst out from behind the bush and ran a zigzag course toward the hedges bordering the walkway to the statue's entrance, where the two guards' bodies still lay. Quickly he bent to check their holsters, but the guns of both had been taken by the invaders. Malcolm spun around in time to see Paolo slipping through the shadows fifty yards away. Then he dived around the end of a row of hedges so that, out of sight, he could scurry along the length of the hedge and cut back around to the side where he started, but now at the other end.

Paolo, crouched low, came almost directly toward where Malcolm squatted behind the end of the hedge. He dug into the wet dirt, which had been freshly turned by the gardeners, and grabbed up a handful, which he compacted into a sizable ball of 'mud. When Paolo was somewhat closer, Malcolm lobbed the mudball overhand toward the opposite row of hedges, where it landed with an audible crash. Paolo, thinking it was Malcolm, fired two nearly silent bullets toward the sound and leaped over the hedge, no doubt thinking to take Malcolm totally by surprise.

Behind the opposite hedge, Malcolm stood and calmly drew back one of the arrows in the bow. *He will stand up for an instant to see where I've disappeared to*, Malcolm thought. *He has to—it's what any animal would do*. And when Paolo's torso rose slowly above the hedge, almost like a shadow, the arrow was already aimed nearly perfectly. All Malcolm had to do was release it, and pray.

The arrow struck Paolo solidly in the chest. Even in his death throes the little man fired his pistol wildly several times, but probably he had never seen anything to shoot at; it had simply been a reflex action.

Carefully Malcolm approached the body and pried the gun out of Paolo's hand. He had no idea how many shots were left in the magazine, if any, and in the dark with an unfamiliar gun he wouldn't have been able to tell even if he could have figured out where the release was. Slinging the sycamore bow across his shoulder, he held the gun in his hand and walked up the sidewalk into the pedestal building.

Once again he avoided the elevator for reasons of silence, though by now his heart pounded heavily and his breath came in labored gasps. At the bottom of the statue itself he began slowly to climb the central spiral staircase, counting each step to himself. At the thirty-first step the edge of the bow caught on a rivet, then snapped in against the center column with a hollow ring. In the shifting glare of the floodlights above, one of the men spotted him and shouted his name.

"All right, Williams, hold it right there!" Bruckner shouted down. "Since you're here and Paolo isn't, I assume he's dead and that you've got his gun. Please back down the stairs and stand out in the open so we can see you."

"So you can kill me?" Malcolm shouted up.

"From up here the angle's almost as bad for us as it is for you, and there's a lot of hardware in the way. But if you don't do as I say within the next thirty seconds, I will untie Bobby from the beam and drop him down twelve stories on his soft young head. Have you ever seen the body of a person who has been dropped from a twelve-story building, Mr. Williams?"

Malcolm touched the makeshift bow across his back, certain that it was not powerful enough to send an arrow straight up against gravity to Bruckner's level. Realizing that the invaders held all the cards, or at least the most important card, he backed down the spiral to the base of the statue and walked out to one side of the staircase as Bruckner had ordered. "What do you want of me?" he shouted up to people he could not actually see.

"We're lowering a rope close to you," Bruckner said. "Tie the gun to the rope."

In a moment Malcolm saw the rope snaking its way down among the girders and iron rods; it touched the floor a few feet away. "I didn't take that other man's gun," Malcolm shouted, hoping he sounded convincing. "It was out of bullets anyway."

Suddenly there was a scream from up above, followed by the unmistakable sound of Bobby crying. "I took the tape off your son's mouth and bent his arm back a little, to show you we mean business," Bruckner shouted down.

428

"Tie the gun to the rope this instant or I will rip his little arm off and throw it down for you to examine, before I toss the rest of him off. I'm perfectly capable of doing that, and much worse, if it comes to that."

"I'm sure you are, you butcher!" Malcolm said softly, tying the pistol to the rope by its trigger guard. He gave the rope a couple of tugs and they hoisted it up above his head. As the pistol rose out of sight, Malcolm tried another tactic. "Bruckner!" he shouted up after the pistol. "You may not believe me, but you can't afford not to. Listen, I had a hidden radio transmitter back at the house that your people didn't find. I managed to reach the mainland, and they'll be sending a huge force to overpower you any minute now. You could make it much easier on yourselves by surrendering now, to me. I'll see that you are treated fairly by the authorities."

"You're right, I don't believe you," Bruckner answered. Nevertheless, Malcolm heard them tune in what sounded like a powerful transceiver to the police band. "Kummel," Malcolm heard Bruckner say, "take your CB and give me a report from the torch." It was several minutes before Malcolm heard the faint sounds from, presumably, Kummel's walkie-talkie, and though he could not make out the words, he felt sure the report from the torch was negative.

Sensing the hopelessness of further delaying tactics, Malcolm moved away from the open area into the shadows at the top of the pedestal, where it would not have been possible for them to see him.

"Williams?" Bruckner shouted. "Show yourself!"

When Malcolm didn't move, there was a second shouted order to show himself and then Bobby screamed again. Gritting his teeth and with his fingers in his ears, Malcolm crouched in the shadows and prayed that they would assume he had gone all the way back down to the ground level, and that hurting Bobby further would do them no good. After what seemed like a very long time he lowered his hands, and listened, and heard nothing.

Crawling out from his hiding place on his hands and knees, Malcolm cautiously peeked up into the vast interior of the statue and was astonished by what he saw. For now the floodlights were no longer shining directly down into his eyes, but were pointed at various odd angles to illuminate the iron framework and small areas of the copper skin. The invaders had obviously set up a kind of weird command post in the crown of the statue, using it as their base of operations. On filaments of gleaming nylon rope the three remaining men, each wearing a miner's lantern strapped to his head and holding a second light powered by a battery pack, swung across the interior space of the enormous metal structure from point to point, beam to beam, their individual lights from this distance looking for all the world, Malcolm thought, like fireflies darting about in the near dusk of a peaceful summer evening.

38

THE CALL CAME IN to the New York Police Department's Harbor Unit at 1:55 A.M., and because it had been a slow night and the communications sergeant was back in the lounge having coffee, Captain Shaner answered the telephone himself.

"Harbor Unit, Captain Shaner speaking."

"Hello, Nick, this is Todd, over in the Eighth Precinct."

"Yeah? Whattya got?"

"Something screwy one of our patrol cars picked up. It's in your area—okay if I patch him through to you right now?"

"You mean I've got a choice? Sure, go ahead—I've got all night. Fourth graveyard shift I've pulled in the past two weeks. You think they're trying to tell me something, Todd?"

"Listen, things down there couldn't run without you, Nick."

"Bet your ass. One of these days they're gonna find out, though."

"Right, Nick. Here comes the patch—the patrolman's name is Mullins."

There was a certain amount of electronic squawking as radio switches were connected and disconnected; then Shaner heard Mullins identifying himself as one of the occupants of car 307. "My present location is just off the intersection of Canal Street and the Bowery. My partner and I have one Henry Spitzer in custody, and also the truck he was driving when we intercepted him."

"This is Captain Shaner," Shaner interrupted the patrolman. "Who told you to intercept the truck?"

"The Eighth Precinct dispatcher. This guy Spitzer called

LAWRENCE DUNNING

in over there voluntarily, I guess, and they wanted us to
check him out. His story to them, and to us, too, was that
he claims to have received a call on his CB from somebody
who insisted that the Statue of Liberty was being invaded
and that he was supposed to call and get help from the
National Park Service or the police or *somebody* as soon
as he got off the bridge."

"What bridge, Mullins?"

"The Brooklyn—that's where Spitzer was driving his
truck when he claims to have received this message."

"Well, it could be legit," Shaner said. "The Brooklyn
Bridge isn't all that far from Liberty Island."

"Yes, sir, I know. The only thing is, when we pulled
a routine search, we found illegal contraband in the back
of the truck."

"You mean dope?"

"Affirmative. Looks like about ten pounds of marijuana
wrapped in plastic and stuffed inside old automobile tires.
The guy's kind of a hippie, don't look too clean, know
what I mean?"

"Did you by any chance have a search warrant on the
truck?"

"Well, no, sir, not exactly. See, there wasn't time or we
might've lost him after he called in."

"Then you're in shit city, Mullins. You may be able
to save your ass but don't count on it. You think maybe
this Henry Spitzer is making up the Statue of Liberty story
to divert our attention from the dope he's hauling?"

"It looks that way to me, Captain."

"Then why do you suppose he called the precinct voluntarily when nobody was onto him?"

"Oh . . . I hadn't thought about that. Maybe he wanted
to turn himself in."

"And maybe you're the king of North Africa, Mullins,
but I doubt it. Here's what you do—bring in the trucker
and the truck to me. I want to talk to him. Meanwhile I'll
try to check out his story if I can. And for God's sake,
don't look in his glove box or his pants pockets."

"Yes, sir. But I already have."

"Somehow, Mullins, that doesn't surprise me," Shaner
said and hung up.

432

The sergeant was still not back at the radio panel controls. "Sergeant Lobaugh!" Shaner shouted, and the sergeant ambled back from the lounge with a huge mug of coffee in his right hand. Across the mug were printed the words, I DIG COPS.

"What's up, Cap'n?" Lobaugh asked. He was a good-natured redhead who didn't seem to mind working the long, lonely nights like Shaner did.

"See if you can find the long glasses back in the supply room."

In a few minutes Lobaugh returned with the unwieldly 10 x 50 binoculars and handed them to Shaner, who took them over to one of the huge windows that looked out onto the waters of the harbor. "Never can adjust these things properly," he said, mostly to himself, as he fiddled with the center focus knob. He braced the glasses against the windowsill and slowly swept the field of vision across the choppy, rain-swept water. He saw two tugs, a large freighter, and then the Statue of Liberty, torch and crown lighted just as they always were. Nothing at all seemed to be wrong.

He went back to his desk and flipped through his telephone list finder. The only two numbers he had for Liberty Island were the Administration Building, which would have been closed for a good many hours now, and the superintendent's home. He picked up the telephone to dial the latter number, then returned it to its cradle. It was, after all, something after two A.M. Malcolm Williams was a personal friend of Shaner's—he and his wife, Lucy, and Shaner and *his* wife had been a foursome on many an entertaining evening when Lucy had still been on the island. Shaner had talked to Malcolm a couple of times since then, and had read the noncommittal voice well enough to know that Malcolm worried about Lucy, worried about his job, in fact seemed to worry about everything these days. Shaner did not want to disturb him at this ungodly time of the morning with what would probably turn out to be a bogus scare concerning the statue. He decided to wait, instead, for the arrival of the trucker with the fantastic story.

*   *   *

Mullins had been right about one thing—the trucker was a holdover from the late sixties, with a gold earring dangling from one ear and his foot-long, greasy-looking hair held back in a ponytail with an Indian ring made of turquoise and silver. He was nervous, as well he might be, sitting on a load of grass that would shortly become the official property of the city.

"I heard it, Captain, exactly the way I told you," the trucker Spitzer said. "This voice was calling out a weak mayday, and I thought it was some kids playing around with their old man's CB, you know, so I hollered back at 'em just to give 'em a thrill. But then this guy starts in telling me how he's the superintendent of Liberty Island and how he's got all these folks there busting up the place, or about to, they've got his little kid up in the statue or something like that, and he said they'd already killed some guards."

"Did he gave his name?"

"Not that I remember."

"How many people were supposed to be on the island?"

"Just the superintendent, his kid, and these four goons, was the way I got it."

"Did he say what they were after?" Shaner asked the man.

"No, I don't think so. See, I still thought it was all a joke of some kind. I just didn't pay too close attention."

"So why did you call in a report to the Eighth Precinct?"

"Well, that was after I got off the bridge, and I got to thinking about how I lost contact with the guy all of a sudden—"

Shaner frowned. "You mean, like somebody hit him or something?"

"No, it was more like he just faded out—see, I was travelin' and I probably just ran outside his range."

Shaner looked down at the few notes he had taken. "Anything else you can tell me that might help?"

The trucker studied his shoe a minute. "This here charge you got against me—possession of an illegal substance—I don't suppose it'd help if I told you it belongs to somebody else?"

"We'd like to know his name," Shaner said.

"Yeah, well . . ." The trucker shifted his weight from one foot to the other. "Seems like to me that since I helped you out all I could, even voluntarily called in like a good citizen to report this matter to the *police*, well, you might see your way clear to just let me and my ol' truck get on out of here and let you fellas get on with your work."

When Shaner didn't change his expression, the trucker tried again. "How 'bout just me? Hell, you can have the truck—it's not much good anyhow."

"We can't make any deals, Spitzer. Course, if this information of yours checks out, then maybe I could—"

"Williams!" the trucker almost yelled. "The guy told me his name was Williams—I just remembered."

"You're sure? Think hard, Spitzer."

"I'm sure it was Williams—Superintendent Williams."

Shaner stared at Spitzer for a second and nodded. "I believe you, and I think what you got was a legitimate call for help." He turned to Sergeant Lobaugh at the communications console. "Where's that patrolman—Mullins, or whatever his name was—that brought this guy in here?"

"I think he's back having coffee, Captain."

"Well, get him out here on the double and have him take Spitzer here back out on the Brooklyn Bridge to the spot where he got the CB traffic. Maybe they can pick up some more, or try transmitting to make contact. They can go in the patrol car—the truck stays here as evidence."

"But, Captain," Spitzer protested, "my truck CB may work different than what you've got in patrol cars."

"He's right, Captain," Sergeant Lobaugh said. "Particularly if it was a freak transmission in the first place—they'd have a hell of a lot better chance picking it up again on the exact same equipment."

"Yeah, yeah, I know you're right. Okay, Spitzer, you can take the truck but the pot stays with me, *permanently*. You read me?"

"Sure, Captain, sure," the trucker said, trying hard to conceal his delight at regaining possession of his truck. As long as he had wheels, he seemed to be thinking, there could always be other deliveries.

When Mullins and the trucker had left for the bridge,

Shaner dialed both the numbers he had for Liberty Island, including Malcolm Williams's private number, but could get no dial tone or ring on either. While Sergeant Lobaugh put in a line check request to the telephone company, Shaner tried to get in touch with the National Park Service district office for Manhattan on Pine Street, but there was no answer, which wasn't surprising. The office wouldn't open for another six hours, probably. Most of the security and police function was located out on the island, anyway.

Shaner's next call was to Captain Herschell at the U.S. Coast Guard facility on Governors Island. As ranking Coast Guard officer in the area, Herschell carried the additional title of captain of the port, which made him essentially responsible for exercising general police powers in the harbor. In addition to six thousand people, Herschell also commanded six fully rigged vessels and a number of helicopters and reconnaissance planes that could and did patrol the Atlantic coastal waters for hundreds of miles.

Capain Herschell himself was on the line a surprisingly short time, considering that it was just after two o'clock in the morning. When Shaner explained his concern for Liberty Island, the statue, and Malcolm Williams and his son in particular, Captain Herschell put Shaner on hold while he discussed the procedures with his subordinates, then came back on the line. "I'm sure we're agreed, Captain Shaner, that the first priority is to have a look at the island, see what we can see close-up."

"Absolutely, Captain Herschell. My people and equipment are at your service."

"Then here's what I think we'll do, Shaner. The Coast Guard will furnish men and boats, for a landing party if necessary, if the New York City Police Department will furnish helicopter support. My choppers are all either down for maintenance or temporarily out of the area."

"We'll be happy to, Captain Herschell," Shaner said with somewhat false enthusiasm. Shaner felt confident his own Harbor Unit people, boats, and choppers could handle almost any emergency in the harbor by themselves, and besides, having to call the younger man "Captain" all the time rankled, even though technically the captain of the port outranked any policeman.

436

"Just a minute, sir," Shaner said, putting his hand over the phone. Sergeant Lobaugh was signaling frantically with a message from the phone company. "Excuse me, Captain Herschell," he said a moment later. "I've just been told that the telephone company has checked the lines to Liberty Island and that they're out of order—no reason given. My own gut feeling is that they've probably been cut by whoever is out there."

"Or," Captain Herschell offered, "the main cable could have simply corroded from the saltwater."

"Yes, sir, that's possible," Shaner agreed. "But with your permission, I'd like to dispatch a single chopper to overfly the island for a close survey. The pilot will be in constant radio contact."

"Very well, Shaner, go ahead. But keep me posted—I want us to stay on top of this thing until we've cleared it up one way or the other. The Statue of Liberty is a symbol of hope and freedom to millions of people on this planet and, of course, is irreplaceable. We mustn't do *anything* to jeopardize her continued existence."

"Yes, sir. Out for now." Shaner clicked off, vaguely annoyed by Captain Herschell's flag-waving speech. It wasn't that he didn't basically agree about the statue's significance, it was simply that he thought Herschell might have shown a little more interest in the living inhabitants of the island. Assuming, of course, that they were still alive.

He made the necessary arrangements to send out one of the unit's light bubble-canopy helicopters with a two-man crew—one to pilot, the other to operate the mammoth ground-illumination spotlight that could turn night into day within any forty-foot-diameter area beneath the chopper. After the craft was airborne, Shaner had Sergeant Lobaugh tie into the helicopter's radio frequency. He picked up a hand microphone and pressed the on switch.

"This is Captain Shaner calling 374-L. How do you read me?"

"Loud and clear, Captain."

"Okay, 374-L. We'll maintain an open mike for the duration of the flyover. Do not attempt to land on the island—*repeat,* do not land. You are to light up every square inch of that rock, flying on the deck, and see what you can see. If there's anything that looks bad, or even that just doesn't look quite kosher for some reason, the Coast Guard will send a landing party on a cutter. Under no circumstances are you to attempt any heroics unaided. Understood?"

"Yes, sir. We're coming up on the southwest side of the island now, just to the left of the statue. All the floodlights look good, torch lights look good. We'll circle the island and dip lower around the north side. We've got the bright eye on the docks—no vessels in sight. Generator building intact, all other buildings seem normal. No sign of any human activity yet. We're circling behind the statue and dropping altitude to four hundred feet . . . Wait! Bright eye's picked out something on the pathway directly behind the statue . . . it appears to be a man lying down, or a body, possibly in uniform . . . I'm circling to the left and coming down another fifty feet for a closer look."

Shaner stood with the mike in his hand, listening to the speaker on Sergeant Lobaugh's communications console. Two other members of the Harbor Unit had drifted into the room and were listening as intently as Shaner to the helicopter's activities. "For God's sake, man, what do you see out there?" Shaner shouted into the mike.

"We don't know what to make of it, Captain," the helicopter pilot's voice came back. "We both saw it, but when we circled and dropped, whatever it was just wasn't there anymore."

"Are you saying you see nothing where you thought you saw a body before?"

"Yes, sir. I can't explain it, but it's definitely gone now. We'll continue to circle the statue clockwise and throw some light into the shadows. I'm telling you, Captain, it's got us spooked up here!"

Pell Bruckner, perched on a transverse ledge beside the metal platform that formed the floor of the statue's crown, listened on the big transceiver to the conversation between Captain Shaner and the helicopter pilot. Beside the equipment the superintendent's son, Bobby, tied to an upright iron brace and with his mouth again taped shut, stared at Bruckner with wild, frightened eyes.

On the walkie-talkie Bruckner ordered Kummel down to the base of the statue to drag the bodies of the two guards inside or at least hide them from the helicopter's dazzling light. Outside the cavernous interior of the statue he could already hear, over his own voice, the beating sound of the police helicopter's rotors. If that fool superintendent, wherever he was, heard the helicopter and knew what it was, he would probably try to signal it in some way. But that couldn't be helped now. He got on the walkie-talkie again and told Gros-Jacques to swing over on his rope harness from the area he had been searching —a dimly lit hole at the spot where the right arm that held the torch joined Liberty's shoulder, a hole approximately twenty feet across containing structural iron straps and a maintenance ladder. While he waited for his orders to be carried out, Bruckner moved over to the platform area where they had laid out all their equipment and began surveying the weapons they had brought, cursing whatever bad luck had brought one of the police's mosquitoes down on their heads.

Meanwhile Kummel, following Bruckner's order, had quickly descended on a rope sling to the base of the statue, which was much faster than using the stairs. He ran to the elevator and punched the button, listening to the deep-throated drone of the helicopter just as Bruckner had and hoping he would be in time. In the base of the pedestal he hurried down the stairs and across the lobby toward the entrance. From the corner of his eye he saw a shadow move near the darkened information desk, and reflex action sent him diving for the floor. An arrow zipped through the air over his left shoulder and skittered harmlessly across the lobby floor.

The silenced pistol was already in his hand when Kummel hit the floor. When he detected a second slight movement in the shadows he fired at the movement, and Malcolm Williams, hurled backward behind the counter by the force of Kummel's bullet passing through the fleshy part of his hip, uttered a muffled scream. The makeshift bow had slipped from his hands and he was in no condition to retrieve it at the moment. From his position of relative safety he listened as Kummel went outside the pedestal building and then returned, dragging something across the lobby floor. Afraid that Kummel might come looking for him when he had finished whatever it was he was doing, Malcolm painfully crawled out far enough from the counter to reach the bow. Back in his hiding place he settled down to wait, an arrow notched in the bowstring. Kummel might still shoot him, but only if he could manage it with an arrow sticking out of his throat.

But Kummel did not reappear.

When Gros-Jacques had reached Bruckner standing by the pile of gear on the platform within Liberty's crown, Bruckner pointed to the half dozen disposable M72 rocket launchers, each of which weighed only four and a half pounds, including the self-contained missile. The weapon was designed to penetrate up to ten inches of armor plate. "Grab two or three of those and get up to the torch," he told Gros-Jacques. "We could hold off quite an attacking force for a while, if we had to. Let's hope we don't."

As Gros-Jacques disappeared toward the ladder inside the statue's upraised right arm, Bruckner used the walkie-talkie to send a message to Kummel. "I'm blowing the interior lights until that chopper disappears. Hold your position—Gros-Jacques is in the torch."

Bruckner cut the switches on their portable lighting system, plunging their aerial workshop into instant gloom, and scrambled up deep inside the crown of the statue to the semicircle of windows. By sitting on the floor he could see up to the lighted platform surrounding the torch, and he also had a clear view of the entire front side of the island. He radioed to Gros-Jacques for a report; Gros-Jacques said the police helicopter was practically on top of the torch with its bright light.

"I can see it from here," Bruckner said. "Stay out of sight."

But as soon as Bruckner had released the talk button on the walkie-talkie, Gros-Jacques was chattering on in half

440

French, half English that the helicopter light had swung around directly and unexpectedly toward the torch platform. "They've seen me, I'm sure of that!" Gros-Jacques whispered loudly. "What should I do?"

"You fool!" Bruckner swore, thinking of the limited options. "All right, Gros-Jacques, your stupidity has left us no choice," he finally radioed back. "Use the rocket."

From his viewpoint on the floor of the famous head Bruckner watched through the windows as Gros-Jacques stepped out of hiding on the small torch platform. The awesome little tube of the rocket launcher, which Bruckner remembered seeing in action in Vietnam, was cradled in the big man's arms like a malevolent baby.

Captain Shaner, standing mike in hand beside the communications console, had heard nothing from the helicopter pilot in more than two minutes and was getting worried. He pressed his talk button again: "374-L, this is Shaner. What the hell's going on?"

"Sorry, Captain. We've just come up on the torch arm at about the level of the top of the flame, and I just saw something move on the platform. Bright eye saw it too —he's swinging the light up for a better look . . . My God, there's a huge guy just standing there in plain sight and he seems to be pointing something at us . . . it looks kind of like a—"

There was an instant of dead air, then a tremendous explosion roared from the speakers in the Harbor Unit office. But Shaner didn't need the radio to confirm that something awful had happened, because even without the long binoculars he could see the brilliant flash out in the harbor. Flaming pieces of debris sailed through the night like the world's largest fireworks display.

"What the hell was that!" Shaner roared, but Sergeant Lobaugh merely shook his head, a desperately pained look on his face. "No small arms fire caused *that*, Lobaugh. What the hell kind of weapons do they have out there? Must be some kind of an army!"

Shaner turned to the forgotten mike in his hand. "For God's sake, 374-L, come in! Lobaugh, do something with that fancy equipment of yours."

He and the sergeant looked at each other as Lobaugh turned a couple of dials on the console to boost the power level on the receivers. But only a faint dry electronic crackle remained of the helicopter that had been on the other end of the open line.

39

"KUMMEL!" BRUCKNER BARKED INTO the walkie-talkie. "Get up here on the double!"

When Kummel swung up onto the crown platform on the end of his rope, as gracefully as a spider traversing its web, Bruckner handed him an M16 assault rifle fitted with a star-scope night vision device. "Find two or three cartridges of tracer bullets for this thing out of the pack and get up on the torch platform with Gros-Jacques," Bruckner told him.

"You are expecting visitors?" Kummel asked.

"I'm certain the Coast Guard will attempt to land an assault party quietly by boat; we just don't know where," Bruckner replied. "There should be enough ambient light from the statue's outside lighting system to actuate the star-scope's electronic image and allow you to see a good distance out into the water—I've seen them work on nights so cloudy you'd swear there was *no* ambient light."

Kummel took the equipment and clambered up the same ladder through the statue's right arm that Gros-Jacques had used. Bruckner twirled the knobs on the big transceiver but heard nothing useful, which wasn't surprising since an assault team would maintain strict radio silence. He was glad neither Kummel nor Gros-Jacques had objected to being ordered out into the open on the torch platform, while he remained inside the statue in relative safety—he wasn't quite sure what he would have done if they had.

Five minutes later Kummel came through in a loud whisper on the walkie-talkie. "I have a clear image of the Coast Guard boat on the star-scope—they are coming up slowly on the dark side of the pier where the tourist ferry docks. Perhaps they use oars, for silence."

LAWRENCE DUNNING

"All right, Kummel. Can you hit the vessel from where you stand?"

"Easily—it is a straight shot down and out, quite within range."

"Good. Lead in with the tracers before they land, to spot the boat's exact position for one of Gros-Jacques's rockets. You understand, Gros-Jacques?"

"Oui," Gros-Jacques answered.

"You mean *yes,* don't you? The first shot will be your only shot, I imagine. Don't miss!"

Bruckner crouched beside the last window on the right side of the crown and by leaning at an angle could see the lights of the dock and the generator shed far below, the black water beyond. Suddenly a bright meteor shower of tracers from Kummel's rifle arced gracefully through the night sky, falling down, down past the far edge of the pier and spewing into the water. Then, raised slightly to find the range, they spattered against the launch and briefly illuminated the men in battle dress crouched amidships. Bruckner thought he could make out the faint outline of a large mounted gun being swung around by the crew on deck, but since they would never shoot at the statue, it was the least of his worries.

He wondered what was taking Gros-Jacques so long. Almost in answer to his thought, there was a different kind of lingering rocket trail blazing suddenly along the dying path of the tracers, and then a brilliant flash far down below in the water, followed a second later by an explosion that rocked the statue enough that Bruckner felt it sway. The Coast Guard boat seemed to leap flaming from the water, then shatter in a thousand burning fragments that quickly settled beneath the black waves.

"Report, please," Bruckner radioed to the torch platform.

After a while Kummel's voice came through. "The vessel was destroyed completely. There has been no sign of survivors reaching shore."

"Okay, Kummel, you stay up there for a while with your star-scope and pick up anything you can. We've apparently won this little skirmish, but there's no way we can win an all-out war. Get back to your search, Gros-

Jacques—we have very little time to discover the hiding place of the metal box, and none of us leaves the island until we do."

Bruckner flipped the switch that again lit the powerful floodlamps they had set up inside the statue. Tuning the transceiver to the police frequency Captain Shaner had been using during his monitored conversations with the Coast Guard and others, Bruckner keyed the microphone on and said very loudly and slowly, "This is Command Post Liberty calling Captain Shaner of the Harbor Unit. Come in, please."

There was a certain amount of electronic chatter before a voice came through on the same frequency. "Captain Shaner speaking. Who is this, and what do you want?"

Smiling to himself, Bruckner pressed the talk switch. "Who we are doesn't matter. What we are capable of *does* matter. As you are no doubt aware by now, we have destroyed one of your police helicopters—the nice blue and white ones—along with its crew, and we have also destroyed the Coast Guard launch that someone was foolish enough to attempt to land on the island. Unfortunately, its entire crew and attack party were killed—an entirely defensive move on our part, I assure you, but a necessary one."

"I repeat," Shaner's voice came back, "what is it you want?"

"Simply this," Bruckner said, "we want you to send a single helicopter, large enough to carry four or five people, to land on the island in the lawn area directly behind the statue in exactly two hours—I make that four-thirty. The chopper will carry full fuel tanks and only the pilot —no funny little police tricks, please. We realize that we are not capable of holding the island indefinitely, and our only concern now is for safe and unimpeded passage away from here to our destination. We will, of course, be carrying a hostage, as well as your pilot, and will have other means of assuring that you do not interfere with us."

"You must be crazy, whoever you are, to think I'd let you get away!" Captain Shaner bellowed through the transceiver. "Who is your hostage?"

"A very nice little boy," Bruckner answered. "Good

manners, quiet . . . he's tied and taped at the moment, of course, which may have something to do with his disposition. Here, he can talk to you himself." And Bruckner reached over to where Bobby was tied to the upright piece of iron and ripped the tape from the child's mouth. Bobby screamed, directly into the microphone, which Bruckner held conveniently close to the boy's face. "Say something, Bobby," Bruckner said, pinching Bobby's jaws open.

"Hel—hello," Bobby said in a tiny, scared voice.

"Tell the nice man who you are," Bruckner ordered.

"My name's Bobby . . . Bobby Williams."

"Malcolm's son," they heard Shaner say, either to himself or someone else at the other end. "Goddamnit, what kind of monsters are you?"

"The kind who believe in insurance, Captain," Bruckner said. "Listen carefully as Bobby here describes a process you may find absolutely fascinating. We brought along quite a number of magnesium bombs with us—are you familiar with them, Shaner? They're very effective in a good many military operations. A magnesium bomb is simply an incendiary bomb, but a rather special one. It's made of a light magnesium case containing a cone of thermite—powdered aluminum and iron oxide—that when detonated flashes at extreme temperatures and ignites the magnesium case. I think a little demonstration, narrated by Bobby here, will serve as an excellent object lesson for those of you or your friends who may doubt our intentions or our resolve. Just tell the nice police captain what you see us doing. Bobby, while we perform our little experiment."

Handed the microphone, Bobby, still tied to the upright, looked as though he might begin to bawl. But then even he became fascinated watching what Bruckner was doing. After calling Gros-Jacques on the walkie-talkie, Bruckner took several pieces of equipment from a large canvas bag, including a metal cylinder, a radio-controlled detonator, and a small black box with a remote-control switch on top.

"They've got all this stuff with them," Bobby said hesitantly into the microphone. "They're letting themselves down off the platform on ropes. Now they're just hanging there . . . now the mean one is wrapping something around this round metal thing, it looks like he's taping it to a metal bar that goes from one part of the statue to another . . . Okay, he's got it taped on and he's hooking some wires to it. Now he's hooking something else to the other ends of the wires . . . It's kind of square and looks a little like a transistor radio. Both of them are coming back up on the ropes now, and the mean one is holding this little black box. He looks like he's trying to give it to me!"

"Take the box, Bobby, and push that little switch," Bruckner said, holding out the remote controller. "Go on, it won't hurt you—I just want to show Captain Shaner how easy it is."

Timidly Bobby reached toward the switch and pushed it. Several things happened immediately: A red light glowed on the detonator; the magnesium bomb taped to the iron strut below ignited in a shower of sparks and smoke; and the magnesium case erupted into white fire so brilliant that it was impossible to look anywhere close to it without being blinded. At Bruckner's insistence Bobby described what he saw, and from the sound of his voice it was obvious that he was awed by the impressive and unexpected fireworks display. Suddenly he shouted into the microphone, "The metal bar burned up! That thing just burned it in half—the two pieces are just sitting up there with a big hole in the middle!"

Bruckner took the microphone then. "I assume you heard it all, Captain. The truth is, by remote radio control I detonated a device—the magnesium bomb—that burns at a temperature of more than three thousand degrees Farenheit for ten minutes or so. And in case you foolishly think we don't know what we're doing, I should perhaps point out that the melting point of iron, which forms the skeleton of this statue, is two thousand seven hundred and ninety-five degrees, while the melting point of the copper skin is a mere one thousand nine hundred and eighty-one degrees. Unless you and the Coast Guard withdraw all planes, boats, and personnel from the vicinity of Liberty Island immediately and furnish the lone helicopter as I previously specified, we shall have no choice left but to connect a number of these interesting devices to strategic points of the statue's skeleton and skin, and destroy it bit by bit. I think we shall start with the head and right arm—that's the one holding the torch, in case your memory is hazy —on a diagonal line from the left shoulder to a point just below the folds in the right sleeve. A rather large part of Miss Liberty's anatomy would end up toppling into the bay, and I'm afraid Bobby would go with her. Do you understand what I'm saying, Captain?"

"I hear you," Captain Shaner replied.

Seeing what he thought was a good opportunity, Bobby grabbed the microphone from Bruckner's hand and started yelling into it: "Please come get me—my dad's disappeared and I'm scared—please help me somebody!"

Bruckner snatched the microphone back. "He's a gutsy little kid, I'll say that much for him. But he'll be a *dead* gutsy little kid if you don't do exactly as I've told you. Agreed, Captain?"

There was a pause, then Captain Shaner's defeated-sounding voice came over the speakers with a single word: "Agreed."

Since the beginning of the Liberty crisis the Harbor Unit office had gradually become more and more crowded as the word spread that something hot was going on. The atmosphere in the communications control room was tense and heavy; Captain Shaner, his tie off and shirt sleeves rolled to the elbow, was sweating profusely as he stood holding the microphone and mopping his forehead with a handkerchief the size of a dish towel.

One of those who came in from outside was Lieutenant Allen, Shaner's second in command. "Hey, Frank, where you been?" Shaner said. "Things are popping like crazy here."

"That's what I heard, Nick. Believe it or not, I was home sleeping like a baby when this jerk I know from WQVD-TV calls me up on my personal number and wants the scoop on whether some group of terrorists has taken over the Statue of Liberty. I figured since I was awake then anyhow, I'd come down and find out what the hell was going on."

"Okay, Frank, I'll fill you in later—I'm trying to reach

his majesty Captain Herschell out on Governors Island. We've got a real thing going here—I don't mind telling you I'm scared shitless something bad's coming down before we're through. Anyway, I'm glad you're here—get me another cup of coffee, will you?"

"Yeah, boy, when the chips are down in a tough situation, old Frank always comes through," Lieutenant Allen said wryly and went off to get his boss a cup of coffee.

Shaner finally got through to Captain Herschell, and explained in detail his conversation with the group who now held Liberty Island. "I don't know about the temperatures and all on a magnesium bomb, but I would guess they've really got 'em out there. Could they actually do what he was saying—you know, burn off the head and arm?"

"I don't know," Captain Herschell said. "We don't have any use for that kind of violent stuff in the Coast Guard. Hang on a minute—I'll have one of my people check it out with the Army munitions people over at Fort Hamilton in Brooklyn."

Shaner hung on while Herschell spoke to someone at his end of the line. Lieutenant Allen looked at Shaner and raised his eyebrows, and Shaner shrugged. He held his hand over the mouthpiece and said, "Captain Herschell says the Coast Guard is a nonviolent organization."

"Did he say whether they're accepting pansies these days?"

Captain Herschell came back on the line. "We've rung through to the munitions CQ at Fort Hamilton—we're getting a reading now . . . What's that? Yes, that will do nicely . . . You're sure, then? Thank you very much . . . Sorry, Shaner, I was talking through my people here. The man at Hamilton says magnesium bombs will do exactly what your mysterious contact at the statue said they would. And, incidentally, the critical melting points for copper and iron were right on the money. If the man you spoke to has a magnesium bomb—even *one*—the statue is in terrible jeopardy."

"I believe he does," Shaner said. "Under the circumstances, Captain Herschell, don't you agree there's really nothing we can do at the moment except to hover out of sight and wait for their next move?"

"That seems to be about it. There's no way that I would be willing to risk another single boat with a landing party, and a full-fledged coordinated air and sea attack would likely result in moderate to severe damage of the statue itself."

"And of course to the hostages," Shaner added.

"Assuming there are any."

Shaner sighed, thinking about the words of the truck driver and of the man presumably speaking from the island. "There's something funny, though, you know, Captain Herschell? These are obviously not your usual Statue of Liberty demonstrators, the political boys who choose Miss Liberty because she's such a terrifically visible symbol. There've been all kinds and sizes of protesting groups out there over the years, from Puerto Rican nationalists to U.S. veterans, all eager to get the eyes and ears of the world focused on them and their causes. But this group fits no known pattern—at least nothing that looks familiar to me."

"What do you mean, exactly? Do you know something you haven't told me?"

Shaner couldn't believe the man. "No, of course not. It's just that, for one thing, it's not taking place during the daylight hours like all the other demonstrations have. And they don't seem to want any publicity. Far from it —they only contacted the outside world when they felt threatened. No, I definitely have a feeling that something else is going on out there, something we don't even begin to understand."

"There's another thing," Captain Herschell said. "Whatever guards the Park Service maintains out there on the island have obviously been neutralized. Was there any mention of guards being held hostage?"

"No."

"Then I think we can safely assume the guards have been killed, and to my knowledge that hasn't happened before."

"My pilot reported seeing a body in uniform. It wasn't

450

there the second time around, but the invaders probably moved it out of sight."

"Well, I assume you'll keep me informed if you receive further word from the group in the statue—by the way, any idea how many of them there are?"

"I should think few, but highly prepared. Commando types, probably."

"We call them 'special forces' these days," Captain Herschell said with the assurance of a career military man talking about military matters.

"Whatever. I'm really worried about Malcolm—they didn't mention him at all."

"Who's Malcolm?"

"Williams—the Liberty Island superintendent. There's been no word about him since that trucker called in with the message from him that we all thought was a phony. I just hope Bobby Williams isn't already a daddyless little fellow—the poor kid sounded scared to death."

"Wouldn't you be?"

"Sure . . . sure I would. Have you ever been all the way up inside the statue, Captain?"

"Not since I was a kid in the Bronx," Captain Herschell said.

"Damned spooky place," Shaner admitted, "even in the daytime. On a rainy afternoon, with the lightning bouncing around, it's like something out of *Frankenstein.* I'll brief you before we send them the escape chopper."

"I may contact my superiors in the Pentagon," the Coast Guard captain said. "They may not want us to go along with the invaders' demands."

"I think they will," Shaner said dryly. "Talk to you later."

He rang off and shook his head at Lieutenant Allen. "I feel so damned *helpless,* Frank. They're holding all the cards right now, and the Coast Guard doesn't have any more idea what to do about it than I do. Captain Herschell's talking about alerting the Pentagon, and that would probably mean the FBI and everybody else in this part of the country would get involved. I don't know—I just have a gut feeling we ought to keep this whole thing on a kind of personal, one-to-one level."

451

Allen nodded. "You're probably right—at least until we get a better handle on what we're dealing with, and who."

"Call for you on sixteen, Captain," Sergeant Lobaugh interrupted.

"Yeah, Captain Shaner here."

"Yes, Captain," the voice on the phone said. "This is Bill Rice with the news department of station WQVD-TV. One of my reporters was speaking with a Lieutenant Frank Allen of your department earlier about a possible siege and takeover of the Statue of Liberty—I understand that would be in the jurisdiction of the NYPD Harbor Unit, am I correct?"

"Close," Shaner grudgingly admitted. "But we have nothing at all for you at this time. Maybe if you called back around eight o'clock in the morning . . ."

"Come, come, Captain, we both know the news media are entitled to whatever you have that might be newsworthy—and certainly the fact that some group is threatening our beloved symbol of freedom, Miss Liberty, out there in the harbor would be the lead story for anyone who had it. Naturally, WQVD would like to be the first to give our viewers the facts. If you could just fill me in on what's happened to this minute—"

"Look, Rice or whatever your name is . . . we're working on a rumor at the moment and we're doing everything possible to check it out and verify the facts. When we have something concrete you'll certainly be the first to know."

"What is the rumor, Captain Shaner?"

"You may be entitled to facts, sir, but certainly not to unsubstantiated rumors. As I told you, we'll let you know—"

"Of course, if you won't cooperate with us, Captain Shaner, you just make our job of informing the public —the American public—a little tougher. But we *will* get the story, with or without your help. Our instant cameras are being loaded on board a helicopter this very minute for a close look at Liberty Island and the statue. If there's anything out there I think we'll find it."

With a huge sigh for the hardheads of the world who

made his job so much more difficult, Shaner wiped his forehead with the oversize handkerchief and spoke very distinctly into the telephone receiver. "Mr. Rice . . . that is correct, isn't it? Mr. Rice?"

"Yes, sir."

"Mr. Rice, the Statue of Liberty, the air space above it, and the waters surrounding it within a radius of a couple of miles, are as of this minute off limits to everyone, including the media. *Especially* the media. If your helicopter approaches the island, it will be buzzed off by one of the police choppers in the area. If your pilot should be foolish enough to continue heading in toward the island after being warned, your helicopter will be blown out of the air. Is that sufficiently clear for you, Mr. Rice, or would you like me to repeat it?"

"I doubt that you have that kind of authority, Captain Shaner. In any case I will certainly check with your superiors—and I believe the Coast Guard has some interest in matters of this kind. Has the captain of the port issued a public announcement to the effect that the Port of New York is closed?"

"I didn't say that," Shaner said, wondering where they got creeps like Rice.

"I'm sorry, Captain, but this story has the smell of something a lot bigger than either of us," Rice said at last. "I dislike going live with facts we're unable to verify, but you leave me no choice."

"What kind of double-talk is that, Rice? Facts that you can't verify couldn't possibly be facts. Is this what you call in-depth news reporting?"

"Thank you for your cooperation, Captain. We'll be issuing a special news bulletin in about fifteen minutes. I hold you directly and personally responsible for any misstatements of fact due to your concealing pertinent information from us. If you should change your mind, I'll be at my desk in the WQVD offices. Good night."

Shaner slammed the phone into the cradle and cursed. "Arrogant sonofabitch—he wouldn't mind at all endangering people's lives as long as he got his little scoop. I don't think he gives a goddamn whether his facts are straight or not, just so long as he's first."

"Was that the same one who talked to me?" Frank Allen asked.

"His boss. Irresponsible TV bastards. The newspaper reporters are just as bad, though."

"Not quite," Allen said. "At least they don't wear makeup."

Shaner had Sergeant Lobaugh patch him back in to Captain Herschell on Governors Island. "I couldn't wait for your confirmation, Captain," Shaner said with regard to his imposed blockade of Liberty Island. "That jerk would have gone out there and probably gotten himself and a lot of other people killed. Are you in agreement—enough to make it official?"

"Yes, I am—but I believe we should not announce it publicly but only as it comes up. We don't need panic at a time like this."

"I have a feeling we may not be able to avoid it," Shaner said.

"Just don't tell anybody anything—that ought to be simple enough," Captain Herschell said with such conviction that he was almost convincing.

Shaner gave the instrument back to the communications sergeant and went to his desk, where he sank down into his chair for the first time in what seemed like days. He consulted a mechanical number finder beside his desk calendar and used his own telephone to dial the number of Lucy Williams's apartment in Greenwich Village. While it rang he glanced at his watch, saw that it was getting on toward three o'clock, and winced. But he let it ring anyway—eight, nine, ten times—until finally a sleepy Lucy answered on the eleventh ring.

"Lucy, is that you?"

"Who the hell is this? What time is it?"

"This is Nick Shaner, Lucy," he said, and stretching the truth added, "it's after two, and I apologize, but it couldn't be helped."

"Okay, I guess I'm awake now," a sleepy Lucy said. "But this had better be good, Nick."

"I'm afraid it's not good at all—that's why I'm bothering you like this." Shaner took a deep breath and then told her as briefly as possible all he knew about what had happened at the statue, leaving out only the parts having to do with the people who had been killed. "Bobby's okay, at least for the moment—I talked to him myself and he seemed fine, very brave and a real little man. You ought to be proud of him, Lucy."

"What . . . what about Malcolm?"

"We don't know. It's a tough thing to say, but we just don't have any way of knowing where he is right now, or what he's doing . . ."

"Or whether he's even alive. That's what you mean, isn't it?"

"We don't know, Lucy."

"Have they killed anyone that you know of?"

"We don't know that either," Shaner lied, knowing that it couldn't help Lucy if she did know. "We're doing the best we can, but right now we don't have much to go on. We don't even know what they want."

"Maybe they just want the statue."

"That doesn't make any sense, Lucy."

"Lots of things don't make sense these days."

"Well, I just wanted to let you know as much as *I* know, up to now. Is there anything we can do for you?"

"Sure—tell me this is all a nightmare, and that I'll wake up in a minute."

"I guess it's one of those real-life nightmares, Lucy. I can't tell you how sorry I am. I know how much you two love each other, in spite of this business lately."

Suddenly Lucy was crying on the other end of the line. "Nick, I feel *awful*," she sobbed. "Malcolm and Bobby were here, in the apartment, just tonight. Malcolm wanted to stay but I wouldn't let him, and we had a bad argument. I almost feel responsible for what's happened now —do you see what I mean?"

"I think so. But you mustn't blame yourself, Lucy. This was nobody's fault. Anyway, it's probably going to turn out fine—these things usually do. You know, don't you, that there's never been a really serious incident at the statue?"

"That's what I've been told. Nick, can I come down there where you are? You know, just to be around in case there's . . . anything."

"I'd rather you didn't, Lucy. There's nothing you could do, and it might be harder on you."

"Please, Nick. I'll go crazy if I sit here alone."

"Okay. We're trying to keep people out of here, but just tell whoever you see that I sent for you."

"Thanks. You're a real friend, Nick. The best."

"You're pretty special yourself, you and Malcolm both. I'll see you later."

Shaner hung up and called Lieutenant Allen over. "That was Lucy Williams, Malcolm's wife. She's pretty busted up over this, as you might expect. I told her she could come down here—she'll be in the way, but I couldn't say no. If I'm busy you'll have to take care of her. The thing that worries me now is that we've obligated ourselves to send a pilot and a helicopter out to the island."

"Isn't there some way we can fake it, to get inside their defenses?"

"There's just no way, Frank. They've got us cold on this one. There's a good chance we're going to end up sacrificing a man, and I don't see how I can ask anybody to do that."

"Hey, Nick, we don't know that they'll just kill the pilot like that. They probably need him to fly them out, right?"

"Maybe, maybe not. Anyway, they'll only need him till they get where they're going. I hate the thought of jeopardizing a good man for a lousy bunch of terrorists or whatever they are."

"They sound like nuts to me."

"Nuts, yeah," Shaner said, frowning. He thought of something that had been bothering him all night, a forgotten incident that had been edging around the back side of his consciousness. The week before he had had a visitor in the office, a man he had assumed at the time was just another of the hundreds of nuts and freaks and paranoid citizens big-city cops came in contact with all the time. The man had babbled on about some kind of attack that might be made on the Statue of Liberty, but there were no details, no suggested time frame except soon, and Shaner had had the feeling that the man was a real Bellevue-type psycho. If he had had more time he might have checked that out—he remembered writing the man's name and number down and putting it somewhere in his desk.

He found the slip of paper buried in his card file and dialed the number. Surprisingly, because it was now after three o'clock in the morning, there was an answer almost immediately, and Shaner wondered briefly what sort of person would likely be awake at that hour.

"Mr. Owens? Peter Owens? Sorry to bother you at what must seem to be a strange time . . . This is Captain Shaner of the Harbor Unit, New York Police Department—you remember you were in my office a week or so ago? Mr. Owens, I think you'd better get dressed and come down here right away—I'm sending a patrol car to pick you up. I think you might be a big help to us in that business about the Statue of Liberty and Project . . . Lamplighter, was it? . . . No, this is not an arrest, Mr. Owens, why would you think that? It's simply an opportunity for you to be a good citizen . . . Thank you."

"Nick, here's something you're not gonna like," Lieutenant Allen said as Shaner was hanging up. "The guys back in the squad room had the TV on, and they just saw a flash bulletin about the statue."

"Oh shit! What'd it say?"

"It was all screwed up. They said the announcer acted as though the station had made the scoop of the century, and that they were right on top of the story—he even implied they had a chopper out there right now."

"They'd better not! I'm not kidding, Frank, I'll blast their ass right out of the sky if I have to."

"They're not stupid, Nick. I think they knew you meant business. Hey, who's this guy Owens you were talking to? I couldn't help overhearing."

"I don't know."

He saw Lieutenant Allen looking at him strangely and repeated himself. "I tell you I don't know who he is—probably some jerk who sees visions about the end of the world. I don't know how anybody could possibly help us now anyway—I'm just pulling at straws, Frank, just pulling at straws. Can you imagine the Statue of Liberty's head and torch and right arm all crumpled up and buried in ninety feet of garbage out there in the harbor?"

Lieutenant Allen shook his head.

"Neither can I, Frank. We just can't let that happen."

"Maybe you could send this Owens out to the island in a chopper—if he knows the terrorists, or knows what they're up to, maybe he could talk to them, reason with them . . ."

Shaner looked at his assistant. "You mean, take a chance with the Statue of Liberty on some unknown quantity, some crazy civilian?"

"Sure, Nick, why not? What else have we got going for us?"

"Nothing . . . not a goddamn thing!"

The telephone rang and Sergeant Lobaugh answered, taking what would undoubtedly be only the first of many calls from people who, having seen the television bulletin, would want to know what sort of new danger lurked outside the windows of New York.

40

THE THREE REMAINING INVADERS—Bruckner, Kummel, and Gros-Jacques—swung back and forth on the ends of their climbing ropes along the length of the iron struts of the statue's skeleton, swooping down in their complicated harnesses and pulleys to hover above a joining of struts, bobbing their heads to illuminate the shadowed crevices with the miner's lamps strapped to their foreheads, then leaping off again across the dismal abysses toward another juncture that represented a potential hiding place for their quarry, the metal box Bruckner had described. The patterns they made in the air resembled the patterns that might be made by some prehistoric spider spinning an endless, imaginary web.

All three were aware of time now, more so than before Bruckner's conversation with Captain Shaner. They each worked alone feverishly and desperately without attempting to maintain contact on their walkie-talkies, which they left open to receive messages from the others. Gros-Jacques worked the lower third of the statue, Bruckner the middle, and Kummel the upper section, with the exclusion of the torch arm, which had already been thoroughly checked. "What happens if we go through the whole statue without finding the box?" Gros-Jacques had asked earlier, to which Bruckner had replied, "Then, *mon ami,* we start over again."

Though he, too, felt pressured by the lack of time, Bruckner also recognized in himself a kind of exhilaration brought on by the act of near-flying and by the unprecedented challenge of what they were attempting here inside the statue. Exhilaration was not common to Bruckner, and he distrusted any such powerful emotion as being

459

potentially harmful to his work, but in this case there seemed to be nothing he could do about it.

As he worked his way along a horizontal path from the right side of the statue toward the cavity in the opposite side made by the left arm bent inward to hold the tablet of law, he switched on a powerful hand-held spotlight dangling from his utility belt and focused it on a massive joint of iron bars and struts joined by iron straps to the thin copper plates of Liberty's left breast. He played the light back and forth across the intersection of the various skeletal pieces, then dropped down on his rope to inspect the underneath side of the joint. It had the same basic appearance as a good many other joints he had checked, but something about it seemed different. Edging closer, he held the spotlight steady above his head, and for a second or two his breath hung suspended in his chest; for there, caught in the circle of bright light, was an oblong metal box snugly welded into the deepest corner of the intersecting beams.

It was the same color as the surrounding beams and could have been simply a strengthening support for the joint, of course, but there was no structural reason for it to be the shape and size it was. Hand over hand in the rope harness, Bruckner pulled himself next to the underside of the joint and pressed his hand flat against the side of the box. It felt cold and clammy, as all of the metal inside the statue did; but when he flicked his index finger against it, there was the impression, however slight, of a hollowness inside.

He held the walkie-talkie to his mouth, hesitated a moment as he checked the positions of Kummel—above him and out of sight on the other side of the staircase—and Gros-Jacques, below him, then pressed the talk switch. "Gros-Jacques, come up to where I am and bring the acetylene torch—there's an area here I want to inspect further."

He knew Kummel would have heard the same message and would wonder about it, but there was no sense stopping Kummel's search when this might prove to be nothing at all. Nevertheless, he was hardly surprised when Kummel appeared, dangling from his own rope, immediately behind Gros-Jacques, who was having difficulty controlling both his ropes and the bulky welding gear.

Gros-Jacques passed the torch to Bruckner and hovered to one side as Bruckner turned the valves until a yellowish flame popped into life. He adjusted the torch to a short, pointed, nearly invisible blue flame and touched the point to the welded bead that joined the box to the iron struts. The metal turned red, then white with the heat, and brilliant sparks of flaming metal spewed out into the dark cavern of the statue.

When two sides of the box had been cut away from the struts, Bruckner slipped on the heavy welder's gloves Gros-Jacques had brought along; although he planned to catch the glowing box in the gloves before it could fall, it was impossible to handle it while he was still directing the torch flame toward it. Gros-Jacques swung in his rope harness as close to Bruckner's work area as he dared, holding his arm and gloved hand bent in front of his face to protect himself from the flying sparks. Kummel was not far away. Both men watched Bruckner's every move with a greedy intensity of which Bruckner himself was only dimly aware.

The box came loose suddenly and unexpectedly and nearly fell free. Bruckner had the flaming torch in his hand to worry about, but Gros-Jacques, executing a surprisingly graceful midair dive in his rope harness, grabbed the box in both gloved hands and held it in front of him, staring at it as the heat slowly dissipated and the metal gradually returned to its original color.

Bruckner smiled. "Well done—a prettier catch I've never seen. Now give me the box, Gros-Jacques."

But the huge Frenchman shook his head slowly side to side. "No!"

"What?"

"I said no—not until we all have a good look at what's inside. We've been risking our necks here, we deserve a little something special."

"You'll get your something special!" Bruckner hissed, grabbing for the box with his own gloved right hand. But the box was heavy, and the motion of the rope slings was difficult to compensate for; his hand only slapped the side of the box, loosened Gros-Jacques's hold on it momentarily, and flapped helplessly in the air as the box tumbled end over end down through the gloomy cavern, clanging against a strut here and there and bouncing off in a slightly different direction, until it crashed into the floor of the statue ten stories below.

"You miserable fool!" Bruckner shouted at Gros-Jacques. "What if the box has split open down there!"

"What if it has?" Gros-Jacques asked. He stared at Bruckner a second, then propelled himself over to the central stairwell, released his harness, and began spiraling down the stairs. Kummel and Bruckner were immediately behind him.

At the bottom spiral Gros-Jacques slowed his descent until Bruckner and Kummel were on his heels, then threw all his massive weight backward in a body block that sent the other two crashing painfully into the metal ironwork of the stairs. Free for a moment, he raced to the spot where the box had fallen and found it still in one piece though dented badly on one corner. He scooped up the box and dashed over to the elevator, which would take him down to the pedestal lobby and eventual freedom.

As Gros-Jacques stepped into the elevator and punched the button that would close the doors, Bruckner ran full speed across the distance from the stairwell to the elevator, fumbling at his belt as he ran. With his left index finger he yanked the ring-pin from a small fragmentation grenade and tossed it accurately through the opening just before the doors closed. The elevator, humming on its cables, descended slowly toward the lobby. In four seconds there was a muffled explosion from somewhere far below; Bruckner, having counted the seconds to himself, nodded once. Kummel said nothing.

The two of them climbed down the pedestal stairs much more slowly than they had come down through the statue. At the bottom landing they saw the doors of the elevator gaping open, as though waiting for someone to enter. Gros-Jacques lay on the elevator floor in a pool of blood, his grossly contorted body cut to ribbons by hundreds of tiny grenade fragments. His open eyes, quite dead, seemed to be staring out at Bruckner. The metal box, spattered with blood, lay beside him.

"He was a stupid man," Bruckner said meaningfully to Kummel. He reached across Gros-Jacques's body and retrieved the box, which he wiped clean on his sleeve. "Let's go back up and see what's inside, shall we?"

To avoid the bloody mess in the elevator they climbed back up through the pedestal and up the spiral stairs, picking up the welding torch on the way. Eventually, both somewhat out of breath, they reached their operational platform in the crown of the statue. Bruckner looked over at where the boy Bobby was tied to the upright strut, and Kummel, following his gaze, said, "Assuming this is what you've been looking for, what happens to the boy?" But Bruckner, already wielding a large mallet and a steel wedge to crack open the box, did not answer Kummel's question.

The box had obviously been welded shut expertly. It took Bruckner nearly half an hour of careful work with the mallet and wedge to open the box along a seam on three sides. Inhaling sharply with expectation, he pried open the box lid and shone the portable spotlight inside.

Thousands of pinpoints of brilliantly colored fire flashed in the strong light. The box was indeed filled with diamonds and emeralds and rubies, some of incredible size, just as the Lamplighter manuscript had said it would be, and the sight was so breathtaking that for several seconds neither Kummel nor Bruckner could speak. Finally Kummel uttered a short sibilant expression in a language that sounded to Bruckner like Russian but was, in any case, a language he had no fluency in. Bruckner reached out and picked up a handful of the gorgeous gems and let them spill through his fingers.

Kummel shook his head. "No wonder you risked so much for the mere possibility of finding these incredible jewels—they must be priceless."

"Oh, no, my friend," Bruckner said, still gazing at the jewels. "Everything of value has a price on the world market. According to our best previous estimates, these pretty little stones should bring ten million dollars, more or less—but don't get greedy, Kummel. They belong to me."

Kummel looked at him. "You said 'our' best estimates —who might *our* refer to?"

"That is information of no concern to you," Bruckner said. Abruptly he closed the box and shoved it into the cloth pouch he wore slung across his shoulder. "Please take the rocket launcher and climb up to the torch—the escape helicopter should be nearing the island soon. Be aware that the police or the Coast Guard may try some trick."

"And what," Kummel asked him, "will you be doing in the meantime?"

"Don't worry, I'll be busy enough," Bruckner said. "I'm going to wire a string of magnesium bombs around the framework of the statue so that, if necessary, we can detonate the charges later by remote control from the helicopter."

Frowning, Kummel said, "Would you really do that? I was under the impression that all Americans are terrible sentimentalists where the Statue of Liberty is concerned."

Bruckner laughed harshly. "For ten million dollars I would do a lot of terrible things, old sport. And to answer your other question—the one you didn't ask—there's no place for me to run away or hide with the jewels, so you don't have to worry just because I have them."

"I want my fair share, Bruckner."

"Of course—there are only the two of us left now, and we'll have ample time to work out the details later. But first we have to get away from this island safely or neither of us will have anything to look forward to except a lifetime in prison. We need each other, Kummel, we need to help and trust each other if we are to escape to freedom successfully."

With a firmly set mouth Kummel looked at Bruckner and finally nodded in agreement. Bruckner watched him strap the rocket launcher to his back and begin climbing the ladder toward the torch still blazing brightly in the wet night outside.

41 _____

DANGLING FROM THE ROPE harness and with the help of the lamp strapped to his forehead, Bruckner fastened the magnesium charges at various strategic points around the statue's upper skeleton and wired them in sequence to the radio-controlled detonator. He had just finished wiring the last charge when Kummel called him on the walkie-talkie from his vantage point in the torch. "There is a single helicopter approaching the island from the north," he reported. "Same configuration as the previous police helicopter, though it is too dark to see the markings."

"Is it still raining?" Bruckner asked him.

"Lightly—more a mist than rain. Not the best weather for helicopters."

"Is there any other traffic in the air at the moment?"

"Not in the immediate vicinity. There appear to be several helicopters hovering at some distance—perhaps slightly less than a kilometer—to the north, east, and south of us."

"Looking for a chance to get at us through a single careless move," Bruckner said. "All right, keep watching that helicopter coming in and let me know when it's close enough to see details. I'm going to use the transceiver."

He propelled himself along the rope webbing to the platform in the crown and switched on the big sending unit that was already set to the harbor police frequency. "Calling Captain Shaner of the Harbor Unit—come in, please," he spoke into the microphone.

The speaker crackled as the electrons sorted themselves out. "This is Captain Shaner. What do you want?"

"We see your helicopter approaching the island—we assume for the moment everything is as we requested.

However, I must inform you that when we depart shortly, we will have with us a remote-control device with which to destroy the statue from the air, should that become necessary. We will also have the boy with us in the helicopter—I suggest you do nothing to interfere with our flight or he will suffer greatly. I demand that you remove all the aircraft hovering on the island's perimeter, since they will only harm both our causes. Agreed?"

There was a long pause as Bruckner listened to the non-human sounds issuing from the speaker. When Captain Shaner still had not replied after thirty seconds, Bruckner angrily broke in. "Don't be a fool, Captain, you have no choice! I'll give you five more seconds to reply—after which the boy will begin to scream."

"All right, you butchers! Agreed," Captain Shaner said. "The perimeter helicopters will be entirely withdrawn from the area, and there will be no attack made on your escape aircraft. Now, for God's sake, let the boy go!"

"One moment, Captain." Bruckner switched off the microphone and called Kummel on the walkie-talkie. "What is the situation now?"

"The other helicopters have just this moment begun to disperse back to the mainland," Kummel reported. "Their lights have all but disappeared."

"And the single incoming aircraft?"

"It is now approaching the torch from the east side—so far as I can tell there is only the one pilot, no passengers in the rear seat."

"Excellent." Bruckner got back on the microphone to Captain Shaner and confirmed that the previous instructions were being carried out. "Our thanks to you, Captain, for your uncommon good sense," Bruckner said. "Please let it continue."

"I'll see you in hell!" Captain Shaner barked and audibly cut off his microphone.

Kummel came down from the torch and joined Bruckner on the platform. "I heard your conversation with the police captain on my small radio," he said. "Tell me, are we actually taking the boy with us?"

Bruckner looked across at the frightened boy tied to the strut and smiled at Kummel's worried expression. "Of course not, but no one will know that except us. The idea, carefully planted in their heads, that the little fellow will be an unwilling passenger on the helicopter will be every bit as effective as if it were a fact, and a lot less trouble."

"And what about the pilot now flying in, who is undoubtedly a police agent? Do we need him further, once he has landed the craft?"

"Not at all, Kummel. I am quite capable of piloting the helicopter myself, and of course we have no need of additional hostages. I simply saw no reason to tell that to the captain."

While he had been speaking, Bruckner several times noticed Kummel staring at the pouch slung across his shoulder that contained the jewels. There was something of desire and envy in that concentrated stare—much the same look that some men had for beautiful women seen in the company of other men. But Bruckner put Kummel's staring down to mere greed, the lowliest of passions; he would simply have to watch Kummel more closely until the situation had jelled.

"We should go down now to meet the helicopter," Bruckner told Kummel. "Bring the transceiver along—there may still be a necessity for further negotiations with Captain Shaner or the Coast Guard."

Bruckner waited until Kummel had strapped the big radio unit on his back so that he, Bruckner, could be last going down the stairs. When Kummel picked up one of the Uzi submachine guns, Bruckner frowned and said, "You won't need that." But Kummel showed no signs of giving it up, and it wasn't worth an open confrontation at the moment. Bruckner patted the handle of the machine pistol stuck in his own belt to make sure Kummel noticed it. In his left hand he carried a small black remote-control switch box that, when turned on, would activate the detonator and ultimately the magnesium bombs sprinkled around Liberty's iron bones like deadly ornaments on a Christmas tree.

When they reached the lobby of the statue's pedestal they could clearly hear the beating of the helicopter's rotors as it gently came to rest on the hedge-bordered lawn behind the statue. The craft's landing lights flashing through the glass doors cast eerie shadows through the deserted lobby. Bruckner suddenly clutched Kummel's arm and, holding his finger to his lips, pointed toward a dimly lit corner of the room next to the information area. A man's leg, partially visible, stuck out stiffly from the floor behind the counter.

Kummel circled back to the far end of the counter while Bruckner cautiously crept to the place where the motionless leg was still visible. With the machine pistol in his hand, Bruckner suddenly pressed his foot down hard on the leg and sprang around the end of the counter. There, sitting propped up as best he could with the bow slung across his shoulder and several arrows dangling from his belt loop, was a tired Malcolm Williams. He screamed, partly from fright at seeing Bruckner and the gun, and partly from the pain of Bruckner's weight on his wounded leg. Kummel was beside them in an instant, his finger on the trigger of the mean little Uzi.

"Well, well, what do we have here?" Bruckner taunted Malcolm. "Robin Hood and his trusty bow? Where are your merry men, Robin?"

Malcolm looked at him steadily. "Where's Bobby? What have you monsters done with him?"

"He's safe, up in the statue," Bruckner said. "We have a little business outside—would you care to join us?"

"No, I think I'll just wait here," Malcolm said. "My leg doesn't work too well, thanks to your friend there."

Kummel shrugged. "You are very fortunate to be alive, Robin Hood."

"On your feet!" Bruckner shouted, grabbing Malcolm's arm and jerking him upright. He smiled when Malcolm winced with the pain. "Leave the bow here and get the hell outside—we're being rescued by helicopter, you see."

Malcolm unslung the bow and left it lying on the floor of the lobby. He walked silently ahead of Bruckner and Kummel, limping on the bad leg.

Outside they could see the helicopter on the grassy area to the right of the middle sidewalk. The rotors had stopped and the landing lights were off. Bruckner and Kummel left Malcolm, who was no threat to them with his wounded leg, and hurried toward the dragonfly-shaped machine that was tinged with a greenish light reflected from the back of the statue. There were only a few scattered raindrops now, but the clouds hanging low in the dark sky seemed to isolate the island from the rest of the world.

The little Plexiglas door of the helicopter swung open and the pilot, wearing civilian-style khaki coveralls, stepped out onto a rung and looked at the men. He had seen their guns, of course, but he must have expected that. He looked around him to see if there were others coming from a different direction, then jumped down to the ground beside the helicopter and stood waiting for them.

Kummel and Bruckner stopped about ten feet from the pilot and watched him for a moment. Then Kummel looked at Bruckner and said to the pilot, "Have you come to rescue us?" Before the pilot could open his mouth, Kummel pressed the trigger of the submachine gun and sent a full burst of 9-mm slugs ripping through the khaki coveralls. The pilot's body was hurled back against one of the helicopter's landing struts and hung there for a moment before crumpling to the grass in a bloody heap.

By now Malcolm had limped his way gradually closer to where Kummel and Bruckner stood. When he saw that Kummel had shot the apparently unarmed pilot at point-blank range, the terror he had felt before was suddenly replaced by a kind of insane rage. Pitifully off balance, he lunged at Kummel with no thought other than that he might knock the man down. Bruckner whirled toward the charging superintendent, the machine pistol tracking the wounded man's movement, and simultaneously Kummel dodged out of the way and swung his submachine gun around to finish the job.

Suddenly a blindingly brilliant light stabbed out at them from the underbelly of the helicopter, momentarily freezing the three of them in mid-action, along with the body of the dead pilot, in a grotesque tableau. A man's voice came from somewhere behind or above the light: "You going to kill me, too? Again?"

Bruckner frowned, momentarily stunned by the familiar tone of the voice. "Toberts?" he said, turning toward the voice.

"Yes, Bruckner, it's me."

Smiling then, Bruckner pointed the machine pistol toward the helicopter and said, "Actually, Toberts, old sport, I think that's exactly what will happen—I'll simply have to kill you all over again."

"But not quite yet," Toberts said, coming into view out of the glaring light, "because we have several things to discuss. Who are your friends?"

Relieved to see that Toberts was not holding a weapon in his hands, Bruckner couldn't help chuckling. "You amaze me, Toberts—still the professional diplomat interested in all the social niceties, aren't you? Well, this gentleman is Superintendent Williams, who sort of runs this island, or used to. The identity of the other gentleman is of no concern to you."

But Toberts was staring at Kummel with a puzzled look on his face, shaking his head. "So," he finally said to Bruckner, "you really did go over to the other side. Somehow I always figured you for a lone renegade, not a double."

Bruckner squinted at the still silhouetted Toberts. "What the hell are you talking about? If this is some kind of double-talk to save your lousy skin, it won't work."

"Bruckner, I'm as surprised as I can be, frankly, but there's no mistake—the man standing there with the cute little death-toy in his hands is named Boris. I never knew his last name. All I know is that he's a KGB agent with Colonel Balachov's Paris organization—he was at the Russian Embassy when they were holding me there after you left me for dead in the Bois de Boulogne."

Bruckner, obviously not believing it, looked at the man he knew as Kummel. "Boris?" he said.

Kummel/Boris shrugged; his face displayed no emotion at all.

"If you didn't know about him," Toberts said, "then I guess you've been set up, old boy. Don't take it so hard—it happens to the best of us."

Boris turned the blunt little Uzi toward Bruckner's stomach. "I will take the jewels now, Mr. Bruckner, and the control box with the remote detonator switch. The jewels, of course, rightfully belong to the people of the Soviet Union. Fortunately, I received an excellent course in piloting American helicopters at the training school outside Leningrad. You will very carefully drop the pistol and hand to me the items I have mentioned. Now!"

It was Bruckner's turn to shrug. He let the machine pistol fall from his hand flat on the ground by his feet. Holding the control box in his left hand, he reached for the box of jewels with his right, then almost casually tossed the two articles toward Boris, one slightly to either side of the Soviet agent.

It was enough, as he had planned, to distract Boris that fraction of a second which was all Bruckner needed. Boris tentatively stepped to his left to catch the tossed jewel box, then thought better of it as instinct told him to glance back at Bruckner. But his tiny tactical mistake proved crucial, for by then Bruckner had dived to the ground and scooped up the pistol. Rolling once, he placed a short burst squarely in the center of Boris's chest. The Soviet agent toppled over without firing a shot.

Malcolm and Toberts had both dropped to the ground to remove themselves from the line of fire. When Malcolm stood up again, staring wide-eyed at the bloody, dead Boris, he was holding in his hand the remote control detonator box that Bruckner had tossed to one side of Boris. Toberts was staring at something else—the metal jewel box had hit the ground and popped open, spilling its contents in a rough, sparkling circle in the wet grass. "My God!" he said, and Malcolm and Bruckner both turned their attention to the fortune in gloriously brilliant gems that lay glistening with tiny drops of rain in the glare from the helicopter light.

Suddenly Malcolm, as though coming out of a deep trance, realized what he was holding in his hand and with all the power in his arm hurled the control box toward the nearest point of the seawall. The box cleared the wall by a foot or so and sailed out into the black ocean, where it disappeared without making a sound.

"Fool!" Bruckner shouted, delivering a powerful savage kick to Malcolm's wounded thigh and causing him to groan with pain. "The radio signal was preset—I wired it myself. All that's needed to activate the detonator inside the statue is for the electrical switch in the control box to be closed.

The seawater, good conductor that it is, will seep into the box and close the circuit in a matter of minutes. Then boom goes the statue, and with it your little boy."

"No! No!" Malcolm shouted. "You can't mean you've done that. Kill my son? Destroy the Statue of Liberty? You crazy son of a bitch!"

Bruckner gripped the trigger of the machine pistol that was pointed directly at Malcolm, but then shrugged. *"C'est la guerre,"* he said. "I'm leaving you now. They don't know on the mainland that I no longer have the control box so they won't stop me. And neither will either of you."

But Malcolm paid no attention to Bruckner's words. Limping badly from the double injury to his leg, he began to hobble and drag himself in a near run toward the entrance to the statue. Toberts looked steadily at Bruckner and said, "Don't you think you've caused enough suffering and death for one lifetime?" Then he turned his back on his former teammate and ran to catch up with Malcolm, who would obviously never be able to reach his son in time. Toberts looked back once and saw that Bruckner, kneeling over the spilled jewels, had raised the machine pistol and was taking aim. Almost immediately something knocked Toberts down, but he jumped up again and kept running, grateful that he was still alive.

He passed Malcolm, who had gotten as far as the elevator only to discover the bloody body sprawled inside. The elevator apparently did not work. "I'm going up—you'd better stay here," he shouted to Malcolm in passing. "Where's your son?"

"On the platform in the crown," Malcolm said, "tied to a vertical beam—unless they moved him. Please hurry."

"And the radio receiver for the detonator?"

"I don't know."

Toberts raced up the stairs inside the pedestal, taking two and three at a time. After the fifth level he noticed that he was slowing down, that his legs were beginning to feel heavy and slightly numb, but he willed them to keep pumping beneath him. He had had almost no exercise since the surgery on his chest in Paris, and now the old wound began to throb with pain. He tried running with his left hand clutched against his chest, as though that might somehow hold him together, but shortly he discovered that he needed both arms for balance and so resigned himself to the steadily increasing pain.

He reached the top of the pedestal and for a moment became disoriented in the dim light. Then he remembered where the spiral staircase started and ran toward it, his breath coming in great gasps like that of the dying beached whales he had seen once in Oregon. Now the pain in both his chest and the calves of his legs was constant, so intense that at times he was certain his brain would simply shut down to provide his body with an automatic rest stop. Around and around the spirals he ran, sometimes clawing blindly at the handrail as the sweat drained profusely into his eyes. His shoes clanged heavily on the metal steps, and the rhythmic sound became a kind of metronome for the blood pulsing through his straining arteries.

After a while he heard an interfering rhythm, a second progression of sounds coming from somewhere below. Stopping for a moment to catch his breath, he leaned out over the stairs to look down at where he had been and saw that Malcolm, obviously in worse pain than Toberts, had started up the spiral stairway, reeling dizzily, his arms wrapped and locked around the center column. "Go back—you'll kill yourself!" Toberts yelled down at him, but realized that nothing he could say would stop the man from trying to reach his son in time to save him.

Toberts grabbed the handrail and jerked himself forward and upward into the gloom of the statue's interior, hardly noticing as he climbed that heavy ropes had been strung and left hanging from many different points along the metal framework of the interior skeleton. It was all he could do to keep his eyes focused on the next wedge-shaped step, and the next after that, to keep his feet from striking the edge at a bad angle, sending him toppling. And all the while his mind was on the square control box sunk deep in the ocean, the water even now invading the box's mechanism and closing the electrical switch, so that somewhere beside him in the dark reaches of the statue another switch was being thrown that would detonate the charge and destroy them all.

Finally, at the moment he knew that his lungs were going to burst, he glanced up above him and saw a pair of huge eyes staring down at him. The eyes were sunken in a tiny face, the lower half of which was covered with adhesive tape. The boy was bound tightly to an upright beam of some sort, just as Malcolm had said he would be. Toberts reached the crown platform and raced toward the boy, ignoring the pains in his chest. "You'll be okay now!" he gasped as he ran. "It's all right . . . we're here with you, you'll be fine now . . ."

Knowing there were only seconds left, or microseconds, or perhaps no seconds at all, Toberts ripped the adhesive tape from the boy's mouth and shook him to overcome the painful shock. "Where's the receiver, the detonator? It probably looks like a pocket radio—where'd they put it, do you know?"

"Down th-there," the boy stuttered, motioning with his head toward what looked like an inaccessible open area lower on the framework that was traversed only by a single iron beam the size of a two-by-four. "Do you see it?" the boy asked, and finally Toberts's eyes distinguished a small object attached to the beam from which wires radiated in several directions. It had been one thing to race up the spiral stairs at breakneck speed, but launching himself out over the terrible void stretching down to the base of the statue was quite another matter.

He grabbed one of the ropes hanging from the platform, and hesitated only a second before lowering himself hand below hand to the level of the traversing beam. When he found that he could not reach the beam from the rope, he deliberately began to swing back and forth, until finally the arc of the rope brought him close enough to grab the beam with one arm, then the other. He looped the rope over the beam for the return trip; then he wrapped his legs around the beam and, hanging upside down, began inching his way out to the box wired to receive a signal from the mechanism now being activated on the ocean floor off the island.

When he was close enough to touch the box, he discovered there was an indicator lamp covered by a red plastic bubble on the face of the box, but no switch to deactivate the mechanism. Hanging desperately by one arm hooked around the iron beam, he dug in his pocket for his penknife, opened the tiny blade with his teeth, and began sawing frantically at one of the wires leading from the box to the magnesium charges. His legs began to cramp from clutching the beam so tightly, and he knew that when he could stand the pain no longer, his trembling muscles would relax their hold and he would plummet seventy-five feet to his death.

He had cut through one of the wires and was sawing at the second when something blinked red in the corner of his eye. His heart pounded so hard his hand jumped; the red blink could only be the indicator light on the detonator showing that the current was starting to flow. From sheer frustration as much as any deliberate and rational action, Toberts held onto the beam with his left arm and swung his right fist in a roundhouse punch that caught the detonator box squarely and ripped it loose from the remaining wire. As it tumbled down into the dim void beneath him, he saw the box suddenly suffused in a bright red glow. He held his breath until the detonator crashed into the floor seven or eight stories below.

When nothing happened, Toberts sighed deeply and felt his muscles giving way. He reversed his previous course, along the bottom of the beam, grabbed the rope, and using every ounce of strength left in his arms, he began to hoist himself up toward the platform. It seemed a much longer journey than when he had let himself down, and at least twice he all but decided it was impossible, that he could not raise his arms another inch, he would simply have to drop. But he willed his forty-five-year-old body to do things it shouldn't have been asked to do, and at last found himself crawling out on the platform toward the superintendent's son.

"Thank you," the boy said very politely after Toberts had cut him loose with the little penknife. Toberts started to tell him about his father when the top of Malcolm's head appeared over the rim of the spiral staircase. Somehow Malcolm dragged himself up onto the platform, looking exhausted and deathly pale.

"Daddy! Daddy!" the boy shouted, running toward his father. "You did come to rescue me, didn't you!"

Malcolm swept Bobby up in his arms and rocked him back and forth, softly calling his name. Toberts saw that tears were streaming down Malcolm's face and he looked away. His own child, if she had lived, he thought irrationally, would have been older—about eighteen now, surely a beautiful young woman, the image of her mother.

The three of them began the long climb down the spiral stairs and then the stairs down through the pedestal. Toberts helped Malcolm as well as he could while Malcolm held on tightly to Bobby's hand. "He seems to have survived his ordeal remarkably well," Toberts said at one point, to which Malcolm simply answered, "Thank God!"

When they reached the lobby, Toberts went on ahead to the door leading out behind the statue. He could see that the bright ground-illumination light from the helicopter was still on. Suddenly, as he watched, the huge overhead rotors began to turn as the engine whined into life. Keeping low so that Bruckner could not see him from the pilot's seat, Toberts rushed out to Boris's body to find the submachine gun. But Bruckner had obviously thought of everything—the gun was not there, and neither were the jewels. And even though he had lost a brief argument with Captain Shaner before leaving the mainland, Toberts was sorry now that he hadn't brought along at least a pistol anyway.

Toberts saw that Malcolm and Bobby had come out to join him and he motioned them to stay out of sight. "I can't believe we're just going to let that murderous monster get away free!" Malcolm shouted over the noise of the engine warming up.

"Shoot him, Daddy, shoot him!" Bobby yelled.

"With what?"

"Your bow and arrow, Daddy!"

Enraged beyond logic by what Bruckner had almost done to his son, Malcolm retrieved the makeshift bow from inside the pedestal lobby where Bruckner had made him drop it and limped back outside toward the helicopter, fitting one of the arrows from his belt loop to the string as he went. He tried to remember where he had seen Coast

Guard helicopters refuel—which would tell him where the gas tanks were located—when suddenly the engine revved up with an earsplitting roar and the helicopter lifted off the ground. Kneeling to brace himself against the downwash from the rotors, Malcolm took careful aim and fired an arrow into the skin of the helicopter, where it lodged half in and half out.

But the machine kept rising, then tilted to one side and left the island, heading out over the harbor south toward The Narrows.

"Damn!" Malcolm cursed, watching the helicopter disappear.

"Did you miss him, Daddy?" Bobby wanted to know.

"It'll be all right," Toberts said. "We—the police technicians and I—made a few modifications to the helicopter before we took off, so that all on-board instruments and controls can be completely taken over by radio command from the mainland. In a minute or two they should have Mr. Bruckner locked in on their signal—they'll be able to set him down where they want him and there won't be a thing he can do about it."

Malcolm shook his head. "I didn't know such things were possible."

"Sure. Haven't you ever seen a radio-controlled *model* airplane? This system is just a little bit bigger and more sophisticated."

Toberts knelt down beside Boris's body and, rolling him over on his face, unstrapped the big portable transceiver he had been carrying on his back. "It doesn't seem to have been hit," he told Malcolm. "I'm going to try to contact Captain Shaner—no doubt Bruckner already tuned the set to the right frequency."

He turned the power on and broadcast an appeal for Shaner to contact him, then moved the dials slightly and tried again. After a few minutes the speaker squealed and Captain Shaner came on, asking who was calling.

"This is Peter Owens, Captain. A man named Bruckner has taken the helicopter and is heading south over the harbor—can you pick him up?"

"Yes, Owens," Captain Shaner said. "We're tracking him on shipboard radar from a Coast Guard cutter out in the harbor. We had him locked in to the radio-control system but then something happened—he just slipped right out from under us. What I think is that a wire may have come loose from the vibration."

"Or," Toberts said, "what's even more likely, Mr. Bruckner found our clever little black box and ripped it out as soon as he felt the loss of control. The clouds are low enough that we can still hear his engine from out here on the island."

"We can't move in, though, as long as he's got that remote-control detonator switch."

"He doesn't have it, Captain," Toberts said, "and Bobby Williams is safe. Go ahead and scramble some pursuit, if you want, but keep this in mind—Bruckner is carrying a small metal box with about ten million dollars worth of jewels in it."

"Oh, Christ!" Shaner said. "Well, it looks like we'll just have to wait him out."

Malcolm shook Toberts's arm. "The engine sounds different—hear it? It sounds like something's wrong with it."

Toberts, too, heard the different pitch of the whirring rotors. "It sounds like the engine's missing every other stroke—I think he's in trouble out there."

"You did it, Daddy!" Bobby shouted. "You did it with your bow and arrow, just like I told you!"

"Maybe," Malcolm said, the beginnings of a smile lighting up his face.

They watched the running lights of the helicopter, tiny in the distance, bob sickeningly in the air through a few desperate spirals, then plummet straight down into the cold black water of the harbor.

"Radar's lost him," Captain Shaner reported over the radio. "They say it looks like he spun into the bay. I don't understand it."

"It's a little complicated, Captain," Toberts told him. "We'll explain it later."

"Is everyone out there on the island okay? Give me a report, Owens."

"Malcolm needs medical attention to his leg, but apparently it's a flesh wound. Bobby's okay, I think—just exhausted from the ordeal."

"Okay. Stand by on this same frequency—I may have a message for you in a minute."

Malcolm and Toberts settled down on the ground beside the radio, and Bobby climbed into his father's lap. Toberts lit a cigarette. "What a night!" Malcolm said. "Look at me —my hand's shaking so hard you'd think I had palsy."

"We're all lucky to be alive," Toberts said.

Malcolm nodded. "You know, there's something I don't understand—when we were running back to the statue to get Bobby and try to cut the wires to the detonator, I was sure I saw that guy Bruckner draw a bead on you with his gun. I couldn't figure out why he didn't shoot when he had the chance. But now I think maybe I know the reason —I think Bruckner had a deep-down feeling for the statue after all. He was American, wasn't he?"

"Yes, he was," Toberts said. "But Bruckner had no patriotic feelings, no respect for the freedom of others or any of the other decent things the Statue of Liberty stands for. He was the most totally amoral man I've ever met."

"How do you know that? Maybe he did, when it finally came down to a do-or-don't situation. Maybe you misjudged him."

Toberts slipped off his jacket and sweater and showed Malcolm the bulletproof vest in which he was encased from just under his chin to his abdomen. In the back was a place where the fibers had been flattened out and nearly ruptured by two or three bullets, one of which was still embedded in the fabric. "Sorry to disappoint you, Malcolm," Toberts said.

Captain Shaner came back on the radio and asked if Malcolm Williams was there. Toberts said yes and handed the microphone to Malcolm.

"I have a message for him from his wife, Lucy."

There was a pause, then Lucy's voice came over the speaker, tentatively, as though she was not sure anyone was listening to her. "Malcolm, are you there?" she asked.

"Yes, Lucy, I'm right here," Malcolm said.

"Is Bobby really okay?"

"Yes, I think he's fine—still a little shaken up, but otherwise fine. Just a second, I'll let him say hello."

Malcolm held the microphone to Bobby's mouth and Bobby said, "Hi, Mom, I'm fine."

"Oh, darling, it's so good to hear your voice again. Malcolm, what about you? Captain Shaner said you were wounded."

"I'm okay," Malcolm said. "Just a little tired."

"Thank God! I was so worried . . ."

"Lucy, listen to me . . . I'm sorry about everything. All night long, when I wasn't sure we'd ever make it off the island, I worried about that."

"Oh, Malcolm, I'm sorry, too. I've been . . . all mixed up, I guess. If you want me, I think I'd like to come home now, with you and Bobby. I tried to make them let me come out to the island earlier but they wouldn't let me."

"I can vouch for that!" Captain Shaner added. "She just about drove me crazy."

Smiling happily, Malcolm hugged Bobby to him and said into the microphone, "That would be very nice, Lucy —the nicest present I can imagine."

Shaner came back on the air. "We'll send out a chopper to pick you up shortly. Don't go anywhere till we get there."

Toberts took the microphone from Malcolm. "You'd better send a good-sized boat for the dead, too, Captain —we've got five or six bodies out here."

"Affirmative, Owens. I'm signing off for now."

Toberts hung the microphone back on its hook but left the receiver's power on in case there should be further messages from Shaner.

Staring out at the ocean south of the island where the helicopter had gone down, Malcolm shook his head. "I suppose they won't have too much trouble recovering the helicopter and the jewels—the water's only eighty-five or ninety feet deep in the deepest part of the harbor. What do you think will happen to the jewels if they're found?"

"Oh, you can bet they'll be found—anytime there's that much money involved . . ." Toberts stared out at the water, too. "There'll be a lot of questions, of course. You and I will probably have to answer our share. After the immediate facts are determined, I expect the rightful ownership of the gems will be discussed in and out of the international courts for a good many years. France, the Soviets, and the U.S. all have at least a partially valid claim."

Toberts turned his attention to the back of the statue soaring up above them. "She's had the jewels almost a hundred years now—I guess that's long enough for any woman."

"Yeah," Malcolm said, "I guess they belong to the people now."

Toberts nodded. "The question is, *what* people?"

As they watched, the sky lightened in the east and a pinkish glow tinged the soft green of Liberty's weathered copper skin. The clouds had been breaking up for the past hour, and there was every indication now that the day would be beautifully clear. Photoelectric sensors in the base of the statue felt the first rays of the sun's light and quietly and efficiently turned off the nighttime illumination floodlights in a prearranged sequence, just as they did every morning.

"There the old girl goes, waking herself up again," Malcolm said. "It's a little joke Bobby and I have—isn't that right, son?" He rubbed Bobby's hair, and Bobby, smiling happily, snuggled deeper into his father's arms.

"It won't be so awfully long before the first boatload of tourists shows up," Malcolm continued. "Oh, we'll have to start late today—keep them all outside until the maintenance and security crews can take down those infernal ropes, remove the detonation charges, and do an inspection to see what other damage those people may have done to her. Otherwise, though, I suppose it'll be a pretty ordinary day here."

"Yes, I suppose it will," Toberts said, thinking about what sort of day he could look forward to. Sooner or later —probably sooner—he would have to make an attempt to clear himself with Langley, which shouldn't be too difficult with Malcolm's and Shaner's testimony. The truth was, though, that the CIA never completely forgave you for something like this—there would always be a question in their minds as to whether you had been even cleverer than they suspected and had gotten away with something. Maybe now would be the perfect time to retire from the agency, think about heading his life in a new direction, maybe discover something else he would really like to do. He would have to straighten things out with Jessie, too, once and for all. It was odd, but Jessie seemed little more than a stranger to him now, someone he had known a long time ago and no longer cared about one way or the other. He wondered what life would be like without her; better, he was sure of that, much better. She would fight him, of course, but that was nothing new. What he needed more than anything else now was time by himself, time to sort out his life and his thoughts, to let all the old wounds heal. And that might take a while.

The statue's magnificent face was bathed in sunlight now. For the first time Toberts noticed how Liberty stood eternally gazing out toward the far shores of Europe, and he suddenly thought how terribly much he missed Solange and how he wished that she could be here now, beside him. She had been only one of the many casualties of Project Lamplighter, if anyone could be cold enough to dismiss her death that way. But for Toberts she was still very much alive deep inside him where no one could ever harm her again; and though he would miss her and ache with longing for her for the rest of his life, in a very real way she would always be with him.

"Mr. Owens," Malcolm said, "would you like a drink?"

"The name's Martin," Toberts said. "It's a long story. Yes, I would very much like a drink. Strange—I didn't know employees of the National Park Service usually began their drinking at six o'clock in the morning."

"Well, you know," Malcolm said, "some days are just worse than others."

The three of them—Malcolm, Bobby, and Toberts—stood up on the neatly bordered lawn, and with a final look at the back of the statue's flowing green robes they went off arm in arm toward the superintendent's house to wait for the day to begin.